Praise for the novels

"*Poison Study* is a wonderful and lively read. Highly recommended!"
—World Fantasy Award finalist Kate Elliott

"Snyder's clear, straightforward, yet beautifully descriptive style is refreshing, while the story itself is completely engrossing."
—*RT Book Reviews* on *Magic Study*

"Snyder delivers another excellent adventure."
—*Publishers Weekly* on *Fire Study*

"Snyder deftly weaves information about glassblowing into her tale of magic and murder."
—*Library Journal* on *Storm Glass*

"A compelling new fantasy series."
—*SFX* magazine on *Sea Glass*

"Snyder's storytelling skills continue to build an involving story line."
—*Library Journal* on *Spy Glass*

"Filled with Snyder's trademark sarcastic humor, fast-paced action and creepy villainy, *Touch of Power* is a spellbinding romantic adventure."
—*USA TODAY*

"The action in this book is non-stop, with many twists and turns to keep the reader guessing about what's in store on the next page."
—*Examiner.com* on *Scent of Magic*

"Snyder draws us in with her excellent, efficient storytelling, amusing dialogue and distinctive characters, all set within a well-crafted plot. A delight of a read!"
—*RT Book Reviews* on *Taste of Darkness*

night
study

NEW YORK TIMES BESTSELLING AUTHOR

MARIA V. SNYDER

MIRA

Recycling programs
for this product may
not exist in your area.

ISBN-13: 978-0-7783-1875-0

Night Study

Copyright © 2016 by Maria V. Snyder

Printed in U.S.A.

First printing: February 2016
10 9 8 7 6 5 4 3 2 1

To my inspiring and awesome writers' retreat ladies—Nancy Hunter, Mindy Klasky, Jeri Smith-Ready and Kristina Watson. Remember...what happens during a writers' retreat *stays* at the retreat!

night study

1

YELENA

Valek blinked at me. "You're what?"

I drew in a deep breath and held up the glass vial filled with moon potion. My hand trembled, sending waves through the white liquid inside. "Pregnant... I think."

"Before we celebrate, love, let's go over your logic."

Surprise pierced my growing panic, and I glanced at him. "You want to celebrate? I was taking the moon potion to *prevent* this."

He took the vial from me and set it on the bed. Then he laced his fingers in mine and pulled me close. "Of course it would be a cause for celebration. Well, a *quiet* celebration." Valek gave me a wry smile—we both had so many enemies, it wouldn't be smart to announce my condition to the world.

My anxiety eased a bit.

"Now, why does that vial mean you're with child?" Valek asked.

"Healer Hayes told me to take the potion after I...bled... so I'd be protected for another year. But I haven't yet, and it's been..." I calculated in my head. It'd been six weeks since I'd last had my blood cycle. "I'm two weeks late." My stomach churned with distress—talk about the worst possible time to be pregnant.

"A lot has happened to you in the last four weeks. Maybe you're late because of the stress."

Valek had a point. It had happened to me before during trying times. And recently I'd been the target of an assassination attempt. Twice. The first occurred a month ago, when I was shot with an arrow that I suspected had been filled with a poison that blocked my magic. Or so I'd thought. I tightened my grip at a sudden notion. "Could the loss of my powers be due to being pregnant?"

"If that was the case, wouldn't Irys know that's a side effect? You said she was as baffled as Bain was about why your magic is blocked."

He was right. If magic loss was a common side effect during pregnancy, the Master Magicians would be aware of that. Disappointment deflated my brief surge of hope. I'd been searching for a poison or substance that explained my current predicament without success for the past month.

Correctly reading my expression, Valek squeezed my fingers. "It still might be possible. I'm immune to magic. Maybe Junior takes after his dear old dad."

Ignoring the *Junior* comment, I asked, "In that case, wouldn't I be immune, as well?" That protection would have been more than welcome four days ago when Owen Moon's magic had sliced right through me. If it hadn't been for Valek encouraging me to survive, I'd be a mindless, drooling mess right now.

Valek shrugged. "We've encountered so many different… quirks of magic over the years, this may well be one of them." He grinned. "Time will tell. And during that time, you'll be safe. No assassin would dare target you while you're with me."

I was more worried about Owen Moon. The rogue magician had managed to escape after attacking me. He had been growing the Curare vine in a hothouse made of glass. When a person was pricked by Curare, it caused full-body paralysis, which was an effective and nonlethal weapon, since the victim could still breathe.

When Owen had been captured in Ixia four years ago, the Commander assured the Sitian Council, Valek and me that Owen had been executed. Instead, the rogue magician had negotiated a deal with the Commander to manufacture and produce Curare for Ixia's army.

A nice little arrangement, until Owen turned greedy. He sold the drug to other interested parties, and it upset the Commander so much he sent Valek to shut down Owen's entire smuggling operation. Too bad the Commander failed to inform Valek of who had really been in charge of the operation.

We'd all had our share of nasty little surprises in the past week.

"What if Owen shows up?" I asked.

The muscles along Valek's sharp jaw tightened as fury flared in his sapphire-blue eyes. "Don't worry about Owen. Janco and Onora will be traveling with us."

I understood his anger. Owen also knew Valek's weakness. Because he was immune to magic, a null shield cast around him would trap Valek as if he'd been imprisoned in an invisible cell. It was just a matter of time before the word spread to other magicians, and those who could erect a null shield bubble would have an easy way to stop the infamous Ixian assassin.

"Speaking of traveling," I said to lighten the mood. "If you want to leave tomorrow morning, I need that bath."

The hard lines on his angular face softened. "I'll show you the way." Valek let go of my hands.

"Uh-huh. Mighty nice of you."

"I aim to please." He leered, but it soon turned into a more contemplative expression.

As I gathered my clean clothes and soap, Valek picked up the vial of moon potion.

"What about this?" he asked.

"If stress has delayed me, then I should drink it afterward like Healer Hayes instructed."

His brow puckered. "How long does it last?"

"A year, but I usually take it about a month before the year is up just to be safe."

"Is it a hundred percent effective?"

Odd questions, but I humored him. "No. For some, it doesn't work, but I've been taking it for eight years now without a problem." Until now.

"Oh." He set it on the top of the dresser. "What if you wish to have a child sooner?"

"Don't you know all this?"

"No. We use different substances in Ixia."

"In that case, there is another potion called starlight that reverses the effects of the moon potion."

Valek stilled. "How fast?"

"I think it's within hours. I'm not sure. Why all this interest?"

"Just curious."

There was something in the taut line of his body that caused me to suspect there was more to it than mere curiosity. But I decided to let it go. Besides, after lying in bed recovering for the past four days, I really needed that bath. And a change of scenery. The bedroom I'd been occupying had bland yellow walls, a single bed, night table, dresser and no decorations.

Valek escorted me down to the ground floor. The farmhouse had plenty of rooms, which was probably why Owen had bought it for his base of operations. The complex of stables, barns and other structures hid his movements from public view while the large chain-link fence kept curious neighbors from stopping by for a visit. Not that there were many people around. The farm was in a remote area in the northern part of the Moon Clan's lands, near the border with Ixia.

"What's the closest town?" I asked Valek. I'd been tied down under a tarp while being transported here, so I'd counted towns by the vibrations from the wagon wheels trundling over the cobblestones, guessing we were three towns east of Lapeer.

"Broken Bridge is just west of here."

I glanced at him. "Interesting name."

"An accurate name. There was a bridge spanning the Sunworth River at that location, but a flood cracked it in half a long time ago. One half floated down the river, but the other remains on the far bank. No one remembers the real name of the town."

"How do you know all this?"

He grinned. "I've been talking to the locals. Mostly to discover how long Owen's been here, if they'd seen any other strangers around town and if they know about other places he might own. Town gossip can be very informative."

When we reached the washroom, I sighed in contentment when I spotted the glowing coals under a large metal tank. Hot water was just an open valve away. An oval tub sat in the middle of the stone washroom. A row of hooks lined the wall above a bench. Towels had been stacked in a cabinet next to it.

Valek filled the tub while I peeled off my sweat-stiffened tunic. The crisp air caused goose bumps to coat my skin. It was just two weeks into the warming season, and while each day would be a bit warmer than the last, it would be another month before I wouldn't need a cloak during the day. Nights would remain cool well into the warm season.

The rest of my clothing soon joined my tunic on the floor. Before I could even shiver, Valek wrapped me in an embrace. Warmth enveloped me and I gazed up into his eyes.

He swooped in for a kiss. I hooked my arms around his neck and laced my fingers in his shoulder-length black hair, deepening the kiss. My worries melted as heat spread throughout my body.

Too soon, he pulled back. "Your water's getting cold."

"I'm not the one still wearing clothes."

Regret flashed across his face. "I've a few things to take care of before we leave tomorrow."

"But—"

He silenced my protest with another kiss. "Tonight. I promise."

After he left, the cold rushed in with a vengeance. I grabbed a towel and my supplies and hurried to the tub, setting the items on a nearby table. Steam curled from the water and I stepped into bliss, sighing as I submerged up to my neck. I closed my eyes and enjoyed the soak until my worries once again solidified. The biggest one pushed all the others to the side, and I rested my hands on my lower abdomen.

A baby.

No. Valek was right. Stress and trauma had upset my monthly cycles before. This time was no different. Besides, the moon potion had worked for eight years; no reason to doubt its potency now.

A baby.

Fear stirred in my chest. I couldn't be pregnant. Not now. Assassins had been hired to kill me, I had no magic and Owen Moon—a dangerous and powerful magician who also wanted me dead—was at large. Plus this new girl, Onora—yet another assassin—was after Valek's job as Ixia's security chief. And he had dozens of enemies.

Then again, I couldn't imagine our lives ever settling down enough for the timing to be perfect. A child of ours would never be safe. But no need to jump to conclusions just yet. As Valek had said, *time will tell.*

And if I wasn't…?

It'd be for the best. Yet a faint pang of disappointment poked my chest at the thought. Silly.

When the water turned lukewarm, I grabbed my soap. Careful of the scabbed-over rope burns and multicolored bruises around my wrists and ankles, I scrubbed off a few layers of grime. Old scars crisscrossed my stomach, ribs, legs and arms. I'd seen more than my share of action. The newest scar, a roundish shape just below my left clavicle, had been made by the first assassin's arrow just a month ago.

I fingered the ridges, remembering the force of the impact that had knocked me from Kiki's back. The shaft had been filled with an unknown liquid poison. My magic expelled most of the drug—or so I'd thought—and healed the wound. That had been the last time I drew from the blanket of power that surrounded the world and fueled a magician's magic. Once I recovered from the injury, Valek and I enjoyed the remaining day of our vacation before he left for Ixia. That morning, the symptoms of the poison began, and I spent the day suffering from intense hot and cold flashes. When they finally ceased, my ability to draw power was gone.

A delay between poisoning and the onset of the symptoms was not unheard-of. Many assassins liked to be well away before anyone suspected foul play. Yet in this case, shooting a victim with an arrow was far from subtle. I considered. The poison may have nothing to do with my blocked magic. Perhaps it was just added insurance, in case the assassin missed my heart. My ability to drain the substance from my wound then turned a lethal dose into a sick day in bed. That scenario implied there was another cause.

Conception? If I was with child, the timing coincided. But

again, if magicians lost their powers while pregnant, it'd be well-known. Unless, as Valek had said, there was some quirk in the magic. Perhaps First Magician Bain Bloodgood would know, or he could search through his history books for a reference to a similar occurrence. It'd be too dangerous to send him a message right now, and it might be a bit premature at this point. Once I had confirmation of my condition, then I'd talk to Bain.

Clean, I rinsed off the soap and dressed in record time. My stomach growled, so I searched for something to eat. No surprise that my brother, Leif, stood at the kitchen's long counter with his hands in a large metal mixing bowl.

Leif was never far from the food.

His strong forearms flexed as he kneaded the dough. About six inches taller than me, his broad shoulders and square jaw gave him a stocky appearance, but despite being obsessed with eating, it was all muscle under his brown tunic.

"You going to stand there all day?" Leif asked without glancing in my direction. His magic sensed a person's proximity, as well as intentions, moods and guilt. He frequently aided the Sitian Council in their investigations.

"I'm still recovering from the shock of seeing you cook."

He grunted. "Who do you think has been feeding you the last four days?"

I stepped into the spacious kitchen. A mammoth stone hearth comprised the entire far wall. Coals glowed red-hot under a large-sized white brick oven, above which hung an assortment of black iron pots. The scent of baking bread filled the air. A long wooden table with seating for at least two dozen bisected the room.

"I know you're famous for your wet-dog tea and rabbit stew, but I thought you'd rather eat other people's cooking."

"It's *corgarviy* tea, and without it, you'd still be drooling on your pillow."

True. Even though it smelled awful, it had helped rejuvenate me. I joined him at the counter. An impressive array of utensils, tools, bowls and equipment lined the shelves.

"Besides, if I had a kitchen like *this*, I'd cook all the time." Leif studied me. "Hungry?"

"Very."

He gestured to the bench near the table. "Sit."

I didn't waste any time, and he laughed. In that instant, he looked much younger than twenty-nine, which was two years older than me. He grabbed a bowl and uncovered one of the pots on the hearth. Ladling a heaping portion into the bowl, he then placed the steaming goodness in front of me, along with a spoon.

After I inhaled a few bites of the beef-and-vegetable soup, I asked him if he'd identified any more of the other plants inside the glass hothouse Owen had constructed to grow the Curare vine. Before this invention, Curare only grew in the Illiais Jungle far to the south, where it was warm and humid all year round. Another benefit of the vine being confined to one area was that the Sitian Council could limit its availability, which it did. The Council kept strict control of who was allowed to carry it as a weapon. A watered-down version was also manufactured and given to healers in order to reduce a patient's pain, which I thought was the best aspect of the drug. It was the reason my father had hunted for the vine all those years ago.

"I know all but four. We'll have to wait until Father arrives to identify the rest." Leif filled another bowl and sat opposite me. He fiddled with his spoon, twirling it around on the table.

"What's wrong?"

"I keep thinking of that factory in Lapeer. In order to produce so much Curare, Owen must have more of those hot-houses. Lots more."

I'd suspected as much. "We'll find them. Has anyone interrogated Ben? He may know where the others are." Owen's brother had been caught, along with Loris and Cilly Cloud Mist. Ben wasn't as powerful as Owen, but he could erect a null shield, light fires and move small objects. The Cloud Mist siblings' abilities to mentally communicate and manipulate a person's thoughts and memories had aided Owen in maintaining the deception of his death.

"No. The three magicians were taken to Lapeer and incarcerated in a cell with a null shield. The authorities won't let any of us near them, although Devlen left this morning to try again. The Captain claims he's waiting for orders from the Sitian Council."

I cursed under my breath. "I hope the Captain's a patient man." The Council took far too much time to make a decision on anything.

"I'd bet they're in a panic," Leif said. "The Commander has Curare, and he won't be afraid to use it. Unlike our soldiers, I'd bet every single one of his soldiers will have darts laced with the stuff in no time. He could be preparing to invade Sitia as we speak."

As the Liaison between Ixia and Sitia, I found that scenario to be unlikely. However, with the Commander keeping secrets from even Valek, I might not know the Commander as well as I'd thought. Still... "Or he could just want to even the playing field. Having both Curare and magicians, Sitia has had the advantage for years."

Leif picked up the spoon. "Which has made me feel all safe and warm. Now I'm wondering what type of uniform I'd have to wear when we're conquered."

Considering the Commander had banned all magicians, ex-

MARIA V. SNYDER

cept me, from Ixia and executed most of those caught inside his borders, I knew that, at best, Leif and the others would be incarcerated in a magic-proof cell for the rest of their lives—or, at worst, they'd all be killed. I decided not to sour his mood any further.

Instead I said, "I'm sure the Commander will find a job that's perfect for your qualifications. You'd look good in a stable boy's uniform, or spiffy as a chamber pot manager."

"Sure, you can laugh. The Commander likes you. And now you…" Leif ducked his head, focusing on the bowl in front of him.

"What? Now I'm not a Soulfinder anymore, the Commander will welcome me with open arms?"

He wouldn't meet my gaze. "Something like that."

"Then say it. I don't want people dancing around the subject or treating me different…or locking me in jail 'for my own protection.'"

"I was under orders from the Council," Leif protested.

It had backfired. The second assassin had found me in no time. "And look how well *that* turned out." Thank fate I still had a few tricks up my sleeves.

"Sorry. Won't happen again," Leif promised.

"Good." I changed the subject. "Are you staying here until Father comes?"

"Yes. I expect he'll arrive in about fifteen days."

That was a long time to wait. Leif's wife, Mara—a real sweetheart—wouldn't ever complain, but she couldn't be happy. "What will you do all that time?"

"We plan to search the surrounding towns and villages, looking for more of those hothouses."

"We?"

"Devlen believes it's a good idea. And he's got a way with the locals. They talk to him."

With Owen at large, Devlen's daughter, Reema, would have to remain with Ari in the Commander's castle until it was safe. Owen had threatened to kill her.

"Have you found any records here? That would make it easier." And so would interrogating Ben. I wondered if Valek had "talked" to him before the authorities swooped in.

"It appears Owen didn't keep any records at this location. Which is why I'm hoping to find another place where he may have left information behind."

"Or you might find him." The thought of the two of them hunting Owen alone caused a queasiness to roll in my stomach. Leif had been kidnapped by Owen before. And while Devlen was skilled with a sword, Owen's magic outmatched Leif's.

"Even better," he said in a low, dangerous tone.

Not good. "At least make sure you take Hale with you." I was glad Hale had been assigned to travel with us for added protection.

"Hale's gone. He was ordered back to the Citadel."

Interesting. "And you weren't?"

"Oh, I was."

"Leif—"

"Don't 'Leif' me." His green eyes sparked in annoyance. "You know as well as I do the Council will debate what to do for months. Meanwhile, Owen's out there—"

"Along with Rika Bloodgood and Tyen Cowan. Two powerful magicians, which brings the total to three against you and Devlen."

He squared his shoulders with that stubborn Zaltana determination.

I tried another tactic. "Owen's smart. He knows both the Commander and the Council will be searching for him, so he's going to lay low for the next few months while he figures out his next move."

"That's why we need to stop him before he can *act*."

Leif had a point. I considered the situation. "Then the best use of your time would be to convince the Sitian Council to let you use your magic to interrogate Ben and the others."

He grunted, but I wasn't sure I'd convinced him.

We ate the rest of our soup in silence. After a few minutes, Devlen entered the kitchen. A deep scowl etched his dark face, and tension radiated from his powerful build.

"Still no luck?" Leif asked him, referring to Devlen's repeated attempt to speak to Ben.

"Yelena, where is Valek?" Devlen asked, ignoring Leif.

"He said he had to take care of a few things. Why?"

Devlen cursed.

"What's going on?" Leif asked.

"Ben, Loris and Cilly have all been assassinated."

2

VALEK

As he prepared for the trip, Valek's mind whirled with the implications of becoming a father, even though he knew Yelena might not be pregnant. Just the thought of a baby sent a giddy, wild happiness mixed with fear pulsing through his veins. No surprise his immediate instinct was the intense desire to protect both his heart mate and the baby. He imagined locking them both in a tower so no one could harm them. Pure fantasy at best.

His second reaction was to plan the logistics. Yelena would stay with him, of course, and they'd raise the baby together. Where would they live? In the Commander's castle? No. In their cabin in the Featherstone Clan lands? No. That location was too well-known. And what if he was on assignment for the Commander?

Valek banished all his crazy thoughts with effort. Yelena needed to be a part of this discussion. And he needed to confirm a suspicion.

When he'd finished gathering supplies, he searched for Onora. She had offered to get the horses ready. Leaning on the side of the stable, Valek studied Onora as she groomed Onyx. The black horse allowed her to inspect the underside of his hooves, lifting each in turn. Kiki and The Madam grazed nearby in the farm's pasture. Their coats gleamed. In order for each member of their traveling party to have a mount, Onora had picked a chestnut-colored Thoroughbred from those Owen had left behind. The gelding displayed a gentle manner and appeared to be strong and healthy. Valek approved of her choice.

Just about everything was ready for their trip east. They would leave at dawn and set a fast pace to catch up to his operatives already in the field. The Commander wouldn't be happy about the delay. Valek straightened as anger rolled through him. If the Commander had confided in him, this entire fiasco would never have happened, and Yelena wouldn't have been in danger. Instead the Commander chose to reveal his plans only to Onora, the twenty-year-old assassin whose sole desire was to take Valek's place.

At this point in time, Valek would be happy to give it to her. The Commander has been using her to test Valek's loyalty for the past month. First by attacking Yelena, to determine if Valek would disobey a direct order, and then with a fake assassination attempt on the Commander. Tiresome, to say the least. Then the Commander assigned him the task of shutting down a new smuggling route into Ixia without informing him of crucial details…

Valek drew in a deep breath to calm the rising fury. No need to waste the energy now. He planned to confront the Commander on his return. In the meantime, he needed to clarify one vital detail with, as Janco liked to call her, Little Miss Assassin.

Onora glanced up as he approached. She continued to comb Onyx's tail, but a wariness crept into her gray eyes despite her attempts to neutralize her expression. Barefoot even in the cold air, Onora had pulled her long brown hair away from her narrow face. A pretty girl and almost unflappable, it was difficult to discern Onora's thoughts.

"The horses are almost ready." She pointed to Kiki. "She won't let me put shoes on her."

Her horse knowledge must be considerable if Onora felt comfortable enough to shoe a horse. "Kiki's a Sandseed horse—they dislike shoes," Valek said.

"Yeah, she made that quite clear." Onora pushed up the sleeve on her right arm, revealing a bright red, horse-teeth-shaped bruise.

Valek suppressed a smile. "That's not for the shoes. Sand-seed horses also have a keen sense of smell. That bite is for shooting Yelena with an arrow. Be glad she didn't decide to kick the side of your head in, as well."

Kiki snorted as if in agreement. Onora shifted away from Onyx's hindquarters. She tensed, probably sensing from Valek's tone that he wasn't there to talk about horses. The young assassin had helped rescue Yelena and Janco from Owen, which weighed in her favor, and she had been acting on the Commander's orders when she shot his heart mate. Valek, more than anyone else, understood the advantages and disadvantages of being loyal to the Commander. However, he suspected Onora had lied to him about a few details.

Valek strode right up to her. "The Commander didn't give you that arrow, did he?"

Dropping the comb, she reached for her knives, but Valek already had his pressed to her throat. She froze. Smart girl.

"*You* filled the arrow with starlight, hoping Yelena would become pregnant, hoping I'd be happy to retire from my position to raise a family."

Onora didn't deny it.

"Are you that hungry for my job?" he asked.

"Yes."

MARIA V. SNYDER

"Show me."

She hesitated.

"Show me or I'll slice your tunic open."

Giving him a nasty glare, she yanked down the collar of her shirt. A purple C-shaped scar marked her chest. From his own experience with scars, he calculated that it'd been done approximately six months ago. Probably when she first started working for the Commander. Emotions boiled in his stomach. Betrayal and relief dominated. Betrayal over the Commander marking another without discussing it with Valek or even informing him. Relief that he no longer needed to fear for the Commander's safety whenever Onora was near him, because she had given her life and loyalty to the Commander.

Onora braced for his reaction.

"That scar won't protect you from *me*. Don't lie to me again. Understand?" he asked.

"Yes."

He pressed harder. Blood welled under the sharp blade.

"Yes, sir," she said.

"Hey! What's going on?" Leif asked.

In one quick motion, Valek sheathed his knife and stepped away from Onora. Leif, Devlen and Yelena hurried to join them. Color had returned to Yelena's cheeks. It was much better than the deathly paleness that had clung to her skin over the past few days. Of course, it would be even better if she wasn't staring daggers at him. Probably not a good time to inform her that the Commander and Onora had plotted against her.

"Haven't you assassinated enough people today?" Leif glared at him, then yanked out a handkerchief to dab at the blood on Onora's throat. "It looks shallow, but I should put a poultice on it just in case."

Onora shooed him off. "I'm fine."

Uncertain about what had caused all this hostility, Valek mulled over Leif's question. "Who died?"

"Oh, come on. Don't play the innocent, Mr. *Assassin*," Leif said. "I get that you're all protective of my sister and think anyone who hurts her should die. But they had vital information that could have led us to Owen, you idiot!"

Ah. "All three?"

Leif opened his mouth, but Yelena stopped him. "Yes, Ben, Loris and Cilly."

While not in the least bit upset over their deaths, Valek did regret not having more time to "talk" with them. He'd used goo-goo juice on Ben to learn the location of the escape tunnel's exit point, but by the time he'd returned from his failed attempt to track Owen, the Sitian authorities had arrived.

Valek suppressed the urge to glance at Onora. Was she responsible? And, if so, was she acting on her own or following the Commander's orders? Now was not the time to ask. "How were they killed?" he asked Leif instead.

Leif huffed in annoyance, but Devlen said, "Puncture wound to the jugular. They died of rapid blood loss."

Yelena touched her neck—a gesture her mother often used when feeling anxious or vulnerable.

None of the assassins he knew killed that way. "Sound familiar?" he asked Yelena.

"When The Mosquito attacked me, he aimed an ice pick at my neck. If he'd succeeded, I probably would have died the same way," she said.

Valek vowed to find the assassin and squash him. But first... "Didn't Bruns Jewelrose hire him to target you?" Another whom Valek needed to have a little chat with—he planned to let the sharp point of his knife do all the talking in that conversation.

Her hand remained around her throat. "Yes. Do you think

MARIA V. SNYDER

Bruns sent him after the magicians? That doesn't make any sense."

"You're right, it doesn't. And an assassin rarely works for one client. Owen has the most to lose if they talked to the Council. Plus, he has the money to hire The Mosquito," Valek speculated.

"He wouldn't kill his own *brother*," Leif said. "He rescued Ben from Wirral Prison."

"Which alerted the authorities," Valek said.

"Who would have lost him if Ben had not gone after Yelena," Devlen added.

"Brothers," Yelena said, gazing at Leif pointedly, "can be troublesome and have the tendency to jump to conclusions. You need to apologize to Valek."

Leif crossed his arms as two red splotches spread on his cheeks. "It wasn't a jump. It was a perfectly reasonable assumption. One you made, too."

"I suspected Valek, as well," Devlen said. He towered about six inches over Leif, and his blue-eyed gaze held contrition.

"No need for apologies." Valek considered. "I don't suppose they would let me examine the crime scene?"

"That would be...unwise at this time," Devlen said. "They would not even let me near it or the bodies."

Which meant Captain Fleming suspected Valek and would probably report his suspicions to the Council. "Should we leave tonight?"

"No," Yelena said. "By the time they make a decision, we'll be in Ixia." Her matter-of-fact tone belied her heated gaze. She hadn't forgotten his promise.

Warmth spread throughout his chest. He'd risk being arrested for a night alone with Yelena. Hell, he'd risk his life. Once they left in the morning, there would be no privacy on the road.

Yet there was no sense in taking an *unnecessary* risk. Setting a watch tonight would provide Valek with ample time to escape should the captain decide to arrest him. "All right, we'll proceed as planned. Onora, where's Janco? I thought he was helping you with the horses."

She gestured to a two-story barn to the left. "He's pouting."

Should he even bother to ask?

Yelena did. "About what?" She fed an apple to Kiki, who cleaved the fruit in half with one bite.

Onora rubbed her right arm as she watched Kiki chew. "He wanted to name the horse we're taking with us 'Beach Bunny,' after some stuffed rabbit he had growing up, and I said it was a stupid name for a horse. Then he claimed, if it was his horse, he could name it anything he wanted, and I said he should ride The Madam because she's the easiest to handle, and—"

"You offended his pride and he stalked away in a huff," Yelena finished.

"Yup."

As Yelena scratched Kiki in all her favorite spots, Valek gestured for Onora to follow him to the barn. He stopped outside the oversize doors that had been painted green with white trim.

"Tell Janco to set up a watch schedule for tonight. I'll take the last shift," he said.

"Should he include Yelena?"

"No. She needs her rest."

Onora bit her lip, clamping down on the question dancing behind her eyes—was Yelena with child? Valek walked away without answering. It was too soon to tell, and, as far as he was concerned, Onora would be the last to know. Though a part of him was impressed by the twenty-year-old's ambition and cunning, he also wished to throttle her. But the Com-

MARIA V. SNYDER

mander had chosen her as Valek's successor. And now it was up to Valek to decide if he agreed.

Valek rattled the doorknob so he wouldn't scare Yelena. She lay in bed reading, but she glanced up from her book when he entered. He recognized it as the plant guide her father had given her.

"What took you so long?" she asked, setting the book on the night table with a thump. The low flame in the lantern jumped.

He'd been checking the perimeter, confirming the gates had all been locked and the buildings secured while Janco did a sweep of the surrounding forest. "Ensuring Captain Fleming isn't at the gate with an arrest warrant."

"Good." She peeled back the covers, exposing her naked body. "Join me."

His heart thudded so hard he feared his sternum would crack in two. Breathing became difficult, and the desire to rip the rest of the blanket off and press her to him trembled through his body. Yet he remained rooted in place. She needed to know about the starlight and Onora.

"What's wrong?"

"I need to tell you—"

"Is it important?"

"Yes."

Yelena pulled the blanket up, covering herself. "All right, tell me."

He kicked off his boots and lay down next to her. She scooted closer and rested her head on his shoulder as he wrapped his arm around her. Valek informed her of Onora's nasty little trick.

"I'm going to wring her neck," Yelena muttered after he'd finished.

"You can try. I doubt you'd get close to her."

"Is that why you had the knife at Onora's throat?"

"Yes. She needed to understand that will be the last time she lies to me. And I needed to remind her who is in charge."

"Until the Commander says otherwise."

"True."

"And will you take orders from her?"

"No. By that time, I suspect I'll be taking orders from another woman."

Yelena lifted her head from his chest and met his gaze. "Is that so? What type of orders?"

"You have a dirty mind, love. I'm thinking of orders to change a diaper or rock a baby to sleep. Things like that."

"Not near as exciting as assassinating a criminal."

"Not as dangerous, either. Besides, I think the teen years could be quite exciting. No one is going to mess with my son or daughter."

She laughed. "You can't assassinate bullies or boys who kiss your daughter."

"Pity."

A brief smile flashed, then she grew contemplative. "Since I was hit with starlight, that increases the possibility I'm pregnant. What will we do?"

"I expect we'll do what most people do in that situation—become a family."

"Easier said than done."

"We'll figure this out—I promise." He pulled her tight against him.

She snuggled in and fell asleep. Valek took comfort in the steady rise and fall of her chest, but far too soon, it was his turn on watch. He slipped from her embrace, pulled his boots on and searched for Janco.

A half-moon cast enough light to avoid tripping and walking into tree trunks. Valek found Janco near the glass house.

Condensation misted the outside panels of the structure. Inside, coals burned to keep it warm, and the pans of water added moisture to the air. Leif had been maintaining the equipment in order to keep the plants alive until his father arrived. The whole idea of the house and growing Curare far from the jungle was genius. He wondered if Owen had the original notion, or if the Commander had speculated about the possibility and sent Owen to put it all together.

"Any trouble?" Valek asked.

Janco rubbed the scar where the bottom half of his right ear should be. "Just thinking."

"That could be dangerous."

"Ha, ha. Not funny. What I'm wondering is, if all those plants inside came from the Illiais Jungle, then who brought them here?"

"Owen has been working on this for over three years."

"Yeah, I get that. But wouldn't the Zaltana Clan know strangers were digging around their jungle? Doesn't the Curare vine only grow in a certain section? And isn't Yelena's father the only producer of the stuff?" Janco tapped on the glass. "These are far from seedlings. And then I'm thinking, how many people have enough knowledge of all these plants? Can't be many outside the jungle."

All excellent points. Valek considered. "Tyen Cowan might have the knowledge, depending on where he grew up." The jungle bordered the southeastern and southern sections of the Cowan Clan's lands.

"Or a Zaltana was working with Owen."

Deceit and betrayal were all part of his job; however, Valek had a difficult time believing that one of Yelena's clan members would cooperate with Owen or be involved in illegal activities. Unless they'd been tricked. "Before we leave, we'll ask

Leif to look into it. If Leif finds the expert, he or she could lead him to where the other hothouses are located."

Janco flashed him a bright smile. "See? I have good ideas, too."

"I never said you didn't."

"But you never said I did."

"I don't have to. You're very good at self-congratulation," Valek said.

"I am?"

"Yes."

Janco preened.

"Go get some sleep," Valek said. "It'll be dawn in a couple hours."

At the mention of dawn, Janco's shoulders drooped. "You know, midafternoon is a perfectly respectable time to leave," he grumbled as he headed back to the house.

Valek looped around the complex, testing locks and seeking signs of a disturbance. Satisfied that all appeared secured, he stopped at the stables. Both Kiki and Rusalka, Leif's horse, snoozed in their stalls unperturbed. He'd learned to trust the Sandseed horses. If a strange scent tainted the air, they'd be agitated.

When the sky lightened, he returned to the house. The smell of sizzling bacon reached him. He followed the wonderful scent to the kitchen. Leif filled plates with sweet cakes, bacon, eggs and toast. Everyone was awake and sitting at the table.

Happy to see Yelena tucking into a heaping portion in front of her, Valek joined them, letting the conversation flow over him.

"I'd wake up every morning at dawn if I knew *this* was waiting for me," Janco said, helping himself to another stack of sweet cakes. His salt-and-pepper-colored goatee was sticky with syrup.

"You're going to make yourself sick," Yelena teased.

MARIA V. SNYDER

"Not possible."

"Enjoy it," Leif said. "Tomorrow you're all going to be eating dried jerky, stale bread and hard cheese."

Janco groaned. "Nasty, Leif."

"I'm sure we'll be stopping at a few inns. Right?" Yelena asked Valek.

"We'll see."

"That's Valek speak for 'no way in hell.'" Janco stole a slice of bacon from her plate.

She stabbed him with her fork.

"Owww."

Valek turned to Leif and asked him about other jungle experts.

Leif chewed his food while he thought. "I'll ask my father. Compared to the rest of Sitia, most of the Zaltanas are experts. However, in order to transport plants, you need a higher level of knowledge." He tapped a fork on the table. "And, thinking about it...some of those unfamiliar plants might be crossbreeds." Leif tossed the silverware in disgust. "Of course, that's why I couldn't identify them!"

"Crossbreeds?"

"When you graft one plant onto the other and create a new type of plant. And that's an even rarer specialty." Leif sobered.

"How rare?"

The mulish set to Leif's jaw meant he wouldn't answer without more prompting. "How many people can do it?" Valek asked.

"A few," Leif hedged.

"Two," Yelena said.

Leif shot her a nasty look.

"Do you know their names?" he asked.

"Our cousin Nutty Palm Zaltana, and our Councilman, Bavol Cacao Zaltana."

3

LEIF

Anger boiled. Leif shot from his chair. "There's no way either of them is involved with Owen!"

"Probably not directly," Yelena, his traitor of a sister, said.

"Not at all. They both know how dangerous Curare is." And Leif wasn't going to let anyone cast suspicion on them.

"All right, then prove it," Valek said. "Rule them out of the equation and we'll look elsewhere."

Except all the experts were fellow Zaltanas. His appetite gone, Leif pushed his plate away.

Janco chimed in between spoonfuls of eggs. "It should be easy to do with your lie-detecting mojo."

A queasy expression pinched Yelena's face. "He can't use it unless he has reason to believe they've committed a crime. It violates the Magician's Ethical Code."

"They *follow* a code of ethics?" Janco asked in surprise.

"You should know about it," Yelena said.

"Oh, I know about it. I just figured they all *ignored* it."

"Because, according to you, they're all evil and corrupt?"

"Not all. There are a couple exceptions." Janco inclined his head, indicating her and Leif. "I assumed they ignored it because it's what *I'd* do if I had magic."

"How do you know you don't have magic?" Onora asked, speaking for the first time that morning.

"I don't have magic." Janco huffed.

"But you can sense it."

"And you can sense the cold air, but that doesn't make you a snowman...er...woman."

As they argued over the definition of a magician, Leif collected the empty plates, stacking them in the sink. The thought of interrogating his family sat heavily in his stomach. Maybe a casual visit would work. But then his certainty of Bavol's innocence faded. He remembered how Bavol had dodged their questions when he and Yelena had visited. The man had lied to them, but at the time, Leif had thought it was regarding the Council's knowledge of Yelena's blocked magic.

After everyone finished eating, Leif followed them to the stables. The sun poked from the horizon. Cold air bit through his tunic. He handed Yelena a pouch full of herbal medicines with instructions on how to use them.

She raised an eyebrow at the unexpected weight.

"Just in case you run into trouble," he said.

"I'm traveling with two assassins and a master swordsman. How much trouble do you think we'll get in?"

He gave her a flat look.

"Yeah, okay." She hefted the pouch. "Feels about right." Yelena opened it. "Did you include the ginger tea that helps with nausea?"

"There are a few bags. Why? Are you still feeling sick?"

"Oh, no. Not at all." She tucked the medicines in her saddlebag.

The faint scent of licorice swirled around her. His magic mojo—as Janco called it—sensed she was hiding something. "Are you sure?"

"Yes. I'm healthy."

The sweet smell of truth. "Good. Although you might need that tea after it's Janco's turn to cook."

"I heard that," Janco called. He swung up into Beach Bunny's saddle and shot Onora a triumphant expression.

The quiet woman merely ignored Janco's posturing as she saddled The Madam. Kiki stood head to head with Rusalka, who remained in her stall. Her body language made it quite clear she wanted to go with Kiki and the others. Leif stroked her neck and fed her a peppermint.

Just before the group departed, Leif hugged his sister and made her promise to be careful.

"I will if you will," Yelena said. "If you discover Owen's hiding place, don't go after him with just Devlen for backup. Take Irys and at least another magician with you and about a half-dozen soldiers. Promise?" When he hesitated, she added, "If not for me, then do it for Mara."

Ah, hell. The thought of upsetting Mara always hurt him deep down. And if anything happened to Devlen, their brother-in-law, she'd be doubly upset. Not to mention how devastated Devlen's wife, Opal, and his children would be. "All right. All right. I promise."

"Good. Keep me updated on your progress."

"I will if you will," he said.

"It's a deal." She mounted Kiki.

Leif turned and met Valek's gaze. The infamous assassin had been his best man at his wedding, but Leif still didn't know him all that well. However, he would never question Valek's desire to keep Yelena safe. As if reading his thoughts, Valek nodded at him before spurring Onyx toward the main gate.

He watched the four of them leave. An unsettled feeling swirled in his stomach. Every time he and Yelena parted, one painful memory from his childhood always darkened his thoughts—the time he'd witnessed Yelena's kidnapping and done nothing to help. Each time she left him, he relived his shame and guilt. Fourteen years later, she'd returned and eventually forgave him. But though he'd only been a terrified eight-year-old at the time, he could never fully forgive himself. Instead, he'd made an uneasy peace with his actions. And he accepted that every time she left him, he'd worry that he'd never see her again.

"The horses need to be fed," Devlen said, bringing Leif back to the present.

Devlen mucked out the now-empty stalls. Aside from Rusalka, two other horses remained behind. One for Devlen to use, and the other would be given to the Clever Fox stables as a replacement for The Madam. The unflappable horse was now a member of their herd.

As Leif filled the buckets with grain, Devlen brought fresh water, and together they finished cleaning the rest of the stalls. Valek had invited Devlen to travel with them and eventually join Reema in the Commander's castle, but he'd declined, claiming he'd be more useful aiding Leif with the investigation.

"What is next?" Devlen asked.

"I need to check on the coals in the hothouse." And look for signs indicating crossbreeding to determine the purpose of the unknown plants. They had to have a purpose; otherwise, why take up space that could be used to grow more Curare vines? The factory in Lapeer that they'd shut down had the capacity to process twenty times the number of vines that grew in this one house.

Devlen followed him to the glass building. Using a shovel, Leif spread the glowing remains of the coals while Devlen filled the water pans. A puff of smoke stung Leif's eyes as he added more of the expensive white coals to the fire. They burned hotter and cleaner than the black type. The smell reminded him of Mara and he closed his eyes for a moment to breathe it in. The sugary scent always clung to her clothes after she'd spent the day working in the Keep's glass shop.

"How does the smoke escape?" Devlen asked. The tall man peered at the ceiling.

"Probably through the seams in the panes."

Devlen reached up and ran a finger along the wet drops, leaving a clear line in the condensation. "There are small holes in the glass."

Leif groaned. He'd been so focused on the plants, he hadn't considered who might have constructed the house. Devlen, too, creased his face in chagrin. He'd worked with Opal in her glass factory in Fulgor for the past six months.

The sisters had taught their husbands that making holes in a pane of glass after it hardened would shatter it, but while the glass was molten, holes of any size and number could be added. These panels had been made for this specific purpose. If they found the manufacturer, they might uncover the location of the other houses and, even better, Owen's hiding place.

"Not a word to our wives. Agreed?" Leif asked.

"Agreed."

MARIA V. SNYDER

4

YELENA

Valek set a fast pace and, even though Kiki switched to her smoothest gait, after a few hours in the saddle, I clutched Kiki's copper mane to keep from falling off. My recovery from Owen's attack hadn't been as complete as I'd thought. Lack of sleep didn't help, either.

All morning, we'd pause in a series of small river towns as we headed east, paralleling the Sunworth River. Janco and Valek would dismount and poke around, searching for magic. Or rather, seeking Rika Bloodgood's magical illusions, which may have been employed to conceal the three outlaws. Onora and I would visit the local authorities to inquire about any unusual activities and strange glass houses.

I lost track of the number of towns as the day wore on. We finally stopped for the night in one of the larger settlements. Valek checked us into the Anchor Inn and I collapsed on the bed as soon as he shut the door.

He was next to me in an instant. "Why didn't you tell me?"

"I just need to sleep. I'll be fine. You should be more worried about Janco and Onora sharing a room. One of them is going to kill the other by morning."

"Janco's trying to provoke her."

"And when she snaps?"

"He'll have a bruise and an ego to nurse."

"Are you sure it won't be worse?" Despite Valek's assurances of her loyalty, I didn't trust the girl. And since learning she'd shot me with an arrow laced with starlight, I'd wanted to punch her. Frustration flowed through me. If I had my magic, I'd examine her soul and learn just how dangerous she was. The Ethical Code be damned. She'd started it.

"She won't harm Janco, because it would upset me," Valek said. "And right now, she's still scared of me."

"And when she's no longer afraid?"

"Then it will get interesting."

Typical Valek bravado. If I had any energy, I'd argue.

Sensing my mood, Valek said, "Before you form an opinion of her, I'd suggest you get to know her better. Like you, she's been assaulted and raped. But unlike you, she hasn't killed her demons yet."

"Now you've done it." Regret for my earlier dark thoughts pulsed.

"I've done what?"

"You complicated things. My feelings for her were rather simple. It was nice to just dislike her. Now I want to help her. Too bad my powers—"

"Are not needed," Valek said. "You've overcome your difficulties without using magic, so can she. But I'm sure she'd like a friend to confide in."

"You're sure? Why do you care? She's after your job."

"I've always had people after my job, love. And the Commander's been telling me to find a protégé for years. She's the first to have real potential, and if she can step up, then perhaps she should."

I studied his face, searching for regret or sorrow over the prospect. Finding none, I relaxed back into the pillows. Valek tucked me in and left to listen to the local gossip. I fell asleep dreaming of our future together.

Morning intruded. I groaned and tightened my grip on Valek as he tried to disentangle himself from me and the blankets.

"A few more minutes," I mumbled.

"I caught a lead last night," he said, pulling my arms off his waist.

Suddenly wide-awake, I let go and sat up. "You found Owen? Why didn't you wake me?"

"Easy, love. It's never that simple. I talked to a man who knew about a strange house made of glass."

"And? Did you go check it out?"

"No. The man claimed he needed his brother's help to find the place again. He offered to get his brother and take me there in the morning, for a fee of course."

"Smells like a classic setup." Instead of taking the mark to the promised location, the journey would end in an ambush.

"Indeed. However, from his comments, I think Owen may have tried to erase his memories, which is why he needed his brother to find the location again."

"Still might be a setup."

He smiled. "There will be four of us."

"And if it's a trap, we'll be facing three magicians." I flung the blankets off and dug through my pack. "Make sure all your darts are filled with Curare."

"Yes, sir."

We dressed and met Janco and Onora for a fast breakfast. The man joined us at the stables. He was in his forties, broad-shouldered and good-natured despite the tension. He introduced himself as Tex. I checked that his shadow matched his physique, ruling out a magical disguise. A short sword hung from his waist, but he might have other weapons tucked in his clothes or boots. I drew my cloak tighter around my shoulders. Or rather, Reema's cloak. We had switched garments when I'd sent her to Ixia and out of danger.

Tex's brother was named Jax—a thick, muscled man the size of Ari, whose shadow also matched. A rolled-up horse whip was tied to Jax's belt. Janco eyed the whip with trepidation, rubbing his arms.

Valek introduced us. He used Janco's and Onora's real names, but changed mine to Elliona and referred to himself as Ilom. The men brought their own horses. Jax mounted a beefy gray quarter horse, and Tex rode a dark brown stallion.

Tex gazed at Kiki. "Is that one of those Sandseed horses?"

No sense lying. "Yes."

"Is it true they can go twice as fast as a normal horse?"

"Only when they're in the Avibian Plains, otherwise, no."

"Huh? I thought no one can go into the plains without getting lost."

"That's true, but if you're riding a Sandseed horse, they never get lost."

"That's handy," Tex said.

We discussed horses as Tex and his brother led us south. From the way Janco scanned our surroundings, I knew he was searching for any magical traces. Valek remained quiet, content to let me chat with the brothers. Onora appeared to be bored, but the stiffness in her movements said otherwise. She also kept well away from Jax and I wondered if the man who had assaulted her had been his size.

As Tex had said, he couldn't quite remember the route through the farmlands and forest. At one point, Tex and Jax argued on the right direction. I asked him how they'd found the place before.

"We've been working the river," Tex said. "Loading and

MARIA V. SNYDER

unloading the barges. Last season, a man hired us to transport these bundles of vines from this glass house you're so interested in to the river. I don't remember picking them up, but Jax does—that house really intrigued him. Apparently we did one trip. I collected the payment, but the man didn't pay enough, so we quit. I guess."

"Do you remember what the man looked like?" Valek asked.

"No. And Jax never met him, so, like I said, I don't remember much. It sounds crazy, I know."

It did, but if Owen had erased Tex's memories, and hadn't known about Jax, then it made sense.

After a few hours we crested a hill and stopped. Down below in the middle of a valley was a large glass house twice the size of the one near Broken Bridge. The afternoon sunlight reflected off its roof. Next to it stood another structure that resembled a barn. No one was in sight.

"There should be a…gardener around here," Jax said. "I think."

"We need to head back for another job," Tex said. "You folks okay with finding your own way from here? We're not in the plains." Concern creased his brow.

Genuine? Or a hell of a good actor? "Yes, thank you. Sandseed horses have an excellent sense of direction regardless of location," I said.

Valek paid Tex a generous sum. The man flashed him a grateful smile and headed back with his brother right behind him.

Janco rubbed his goatee, frowning. "Does anyone else think that's odd?"

"What's odd?" Valek asked.

"Those guys. They were…"

"Nice," I finished for him. "Don't tell me you've never met friendly people before."

"Not in my line of work. Who wants to bet me that there's an ambush waiting for us below?" Janco gestured to the valley.

"Do you sense any magic?" Valek asked.

"No, but we're pretty far. You?"

"Nothing."

A pang touched my chest. If I still had my magic, we'd know for sure if this was a trap.

"How do you want to proceed?" Onora asked Valek.

"You and Janco cut through the woods on the left side, check for any unfriendlies. I'll check right. Meet back here." Valek dismounted.

"And what about me?" I asked.

"Stay with the horses."

Red-hot anger flared. "Kiki can *stay* with the horses. I'm coming with you." I didn't wait for his permission. I swung down from Kiki's back, removed my cloak and yanked my bo staff from its holder on her saddle.

Valek studied me and I prepared for an argument. Instead he nodded. "Let's go." He untied his gray short cape and slung it over Onyx's saddle.

Onora and Janco melted into the woods, and I followed Valek. He wore Sitian clothes—a plain tan tunic and brown pants that blended with the surrounding forest. The trees and bushes remained bare of leaves, but a few buds dotted a number of branches, promising warmer days ahead.

Valek traveled through the underbrush without making a sound, his movements graceful and balanced like an acrobat's. I rustled behind him. My woodland skills had grown rusty with neglect. No need to slink about the woods when I'd already known exactly what creatures lurked inside. Since

I could no longer rely on magic, I suspected many hours of training would be in my future.

Using hand signals, Valek communicated when to stop, wait and go. We encountered no one, and didn't see tracks, broken branches or any other sign that another person had been here.

We returned to the horses and, soon after, Janco and Onora reported the same thing—no ambushers. Mounting our horses, we rode down into the valley. As we neared, Valek asked Janco if he sensed a magical illusion.

"No. I'll let you know if I do," Janco said.

Valek stopped us about fifty feet from the barn. He signaled for us to wait, dismounted and circled the buildings. I peered at the glass house. No condensation coated the panes and no greenery pressed against the sides. From this angle, it appeared to be empty.

When he reappeared he said, "No signs of activity anywhere and the barn door is locked."

"Let me," Janco said with a grin. He jumped off Beach Bunny and hurried toward the barn.

"He does know we can all pick a lock, right?" I asked Valek. Janco had taught me the art, and my set of picks held my hair up in an intricate knot.

"This one's a swivel." Valek drew his sword. "Come on."

Onora and I followed him around the building. Janco knelt next to an oversize door, working on a shiny new padlock. We waited behind him until he made a small sound of triumph. He removed the lock and glanced at Valek, who signaled him to open the door.

Janco yanked it open with a whoosh. We braced for an attack, but nothing happened. Instead a foul odor wafted from the entrance—the unmistakable rancid smell of death.

With a grim expression, Valek ventured inside. After a moment, he returned. "It's safe."

Covering our noses with our shirts, we filed in. From the overturned chairs and scattered trash, it appeared as if they'd left in a hurry. Valek crouched by the body of a man whose throat had been sliced open.

"The gardener?" I asked.

"Probably. He has dirt under his nails. No defensive wounds, which means he knew his attacker."

"Or he was trapped by magic," Janco said. "How long has he been dead?"

"Three or four days." Valek straightened. "Take a look around. See if they missed anything."

We spread out. A small bed and night table lined the far wall. Gardening tools hung near the door. I poked at the ashy remains of the fire, uncovering a half-burned parchment. Fishing it from the pile, I smoothed it flat, revealing a picture of a hobet plant, along with instructions for its care.

My shirt slipped down and the putrid smell filled my nose. It flipped the contents of my stomach and I bolted for the door. Once I reached clean air, the need to vomit slowly disappeared. Shivering with the cold, I retrieved my cloak from Kiki. Once ensconced in its warmth, I strode to the glass house. I peered through the clear walls. Leaves and broken stems littered the dirt floor. It appeared as if plants had been wrenched out by their roots. I spotted something white in the middle of the mess.

Wagon wheel tracks lined up next to the entrance. I guessed they'd loaded everything up that had been in the glass house and didn't bother to lock up. The knob turned with ease and I entered. The air was colder inside. Boot prints marked the muddy spots.

The white object was a sheet of parchment folded in half. When I picked it up, a loud pop sounded. I straightened.

Thousands of cracks raced through the glass like lightning. Fear sliced through my heart just as fast.

"Yelena!" Valek yelled from the doorway, too far away.

I yanked my hood over my head and dropped to the ground. Pressing my forehead to the dirt, I curled up like a turtle, lacing my fingers behind my neck as an explosion of glass roared.

5

VALEK

The glass walls and ceiling of the house shattered with an eruption of sound. Unable to reach Yelena in time, Valek watched in horror as razor-sharp shards and jagged chunks crashed down onto her huddled form. The force of the impact sent glass flying in all directions. He stumbled back, covering his face with his hands. Pinpricks of pain pierced his legs, arms and torso.

"Holy snow cats!" Janco yelled next to him.

When the noise died, Valek yanked his hands down. He raced along the side of the house, searching for Yelena in the heaping piles of broken glass. The gray fabric of her cloak poked through a mound. An ice-cold dread filled his heart when he spotted the blood. Without hesitation, he waded into the ruins. The glass crunched, popped and cracked under his boots.

"Careful," Janco said as he followed.

They reached Yelena's side. She was buried. They removed the big slabs and brushed off as much as possible. She tried to move, but her cloak was still pinned.

"Easy, love," he said, relieved she was conscious. "Let us free you first."

Yelena stilled. Blood soaked her back from dozens of slivers, but the real concern was a large triangle-shaped piece that jutted from her left side, just below her ribs. Janco pointed to it and mimed a yanking motion. Valek shook his head. They'd remove the dangerous one after they assessed where it had hit her.

Working together, Valek and Janco cleared the rest of the glass and freed her. By the time they finished, blood dripped from his and Janco's hands from the numerous cuts they'd gotten.

"Can you stand?" he asked her.

"Yes." She pushed up to a sitting position. All the color drained from her face. "Uh...maybe not. How bad—" She noticed the shard.

"Let's get you out of here first." He helped Yelena to her feet and supported her as they navigated the uneven debris.

Onora waited for them. She had retrieved the first-aid kit from Kiki's saddle. Once they cleared the house, Valek removed her ruined cloak and she sank to the ground. He cut away part of her shirt to expose the worst injury. It looked deep, and he worried it might have pierced her stomach. At least it wasn't close enough to endanger the baby, if she was in fact pregnant.

Yelena inspected the damage. "It shouldn't bleed out when it's removed, but the wound will need to be sealed."

Good thing the first-aid kit contained a jar of Rand's glue. The Commander's late chef had invented an edible adhesive for his cakes that also worked on skin.

"Let's take care of these others first," Valek said. "Do you want me to pour the medicinal Curare on your back?" Yelena's father had supplied them with a watered-down version of the drug for this contingency.

"Save it for when you seal the serious wounds."

Being the only one without cuts on her hands, Onora used a pair of tweezers to remove the slivers from Yelena's back and the back of her head. Onora peeled off Yelena's tunic as she worked. Janco hovered, getting in the way.

"Do a sweep of the area. Make sure no one is around," Valek ordered him. "If it's secure, we'll camp here for the night."

"Yes, sir." Janco dashed off.

"Thanks," Onora said. She continued, creating a pile of bloody pieces next to her. "It could have been worse. The cloak's fabric stopped a bunch." Onora continued to pluck glass from Yelena's skin and then her hair.

Valek hated seeing Yelena hurt. A helpless frustration boiled up his throat, and the desire to murder the person who'd harmed her pulsed with every heartbeat. If she reclaimed her magic, he'd never take her healing powers for granted again.

"Valek, attend to your wounds," Onora said, shooing him away. "You can't help me with bloody fingers."

He stifled a protest—she had a point. And now that she had mentioned them, pain flared to life. Multiple stings peppered his body and blood stained his clothes. Valek pulled glass from his skin, then washed his hands and wrapped a bandage around his right palm, which had sustained the largest gash. He'd save the glue for Yelena.

When Onora finished, he knelt next to his heart mate and met her gaze. "Ready?"

She nodded.

He grasped the triangular shard and yanked it out in one quick motion. She gasped. Blood poured from the wound. Pressing a bandage on it, Valek stanched the flow as she lay on her uninjured side. When the surge eased, he rubbed Curare around and in the injury, then inspected it. It wasn't as

MARIA V. SNYDER

deep as he feared. Relieved, he used Rand's glue and sealed the gash before tending to the others.

In the time it took for Janco to return and build a campfire, Yelena's cuts had been cleaned and wrapped in bandages, and she'd changed into fresh clothes. Despite her protests, Valek tucked her into her bedroll, insisting she rest. The sun balanced on the crest of the hill and darkness would soon fill the valley.

Janco boiled water for one of Leif's healing teas. "I knew those brothers were up to no good. They must have doubled back after they left us."

"Did you see them?" Valek asked.

"No, they were gone by the time I did my sweep. The crossbow must have been hidden somewhere nearby."

"Crossbow?" Onora asked Janco.

"Of course a crossbow. How else could they have shattered the glass from a distance? It had to be a bolt."

It made sense, but Valek had felt a brush of magic right before the walls exploded. "I think it was magic."

"But I thought you checked," Janco said.

"I did." He'd not only circled the building, but touched the glass walls to ensure no magical alarms had been installed.

"It was a booby trap," Yelena said, pushing up to her elbow.

"Then what set it off?" Janco asked.

She gazed at the fire as if in thought. "There was a piece of parchment on the ground. As soon as I picked it up, the glass started cracking. It must have triggered the trap."

"A magical booby trap?" Janco cursed. "Oh, that's just wonderful. The more I learn about magic, the more I hate it."

Valek considered. "Was there a message on the paper?"

"I didn't have time to look," Yelena said. "It's probably still there."

Janco sprang to his feet. "I'll get it." He crunched through the debris. Cracks and pops marked his noisy passage. After a few minutes, he returned with the folded note and a murder-ous expression on his face.

Janco handed it to Valek. "Read it."

Valek unfolded the parchment. One word had been writ-ten in black ink.

"Gotcha."

Fury burned in his chest. Owen would pay for this little stunt the next time Valek encountered him. And he wouldn't allow Owen to catch him in a null shield. Oh no. Valek had no intention of letting the magician know he was in mortal danger. Not even with a note.

"Let me see." Yelena held out her hand. Small cuts criss-crossed her knuckles.

He passed it to her.

She huffed. "Typical Owen."

"How do you know it was Owen?" Onora asked.

"He's the only one of the magicians who can set a trap like this," Yelena explained. "Rika is limited to magical illusions, and Tyen can only move objects."

"What else can Owen do?" She poured hot water into a teacup and gave it to Yelena.

Valek approved of her question. One of the lessons of being an assassin was to know everything possible about your mark.

Yelena crinkled her nose as she sniffed the tea, either dis-gusted by the smell or the topic. "Owen's quite talented. He can mentally communicate with another magician, which isn't a big deal, but his ability to lie to another when communicat-ing mind to mind is extremely rare."

"He can also lasso one of those null shields around some-one pretty quick," Janco added. "They can block magic, but not objects or people, except for—"

"I know what they are," Onora said, glancing at Valek.

MARIA V. SNYDER

Valek hid his amusement. She was worried about upsetting him.

"Owen can also mess with a person's memories, erasing the real ones and inserting fake ones. Or he can just tear your mind apart, leaving you a mindless idiot." Yelena rubbed her forehead, no doubt remembering Owen's attack.

"So that's what happened to Janco," Onora quipped.

Janco tsked. "Nasty."

"Accurate." She shot back.

"You wish. I can think circles around you!"

"I agree. Your mind spins round and round, like a gnat's. A truly dizzying intellect."

Janco squawked in protest, but before he could respond, Valek said, "That's enough."

Janco clamped his mouth shut, but shot Onora a venomous glare. She ignored it. This time. It was inevitable that Janco would push too far and they'd fight, which would be interesting to watch. However, for tonight, Valek didn't want to upset Yelena.

"Is that the extent of Owen's magical powers?" Onora asked.

"No," Yelena said. "He can heat objects. I once held a knife to his throat and he made the handle so hot, I had to drop it, which means he can also start fires. And apparently set traps. That's new to me, so he might have other hidden powers."

"Gee, what a sweetheart." Janco's tone dripped with sarcasm. "Sounds like the creep could be a Master Magician."

Yelena sipped her tea. "He's not that powerful, but he's close. I wonder if he took the master-level test and failed. That could explain some of his...bitterness and antisocial behavior. It's a brutal test." She covered her expression with the cup.

"Have you taken it?" Onora asked.

"Oh, no. Not really." Yelena glanced at the embers swirling in the hot air above the fire.

Probably searching for the bat that was usually her constant companion when it wasn't hibernating during the cold and warming seasons. Valek wondered if the bat would find her or even if it could find her now that she no longer had magic. He hoped the little creature wouldn't abandon her.

The bat had arrived soon after Yelena's first trip into the fire world. Valek remembered being utterly devastated when she'd disappeared into the fire world after the Warper battle. She'd been gone for months. If she hadn't reached out to Leif... He'd planned to join her there.

"According to Irys, when you returned from the fire world you passed the master-level test," Janco said.

"But I didn't meet all the requirements for being a Master Magician. No, it just confirmed what I'd suspected, that I was a Soulfinder and my job was to find lost souls and guide them to either the sky or the fire world, depending on their deeds while alive."

Janco thumped his chest. "I'm sure I'm destined for the fire world. At least I'll be in good company." He gave Onora and Valek a pointed look.

Yelena frowned. "It's not something to joke about, Janco. It's a terrible place full of pain, despair and utter misery. And you're not destined for it."

"Why not? I've lied, cheated, stolen things. I've killed people."

"You have also *saved* people, sacrificed yourself and are helping to keep the peace by stopping the truly evil people from taking over. It's not so much your actions, but your intentions and your choices." Yelena met Valek's gaze. "And it's a matter of balance. Even if you did terrible things, all the good you do will eventually outweigh it, tipping you toward the sky."

A lovely sentiment, but Valek needed a few decades of good deeds to balance out his years as an assassin for hire. He'd killed to learn how to be a better killer. All in order to assassinate the King of Ixia. Granted, the King had been corrupt and evil, but those others had just been marks to him. Except for the men who had murdered his brothers in the King's name. They deserved to die.

Janco's brow creased in thought—a rare expression for him. "Does this mean I have to be nice to Little Miss Assassin?"

"Yes, because I'm no longer a Soulfinder, so I can't rescue you from the fire world."

Now Janco blinked at Yelena. All humor dropped from his face and he pressed a hand to his heart. "You would have rescued me?" he asked in awe.

"Of course, you idiot! I wouldn't let you suffer."

Despite being called an idiot, he grinned. Or was that in spite of? Hard to tell with Janco.

Onora shook her head. "Now you've done it," she muttered.

To forestall Janco's obnoxiousness, Valek changed the subject. "Onora, you have first watch. Janco, take the second shift, and I'll go last."

"That means I have the third shift," Yelena said in a tone that warned of a major battle if he disagreed.

"All right. In the morning we'll stop at the closest town and send Leif a message, informing him of the booby trap."

"Do you think Owen had time to rig all the houses?" Janco asked Valek.

"He has a six-day head start. And he knows we'll be searching for them. Plus the Curare is too valuable to leave behind, so I'd expect him to gather as much as he can. He'll need money to finance his next endeavor."

Owen had claimed to have discovered something big

enough to make the Commander forgive him for his betrayal. It could have been a boast, but Valek doubted it.

"What about the dead body?" Janco jerked a thumb toward the barn.

"We'll inform the local authorities in the morning and let them handle it."

"Does anyone else think it...odd that Owen murdered the gardener?" Yelena asked.

"No," Valek answered. "The gardener probably had information about the operation. It was smart to silence him."

"Yes, but..." She played with the string on her tea bag.

"Owen murdered his brother and the others," Janco said.

"We still don't know for certain who killed them, but assuming it was him, he *hired* an assassin. Big difference." Yelena gazed at the liquid in her cup. "And I'm still not convinced it was him. In all my dealings with Owen, he never acted like a killer. Think about it. He went out of his way to scare me off by *pretending* to kidnap Reema back in Fulgor. Even when he captured us, his solution was to erase our memories. Why not just slit our throats and bury us?"

"Because if he killed you, Valek would hunt him down and tear him apart," Janco said.

True. Valek's fingers itched to grasp a blade just thinking about anyone harming his heart mate. But what Yelena said also had merit. Did she suspect Onora had assassinated the trio? "If Owen didn't do it, then who did?" he asked her.

"It's just a theory, and you're not going to like it."

With that one comment, he knew. And she was right. He didn't like it, but he had wondered the same thing. "The Commander."

Yelena met his gaze. "Owen is proof that the Commander lied to the Sitian Council about executing the magician four

MARIA V. SNYDER

years ago. He'd want to erase all the evidence that connects them, including all Owen's coconspirators."

Janco added another log to the fire. "But the Sitians know Owen's alive and producing Curare for the Commander."

"There's no proof the Commander has Curare and, as long as Owen isn't captured, it's only our word that he's still alive."

"That should be good enough." Janco puffed out his chest.

"The Commander can say we must have mistaken Ben for his brother. He can order you, Valek and Onora to keep quiet. In the political world and without any hard evidence, the Council can't do anything."

Interesting theory. "Are you saying the Commander hired another assassin to kill Ben and the others?" he asked Yelena, wondering if she suspected Onora of assassinating them. Not that she'd suggest it in front of the girl; nor did she glance in Onora's direction.

"I'm not accusing him. I'm just speculating. But if he wishes to keep the relationship between Ixia and Sitia civil, he would need Owen to disappear forever."

"He went to a lot of trouble to get all that Curare," Janco said. "I don't think he's worried about being civil."

The rest of the evening passed without incident. When Yelena woke him for his watch shift, lines of strain marked her face.

Concerned, he sat up. "What's wrong? Do you need something for the pain?" He kept his voice low so he wouldn't wake the others.

"I already dipped into Leif's goody bag," she whispered.

"That bad?"

She waved off his comment, which meant it had been bad and she didn't want to worry him. Too late. He'd never *not* worry about her.

Yelena settled next to him. "I've been thinking about Owen. He's too smart to hire a couple of locals to transport the Curare vine from the hothouse to the river. Locals get curious, ask questions, gossip in the taverns. All things he avoided. Otherwise we would have gotten wind of his operation before."

"You think he paid the brothers to bring us out here? Pretend they didn't remember everything?"

"Yes."

It made sense. "We knew it was a risk coming here."

She agreed, but something was off. He studied her. Her movements were stiff, and she held herself as if she'd break. His own cuts throbbed, so he could only imagine how much more pain she was in. Despite that, he sensed another problem.

"You liked them," he said.

A brief, wan smile. "Yes. And, even though I didn't completely trust them, I relaxed and wanted to believe they were genuine. Did you know they lied?"

"I suspected, but thought finding one of the glass houses was worth the risk."

"I know I should trust no one, but…it's exhausting."

Ah. The real reason for the melancholy. "You've been relying on your magic to assess people you meet and now that's blocked, so you're at a loss and probably second-guessing yourself. Right?"

She nodded.

"Then I'll teach you how to read body language. Most people give themselves away when they're lying."

"Most people?"

"I've only encountered a few who can lie to me." Eventually, he would discover the ruse, but, at the time, they'd convinced him.

"Who?" she asked.

MARIA V. SNYDER

"The Commander. Onora. The others are...gone."

She arched an eyebrow. "Gone?"

"I don't like being fooled."

"And the Commander?"

Valek glanced at Onora. Curled up on her side, she appeared to be asleep. "The Commander's lying is a more... recent event."

"But he didn't tell you about Owen."

"Oh, he's kept things from me before, but he's never looked me in the eye and lied."

"What changed?" she asked.

What indeed? "I suspect a few things."

"Such as?"

"Not here, love. Janco's far more interested in our conversation than his dreams."

"Am not," Janco said, not in the least embarrassed he'd been caught eavesdropping. "Besides, I don't have dreams, I have nightmares."

Before Janco could launch into a detailed description, Valek said, "Then we'll let you get back to them." He stood to allow Yelena to take his place under the blankets.

She untied his short cape and handed it to him. They'd have to buy her a new cloak to use during their trip to Ixia. Once there, she could reclaim her own cloak and give the new one to Reema. Too bad she didn't have it with her before. The special resistant fabric of her garment would have stopped many of the smaller shards of glass.

Valek added a few logs to the dying fire. The air had grown quite cold. Then he moved away from the light, letting his eyes adjust to the darkness. He did a sweep of the surroundings and, when he was satisfied no one lurked nearby, Valek found a spot to watch over the camp until dawn.

When the sun rose, he woke the others. Janco grumbled.

Onora said nothing as usual. Yelena sat up and winced, pressing a hand to her side. Valek insisted she drink a cup of Leif's wet-dog tea. He checked her bandages. With a bit of sleight of hand, he rubbed a couple drops of the watered-down Curare along her injuries before applying fresh bandages.

"I saw that," she said.

"No, you didn't." When she opened her mouth to protest, he said, "We have a long day ahead of us."

They packed up and headed northeast, returning to follow the Sunworth River. At the first decent-sized town, Valek sent a message to Leif, warning him of the booby trap inside the glass houses while Yelena informed the local security forces about the dead gardener.

As they continued east, Janco asked him, "Are we going to keep searching for more of those hothouses?"

"No. Owen's probably cleaned them all out. We'll let Leif and Devlen hunt for the rest of them. We need to rendezvous with my team and locate that other tunnel into Ixia." His team had expected him days ago, and he'd have to eventually report his detour to the Commander. At least they had collapsed the hidden tunnel located near Lapeer. Owen had been making a tidy profit by allowing smugglers to use his tunnels for a fee. Valek loved it when criminals turned greedy. It made his job of catching them so much easier.

"Then we should cross to the north side of the river," Janco suggested. "The other tunnel was on that side near the Ixian border."

"Ari said they traced the smugglers to the foothills of the Soul Mountains. We can travel faster on the road than in the forest." Valek considered. The intel from Ari and his corps had only pinpointed one location. Janco had discovered the Lapeer tunnel by accident. It might be possible there were more. "Actually, you—"

"Don't say it," Yelena said.

Affronted, Janco asked her, "Would it kill you to give a guy a bit of praise?"

"If that guy is you, then yes. Humility is not one of your personality traits."

"You're just mad because now we're going to travel through the woods, which means sleeping on the ground and not in an inn."

"I can handle it better than you. Your joints crack and pop every time you stand up, old man."

"Old man! I'm only seven years older than you."

"Are you sure it's not seven *dog* years? You have a lot of gray in your muzzle," Yelena quipped, referring to Janco's salt-and-pepper goatee.

"Every single one of these gray hairs is directly linked back to saving you or being involved in one of your schemes."

"Oh no, you don't. I distinctly remember the time…"

Valek ignored the rest of their bickering. Usually Yelena avoided verbally sparring with Janco, but, by the glint in her eyes, she enjoyed needling their friend.

Instead, Valek concentrated on the terrain along the northern bank of the Sunworth River. Not far from their location, the waterway turned southeast and became the actual border between Ixia and Sitia near the Soul Mountains. There wouldn't be any bridges along that segment. Plus, the forest had been cut down for a hundred feet past the bank, so anyone attempting to cross the border at that point would be seen by the Ixian patrolmen. Which was why the tunnels worked so well.

When the Commander closed the border after the takeover, he cleared the land from the Sunset Ocean in the west all the way to the mountains in the east. Valek doubted Owen would build a tunnel in the open area between the countries or under the river. Which meant that the only logical place for a tunnel would be in the foothills of the Soul Mountains.

"We'll keep to the road," Valek said, interrupting one of Janco's rants. "Speed is vital at this point."

"And beds," Janco added.

Valek gave him a flat stare.

"Nothing wrong with that." Janco thumped his stomach. "Better sleep means a better response to danger. We've no idea what nasties are lurking in that tunnel."

"Hate to say this, but Janco has a point." Yelena grimaced as he puffed his chest out. "Owen knows you're searching for the tunnels. He booby-trapped the glass house, so it makes sense that he'd rig the tunnel, as well." She gestured to Janco. "We can send him in first since he's the Master Illusion Detector."

Air hissed as Janco's chest deflated. "Me?"

"Yes, you. Weren't you just boasting that—"

Valek spurred Onyx into a gallop. If Yelena had the energy to tease Janco, then she'd be okay for another couple of hours and they could reach the next town by nightfall.

They rendezvoused with Valek's team two days later in a mining camp located in the foothills just a mile inside Ixia. The small unit had spent the extra time searching for signs of the tunnel without success.

"Have you heard from Bravo team?" Valek asked Ivon, Alpha team's leader.

The wiry man snapped to attention. "Yes, sir. Qamra sent a message four days ago. Her team located two warehouses used by the smugglers in MD-5 and burned them to the ground as ordered."

Interesting. Ari had found only one. "And her assessment?"

"At the time of the missive, she was unable to confirm if

MARIA V. SNYDER

General Ute had any knowledge or involvement in the operation. Her plans were to continue the investigation."

"Very good."

Ivon's steel-gray gaze never wavered from Valek's face. Very little slipped past the man's notice. "I'm sorry we were unable to be as effective, sir."

"No need to apologize. Show me where the trail ended."

"Yes, sir." Ivon unrolled a map marked with the place Ari had identified and handed it to Valek.

The spot was about a mile east. The map also indicated the locations Ivon's team had checked. Valek planned to leave Yelena in the camp with Onora nearby, protecting her. Smudges of exhaustion darkened the area under Yelena's green eyes. The fast pace hadn't been conducive to healing.

However, in order for Yelena to agree to his plan, he'd have to choose his words with the utmost care. "No need for all of us to go traipsing around. Janco and I will home in on any magical illusions that might be hiding wagon tracks or the entrance and we'll return once we find it so we can go over options."

"I'm pretty sure there'll only be two," Janco said. "Enter or cover the entrance with a bunch of rocks. Frankly, I'd vote for just blocking the damn thing. No reason to go inside."

"Unless that's where Owen is hiding," Yelena said.

"Even more reason to collapse it."

"Why would he hide inside when he knows we're searching for it?" Onora asked.

Valek met Yelena's gaze. Was she remembering the time they had hidden inside a dungeon? She smiled. That would be a yes.

"Sometimes the best places to hide are the most obvious," she said. "Owen's smart. He knows Valek has orders to put the tunnel out of commission and blocking the entrance is the easiest way. Why look inside? And don't forget Tyen can move those boulders with his magic."

"Lovely." Janco scratched the scar where the bottom half of his right ear used to be. "And what happens if they are hiding there? Let's face it. Between Owen's ability to trap Valek, Rika confusing us with her illusions and Tyen tossing boulders at us, we're fu...er...outmatched."

Valek agreed. Head-to-head, *outmatched* didn't even begin to describe it. However... "The trick is to avoid detection."

"And how exactly do we do that?" Janco asked.

"Carefully. Come on, it's getting late. I want to cover as much ground as possible before the sun sets." Valek consulted the map.

"How can my team aid you, sir?" Ivon asked.

"Talk to the locals and the miners. See if anyone noticed or heard anything that might point us in the right direction."

"Yes, sir." Ivon called to his men.

"What about us?" Onora asked.

"Find a place in the camp where we can set up and make sure the horses have a comfortable spot."

"Busywork," Yelena said. "I know what you're doing."

"You do?"

"Feigning innocence doesn't work on me." She waved a hand. "Don't worry. I'm not going to insist on accompanying you. You're right. I'd be useless for this mission."

"That's not the reason." He tried to explain, but she strode away.

Onora remained. "I'll keep a close watch on her."

"Good."

She hurried after Yelena.

Janco watched her. "You're trusting her?"

For now. "Why do you ask?"

"That hit on Ben Moon and the others."

Valek waited.

"You're gonna make me say it, aren't you?"

"Yep."

Janco scrunched up his face as if in pain. "The Commander ordered you to shut Owen's entire operation down. It makes sense he ordered his shiny new assassin to do the same thing. It'd be dead easy for Onora to make it appear as if The Mosquito was the culprit. And you already know all this, don't you?"

Valek kept his expression neutral, but he was impressed. "I thought Ari was supposed to be the smart one."

"Yeah, well, he isn't here, so I gotta do all the thinking. And I'm not happy about, either. It makes my head hurt."

Valek and Janco spent the rest of the day hunting for the familiar sticky feel of magic in the foothills. They returned late and left early the next morning to resume the search. Another two full days passed before Janco stopped Beach Bunny.

He pressed his hand to his right ear. "Son of a snow cat!"

"You're not thinking again, are you?" Valek drew next to Janco, halting Onyx.

"Not funny. It's gotta be a superstrong illusion."

Valek dismounted. "Which direction?"

Janco pointed to the right. Nothing appeared out of the ordinary. The bare branches of the trees dipped and swayed in a cold northern breeze that smelled of snow, despite it being a couple weeks into the warming season. High, thin clouds filtered the sunlight.

Valek pulled his sword. Janco slid off Beach Bunny and yanked his weapon from its sheath. The rattle and tumble of dried leaves filled the air. This patch of forest grew in a dip in the rolling terrain near the base of the Soul Mountains. To the east, the jagged snowcapped peaks stretched high, like a row of gigantic corn plants reaching for the sun.

The mountain range earned its name from old legends. Folklore claimed the peaks snagged souls as they ascended toward the sky. These trapped souls haunted the frozen heights and sucked the life from anyone who dared climb past the tree line. Valek believed it to be just a story to explain why no one who tried to reach the summit ever returned. The lack of breathable air was the more likely explanation. Although some also asserted that mysterious people who supposedly lived on the other side of the mountains patrolled the upper regions to prevent anyone from crossing into their homeland, keeping their existence a secret.

Pure nonsense. Valek returned his attention to the task at hand. He hadn't expected Owen's tunnel to be this high in the foothills, but the isolated location was ideal.

Janco aimed for an ordinary group of trees and hissed in pain as he disappeared from sight. Increasing his pace, Valek hurried after him and encountered magic. The invisible force pressed against his skin. Pushing through felt like swimming in mud. He found Janco rubbing his temple on the other side. Valek scanned the area for possible threats. Nothing so far.

A mass of oversize boulders was piled next to a hill. At first glance, it resembled a natural rock slide from the mountains, but upon closer inspection the heap was too neatly stacked. It must be blocking the tunnel.

"Looks like someone beat us to it," Valek said.

"No." Janco's voice strained with effort. "Move closer."

He did. The air thickened. Another illusion. "Clever." It would stop the smugglers from using it, but it kept the tunnel open in case Owen needed it again in the future.

"Could be a trap."

"Indeed." Valek tightened his grip on his sword and drew

MARIA V. SNYDER

a knife with his free hand. "I'm just going to confirm there's a tunnel behind it."

Janco straightened. "Then I'll come confirming with you, just in case."

The pressure on his body increased with each step. Janco paled when they reached the authentic-looking rocks. Even knowing it wasn't real, Valek braced for impact as he strode right into the pile. He muscled through the magic.

No one ambushed them. The tunnel's entrance was empty. Valek crept inside a few feet and listened for any noises that would indicate people were farther inside. No sounds bubbled up from the solid darkness.

Wagon wheel ruts warped the ground just past the opening. Janco drew in a deep breath. Relief smoothed his features and he crouched down to inspect the marks, running his fingers along the smooth grooves.

"How old?" Valek asked.

"Eight to ten days."

"Probably the last smugglers before Rika set the illusion."

"Now what?"

"Return to camp and discuss the next step."

"How about we inform the Sitian authorities and let them deal with it? After all, they have all those magicians," Janco suggested.

"That's one option."

They mounted their horses and headed back to camp. It was late afternoon by the time they arrived. Valek slowed Onyx. A number of people milled about the camp. More than he'd expected. Concern for Yelena pulsed in his chest until he recognized Ivon.

"Report," he ordered his lieutenant.

"We've been talking to the other mining camps, sir. Two of them had a significant amount of food stolen from their stores."

"And why is this relevant?"

Ivon snapped his fingers and signaled one of his men, who dashed away. "A witness caught sight of the culprits."

An uneasy sensation brushed his stomach. He met Janco's gaze.

"Can't be good," Janco said.

Ivon's sergeant approached with a grubby teen boy wearing a torn miner's jumpsuit. The all-black material had a row of green diamond shapes down each sleeve, indicating the miner worked for MD-5.

"Tell Adviser Valek what you told me, Lewin," Ivon ordered the teen.

Under the coating of dust, the young man's face drained of color. Lewin stared at Valek as if he peered into the mouth of a dragon just about to eat him. "Um...uh...it was the... the middle of the night and I was on the...the way to the latrine," Lewin stuttered. "I heard voices ar...arguing near the supply shed, so I crept up tr...trying not to make noise, but I couldn't see nobody." He rubbed his chin with his sleeve. "Yet the...the voices kept at it as if there were a couple of invisible ghosts." Lewin glanced around as if expecting them to tell him he was crazy.

No one said a word. Valek's unease turned sharp, jabbing his guts. "Go on," he urged Lewin.

"There's been lots of ac...activity around here and weird... stuff. So I followed the voices to the...the edge of the camp. And..." He shuddered. "Three people step...stepped from the air. Bulging sacks floated behind them. They con...continued into the woods, heading west. I found out later the stores had been raided."

Valek and Janco exchanged another glance.

"I hate it when I'm right," Janco said.

"Can you describe them?" Valek asked Lewin.

MARIA V. SNYDER

"Yes, sir. Two men and one lady."

Valek tightened his grip on Onyx's reins. "Did you see their faces?"

"Yes, sir." Lewin described the thieves.

Janco cursed under his breath.

"Anything else?" Valek asked, almost hoping the answer was no.

Lewin scuffed his boot in the dirt. "Yeah. Their uniforms. They wo...wore the Commander's colors."

The information rendered Janco speechless. However, Valek knew Janco would say *holy snow cats*. If Valek considered the bright side, at least they knew where Owen, Rika and Tyen were. Too bad they were in Ixia and appeared to be heading toward the Commander.

6

LEIF

"Nope, haven't seen anything like that before. Good day." The glassmaker hustled Leif from his shop, closing the door right behind him.

At least he didn't slam it, Leif thought. He wiped the sweat from his brow with the back of his hand. Between the heat pumping from the glass factory's brick walls and the unseasonably hot afternoon sun, his tunic was soaked. Leif returned the small square of glass with the miniature holes to his pack. He'd cut a couple of pieces from the glass house's ceiling for him and Devlen to take along and show to the glassmakers.

He scanned the street. A few people walked along the row of factories and businesses in Whitestone's small downtown. Over the past nine days they'd been checking with every glass factory and workshop in ever-widening arcs from Owen's farmhouse. They hadn't been back there in the past four days, and Leif planned to return after this stop. There hadn't been any messages from Yelena, and that worried him.

Whitestone was located two days southeast and about a half day from the border with the Cloud Mist's lands.

Devlen rounded the corner. Hard to miss the tall Sandseed among the paler Moons.

"Any luck?" Leif asked when his brother-in-law drew closer.

"No. You?"

"Think I've found something."

"Oh?"

"Guy in there showed me the door faster than I could eat a slice of apple pie."

"That is an impressive amount of speed," Devlen agreed.

"And he smelled like black licorice."

"Which you do not like."

"Not at all." He'd always hated it. The candy tasted of fear and deceit.

"Shall we go talk to him again?" Devlen asked.

"Thought you'd never ask."

They entered the thick air. Five kilns roared, masking the sounds of the glassworkers who sat at benches and shaped the molten slugs of glass gathered onto the end of their pontil irons. Assistants scurried, fetching tools, cracking off pieces and filling the annealing ovens to cool the piping-hot glass slowly. The open windows did nothing to dispel the force of the heat.

The older man Leif had spoken with earlier directed the traffic, but once he spotted them he hustled over with a scowl. The spicy scent of red pepper burned the inside of Leif's nostrils. Anger had replaced the man's fear.

"Get out," he shooed. "I've no time for your nonsense. I've orders to fill."

"This will not take long." Devlen projected his voice through the noise. "Your office." When the man hesitated, he leaned closer and said, "Now."

The man bolted for an open door to the left. Nice. And it'd been the reason Leif waited for Devlen before confronting the lying glassmaker. They followed close behind. Leif shut the door on the din.

The neat and utilitarian office lacked personality. No pictures hung on the walls. No decorative glass lined the shelves.

Devlen laid his square sample on the desk.

The glassmaker jabbed a finger at it. "I've told you—"

"Look again," Leif said. "Closer this time."

The man huffed with annoyance and picked it up, pretending to inspect the piece. A fog of black licorice almost gagged Leif. The man was terrified.

"The person who ordered those panels is no longer a threat," Leif said in his most soothing tone, letting his magic mix with the words. "We've halted his operations and are in the process of determining how extensive it is."

"We who?" he asked.

"Me, Leif Zaltana and my colleague, Devlen Sandseed."

The man's fear eased only a fraction. Leif would have been insulted, but unfortunately he'd dealt with Owen and understood just how much of a scary bastard the magician could be. And with the size of this operation, Owen couldn't erase all the staff's memories—too many people.

"Also the Sitian Council and the Master Magicians," Leif added.

"Have you arrested him?" the man asked.

"Not yet. He's on the run, but every city and town has been alerted and he'll be caught soon." Leif hoped.

"Then he remains a threat."

"I'll order the local security forces keep a close watch on you—"

"Not me. My family."

Typical. At least Owen stayed consistent. "Your family, then."

"And in exchange?"

"A list of locations where you delivered those special glass panels."

The silence stretched and Leif sensed a variety of emotions. The bitter tang of fear dominated.

Finally, the man pulled open a drawer and rummaged through the files. He handed Leif a stack of papers. Leif scanned the pages and counted enough panels to construct at least ten glass houses. Delivery dates and locations had been written on the orders. The closest one was about a day's ride west. The others were scattered north and east, up toward the Sunworth River.

"Can I keep these?" Leif asked.

"Yes."

"Thank you. I'll inform Captain Ozma of the situation right away. We talked to her this morning and none of her forces have seen anyone matching Owen's description in this area."

The man's relief smelled of sweet grass. "Good."

They left and stopped by the security offices. Captain Ozma sent a detail to the glass factory to collect more information.

Leif studied the sky. "We won't be able to reach the closest hothouse today, but, if we leave now, we can make it to the town of Marble Arch in time for supper."

"Let me guess, there is an inn there that serves some type of delectable dish that you cannot find anywhere else." Devlen's tone rasped with smugness.

"Wrong, Mr. Know-It-All! It's a *tavern*, not an inn."

"A thousand apologies."

"Can you say that again without the sarcasm?"

"No."

They had stabled their horses in the guards' barn. Devlen had picked a sturdy cream-colored horse with a dark brown mane and tail. She had lovely russet eyes and she watched Devlen's every move. Leif had teased him that it was love at first sight. Devlen named her Sunfire, which was a heck of a lot better than Beach Bunny.

Mounting the horses, they headed east and, as predicted, they sat at a table in the corner of the Daily Grind tavern just in time for supper.

"Lots of stone carvers come here." Leif explained the name to Devlen. "Marble and granite fill this whole area of the Moon Clan's lands. These people earn their living either quarrying it from the ground or chiseling, shaping and grinding it for use."

A server approached and Leif ordered without consulting Devlen. "Two ales and two extra-large portions of pit beef, please."

"Pit beef? Sounds...unappetizing," Devlen said.

"Have I ever *steered* you wrong?"

Devlen groaned. "You have been spending too much time with Janco."

While they waited for the food, Leif spread out the pages they'd received from the glassmaker and they marked the locations of all the glass houses on a map.

"My father will be here in roughly five days." Leif traced a route with his finger. "We have enough time to check three of them on the way back to the farmstead."

Late-morning sunlight glinted off the glass panes of the hothouse. Leif stopped Rusalka before drawing too close. No need to tip anyone off that they were nearby. The long, thin structure sat in the middle of an open clearing along with a small wooden building. Forest surrounded the complex. This was the first of the three they planned to check on their return to Owen's ex-headquarters.

From this angle, it seemed as if the place was deserted. No greenery stained the inside of the glass house and, after an hour of observation, no one appeared.

Devlen returned from doing a reconnaissance. "Nothing. All's quiet."

"Suspiciously quiet?" Leif asked.

"No. Abandoned quiet."

They ventured closer. Leif tasted the wind, seeking the flavors of past intentions. He drew in deep breaths, sensing the echoes of emotions. The trees rustled and the dry grass crackled under Rusalka's hooves. Otherwise, all remained undisturbed.

Peering through the glass of the house, Leif confirmed that nothing grew inside. A crate filled with an assortment of objects sat in the center.

"Perhaps there is information in the box," Devlen said next to him. He strode to the entrance.

Leif followed. When Devlen opened the door, stale musty air puffed out. They entered.

"Looks like they yanked the plants in a hurry," Leif said. He bent to grab a handful of soil, testing the moisture. He freed a root that had been left behind. It was brittle. "It's been about two weeks since this place was in use."

"That fits the timeline," Devlen said. He knelt next to the crate.

"There's...something...off." Leif wiped the dirt from his hands.

Devlen paused. "Off?"

"I can't pinpoint it. It's...subtle." Leif joined his brother-in-law. "Is there anything in there of value?"

Devlen reached into the box.

"Malice," Leif said. "That's what's off. The air is tainted with malice."

"Considering Owen was in here, I am not surprised." Devlen pulled a broken shovel and tossed it aside. He dumped the rest of the contents—mostly old gardening tools.

"Let's check the other building," Leif said, exiting the glass house.

The oversize wooden barn door gaped open.

Leif halted. "The air reeks of death. And there's nothing subtle about that."

"I smell it, too."

They exchanged a glance. Leif yanked his machete from his belt and Devlen brandished his scimitar. Devlen eased the door wider and signaled him. Leif held his breath and crept inside with the Sandseed right behind. Dim sunlight trickled through the dusty windows. The large single room contained furniture and gardening supplies and a dead body.

Leif cursed aloud. Then he gagged on the rotten stench. "Check." He motioned to search the room. "Quick." Covering his nose with his hand, he took the right side while Devlen went left.

Not much to see. An old frayed couch, a couple chairs and a desk. Although the stack of files piled on top might be interesting. Leif sheathed his machete. He opened the first file.

A loud *pop* sounded. The sharp, acrid smell of malice sliced right through death's foul odor. Inside the file was a single piece of paper.

"Run," Leif yelled, just as a whoosh vibrated through the air.

The barn's walls ignited. Flames ripped up the sides, surrounding them.

MARIA V. SNYDER

7

YELENA

One look at Valek's hard expression and I braced for bad news. He didn't disappoint. Unfortunately. "Are you certain it was Owen and the others?" I asked Valek. "It was dark and the boy is very young." The thought of Owen in Ixia coiled like a snake in the pit of my stomach.

Onora and I had been relaxing by the campfire when Valek and Janco returned from searching for the tunnel. They'd found it, but also learned one of the teen miners had reported spotting three strangers that had appeared right out of thin air the same night his camp's food stores had been raided.

"It's not a hundred percent, but it makes the most sense," Valek said, sitting next to me. He held his hands close to the fire, warming them.

"Why did Lewin see them at all?" Janco plopped down between me and Onora. "That Rika chick should be hiding them behind an illusion all the time. That's what I'd do if I were her."

"It's difficult to maintain an illusion when the subject is in motion," I explained. "The magician has to constantly adjust it to match the surroundings. It's exhausting. While something static, like covering the mouth of the cave with an illusionary rockfall, is much easier."

"But what keeps it going?" Onora placed the cook pot on the fire, reheating the beef stew the cook from the miner's camp brought over for supper. "Once the magician leaves, shouldn't the illusion dissipate?"

"In most cases, the illusion disappears," I said. "However, some magicians can loop the magic back to the power blanket. This loop keeps the illusion intact by drawing power from the source. Booby traps work in a similar fashion, except when one is triggered, it connects to the source to fuel the trap and then disintegrates. There's no loop."

"Yeah, yeah, this is all very fascinating," Janco said, "but why would Owen even be in Ixia? The Commander is angry at him for getting too greedy. His best play is to lie low in Sitia."

"Owen claimed he has something that would make the Commander forgive him," I said, remembering that smug, cocky tone he'd used. And now that I thought about it... "Makes sense for him to want to reach the Commander before Valek reports in. He can spin his story, skewing it in his favor."

"Or he can just use his evil mojo and put the Commander under a spell." Janco waggled his fingers.

That wasn't quite how it worked, but Janco had a good point. I met Valek's gaze. "When were they spotted?"

"Three nights ago, and they're on foot," he said.

If they wished to keep a low profile, they would avoid riding horses. In Ixia, only generals and top-ranking advisers rode horses. Merchants used them to pull their wagons, but everyone else walked.

"If we leave now, we can easily catch up," I said, gesturing to Kiki and the others grazing nearby.

"Yeah, but can we stop them?" Janco rubbed his ear. A

queasy expression creased his face. "Leif's not here to make those null thingies that protect us from their magic."

"We have Curare, darts and blowpipes. As long as they don't suspect we're close, we can incapacitate them," Valek said.

"Can we find them?" Onora asked.

Janco huffed in annoyance. "Of course we can track them. That won't be a problem. If they cover their tracks with illusions, Valek and I can sniff out their magic, and I can follow them if they don't. No, the real problem will be if they can sense us coming."

Everyone turned to me. I considered Owen's magical powers. Back when Owen had coerced me into helping him search for the Ice Moon in the MD-3 mines, he had failed to locate Valek's hiding place on the ceiling.

"Owen can't, but I'm not certain about Rika and Tyen," I said. "Many magicians don't reveal all their powers. They like to keep one or two hidden from public knowledge so they have an advantage."

"Not helping, Yelena," Janco said.

"Owen's been one step ahead of us the entire time," Onora said.

"That's what happens when he has a six-day head start," Janco snapped.

She pressed her lips together and shot him a nasty glare. Onora wasn't the type to state the obvious, so I sensed there was more.

"What are you thinking?" I asked her.

"They argued while stealing food and under a cloak of illusion. That's just stupid. Owen's many things, but he's not stupid."

Valek nodded in agreement. "You think he wanted the boy to see them?"

"Yes, so he can lead us into another booby trap," she said.

Sounded like Owen. "Do we follow the bread crumbs or dash ahead and set our own trap?"

"How far ahead?" Valek asked.

"The castle?" Janco suggested.

"That's dangerously close to the Commander," Onora said.

"Yeah, but it's our home territory. Nobody knows it as well as *we* do." Janco thumped his chest. "And there are a gazillion soldiers there to protect the Commander."

"Yet we're just guessing that they're heading to the castle. The red and black colors on their uniforms could be a diversion," Onora said.

As they discussed options, I mulled it over. Why else would Owen be in Ixia? To hide from the Sitian authorities. Possible, but Ixia kept a close watch on its citizens, making it difficult to blend in and disappear. Owen had managed to avoid execution before; he must believe he could do it again in order to risk the journey. I knew Owen the best, so I put myself in his boots and contemplated the problem.

"Owen's heading to the castle," I said, stopping the discussion.

"Then we need to beat him there," Janco said.

"They're on foot. How long will it take them to reach the castle?" I asked him.

"On foot, it would take about ten days to get there from here."

"With their head start, they'll be there in seven days," Valek said.

"And it will take us five days on horseback. Is two days enough time to prepare?" I asked, already worried about it.

"It should be plenty of time. Plus if they're planting booby traps, using magic to cover their tracks and avoiding detection, it'll take them longer than seven days." Valek lifted the pot's lid and stirred the stew with a spoon.

MARIA V. SNYDER

A puff of steamy goodness wafted up. My stomach grumbled in response. It was nice to have an appetite for a change, but I wondered how long it would last before another bout of queasiness swelled. The nausea came and went, but was never bad enough to make me vomit. Thank fate.

Valek ladled stew into the bowls and passed them around the fire. Every day it was harder to ignore my sensitive stomach. By now, I was four weeks late. Hard to pin the delay on stress when I'd just spent most of the past two days resting. And what would I feel if it was confirmed? I shied away from those thoughts. Too scary.

Instead, I decided to wait until we reached the castle to indulge in any more speculation. Once there, I'd visit the medic and seek advice. Lots of advice.

"When do we leave?" But then Janco waved his hands at Valek in a stopping motion. "Don't say it."

"At dawn."

He groaned. "I told you not to say it!"

No one talked while we ate. When we finished the stew, we prepared to turn in early. Valek insisted on checking my cut. The wound remained painful to the touch and throbbed if I made any big movements, but there weren't any signs of infection. He changed the bandage, then pointed to my bedroll. An unspoken order.

Despite my initial annoyance that he'd left me at camp while he and Janco searched for the tunnel, I had to admit the downtime helped restore some of my energy, which I would need for the next five long days in the saddle. I lay down facing the fire.

"What's the watch schedule?" Onora asked.

"I've assigned Ivon and his men to patrol the camp. We all could use a full night's sleep." Valek joined me, spooning in behind and covering us both with the blanket. He draped his arm over my shoulder.

Ah. My favorite time of the day. I snuggled closer. "What are they going to do once we leave?" I asked.

"Continue investigating and track down any smugglers who used the tunnel before Owen and his companions blocked it with the illusion."

A good plan, but what if they found more than they bargained for? I remembered the brothers, Tex and Jax, and how they might have been planted by Owen. What if Lewin was, as well?

"What if Owen is still nearby?" I whispered to Valek, clutching the blanket. Ivon and his men wouldn't stand a chance against the three magicians.

"He's not. Stop second-guessing yourself." Valek kept his voice low, as well.

Easy to say, so hard to do. "I just don't want anyone else to get hurt."

"Unfortunately, that's not going to happen. But it's not your fault or mine. *Owen* is responsible for his own actions," Valek said.

Again the logic made sense, but my heart failed to agree.

Valek smoothed my hair away from my face. "What's really bothering you, love?"

"That we won't be able to stop him. That he teams up with the Commander and…" Horrible scenarios bubbled, but one stood out.

"And?"

"And the Commander orders you to execute me." When the Commander had written my execution order eight years ago, he hadn't given it to Valek. If he had, Valek would have killed me. No doubt. His loyalty to the Commander was absolute. And I understood and have accepted it.

MARIA V. SNYDER

"It's highly unlikely."

I turned to face him. "But not impossible."

He met my gaze with an unwavering intensity. "Then it will be the first time I've disobeyed a direct order." His words a promise.

That was new. Warmth spread throughout my chest, and it wasn't because of the fire.

We reached a travel shelter after three exhausting days on the road. The horses had set the pace and we arrived near midnight—a half day ahead of schedule. Sweat stained Kiki's copper coat and her sides heaved with the effort. She'd adjusted her gait, keeping my ride smooth. Even without our magical link, Kiki had known each stride sent a jolt of pain through my side.

Onora and I walked the horses to cool them down while Valek and Janco checked the area around the small wooden building for magical booby traps. After signaling the all-clear, they entered the structure.

They returned in no time and joined us.

"All's quiet," Valek said. "There's a couple travelers from MD-2 sleeping, but there's not a whiff of magic anywhere nearby."

The Snake Forest surrounded the shelter on three sides. The fourth side faced the wide fields of cotton and flax plants. The rich soil and weather was ideal for growing both, and with their overabundance of sheep, MD-5 produced and dyed all the thread for the Territory of Ixia. The skeins were then sent to MD-3 to be woven into fabric.

"Let's take care of the horses and get some sleep. I'll take first watch. Onora second, and Janco third," Valek ordered.

"And I'll take fourth," I said.

He frowned, but kept quiet.

The stable next to the shelter had room for six horses. The straw smelled musty, and I hoped no critters had nested inside it. We filled water buckets from the well, removed tack and groomed our horses, all in silence. No one had the energy to talk.

When we finished, we headed into the shelter. The one room contained two rows of bunk beds along the walls on the left side, and a large stone hearth with chairs ringed around it on the right. We found three empty bunks next to each other and away from the two occupied ones close to the hearth.

Valek sat on the edge of mine and tucked me in. He'd always been protective, but on this trip, he seemed overly concerned. Perhaps he shared my worries about Owen and the Commander. Right now I was too tired to ask him.

Instead, I wrapped my arms around his neck, trapping him when he swooped in for a quick kiss good-night. Might as well take advantage of the extra attention. I deepened the kiss.

He broke away. "No fair, love."

I acted innocent. "I'd thought you could use a little extra warmth before you went out into the cold night air."

"You mean the cold *lonely* night?"

"You set the watch schedule. I'd be more than happy to work in teams."

He raised an eyebrow. "You would?"

"Yes, you know how much I enjoy Janco's company."

"Ouch. I walked right into that one, didn't I?"

I smirked my best Janco impression. "Yes, love."

My turn on watch arrived in what felt like a matter of minutes. I had a vague memory of Valek sliding under the blanket, but otherwise nothing until Janco poked me on the shoulder. Movement jolted me wide-awake as Valek brandished a knife.

"It's me," Janco whispered, jumping back.

MARIA V. SNYDER

"Sorry," Valek mumbled before turning over and taking the blanket with him. The knife remained in his hand.

The cold air rushed in and I fumbled for the gray cloak we'd purchased at a Sitian market near the border.

I joined Janco outside. "Anything?"

"Nope. It's been quiet."

I peered into the darkness that wasn't as black as it should be. Predawn light seeped in through the edges of the world. "You didn't wake me early enough."

He shrugged. "It's such a beautiful night, I lost track of time."

"Did Valek order—"

"No, but if you're going to take a watch shift, maybe you shouldn't share a bed with a superlight sleeper who has fast reflexes and is well armed."

"You're just jealous."

"Damn right I am. Now, if you don't mind, I need my beauty sleep." Janco slipped back inside.

I checked on the horses. They slept in their stalls unperturbed—a good sign. Looping around the buildings, I ensured no one lurked nearby or had set up an ambush. Although my rustlings and crunchings on dead leaves would have alerted anyone within a mile of my presence. I'd taken my magic for granted. Being on watch had been much easier when all I had to do was scan the surroundings with my awareness.

No sense moping about it; I would just need to learn how to move through the forest without scaring away the wildlife. And instead of doing sweeps, I found a perfect spot to watch for movement and to listen for sounds.

Dawn arrived. I fed the horses and inspected them for cuts or hot spots. Kiki nuzzled my ear and tugged on my braid. I didn't need our mental link to know what she desired.

"I only have a few left, and you'll have to share them with the others," I said.

She nudged me toward the tack room.

"All right." I dug in my saddlebags and removed the sack of milk oats. "You're spoiled."

Kiki sucked hers down in one bite. The others crunched on theirs. Good thing the Keep's Stable Master had given me the recipe for Kiki's favorite treat. I didn't know how long I'd be in Ixia. Could be seasons. Had Irys sent me a reply by now? My message about traveling with Valek to Ixia would have reached her last week. Did she think I stayed with him because I was terrified or because I didn't trust her to keep me safe in Sitia? Did I know the answer?

Why did I agree to stay with Valek when Sitia needed me? The Council was probably panicking over the news that the Commander had Curare. No. Not probably. Definitely.

So why wasn't I rushing to the Citadel to do my job and smooth relations between the two countries? And then there was Owen. What could I do to stop him? I'd actually be safer in Sitia.

I thought about it. I'd been in plenty of dangerous situations without Valek. But this time... This time I was vulnerable. The most vulnerable I'd been since I'd been a lab rat for Reyad.

And every time I'd been in mortal peril, Valek had saved me. Not always physically, but even just hearing his voice gave me the strength to stop Owen. When I'd been trapped in the fire world, the thought of never seeing him again motivated me to find a solution.

Besides, what was wrong with being selfish? Someone else could be the Liaison. Someone else could be a target for assassins. I could just be with Valek.

Except... Yeah, that was the kicker. Except, I couldn't. Even

MARIA V. SNYDER

without my powers, I remained in a position to help, and the last thing I wanted was war between Ixia and Sitia. Not when I might have a child. A country at war was no place to raise a child. Eventually, I'd need to return to Sitia.

My courage had scattered on the ground like leaves fallen from the trees. I gathered my bits of mettle, tucking them into my heart. Each one increased my motivation to learn how to survive without my magic. Bonus that the perfect person to teach me also happened to be my heart mate.

The door to the shelter creaked. I turned. Valek strode out into the sunlight. He combed his fingers through his sleep-matted black hair, but his alert gaze scanned the area. His stiff posture relaxed when he spotted me by the horses.

"Any trouble?" he asked.

"No."

"Good."

"Anyone else awake?" I asked.

"The people from MD-2 are packing their bags. Onora and Janco are still asleep. Since we're ahead of schedule, I'm going to find a local patrol, see if they spotted Owen. Can I borrow Kiki?"

She would sense any magical traps. "You have to ask her. And I suggest you bribe her with milk oats."

He smiled. "Sounds like your brother."

As he offered Kiki the treat, I thought of Leif. One good thing about Owen, Rika and Tyen being in Ixia—I didn't have to worry about Leif running into the magicians. I hoped he'd received Valek's message about the booby traps.

What if he didn't?

A vision of shattered glass piercing his body flashed. My stomach rolled with nausea. I swallowed and dismissed the horrible scene. Just my overactive imagination. Leif would smell the trap and not be skewered as I'd been. I hoped.

Kiki allowed Valek to saddle her. But before he left, he drew me close. "What's wrong?"

"I'm concerned about Leif."

"He's quite capable of taking care of himself. And Devlen is with him."

"I know. It's just…" I fisted my hands.

"Just what?"

"It's been forty days since I woke up without my magic. And just when I think I've come to terms with it, or just when I've mustered enough gumption to learn how to live without it, some comment or some incident sets me back, and I realize just how much I lost and it feels like day one again—all raw and new."

Valek embraced me. Winded from my outburst, I rested my head against his chest and breathed in his spicy musk.

"You're frustrated, love, and that's understandable. We'll figure it out one way or another. We always do."

"But—"

"Tell me one mystery we haven't solved."

I searched my memory. About to concede the point, I thought of one. "Onora. Is she friend or foe?" And another I wouldn't voice—*Am I pregnant?*—because I suspected I already knew the answer.

"Too recent. I'm still working on it, but I'm confident I'll know in time. Just like your problem. The solution may be revealed tomorrow, or not for seasons, but it will be. No doubts."

Wrapped tight in Valek's arms, I believed him. But I expected that my doubts would creep back in. For now, though, I allowed hope and his warmth to sink into my bones.

Far too soon, he released me. Valek tucked a loose strand of my hair behind my ear. "I'll be back soon." He kissed me, then mounted Kiki.

She butted my cheek with her muzzle before heading out.

I wiped horse slobber from my face. The shelter door creaked again. Two men, wearing cloaks marked with tan-colored diamond shapes, exited. They glanced at the horses with worried expressions before heading for the road at a fast pace. I wondered if they'd recognized Valek.

When I entered the shelter, Onora was crouched next to the hearth, poking the ashy remains for a sign of life. A small flame erupted and she added logs until flames danced brightly. Pouring water into a pot, she set it near the fire. A cup with a tea bag rested nearby.

"Have I turned you into a tea drinker?" I asked in a low voice as I joined her. Janco remained asleep.

"It's for you."

"Oh?"

"I noticed you drink that ginger tea every morning, so…"

"That's nice. Thank you." Or was it nice? Was she waiting for confirmation that her little stunt had worked? That I needed the tea to soothe my uneasy stomach? I vowed she'd be the last to know.

Onora sliced cheese and bread, assembling breakfast for us. I regretted my harsh thoughts a little. While Valek and Janco searched for the tunnel, she'd taken care of me, letting me sleep and recover my strength. Perhaps she felt guilty? With her it was hard to tell. She said little and we hardly talked, which seemed to suit her just fine. No wonder Janco bugged her so much. I grinned, just thinking about it.

"What's so funny?" Onora poured steaming water into my cup.

"Janco. He's determined to annoy you."

"He's succeeded. Many times." She handed me the tea.

"He's looking for a reaction and for attention. You're like The Madam, unflappable, and that irks him, so he tries hard to…er…flap you."

Onora smiled. The first genuine one I'd seen. It reached her gray eyes and transformed her. The carefree expression was a glimpse of the young girl she used to be before her life soured and turned tragic.

"And ignoring him is the ultimate affront," she said.

Ah. She'd figured him out. "Which is why you do it."

"Exactly." She sobered. "And I am an assassin. Being quiet and still for hours is all part of the job."

"True." I sensed there was more, so I took a risk. "Why did you decide to become an assassin?"

Onora met my gaze. All animation left her face, but uncertainty lurked behind her eyes. I guessed she contemplated what to tell me. The truth or some offhand comment.

She lowered her voice. "I didn't want to be afraid anymore."

That I understood. "And did it work?"

"No one can touch me."

Not quite an answer. I remembered what Valek had said about her past and how she hadn't killed her demons yet.

"Have you faced your fear?"

She scoffed, "Don't you mean, have I assassinated the bastard I was afraid of?"

"No. I know murdering a tormentor doesn't mean the problem is solved."

"Sorry, but I don't agree. Death is the final solution."

"Then you are luckier than me."

"Luckier?" Her voice rose in anger.

"Yes. When I killed Reyad, my problems didn't disappear with his death. He continued to haunt me."

"That's because you're the Soulfinder."

"I wasn't then. Then I was a terrified nineteen-year-old, fearing I'd lost my soul and would always be a victim. Those doubts clung to me until I faced it. And I'm still learning that running away from my fears is never a solution."

"That's you. Not me." She stood up. "I better do a perimeter check." Onora left the shelter.

I'd struck a nerve. Interesting.

Janco crept from a shadow. "She's a tough clam to pry open. I've a feeling, though, once we do, we'll find a pearl."

"Pearls form in oysters."

"Oysters, clams..." He waved dismissively. "It's all seafood. You know what I meant."

I did. Yet, I wasn't as certain about the gem inside the hard exterior.

Valek and Kiki returned after breakfast. We joined him in the stable. "What's the buzz?" Janco asked without preamble.

"No sign of Owen." Valek swung a leg over and dismounted.

"Is that good or bad?" Janco asked.

"You tell me."

Janco paused. "Bad. They could be anywhere. What about the local patrols?"

"They haven't encountered anything unusual in the last couple of days."

Nor had any of the other patrols we'd encountered the past three days. "Maybe Owen hasn't traveled this far yet," I said.

"That's a possibility," Valek agreed. "Are you ready to go?"

We gathered our supplies and mounted. As we traveled, I considered another explanation for no signs of Owen. Perhaps he had used magic to erase the patrolmen's memories. Could he erase memories without Loris and Cilly Cloud Mist's help? I remembered that the three of them had each picked one of us to restructure our memories so we'd forget. Which meant he could. And then it hit me. He'd also mentioned inserting *new* ones.

Then why would he be careless enough to let that miner see him and the others? Why not erase the teen's memories?

I snagged on an idea. "Holy snow cats!"

The others slowed their horses and turned to me, waiting.

I rushed to explain, "That boy, Lewin, said he saw Owen three nights before we talked to him. What if Owen planted that memory and it wasn't really three nights, but longer? In that case, Owen, Rika and Tyen might have reached the Commander by *now*."

8

VALEK

Alarmed, Valek stopped Onyx. The real possibility that Owen and the others had reached the Commander sent an icy pulse through his heart. "Holy snow cats, indeed."

"It's pure conjecture," Onora said.

"Based on Yelena's knowledge of Owen," Valek said.

Kiki moved closer to Onyx, and Yelena put a hand on his shoulder. "I'm sorry I didn't remember about his ability to plant new memories sooner."

He covered her hand with his own and squeezed. "Trying to outguess your enemy is all part of the fun, love."

"Oh, so that's what we've been doing? Having fun? Who knew?" she teased.

"Gee, Valek, you ought to show your girl a better time if she doesn't even know what fun is," Janco said.

"All right," he agreed, getting into the spirit. "Next time, love, I'll take you along on a raid."

"Oh my." Yelena fanned her face with a hand. "Slow down, handsome, or I might swoon from all the excitement."

Even though she smiled, it did nothing to dispel the dark smudges lining her green eyes and her sunken cheeks. She hadn't been eating or sleeping well. But once they reached the castle, he'd ensure she got plenty of both.

"The castle, Kiki. As fast as possible. Please," Yelena said.

He spurred Onyx, following Kiki. Janco and Onora rode close behind him. On horseback, the trip would take two full days if they stopped to sleep, a day and a half if they didn't. The decision would be Kiki's. She understood their desire to hurry while she also knew not to exhaust or injure the horses.

Kiki stopped for water around midnight, and Valek decided they should get a few hours of sleep. Nothing good would come from them arriving at the castle completely drained and useless.

"There should be a patrol west of us," he said to the group. "We can overnight with them. That way we all can sleep."

"Hoorah." Janco pumped his fist.

Kiki found the patrol an hour after midnight. Their unexpected arrival caused a considerable stir, and Valek had to explain and soothe the nerves of the young lieutenant in charge. Another hour passed before they spread their bedrolls.

Teetering on the edge of sleep, Valek was roused by Janco's voice.

"Just for the record, *holy snow cats* is my line," he said. "You need to find your own."

"And you had to tell us this *now*?" Onora grumbled.

"I thought it was important. I don't like people stealing my lines."

"It's a *compliment*, you dolt. Did you ever think of that?"

"No."

"Not quite the boy genius over there. Make sure to put *that* in the record."

With Yelena sleeping in his arms, and Janco trading insults with Onora, Valek enjoyed a moment of peace. He suspected he wouldn't get many more once they reached the castle.

MARIA V. SNYDER

★ ★ ★

The guards at the castle's east gate reported no suspicious activity in the past two weeks. No surprise. If Owen had breached the walls using magic, no one would have spotted him.

After riding all day, the horses needed to be cared for. Yelena and Janco volunteered to take them to the stables while he and Onora checked on the Commander. At this late hour, he had probably retired for the night, but Valek didn't care.

They raced to the Commander's apartment. Two members of his detail stood outside his door.

"It's been quiet, sir," Private Berk said to Valek. "But he's probably still awake."

Valek exchanged a glance with Onora. She held her hands close to her daggers. He knocked on the door and a faint "Come in" sounded. They entered, ready to fight if needed.

The Commander sat in his armchair by the fire, sipping a glass of brandy and still wearing his all-black uniform. A book lay across his lap. No one else was in sight.

Ambrose set the glass down and studied them with his golden gaze. "Where's the emergency?"

"We're hoping not here." Valek strode into the room, seeking magic and scanning for intruders. "Has anything unusual happened? Has anyone been here? Or tried to get in?"

"There's nothing to worry about, Valek. All is well."

Valek paused and stared at the Commander. "I'd still like to—"

"No need. I'm sure you have quite the story to tell, but it's late and I'm in no mood to hear it. Report to the war room first thing tomorrow morning." He glanced at Onora. "Just you, Valek. You're dismissed."

The Commander's complete lack of curiosity about Valek's mission alarmed him along with the comment that there was nothing to worry about. The Commander never believed *all is well*. Ambrose considered relaxing your guard to be something that would be exploited by your enemy in no time. However, Valek couldn't press the issue. Not with Onora standing there.

"Yes, sir," Valek said.

They left and closed the door. Valek remained in the hallway, considering his next move.

"Magic?" Onora asked him with concern.

"Not that I felt."

"Then what's wrong?"

"Everything."

Valek sent Onora to help with the horses and to instruct Janco to complete a perimeter check of the castle, including the barracks, stables, kennels and training areas, seeking magic. If Owen was here, he'd be hiding behind one of Rika's illusions. Valek concentrated on all the interior rooms and halls inside the castle. The odd-shaped structure had more hidden places than a labyrinth. Starting in the dungeon and working his way up, he searched for a stickiness in the air that meant magic was in use.

The air remained clear until Valek encountered a brief touch near the rooms reserved for his officers. He followed the tackiness down the hallway. One lantern remained lit, casting a sickly yellow glow on the gray stone walls. A door jerked open, and Valek yanked his knives from their sheaths.

Ari's six-foot-four-inch frame filled the threshold. He brandished a long dagger, but relaxed when he spotted Valek. "I'll be damned. You were right."

"I was right about what?" Valek asked.

"Not you." Ari stepped aside. "Reema. She said you were creeping around."

Reema poked her head out from behind Ari. Her blond

MARIA V. SNYDER

corkscrew curls fanned her face like a lion's mane. That explained the magic. While no one, not even Master Magician Irys, could pick up on Reema's magic, both Valek and Opal suspected she used it. But it didn't explain the strength. Before, Valek had to be standing right next to her in order to sense her power. That puzzle would have to wait.

"I wasn't creeping. I'm checking for intruders," Valek said.

Ari straightened. "What can I do?"

"Stay with Reema."

The big man pressed his lips together, but kept quiet.

"Are the others back, as well?" Reema asked. "My dad and Janco?"

"Janco and your aunt Yelena are with the horses." Valek crouched down to her level. "Your father didn't come. He's in Sitia with your uncle Leif. You'll have to stay here a little longer."

"Oh." She stared at him a moment. "Does that mean the bad men who are after Aunt Yelena haven't been caught?"

Valek glanced at Ari.

"I didn't tell her," he said.

She huffed. "I'm not stupid."

No, she wasn't. "Yes. And you're safe here. That's why your father wants you to remain with us." Valek hoped.

"Can I see Aunt Yelena?"

"Tomorrow. Right now you need to get back to sleep." Valek followed her into Ari and Janco's quarters, which included two bedrooms and a large living area with couches, armchairs, tables and desks. No need to guess that the one overflowing with papers, books and files was Janco's.

Ari's bedroom door stood ajar and Reema headed toward it. Valek turned to Ari, questioning.

"You ordered me not to let her out of my sight," Ari said. "I brought in another bed for her."

"Good. Has there been anything strange going on?"

Ari ran a meaty hand over his short, curly blond hair. "You mean other than tonight? No. Why?"

"Just checking."

"Come on, Valek, it's me. What's going on?"

"Not now. We'll have a briefing in my office in the afternoon."

"That gives Janco time to tell me all about it from his... unique perspective. Are you sure you want to risk it?"

Valek smiled. "He'll be too tired to tell stories."

Ari laughed. "Janco is never too tired to tell stories."

Valek finished his search of the castle. Not wishing to disturb the advisers and high-ranking officers sleeping, he didn't check inside the rooms. All was quiet in the guest wing, but he touched each door just in case. None of them were sticky with magic. Valek continued ghosting through the hallways, but encountered nothing alarming.

Janco waited for him outside his office. The poor guy sat on the floor, leaning against the hard wooden door, sleeping. Valek nudged him awake with the toe of his boot.

Janco jerked and grabbed the hilt of his sword. "What? Oh." He released his grip and shuffled to his feet.

"Did you find anything?" Valek asked.

"No. No illusions or creepy-crawly magic." He stretched his arms above his head while yawning. "None of the guards saw anything strange or heard voices. Though there was something I wish I didn't see." Janco rubbed his eyes. "Sergeant Falice hooking up with Sergeant Dallin behind the barracks. Yuck."

"Get some sleep. We're meeting here this afternoon."

"Yes, sir." Janco wobbled away.

Valek glanced out the window at the end of the hallway.

MARIA V. SNYDER

About one hour until dawn. He headed to his suite across the hall from the Commander's. Private Berk remained on duty.

"Liaison Yelena is waiting for you inside, sir," Berk said.

"Thank you." Valek entered and closed the door behind him.

Yelena had lit the lanterns ringing the main living area. She'd sprawled on the couch and was fast asleep. He picked her up. She hardly weighed anything. As he carried her upstairs to his bedroom, she muttered a few indecipherable words. Yelena roused a bit when he laid her on the bed.

"Did you…?"

"Sleep, love. We found no signs of Owen."

She patted the space next to her.

"Wish I could." He pulled the blanket over her as he told her about the afternoon meeting. "I'll have the kitchen staff send up a late breakfast for you. I want you to eat it all. Understand?"

"Yes, love."

"That's my line. You'll have to think of something else." He kissed her and left.

Exhaustion dragged on his body like a sopping-wet cloak. Valek stopped at the kitchen for a few bites to eat and to order the tray for Yelena. Sammy, the head chef, promised to send her a huge stack of sweet cakes.

The combination of the food and a cold shower revived him. Dressing in a clean uniform, Valek combed his hair. The wet strands hung past his shoulders. Valek tied it at the base of his neck with a leather string. The Commander had stopped remarking on the length when Valek explained that he might need to go undercover as a female. Since playing Valma, the beautician, had gotten Valek close enough to assassinate the King, the Commander didn't insist Valek buzz it close to his head like all his other male officers and advisers.

Valek arrived outside the Commander's war room just as the sun rose. No surprise the Commander had beaten him there. The man never slept more than five or six hours a night. The two guards nodded at him, but remained silent.

Bracing for the inevitable argument, Valek knocked and entered.

The Commander sat at the head of the large wooden conference table, eating breakfast. His uniform had two real diamonds secured to the collar. Not a wrinkle or crease rumpled his clothing.

A wedge of strengthening sunlight shone through the stained-glass windows that faced east. Colors splashed on the ceiling. The tall, thin windows covered three-quarters of the round room—the Commander's favorite place.

Valek stood at attention.

"Sit down." The Commander gestured to a chair a few places down the table on the left. "Report."

Perched on the edge of the hard wood, Valek detailed the mission to stop the smugglers, including his detour to Sitia after he'd learned from Maren about another tunnel north of Lapeer. He ended with Owen crossing into Ixia. "And I believe he's headed this way, although we've seen no signs of him."

The Commander's gaze grew distant. Valek kept quiet. He'd learned to let the man absorb all the information. Questions were only a matter of time. After that, Valek had many of his own.

"Why do you assume Owen is coming to harm me? If he claims to have something better against magicians than Curare, wouldn't you think I'd be interested?"

A cold brush of dread swept through Valek. "Owen's a power-hungry magician who can't be trusted. He can erase memories and implant new ones. It's…insane to let him close

MARIA V. SNYDER

to you. With that type of magic, he can influence your decisions. He can make you give up command and appoint him as your successor. Owen is the embodiment of all the reasons you hate magicians."

There was no reaction to Valek's outburst. Instead he said, "The magic detector Opal gifted to me, that—"

"Won't provide protection. It just lets you know there's magic in use."

Annoyance flashed in the Commander's golden gaze. He hated to be interrupted. "I know. And I'm also aware that a null shield provides the necessary protection, which is why I have a null shield woven into all my uniforms."

That surprised Valek. "How? When?"

"Yelena's brother provided the protection for me. I asked him to keep it a secret. And, guessing from your expression, Leif hasn't informed his sister."

Ah. There it was. "Yelena and I do not share classified information."

No response.

"You know I wouldn't jeopardize your safety. I'm thrilled you're protected. I would have suggested it, but I believed you wouldn't be...comfortable with magic that close to you."

The Commander brushed his hand along the sleeve of his uniform. "These are dangerous times."

"Indeed." And it was about to get downright perilous for Valek. He drew in a steadying breath. "Which is why I need to know *everything*. Why didn't you inform me about your... arrangement with Owen Moon and the Curare?"

"Why did you disobey a direct order?" the Commander countered.

Thrown, Valek searched his memory. "What order?"

"The one not to get involved with Ben Moon's escape.

You were heading to Sitia to help Yelena before you ran into Maren."

"How—"

"It doesn't matter how I learned of this. What matters is you failed to inform me of your change in plans."

"An assassin was after Yelena."

"That is the answer to your original question, Valek. Why didn't I inform you about Owen? Yelena."

"I wouldn't—"

"You wouldn't have told her? Truly? He's a dangerous magician, and she's the reason he was caught. She's the reason his brother went to prison. You wouldn't have warned her?"

Now Valek didn't have an answer.

"Your loyalties are divided."

"Yes. They are. But I passed all your tests. I returned even after Yelena was shot with Onora's bolt. I found and shut down the smuggling operation as ordered. It wouldn't have been as successful if I hadn't taken that detour to aid Yelena."

"You had no way of knowing that before you left. And Owen still managed to escape."

Valek bit down on his first retort. If he'd known about Owen in the first place, this whole smuggling mess never would have happened. "You used to trust my judgment."

Commander Ambrose leaned back in his chair. "I did."

"What changed? Was it because I didn't tell you that I can be trapped by a simple null shield?"

"No. Everything changed the night an assassin crept through my window."

"Onora?"

"Yes."

But he'd been there with the Commander. Unless... Onora had said she'd been working with him for six months. "You

MARIA V. SNYDER

mean the *first* time she arrived? Not the second time, when I was there, which was just another one of your tests."

"Yes. The first time played out almost identical to the second. But instead of you fighting her, I recruited her just like I had with you."

She had the C-shaped scar to prove it. Just like his. "It scared you."

"Damn right, it scared me. The fact that she could get in so easily and you were in Sitia, helping Yelena. Helping the Sitian Council. Helping your friends solve puzzles while I was in real danger."

Not quite accurate, but Valek knew not to contradict him. "All sanctioned by you. You know if these people gain power in Sitia, it's only a matter of time before they set their sights on Ixia."

"That is no longer a concern of mine. I've decided that there will be no more helping Sitia with their difficulties. You're staying in Ixia and dealing with Ixian problems. If Sitia has a revolt and the victors attack us, then we will defend ourselves at that time. My army is quite capable, and it will give all those young hotheads something to do. As of now, you no longer have the freedom to assign agents and go off on missions as you see fit. You must clear everything with me first. Understand?"

The Commander's words sliced into Valek as if he'd been stabbed with a knife. In all their years together and throughout all their fights, Commander Ambrose had never spoken to Valek in that tone. Had Owen manipulated him four years ago when the magician bargained for his life, promising the Commander Curare in exchange? It depended on when Leif had woven the null shields for him.

Unable to remain sitting, Valek stood. "I understand that you no longer trust me."

"You need to earn my trust again. I need to know that when I give an order, you will follow it without question."

Fear coiled around Valek's chest. The Commander had never wished for him to be a mindless soldier. "Questioning your orders has been the heart of our relationship. The ability to discuss issues and determine the best way to handle them has been beneficial. It's why I'm one of your advisers. You'll ruin—"

In a heartbeat, the Commander shot to his feet and advanced on him. Valek remained in place, even when Commander Ambrose drew his knife and pressed the tip to Valek's chest. Fury radiated in every one of the Commander's clenched muscles. Valek had pushed too far.

"You've forgotten your place, Valek. You're mine. Live or die, *I* decide."

The Commander cut his shirt open, then traced the twenty-four-year-old C-shaped scar on Valek's chest with the knife. Burning pain seared his skin as the razor-sharp tip sliced through his flesh with ease, but Valek refused to utter a sound.

"Do you remember what you pledged to me in that alley long ago?" he asked Valek.

"My loyalty."

"Correct. See that you don't break my trust again."

"Yes, sir."

"Good."

Valek stared straight ahead. "Your orders regarding Owen Moon, sir?"

"You are to leave him and his companions alone. No more investigating. No more interference in his affairs. Owen is my guest and is staying in the guest quarters. He works for me and will continue to do so until I say otherwise. Understand?"

"Yes, sir." Fear pierced Valek's anger and humiliation. He had to warn Yelena.

MARIA V. SNYDER

"Good. Anything else?"

"Who hired Onora to kill you, sir?"

"It's under investigation."

Meaning, Onora hadn't been able to learn the client's name from Hedda. Which explained why she killed the teacher. "Your orders regarding Onora?"

"No change. She's to continue being your apprentice."

"Will she follow my orders?"

"As long as you clear them with me first. We will meet here at dawn every morning and again right after supper to discuss your assignments."

"Yes, sir."

"You're dismissed."

Valek left. He gathered the two parts of his shirt together, fisting the fabric in his right hand and pressing it against the bleeding wound on his chest. Pain flared, but his swirling thoughts distracted him. Possible explanations for the Commander's behavior bubbled. Had Onora's attack affected him that badly? Or was Owen to blame? No wonder neither Valek nor Janco picked up on magic. No need to hide behind an illusion when you were an invited guest. Valek would have to investigate how much Owen was influencing the Commander, which meant violating another direct order and further ruining their relationship.

Confusion warred with anger, which flipped to fear and then to outrage. Valek no longer knew what to think, to believe, to do. He'd always known what action to take, but not now. Too much had happened.

One thing stayed consistent. Yelena. He needed to protect her, to send her to safety, to ensure that she understood that his loyalties were no longer divided.

Valek arrived at his suite without any memory of the trip. Yelena sat at the table. She'd cleared a section off so she could eat her breakfast. Her forkful of sweet cakes paused in midair when she spotted him.

She dropped it. The metal clattered on the plate. "What's wrong? What happened?"

He strode over and knelt next to her. "The Commander has reminded me of my pledge to serve him." Opening his fist, he let his shirt hang open.

Yelena gasped and reached to touch him. "What—"

Valek grabbed her wrist, stopping her. "Please, just listen. I've no idea what's going on with him, but I do know that you're the one who owns my heart and soul. And this—" he gestured to the C-shaped cut "—is not going to be a symbol of my loyalty to the Commander anymore. It's..." Drawing his knife, Valek cut a backward C shape into his skin right next to the other, linking them so they resembled a heart. "It's a symbol of my love, my loyalty, my respect, my trust and my commitment to you and *only* you. Yelena, will you marry me?"

MARIA V. SNYDER

9

LEIF

The air thickened with heat and smoke. Leif squinted through the flames that surrounded them, seeking a way to escape the barn as the fire's roar pounded in his ears and his heart thudded in his chest.

"...your fire magic?" Devlen's face shone with sweat.

"I can only start fires, not stop them." Leif coughed into his sleeve.

"Any ideas?"

"Window." Leif bent low and raced to the nearest one.

The wooden frame burned scorching hot, but the glass behind the flames remained intact. Shielding his face with his arm, Leif kicked the window. A loud *crack* juddered through the sole of his boot. He kicked again. This time the glass broke, and he used his heel to clear the shards.

"Pants," Devlen yelled.

Leif glanced down. An old childhood taunt played in his mind. *Liar, liar, pants on fire.* Guess he was a liar. He almost laughed. Except a snapping and groaning noise shook the rafters. The roof. Fear pierced his inertia.

"Let's go," he yelled, diving through the flames dancing in the window. Leif slammed into the ground. The force knocked the wind from him, but he rolled to the side to clear the way for Devlen. He kept spinning to snuff out the fire clinging to his clothes as he gasped for air.

A thud and a curse sounded to his left. Devlen also spun on the ground to extinguish his tunic. Another warning screech reverberated.

"Run!" Leif scrambled to his feet and dashed away.

Devlen followed. They raced from the burning structure as its roof collapsed. A red-hot whoosh of air pushed them forward. Embers and sharp bits of flying debris pelted their backs. Leif stumbled. Devlen grabbed his arm and pulled him upright.

They continued for another fifty feet before collapsing onto the grass. Leif checked his body for flames while his brother-in-law did the same.

"What...the hell...happened?" Devlen panted.

"Booby trap."

"You sure?"

"Yep." He drew in a breath. "Owen knew we'd investigate his glass houses. That stack of files was just too tempting. As soon as I opened the top one, it triggered the trap. Bastard left a note, too."

"What did it say?"

"Gotcha."

The horses arrived soon after their narrow escape. They cataloged their injuries. Leif mixed up a poultice for their burns. He bandaged the jagged cuts on his leg from the window's glass and removed the splinters from Devlen's back. Draining half his water skin, Leif wiped his mouth with a soot-covered sleeve.

The burning barn polluted the air with thick black clouds. Yet no one arrived to investigate or to help. Odd.

"Owen must have scared his neighbors away," Devlen said.

By the time they were ready to leave, the structure resem-

MARIA V. SNYDER

bled a pile of scorched lumber. Heat rippled the air above it and an angry orange-red glowed deep inside. Without a water source nearby, they couldn't douse it. Instead, they rode to the nearest town and contacted the authorities.

Once they explained what had happened, they checked into a local inn. After a bath and a large meal, Leif dragged his battered body up to their room. He stretched out on the bed. Devlen plopped onto the other one. The springs squealed under his weight.

Pain pulsed from Leif's right leg despite the healing ointment. His raw skin oozed and his throat burned. He felt like a pig who'd been tied to a spit and roasted over a fire. Leif would never eat pork again. Well... At least not for a couple days.

"Are we still going to check those other hothouses?" Devlen asked.

"No. I can't stop a magical booby trap, and anything could be the trigger." Leif considered. "I'll message the locations to Irys tomorrow. Only she or Bain has the power to remove the trap without springing it."

Disappointment panged. He'd been hoping to discover a clue to Owen's whereabouts. Now it would be at least half a season before one of the Masters arrived.

"You think Owen had time to rig all ten?"

The magician had a six-day head start. "It's possible. Best to assume they're all disasters waiting to happen." And if Owen had enough time for that, then he probably destroyed anything that would indicate his escape plans. Damn.

"What if one of the locals decides to investigate?"

"We can message the various security forces to keep everyone away until one of the Master Magicians clears it."

The next morning, Leif sent Devlen to dispatch the messages to the towns near the glass houses while he communicated with Irys via his super messenger. He tapped into the vast magic stored within the black diamond that had been encased in glass. Using the extra power boost, he connected his thoughts to her thoughts. When she dropped her protective barrier, Leif explained about the booby traps.

I'm not sure when one of us can leave, Irys said. *The Council is still reeling from the news the Commander may have Curare.*

Annoyance colored his thoughts. *He has Curare. It's not a guess.*

I know, but there's no proof.

Outraged, Leif countered, *We've seen the factory and the vines growing. Owen boasted to Yelena that he made a deal with the Commander to produce it. What more do they need?*

Evidence, Leif. Not hearsay.

Hearsay? They doubt Yelena's word? Anger flared.

Yelena's been dealing with the loss of her magic and a number of assassination attempts. The Council needs to hear the story directly from her. But she's gone to Ixia instead. Don't you see how that compromises her report?

Unfortunately, he understood the Council's position. They wouldn't accuse the Commander of anything unless they had verification. And it didn't help that Ben, Loris and Cilly had been silenced. The knowledge from Owen's accomplices would have provided plenty of confirmation.

What about the efforts to locate Owen? he asked. *Have they coordinated with the Moon Clan's security forces?*

They're not organizing anything. Aside from Yelena, the people who have allegedly seen Owen alive are all Ixian.

So basically, the Sitian Council has done nothing at all.

They're discussing how to prepare the army if the Commander does indeed have Curare. The first step has already been decided. They agreed that we need to discover a way to mass-produce Theobroma.

Theobroma neutralized Curare, but the substance removed a regular person's resistance to magic and stripped a magician of all protective barriers. Using Theobroma wouldn't be a concern if fighting Ixia. No, the problem would be growing enough of the trees whose pods provided the main ingredient. The tree only thrived in the Illiais Jungle and it required three to five years of growth before it produced pods. Maybe they could grow them in those hothouses. But it would still take years to manufacture enough for an army.

Who is working on the Theobroma problem?

Bavol Cacao Zaltana has volunteered.

No surprise. However, Leif wasn't sure they could trust his clan's leader anymore. Without anything more substantial than his gut instinct, he couldn't accuse the man.

What can I do? he asked instead.

Find proof that Owen is alive and has committed treason, so we can convince the Council to start a manhunt for him.

Easier said than done. *How about Owen's head on a silver platter?*

That will work, too.

I'll sharpen my machete.

Make sure you treat it with Curare and are extremely careful. Owen's more powerful than you.

Yelena had worried about that as well, which reminded him. *Have you heard from Yelena?*

Not since she left for Ixia. You?

Worry for his sister squeezed his gut. *No.*

Let me know if you do.

I will. You, too.

Of course.

Please tell Mara I miss her and hope to be home soon. A pang of longing vibrated in his chest. *Miss* wasn't a strong enough word for how he felt.

I will. Keep me posted on your progress.

Yes, sir.

Irys laughed. *You've been hanging around those Ixians too long.*

Leif and Devlen arrived at the farmhouse two days after he'd spoken with Irys. A young man sat on the steps, but he jumped to his feet when he spotted them and followed them to the stable. When the man approached, Leif rested his hand on the hilt of his machete.

"Are you Leif Liana Zaltana?" the man asked.

"Yes."

"Finally! This is for you." The young man shoved a sealed envelope at him then dashed away.

Devlen joined him. "A message?"

"Or another booby trap." Leif sniffed it, seeking the sender's intentions. It smelled of impatience and boredom—probably from the messenger. Otherwise, there was no malice or magic.

He ripped it open, read the message and laughed. "It's a warning to stay away from the glass houses. Seems my sister also triggered a booby trap."

"Was anyone hurt?" Concern laced Devlen's voice.

"Cuts only. Nothing serious." In comparison to her experience, the fire didn't seem as terrible. Better than razor-sharp glass flying toward your head.

"Does it say anything about locating Owen?"

"They haven't seen any signs of him." And he and Devlen had gotten nowhere with their efforts. Damn. Owen could be anywhere by now.

Devlen decided to return to Fulgor. "Reema is safe in Ixia, and I can tap into my network."

"You mean your band of ex-cons?" Leif asked.

"I prefer to call them friends. And they are able to provide information that the security officials cannot. Perhaps they will have a clue that will lead us to Owen."

"It's worth trying. Plus you haven't seen Opal in three weeks."

Devlen grinned. "Returning home after a long absence is always a delight."

"I hear you, brother."

A touch of envy swirled in his chest when Devlen left the next day. Leif had been away for thirty-five long days, with no set time for his return. Reuniting with his wife, Mara, was the best part of traveling. She was always more beautiful than he remembered. Kinder, gentler, patient—perfect. She filled all the hollow spots inside him, making him a better, stronger man.

Esau arrived three days later. There was no mistaking that the man was Leif's father. They shared the same broad shoulders and stocky yet muscular build. Almost twins, except wrinkles etched tracks across Esau's forehead and laugh lines sprouted from the corners of his green eyes. His father's complexion was also a few shades darker—closer to the color of tea without milk.

As soon as Esau dismounted, he crushed Leif in a bear hug. "So where's this glass house?"

"Don't you want to freshen up first?" Leif asked.

A film of dirt covered Esau's clothes. His shoulder-length gray hair hung in greasy layers.

He waved a hand. "There's time for that later. I've spent the last fifteen days just imagining this invention."

Leif led his father to the glass structure.

Esau exclaimed over the construction as he circled it. "Amazing. Wish I thought of it. The ability to grow the jungle anywhere. Marvelous." Then he sobered. "Too bad it was used to grow Curare." He ducked his head. "Wish I never found that blighted vine."

Leif suppressed a sigh over the old argument. "The good uses outweigh the bad, Father. You know that." No matter how many examples Leif and Yelena cited of the drug helping others, their father clung to his guilt like a child clung to a security blanket.

They entered the house.

Esau paused and drew in a deep breath. "It doesn't quite smell like the jungle. What's that sweet odor?"

"White coal to keep it hot."

"Genius!" Esau walked among the plants, naming them aloud.

The Curare vine with its emerald heart-shaped leaves twisted through the greenery. Underneath the bushy canopy, the Theobroma trees grew. Their thin, brownish-gray trunks blended in, along with their long oval leaves. Tiny white flowers clung to the bark. Once pollinated, these blooms would produce pods filled with beans that would be dried, fermented and roasted, transforming them into Theobroma.

"Nice to see some medicinal ones in here." Esau crawled through the brush with his nose close to the ground.

Memories of accompanying his father on one of his jungle expeditions flashed. Hiking through the underbrush, sweating in the humid air, climbing trees, collecting samples, Leif had trailed after his indefatigable father, who questioned him on the uses and names of every bit of greenery they encountered. And Leif had done nothing but complain of being hot and tired while scratching numerous bug bites. What a brat.

Leif had his father to thank for his knowledge of healing recipes. Those teas and poultices had saved lives and helped others. But he wouldn't tell his father that everyone called Esau's most prized and useful discovery "wet-dog tea."

It didn't take Esau long to find the crossbred plants in the hothouse.

MARIA V. SNYDER

"Odd. Very odd," Esau muttered. He broke off a leaf, sniffed the sap and nibbled on the end.

"Do you know what plants they combined? What they were trying to do?" Leif asked.

"Not yet. It's going to take a while."

"Then I'll see to the horses and fetch you some food."

"Yes...yes...fine." Esau scratched the stem with a fingernail and peered at the wound.

Leaving his father to his investigation, Leif groomed the horses, filled their water and grain buckets and checked the tack for wear. When he returned with a tray of fruit and meats, Esau sat cross-legged in the middle of the house. He stared in shock at the branch in his hands.

Leif rushed to his side. "What's the matter?"

"This." His father held it up.

"What about it?"

"It's a cross between the Curare vine and the Theobroma tree."

It took a moment for it to sink in. "You mean—"

"These people are trying to create Theobroma-resistant Curare!"

10

YELENA

Shocked into silence, I stared at Valek's bleeding chest. His question bounced around my mind, searching for a place to settle. The deep cut resembled a heart—one half carved by the Commander and the other by Valek, creating a symbol of his love for me. Valek had chosen me over the Commander. A warm sensation swept through my body, turning my insides to goo.

"Yelena?" A hitch cracked his voice. He remained on his knees, waiting for my answer.

Valek's face had paled to bone white. I'd never seen him so vulnerable.

Sliding from my chair, I knelt in front of him. I took his knife—still wet with his blood—from his hand and sliced my tunic open. Then I pressed the tip into the flesh in the center of my chest. Pain buzzed like an annoying fly. I ignored it as I carved a fist-sized heart shape directly over my thumping heart and between my breasts. "Yes, Valek. I will marry you."

His tight expression transformed as joy sparked in his eyes. He wrapped his arms around me, pulling me close as his lips found mine. Red-hot spikes of sensation shot down to my toes. My muscles shivered and my skin caught fire. The need to run my hands over his lean, powerful body pulsated over every inch of my being.

Far too soon he stopped. Before I could protest at the interruption, he pressed his chest to mine. My wound burned with the contact and with the sting of his blood mixing with mine.

"Till death. I do swear, love." Valek whispered in my ear.

"Beyond death. My vow to you," I said.

He drew back to meet my gaze. "So we shall be. Forever united."

"We shall be," I agreed.

This time his kiss vibrated to the very core of my soul. Our pledge solidified our connection, creating an unbreakable bond.

"Clothes...off..." I said between kisses.

The speed of our disrobement took what little breath I had away. But then breathing no longer mattered. My senses filled with the intoxicating smell, feel and touch of Valek as he lowered my shoulders to the floor. Nothing in life compared to being linked with him. Together we were one.

Movement roused me, then cold air hitting parts of my body that should not be exposed to cold air. I groaned in protest.

Valek pushed up to one elbow. "Sorry, love. But I need..."

"To what?" I untangled my legs from his. The cut on my chest throbbed. For the first time in my life, I savored the pain. It meant so much.

"...to tell you—"

"What happened with the Commander?" No doubt the meeting went horribly wrong. When he'd arrived, I'd feared the worst. He appeared so devastated. I had never seen him like that, not even when the Commander had signed the order for my execution and extended the document to Valek.

"Yes."

I waited for more, but he stared off into the distance as if searching for a good place to start.

"Why did the Commander feel it necessary to remind you of your oath?" I asked, helping him along.

"He cited a number of reasons, but it pretty much boils down to the fact that Owen's his guest and he wanted to ensure I didn't assassinate him, Tyen and Rika while they are here."

"Oh." So many thoughts jammed into my head. The first, *we were all dead*, summed up the fear and panic that dominated. Owen must have taken control of the Commander's mind. Ixia and Sitia were both in huge trouble and... *We were all dead*. That one was hard to move past.

"Yelena, I want you to leave this afternoon. Return to Sitia where it's safer. I'll message when it's over."

"No. We just exchanged vows and mixed our blood. Leaving you now would be the same as cutting myself in half. We'll figure this out together. We always do. Remember? No doubts."

He struggled to find a reply. I used his own words, so in order for him to dispute me, he would have to discredit his own logic.

"Don't look so smug. What about Reema?" Valek asked.

That was easy. "We'll send her home with an armed escort. I'm sure Opal and Devlen miss her."

His shoulders sagged. "If anything happens..."

I hugged him. "We're stronger together. And shall always be." The last part set a joyful thrill spinning around my heart.

He leaned back. "We need to keep that quiet for now. And I'm sure your family will want a celebration."

"Yes, they will be disappointed if we didn't."

"After this mess with Owen is finished, we'll arrange a big wedding and get married again."

"Sounds like a plan."

"I wish figuring out what to do about Owen was as easy."

I considered. "He won't do anything overt. At least not yet.

　　　　　　　MARIA V. SNYDER

He's a guest for now. We need to determine if he has control of the Commander's mind. And then learn what he is plotting and stop him before he moves."

"We can discuss how to go about it this afternoon with Ari and Janco."

"And Maren?"

He frowned. "It depends on if she knew about Owen's bargain with the Commander."

"What about Onora?"

"I still haven't decided if I can trust her."

"I'll talk to her."

"Then you need to know a few things about her history."

Valek filled me in as we washed and bandaged our cuts. I searched for a clean tunic and finished dressing.

"So the man...this Captain Timmer, who abused her, is in the dungeon and she doesn't know?" I asked.

"Not yet. I haven't had time to tell her."

"And what do you expect her to do once she knows?"

"Kill him."

"I don't think she will."

"Why not? You killed the man who raped and tortured you. I took great satisfaction in assassinating the King and the men who murdered my brothers."

"I killed Reyad to stop him from abusing others. But I still didn't feel better inside. I had to rediscover my sense of self-worth and had to stop thinking of myself as a victim."

Valek rested his hands on my shoulders and squeezed. "Then you're the best one to talk to her. Let me know when I can trust her."

"Just like that?"

"Yes."

"I don't have my magic. What if I get it wrong?"

"You won't."

When I arrived at Valek's office for the afternoon meeting, I paused at the threshold. A few unexpected people sat around his conference table. At least Valek had taken the time to clear it off. The clutter hadn't gone far. Tall piles of books and files wobbled on the floor nearby.

Valek and Maren stood by his desk near the back wall. By their intense expressions and whispered conversation, I guessed he was having his heart-to-heart with her about her involvement with Owen.

Janco waved me over, appearing rather energetic for having had less sleep than I. Sitting between Janco and Onora, I glanced across the table. Another man I didn't recognize sat opposite me. Almost as broad as Ari, he studied me with interest gleaming in his light brown eyes.

I elbowed Janco in the ribs.

"Ouch. What... Oh. Yelena, this is Sergeant Grunt. Grunt, this is Liaison Yelena, the Soulfinder and Valek's heart mate. You do *not* want to mess with her."

Stretching my hand toward him, I said, "Just ignore him. We find that's best for all concerned." We shook hands. "What is your real name?"

"Sergeant Gerik, sir."

The *sir* was a nice touch. I turned to Janco. "Where's Ari?"

"He's—"

"Aunt Yelena!" Reema raced into the room.

I stood in time to get knocked back into my seat by her flying hug. "I've missed you, too." She clutched me tight. "Can't...breathe."

Releasing me, she laughed. "That's my necklace-snake move. I clamp on and squeeze until the person passes out. Do you like it?"

"It's very effective."

MARIA V. SNYDER

She beamed.

"Did you invent it or—"

"Lacole taught me. She said since I'm small, my best defense in hand to hand is to clamp on and not let go."

"Death by hug. I love it," Janco said.

"Which explains why no one wants to date you," Onora muttered.

Stopping Janco's outraged retort, I asked Reema, "Lacole? Hand to hand?"

"Lieutenant Lacole. She and Ari are teaching me how to fight."

"Oh?" I tried to keep my tone neutral, but Janco sensed my concern.

"Hey, Ari. You're in big trouble," he called.

Ari strode into the room. His aimed his scowl at Reema. "Didn't I tell you not to run ahead of me? And to keep in sight?"

She shrugged. "You were too slow."

"I'm not racing through the castle's halls. You need to stay with me."

Reema failed to appear chastised. "Can I take Kiki for a ride?" she asked me.

"We can go for a ride later. And you can tell me all about what you've been doing here for the last month." I glanced at Ari.

"I was following orders," Ari said in his defense. He sat next to Gerik.

"Thanks a lot, Ari. Now I'm in trouble," Valek said as he reached the table.

Maren scraped her chair on the floor as she plopped down, joining us. She had pulled her long blond hair into a ponytail. Her pale complexion stood out against her black adviser's uniform. Nodding at me, she said, "Hiya, Puker. Long time no see. You look soft."

I grinned. "Those are fighting words."

"I certainly hope so. I haven't had a decent bo fight in ages."

"I missed you, too."

Her deep laugh rolled around the room.

"Reema," a woman called from the doorway. "Are you ready?"

"Lacole!" With a quick goodbye, Reema rushed from the room. "Can we do more knife fighting today?"

I glared at Ari and he pointed to Valek, who closed the door after Reema.

"We'll discuss this later," I said to them both.

"That's never good." Janco rubbed his hands together. "Can't wait."

Valek returned and stood at the head of the oval table. I guessed he'd changed his mind about Onora and Maren. He filled Ari, Maren and Gerik in on what had happened in Sitia with Owen. Then he broke the news about Owen and the others being a guest of the Commander's.

Copying Valek, I studied their expressions closely. Onora kept her face neutral. Janco and Ari appeared to be ready to commit murder. Gerik seemed more concerned than Maren, who relaxed in her chair as if this wasn't news to her.

"At least we know where they are," Janco said. "When do we ambush them?"

"We don't," Valek said, then explained about the Commander's orders.

"That's...that's..." Janco was at a loss for words.

"Bad?" Ari supplied.

Janco shook his head. "Beyond bad. Catastrophic. We can't follow *that* order. Owen may have hexed the Commander."

"The order will be obeyed. We will leave Owen alone." Valek's tone left no room for discussion. "Maren, tell everyone what you told me earlier."

Maren leaned forward. "When I worked in the Curare factory in Lapeer, the Boss... Owen had been working on a secret project with someone they called the Master Gardener. I tried to uncover information. But Owen suspected I'd been sent by the Commander to oversee the production, so it was difficult. During the chaos of shutting down the factory and loading my wagon with all the remaining stock of Curare, I overheard him tell one of his men to gather all the Harman saplings."

Everyone turned to me expectantly.

"I've no idea what a Harman tree is used for. My father might. Did you catch the Master Gardener's name or see who it is?" I asked Maren, thinking this person may have been the one to crossbreed those plants in the hothouse.

"No. All I could discover was the Master Gardener had been key in getting the Curare vines to grow in those glass houses."

"Didn't you and Leif speculate about Zaltanas who may have the necessary knowledge and skills?" Janco asked.

"Yes. Our Councilman, Bavol, and our cousin, Nutty. My father would know if there is anyone else."

"Sounds like your father also has this ability," Gerik said.

"Watch your tongue," Ari growled.

"It's okay, Ari. He has a valid point," I said. "If my father is involved, then he was duped. Or his memories altered. Which I'd like to believe is what might have happened to Nutty and Bavol." Better than suspecting them of treason.

"Would Leif be able to tell if a person's memories were magically changed?" Valek asked me.

"It's possible. I'll messenger him about this Master Gardener and Owen's location. My father should have arrived by now."

"What can we do?" Ari asked Valek.

"You, Janco and Maren keep an eye out for any new construction near the castle. If Owen brought Harman saplings and Curare vines, he'd want to build more of those hothouses.

Also watch for any strange deliveries like ones with unusual materials or odd supplies."

Ari nodded. "What about Reema?"

"She's going home as soon as I can arrange an escort. Gerik, you are assigned to the Commander's security detail again. If you hear or see anything about Owen or the others, let me know."

"Yes, sir."

"Onora, you're to stay by the Commander's side during the day. He has a glass magic detector. If it flashes, then magic is in use. That's when you don't follow your instincts and question all your thoughts, as they might not be your own."

"What about at night?" she asked.

"I'll take the night shift."

I suppressed my disappointment over having the bed to myself at night.

"And if he protests?" she asked.

"He won't. Although he may kick you out for sensitive conferences. In that case, stay by the door."

"Yes, sir."

The meeting ended. I waited until everyone left before asking Valek, "Why did you decide to trust Maren and Onora?"

"Maren convinced me she had no idea Owen was alive. Gerik and Onora showed up with Janco. It would have looked suspicious if I'd dismissed them." He strode to his desk.

I followed. "Which explains why you didn't detail your own plans or mine."

Valek paused before sitting in his chair. "You're sending Leif a message and talking to Onora."

"And?"

"And staying far away from Owen. You're not exactly his favorite person, love."

"Fine. What else can I do?" I half leaned, half sat on the edge of his desk.

MARIA V. SNYDER

"Perhaps a repeat of this morning's activities?" He leered.

"I'm serious."

"So am I."

"Valek." A warning tone rumbled in my voice.

He sobered. "You have training."

Ah. "Spy training?"

"Yes. You need to learn all those skills that you had previously used your magic for."

A daunting task. "That could take years."

"It won't. You're smart and a fast learner. Plus you already have plenty of experience."

"I don't—"

"At the meeting today, who was surprised that Owen's here?" he asked.

"I know what you're doing."

"Answer the question."

Annoyed, I recalled the various demeanors that ringed the table and said, "Ari, Janco and Gerik."

"Very good. You picked up on Onora despite her lack of a reaction."

"That was a guess. How did she know about Owen?"

"You tell me."

I bit down on a Janco-inspired sarcastic response. "The Commander told her. Probably after your meeting with him, since she also didn't seem upset that he'd ordered you to leave Owen alone."

"That's my assumption, as well."

"Okay, I get it. I'm not a total newbie. When do my spy lessons start?"

"Tomorrow afternoon."

That gave me the rest of the day off, which I could put to good use. I needed to check on Kiki. And that reminded me of my promise to Reema.

"Why is Reema learning how to fight?" I asked Valek.

"I may have suggested it to Ari before I left."

I waited.

"She would have driven him crazy if she had nothing to do," he said.

"She's missing school. They could have worked on her reading skills, math, history…" I sighed. And she still would have driven him crazy. "If Opal gets upset, I'm blaming you."

"Feel free. But I suspect her lessons have strengthened her magic."

"No one has been able to confirm she has magic."

"No magicians, you mean? I've picked up on it when I'm next to her, but last night, I felt her power in the hallway."

"Are you sure it wasn't Owen's? She hasn't reached puberty yet."

"Do I need to cite all the examples we've encountered of magic doing strange, unexpected and impossible things?"

"No." It would take too long. "If she's a protégée, then she'll be a target. I just…"

"Want to protect Reema?"

"Of course."

"Then it's a *good* thing she's learning how to defend herself."

I huffed. "Don't be all logical when I want to be irrational and overprotective."

"Now you know how I feel."

"You? Irrational?"

He grabbed my hand and tugged me toward him. I settled on his lap.

Valek pulled me close until I leaned on his chest. "Love trumps logic. And when it comes to you, love, I can be extremely irrational."

"Is that so? Give me an example."

"All right. I've put you in incredible danger by marrying

you now. If my enemies discover the truth along with the news about your magic, which is spreading, they will take advantage of this unique, and hopefully brief, opportunity to target you. The logical thing to do was to wait until your magic returns and Owen is dead."

"Finding an ideal time may have been impossible," I said.

"I'd like to believe we'd find a moment of peace in our future. However, waiting would have been torture. I'm empty without you."

I tilted my head back to kiss him, and my cheek brushed the bandage hidden under his shirt. I wasn't the only one in severe danger. If the Commander discovered Valek's altered scar, he might order Valek executed for treason. I'd already experienced the searing pain of grief that burned me from the inside out when I'd thought Valek had died in that barn fire over six years ago. A horrible time I'd rather not repeat.

Ever.

I checked on Kiki after leaving Valek's office. She munched on the grass in the small pasture next to the stables, but trotted over to the fence as soon as she spotted me. Her coat gleamed.

Stroking her neck, I said, "I see your favorite stable boy has been busy giving you a bath. Did he braid your tail?"

Kiki moved to the side and swished her tail, which now contained a number of thin braids and colorful ribbons.

"Pretty." I patted her shoulder. "Are you rested enough to go for a ride with me and Reema later?"

She dipped her head once, then glanced at the stable, clearly signaling yes. While glad Kiki was able to communicate with me, I wished I could tell her about my union with Valek. My happiness bubbled inside me, pushing to escape, fueling the desire to share it with her. But it was too dangerous to voice aloud.

Kiki snuffled my pockets. I fed her a peppermint before

searching for Reema. The young girl practiced in the northeast training yards with Lacole. Reema had wrestled her long curls into a ponytail and sparred the young lieutenant with a rubber knife. Ari leaned on the fence, watching them. I stood next to him. He tensed.

"Relax," I said. "I'm not going to yell at you. I'm sure you've had your hands full with Reema over the last month."

"You've no idea," he muttered.

"Then explain it to me." I kept my tone neutral.

Ari's broad shoulders sagged. "She's the most exasperating child I've ever met. Not that I know a bunch of kids, but I swear, she's like a mini Janco—just with more focus."

"You do know you're not making sense, right?"

"Yeah." He drew in a breath. "She's smart and learns new skills wicked fast. Faster than anyone I know. Look at that." Ari gestured to Reema. "She has Lacole on the *defensive* and they just started knife fighting last week. The kid's a natural. She's a pro at reading body language. Plus, she's stubborn, fearless and manipulative. Reema can turn on the tears in a heartbeat and suddenly act like a four-year-old. And then she has this…this sixth sense about people, knowing if they're lying or bluffing or sneaking around the hallways."

"Wow." I studied the girl with a fresh perspective.

Intense, Reema didn't hesitate to take advantage of Lacole's weaknesses. The lieutenant dodged a flurry of Reema's strikes that reminded me of Janco.

"Opal is going to kill me," I said.

"But Valek—"

"*I* put her in danger and sent her here. I'm responsible."

"Responsible for what?" Janco asked, joining us.

"Reema's new skills." I pointed to the match.

Janco's eyes lit up. "Holy snow cats! Look at her go. I gotta get in on that action." He grabbed the top rail of the wooden fence and hopped over it in one smooth move.

Lacole handed her practice weapon to him and he faced Reema with a huge grin on his face.

"Reema's ego is about to be bruised," Ari said.

"Will she get upset?" I asked.

"She'll be sullen for a few hours, but then it turns into determination and I'll have to drag her to bed because she'll practice all night if I'd let her."

Now his comment about her being a mini Janco with more focus made sense. Despite his grumbling, I had the feeling Ari cared for Reema.

"You're going to miss her," I said.

He remained quiet for a while. "Yeah. I am. And I'm sure Lacole will, too. She's been helping me with more than training. There were times Reema needed...er...female supervision, like in the baths." Red splotches spread across his cheeks.

I suppressed my mirth over Ari's embarrassment. We watched Janco run circles around Reema, but I was impressed with her tactics.

"Do you want to join them?" Ari asked. "Get some practice?"

"Not now. I promised to take Reema riding. And I'm going to need to rest before my training starts."

Concerned, Ari turned to me. "What training?"

I searched his expression. "Didn't Janco tell you?"

"All I've heard from him is complaints about Little Miss Assassin and Owen the Bastard. We haven't had time to catch up. Why? What's wrong?"

The desire to let Janco tell his partner about my situation welled, but Ari deserved to hear it from me. So I told him about the morning I woke up unable to tap into the power source.

The crease between his pale blue eyes puckered into full worry. "And you're not immune like Valek and Opal?"

"No. Magic affects me like everyone else." Unfortunately.

"I'm sorry to hear that, Yelena. Will you get your magic back?"

"Hopefully once I figure out why it's gone, I'll be able to reverse it."

"I'm here for whatever you need. Okay?"

"Okay."

He frowned at nothing in particular, his gaze distant. "Well, that explains why Valek asked you if Leif can tell when a person's memories have been altered by magic. I wondered why he didn't just ask you to check with your Soulfinding abilities, but I've learned to ask Valek those types of questions in private."

Interesting. "In case he has a grander scheme in mind?"

"Yeah. He always has a grander scheme in mind. And I, for one, can't wait to see what he has in mind for Owen." Ari punched his palm. Hard.

After Reema finished her lessons and cleaned up, Kiki took us on a ride through Castletown. We stopped in town and I sent a quick message to Leif. Only an hour of daylight remained, and the air held the crisp scent of cold as we trotted into the surrounding farms.

Reema sat in front of me, still in high spirits after her sparring bouts with Janco. I'd found that even when you were being trounced by him, it was hard to get angry at him, and it appeared he had the same effect on her.

However, her good mood didn't last once she heard the news of being able to return home.

"Don't you miss your parents?" I asked in the heavy silence.

"I do, but..."

She had made friends here. "You'll miss Ari and Lacole?"

"Kind of."

"You'll miss training?"

"Yes, and I'll miss being treated like an...adult."

MARIA V. SNYDER

"But you're not—"

"Forget it. You don't understand. Only Teegan and Fisk understand. Besides, it doesn't matter. I can't refuse to go home."

"It's safer."

"It's boring."

Ah. The heart of the problem. I thought about what she'd said, puzzling over why her brother and Fisk might understand. She had lived on the streets for most of her life. First with her mother and Teegan, and then with just Teegan after their mother died. Fisk, too, grew up on the streets, begging. No time for a childhood when you were fighting to survive.

"Can I make a suggestion?" I asked.

Reema tensed. "Sure."

"In order to be treated like an adult, you need to act like one. Make a deal with your parents."

Her ponytail swung as she shook her head.

"Just hear me out. The deal is that you promise to attend school without complaining and to earn high marks, and in exchange they continue your training. Your mom learned from Valek, and your father is an excellent swordsman."

She twisted in the saddle, meeting my gaze. "That might work!"

"Don't sound so surprised." I smiled. "Reema, can you promise me one thing?"

Her excitement dimmed. "It depends."

"Promise to make a friend and have fun once in a while. Stupid kid fun."

"Does stealing pies with Uncle Leif count?"

"No. You need to make a friend who is closer to your age. And Teegan and Fisk don't count, either. Will you promise?"

Reema bit her lip, then nodded. "Yes, I promise."

"Good."

We returned after dark. Reema helped me take care of Kiki

before we entered the castle. I escorted her to Ari and Janco's apartment. We interrupted an argument about cats. Reema immediately took Janco's side. When I gave her a questioning look, she mouthed, *Stupid kid fun*. I laughed and left them to their debate.

Halfway back to Valek's suite, I stumbled over a wave of exhaustion. Leaning against the wall, I considered my day. Nothing should have drained my energy like this, although I hadn't eaten since I woke. Hunger was an infrequent visitor, and the thought of food created another swell—this one of nausea.

As much as I avoided thinking about it and ignoring it, I realized it was time to visit the medic.

Located on the ground level of the castle, the infirmary treated all the castle inhabitants. Another station in the barracks cared for the soldiers unless the injury was too severe. Then the poor soul was transferred here. The main rectangular room contained two rows of beds along each long side. Lanterns blazed from hooks set into the walls. As I strode down the middle aisle, I nodded hello at the few recovering patients who met my gaze. A medic I didn't recognize checked a man's temperature.

The woman in charge of the infirmary, Medic Channa, also affectionately known as Medic Mommy, jumped to her feet when she spotted me heading toward her desk in the far back corner. An examination table waited in the opposite corner. A white curtain hung from a track so it could be pulled around the table to ensure privacy.

A mixture of surprise and concern creased her long, thin face. "The gossips reported you'd arrived last night, but I didn't think I'd see you so soon."

I laughed at the implication that it was only a matter of time

MARIA V. SNYDER

before I showed up on her examination table. When I visited Ixia, I avoided using magic to heal the cuts and bruises obtained when practicing with Ari, Janco and Maren. Having a wound magically disappear made the Ixians uneasy, and it gave Janco the creeps.

She tucked her short hair behind her ears. "What can I help you with?"

Scanning the beds nearby, I lowered my voice. "Is there somewhere we can talk without being overheard?"

"Yes. My office."

"But…" I gestured toward her desk.

"That's just so I can do paperwork while on duty."

Channa grabbed the lantern on her desk and escorted me from the infirmary. Halfway down the hallway, she stopped and unlocked a door on the left. We entered a small space crammed with instruments, books and a couple chairs. A desk was buried under the piles. She set the lantern on top of a crate.

Clearing a stack of papers from the one chair, she said, "I'm not in here that much. It's more of a storage space." She sat down. "Now, what's going on?"

I perched on the edge of the seat. "You keep your patients' medical information confidential, right?"

"Of course. I only report cases that involve a crime. But you already know that." She studied my face. "Are you worried I'll tell people you're pregnant?"

Jerking as if she'd struck me, I said, "What… How… I'm not even sure!"

Channa took my hand in hers. "I've birthed all the babies born in the castle complex, Yelena. It's not hard for me to spot the signs."

"But I've been traveling. And been the target of two assassins. I haven't gotten much sleep. It could be stress."

"It's possible," she agreed, keeping her professional demeanor, even though she was probably lying to me. "If you wish, I can test your blood. The results will remove all uncertainty. Of course, time will also do the same."

I hesitated.

"It's best to know. This way you can take proper care of yourself, ensuring your baby will also be healthy."

And there was the Medic Mommy we all loved, laying on the guilt. I allowed her to prick my finger and collect a few drops of blood in a glass vial. She added a yellow powder and mixed the contents.

"It'll take about ten minutes, then we'll check to see if it turns blue."

"Blue for boy?"

"No. Blue for positive," she said, placing the vial inside a drawer and closing it. "Light affects the results." Channa relaxed back in her chair. "Two assassins? Isn't that overkill, even for you?"

Nice. "If you're trying to distract me, it won't work. Besides, those assassins are the reason why I can't be pregnant. It's too dangerous."

"Valek's your heart mate. There will never be a time that isn't risky."

"Exactly my point."

"Don't you want to have children?"

Annoyed, I clamped down on my first response—*it's none of your business*. But considering the reason I was here… "I do, but not now. And before you give me a lecture on how I should have avoided it, I was shot with an arrow containing starlight. Except I didn't know it was starlight at the time."

"Oh my." She tapped her foot. "I thought I'd heard every excuse, but that's a new one."

Lovely.

"If you really don't want the baby, there are—"

MARIA V. SNYDER

"No." The word erupted from my throat before my mind even processed it. "I can't do that. Others can make that choice, but…" I recoiled from the thought. In fact, the entire conversation was uncomfortable, so I changed the subject. "When did you hear I was in Ixia?"

"My assistant told me this morning. He learned from the kitchen staff that Valek asked them to make you sweet cakes."

The gossips worked faster than Valek's intelligence network. I remembered how they had bet money on how long it would take me to be captured while I participated in the Commander's fugitive exercise. Rand, the head chef at the time, had explained it to me: *Gambling and gossiping is all we servants do.*

Perhaps it might work in my favor for once. "Has the staff been talking about the Commander's new guests?"

"Oh yes. They're all abuzz about them."

"And?"

The medic gave me a shrewd look. "And I don't spread gossip. How can my patients trust me to keep their health issues confidential if I'm chatting about others?"

"You can't."

"Exactly."

But that wouldn't stop the kitchen staff or the housekeepers. Perhaps a visit to the kitchens was in my immediate future. After all, I haven't eaten all day. Too bad, the sound of a drawer rolling open ruined my appetite.

As Medic Mommy dipped her hand into the drawer, a strange mix of apprehension, fear and excitement flushed through me, leaving the tips of my fingers tingling. She grasped the vial between her thumb and index finger and held it up to the lantern light.

I stared at the liquid inside.

It was blue.

11

VALEK

After Yelena left his office, Valek tried to concentrate on the piles of reports. But his thoughts kept returning to his heart mate. Or rather, his wife. Amazed, he touched the bandage under his shirt, recalling the intense emotions that had ripped through him mere hours ago. Amid the maelstrom of confusion and betrayal caused by the Commander, one thing had been crystal clear.

Yelena.

Nothing else mattered. No one except her mattered. It was liberating and terrifying at the same time. If she'd said no… He shied away from that horrible thought. Instead he focused on the joy of her reply and the passion of their union. It still hummed in his blood. Along with the desire to keep her safe, which would be difficult because of the current situation.

Valek needed to evict the trio of unwelcome guests permanently. But how to do it? He agreed with Yelena that Owen would lie low for a while. Which was why he hadn't insisted that she have an armed guard by her side at all times. Not that she'd allow it, or that the protector would be effective if Owen attacked. Hell, even Valek couldn't keep her safe, not if a null shield was used against him.

Abandoning the reports, Valek descended to the lower level of the castle. He checked the storeroom that Yelena, Ari, Janco and Maren had used to train back when she had been the Commander's food taster. Except for a thick layer of dust, nothing had disturbed the space. Valek would borrow a handful of rags to clean it. Hopefully, they could keep her new training sessions a secret.

Then he headed to the Commander's office as ordered. The room's entrance was located along the back wall of the throne room. When the Commander had taken control of Ixia, he'd removed all the intricate tapestries, the opulent jeweled throne and expensive decorations. In their place, he brought in desks, chairs and filing cabinets for his officers and advisers. The productive sprawl had no discernible organization or path, but Valek had traversed the expanse so many times, he could navigate it blind.

Onora stood with the Commander's two personal guards outside the open door.

She hooked a thumb inside. "Food taster just brought his supper."

"Any problems?"

"Other than being grumped at, no."

"Good. You're dismissed. Report back for duty at dawn."

"Yes, sir." Onora strode away.

When the taster left, Valek knocked and waited for permission to enter—a new aspect of their changed…shattered?… relationship. He concentrated on expelling all his emotions as the Commander remained silent for twenty minutes before allowing Valek to enter.

He approached the desk and stood at attention, keeping his gaze on the tidy surface. A lifelike glass snow cat glinted with the lantern's amber hues, but the interior of Opal's magic detector stayed dark—a relief. However, the pair of black snow cats Valek had carved for the Commander no longer decorated the desk. He noted the missing gifts without reacting, but their absence was like a slap in the face.

"Report," the Commander ordered.

Valek filled him in on a few new items—reports of thieves using storms to cover their activities in MD-1, and a request for more soldiers in MD-5. The rest were all minor details he normally wouldn't bother the Commander with.

The silence stretched. Finally, the Commander asked, "Have these Storm Thieves been caught?"

"No, sir. They've managed to evade capture so far."

"Do you think magic might be involved?"

"It's possible."

"Then I want you to *personally* investigate this problem."

"That will involve a trip to the coast, sir."

"I expect it will. You have permission to travel to MD-1. However, I did not give you permission to assign Onora as my guard. It is a waste of her time. She is to work with you on all your assignments. Except when you leave for the coast—then she is to be in charge of security. Understood?"

"Yes, sir." Valek fisted his hands. Onora wasn't ready for the responsibility, but he couldn't say anything. This was beyond painful.

"And you are not allowed to skulk about, either, investigating my guests." Papers rustled. "Why is Captain Timmer in my dungeon?"

"He's a sexual predator, sir." Valek explained his abuse of Onora and Wilona. "I planned… Permission to inform Onora about his presence, sir?"

"Granted. Tell her she will have the pleasure of executing him in public. It'll be a mandatory event for *all* my soldiers. They need to understand I will not tolerate such behavior."

"Yes, sir." For some reason Valek thought she'd balk at that order.

"Inform Colonel Qeb to schedule Timmer's execution during the fire festival."

Which was six months away. The festival was held every year in Castletown. An execution during the festival would certainly drive the point home. "Yes, sir."

"Also, I want you to assign one of your agents to collect all information received from Sitia about the Council's reaction to the *rumor* about Owen and the Curare. I want to know if there's any discussion about an attack on Ixia. Do you still have an operative working for one of the Councilors?"

"No, sir."

"Why not?"

"Master Magician Irys Jewelrose discovered him, and he was arrested and extradited to Ixia."

"Was this before null shields were readily available?"

"Yes, sir."

"Send another agent to infiltrate the Council. Have him or her obtain a null shield to block the magicians. I want daily reports."

"Yes, sir." He hoped Yelena wouldn't find out. As the Liaison, she'd worked hard to develop a civil and respectful relationship between Ixia and Sitia.

"When is Yelena planning to return to Sitia?"

An alarming question. And the Commander didn't use her title. "Unknown, sir."

"She is a Sitian and a magician and is no longer welcome in Ixia. Send her home with the Sitian girl."

Surprised, Valek lifted his gaze. He could argue the same thing about Owen and his friends, but the Commander's cold stare sent a warning signal. Was Ambrose in control, or was

Owen directing the man's thoughts? The magic detector hadn't flashed. Yet Valek suspected these orders were from Owen.

Valek sensed he teetered on a dangerous edge. "Permission to speak, sir?"

"Granted."

"Yelena is unable to use magic, sir. She will be a target in Sitia if she returns."

"Why didn't you tell me about her this morning?"

Valek toppled off the edge and landed right in the middle of trouble. He suspected the Commander already knew about Yelena and had been testing him. "At the time, I believed it was more important to warn you about Owen. After that, I didn't have the opportunity."

"I see. Will her magical powers return?"

"Unknown, sir."

"Do you intend to marry her?"

Where had that come from? "Yes, sir."

The Commander tapped his fingers on the desk. "If she agrees and remains here, then she must cut all ties to Sitia and become my Sitian Adviser. If she is unable to do so, or if her powers return, then she must leave immediately. Understood?"

That it was harsh? And that there was no way in hell she'd agree to cut all ties? Oh yes—crystal clear. "Yes, sir."

"Good. You're dismissed."

Valek turned to leave. When he reached the door, the Commander called, "Valek, if I discover you didn't have the *opportunity* to inform me of other important issues, I will add your name to Colonel Qeb's execution list. Understood?"

"Yes, sir." Valek left.

He navigated the throne room with his thoughts whirling from his meeting with the Commander. His threat made it clear that if he caught Valek disobeying orders or taking matters into his own hands, Valek would be terminated. Unnec-

MARIA V. SNYDER

essarily severe. Owen must be influencing the Commander, but the magic detector didn't flash. Valek would have to investigate despite the threat. He'd just have to ensure he didn't get caught.

However, he needed to keep up appearances. He spent the next couple hours doing damage control, informing Gerik and Onora that his earlier orders about Owen were no longer valid.

"Report to my office in the morning to begin your training," he said to Onora. "Gerik, you are to remain on the Commander's detail."

He found Maren doing bo staff drills with a group of young women. She started them on another drill and he called her over to explain.

"We're not to do any investigating. Understood?" he asked.

"What happened?" she asked.

"Commander's orders."

She tapped a finger on her chin. "Little Miss Assassin ratted you out, didn't she?"

The possibility had crossed his mind. "I need you to find an agent who can infiltrate the Sitian Council."

"That's gonna be super hard. The Councilors are all wary of new people. When do you need the agent in place?"

"The sooner the better."

"Even harder. We might have to settle for bribing someone already on the inside."

"As long as the information is accurate. Stop by my office tonight with a couple suggestions."

"Okay, boss." Maren returned to her students.

Valek arranged for Reema's escort. The girl wouldn't be safe until she left Ixia. Then he searched for the power twins. Ari and Janco played cards with Reema in the dining room. From the groans and pile of coins in front of Reema, he guessed the little scamp had won many hands.

Janco threw his cards down in disgust. "That's it! I'm tapped out."

Reema grinned and raked in more coins. "Do you want to play, Uncle Valek?"

"And go broke? No, thank you."

"Awww. You're no fun."

"Did Yelena tell you about going home?" he asked.

Her good humor dimmed. "Yes."

"I've assigned two of my most trusted men to escort you."

She perked up. "Ari and Janco!"

"No, sorry. I need them." Did he ever.

Once again she deflated.

"You'll be leaving in the morning, and you'll ride horses so you can get home faster," Valek tried.

"Horses are fun," Janco said.

"I guess." She fiddled with a coin.

"How about I let you borrow Beach Bunny? She's a hoot to ride and she likes to jump."

"Really?" Reema's eyes lit up.

"Really," Janco said. "She'll jump over logs and streams and stuff."

Valek kept quiet, even though jumping would be prohibited. The object was to get her home safe, after all.

Lacole arrived and announced it was Reema's bath time.

"No." Reema crossed her arms. "I don't need a bath."

"You're grubby. You smell. And your tunic is covered in horsehair," Ari said. "Now go take your bath or you won't get the goodbye present Janco and I bought for you."

"Yes, sir!" She hopped off her chair and pocketed her winnings. "Come on, Lacole." Reema grabbed the lieutenant's hand and dragged the woman away.

MARIA V. SNYDER

"Please don't tell me you bought her a weapon," Valek said.

Janco pished. "A weapon? Who do you think you're dealing with? We got her *weapons*!"

Valek sank into a chair. No need to worry about the Commander ordering his execution. Opal would kill him first.

Ari studied his expression. "Something up?"

Valek glanced around the nearly empty room. Lowering his voice, he said, "Yes. All the orders I gave earlier are void. We will ignore Owen and not do any investigating."

Janco laughed. "Yeah, right."

"I'm serious. The Commander made it quite clear that disobeying his orders will be considered treason, punishable by death."

"Owen must be pulling the Commander's strings," Janco said. "Everything about this situation stinks."

"It's dangerous, and you two will obey his orders." Valek's tone was firm.

"Come on, Valek. It's us," Ari said. "We won't let you do it all on your own."

They knew him too well. "I can't ask—"

"You're not. We're volunteering."

"Yeah," Janco said. "We'll play the good little soldiers. No one will suspect a thing."

"You've never been the good little soldier," Ari said. "If you start now, everyone will know something's up."

"Yeah, well, you know what I meant."

"Who else is in on this?" Ari asked. "Maren? Yelena?"

Valek touched his chest. "Yelena, but not Maren. Not until I know where her loyalties lie."

"Yeah, that whole business with the Curare factory and Owen. She's holding something back." Janco rubbed the scar on his right ear. "It's wonky."

"Wonky? Are you three years old? What kind of word is *wonky*?" Ari asked.

"The fact that you don't know what it means shows your limited vocabulary skills," Janco countered.

"I'll assign you regular, Commander-approved tasks," Valek said before they launched into an argument. "Any extracurricular activities must be done on your own time. Understood?"

"Yes, sir," they both said.

Valek then explained about the Commander's directive regarding Yelena.

"Harsh," Ari said. "But she's not going to stay as his adviser."

"She can't go back to Sitia," Janco said in alarm. "Not with that Bumblebee assassin after her."

Valek didn't bother to correct Janco. "She'll come with me to the coast when I investigate those thieves. The Commander doesn't need to know."

"Risky. Very risky," Ari said.

He agreed, but there was nothing else he could do.

Exhausted from the long emotional day and lack of sleep, Valek considered bypassing his office and going to bed. Then he remembered he'd asked Maren to stop by tonight. He changed course.

Valek slowed when he turned down the corridor to his office. Flames glowed from two lanterns. The rest remained dark. An oversight or blown out? A pool of darkness covered the area in front of his door. Uneasy, he yanked his knife from its sheath and pulled a Curare-laced dart from his belt with his other hand, pinching it between his thumb and finger. He paused, sniffing. No strange cologne or perfume tainted the air. Magic didn't stick to his skin.

He approached the door. Nothing happened. Stopping in

MARIA V. SNYDER

front, he waited, letting his eyes adjust to the darkness. He strained to hear anything that might indicate a person lurking in the shadows. Nothing. The three locks appeared to be untouched. Valek put the dart between his teeth and reached for his key.

An invisible force slammed into him from the blackness, knocking him down. He rolled onto his back as the force tightened around his body, dragging him away from his office and deeper into the darkness. He slid to a stop, but was pinned to the floor. Then it contracted again. He lost his grip on his knife. Breathing turned into an alarming effort.

A black form advanced. Then the shadows shifted and Owen emerged. Rika and Tyen stood behind him. The magician had trapped him in a null shield. A helpless rage built inside Valek as he sipped in tiny amounts of air. Not enough. Light-headed, spots swirled in front of his eyes. Death by hug. He would have laughed if he had the breath.

Owen knelt next to him and the pressure on his chest eased a fraction. "You're not going to obey the Commander's orders despite all your *yes, sirs* and *no, sirs*. And I can't have that. So you're going to have an accident. Poor Valek fell while scaling the castle walls near the guest quarters. The next time you wake, you'll be flying through the air. Enjoy the ride."

The null shield compressed around his chest, squeezing the breath from his lungs. A vision of Yelena flashed. With the last of his strength, he spit the dart at Owen. The magician jerked back, cursing. The force lessened. Valek gasped and tried to move, but he remained immobilized.

"You missed," Owen said, increasing the pressure.

Regret pulsed as Valek fought for consciousness. *Sorry, love.*

Boots clacked on the stone floor as Maren strode down the hallway. Owen, Rika and Tyen froze. Once again, Owen's hold on Valek slipped just enough to allow air to revive him, but not enough for him to warn Maren.

Maren muttered something about lazy servants as she used one of the lit lanterns to light another one closer to Valek's office.

"Rika," Owen whispered.

The woman closed her eyes. "Done."

Valek assumed she'd used her magic to create an illusion to hide them. Since the null shield around him blocked magic, he didn't feel its sticky touch.

Maren knocked on the door, waited and knocked again. Sighing, she leaned against the wall. Valek's three captors glanced at each other. Then Owen stared at Maren.

She yawned. Her eyelids drifted shut. With a grunt, she shook her head and straightened. But it didn't take long for her to slide down the wall into a sitting position. Relieved that they didn't plan to kill her as well, Valek watched as she rested her forehead on her bent knees.

"Okay, I'm here," Janco called from the other end of the hallway. "Although I don't know why you need me." He drew closer. "Valek trusts your judg… Are you sleeping?"

"Mmm?" Maren raised her head as if it weighed a hundred pounds.

"What— Ow." Janco pressed his hand to his right ear.

Don't look. Don't look, Valek chanted in his mind, fearing for Janco's and Maren's lives.

But Janco turned and peered into the darkness. He fingered the hilt of his sword while rubbing his scar with his other hand.

No. Don't. Look away.

Janco turned his attention to Maren. "Guess the servants decided to take off early tonight." He pulled Maren to her feet. "Come on. Valek probably went to bed."

"No." Maren resisted. "He said to meet him."

"Yeah, well, he didn't get any sleep last night. We can talk to him in the morning. Besides, dark hallways give me the creeps."

He guided her back down the hallway and out of sight. Thank fate.

"Let's go, before someone else comes along," Owen said. "Tyen, pick him up. Don't use your magic. Rika will keep us hidden."

"He's conscious," Tyen said.

"But he can't move. Hurry up."

The big man hoisted Valek up over his shoulder. As they traveled though the castle, Valek contemplated his very short future. Was being awake when they pushed him from the window better or worse than waking up in midair?

Worse, because now he had time to think about how easily Owen had captured him. How stupid he'd been to think Owen would wait. How Yelena would react to his death—badly. How he'd promised her forever and he didn't last a day. How he always assumed he'd die fighting and not trapped and utterly helpless, slung over a brute's shoulder like a rag doll, unable to curse or rage at Owen. Or at the Sandseed Clan, for teaching the magicians how to form those blasted null shields in the first place.

A whirlwind of emotions spun, making him dizzy. Or was that the lack of air?

The trip to the guest wing took much longer than necessary. Owen and company made a few wrong turns and wasted time arguing about the right way. Their lack of knowledge reminded Valek of Janco's comment about having the home-court advantage. Too bad it really didn't make a difference for his current situation.

When they finally reached the guest wing, Owen opened

the door and they hustled inside. Rika closed and locked it behind them.

"The window," Owen ordered. He unlatched the shutters. They banged on the stone walls, letting in a gust of coldness.

Tyen propped Valek on the window's sill. A four-story drop loomed below. Valek's heart squeezed in triple time, pumping liquid fear through his immobilized body.

The tightness around his chest eased as Owen put his hands on Valek's shoulders. Valek braced for the shove, but instead, Owen asked, "Any last words?"

Oh, yes. About a million. And all for Yelena, but this might be his only chance to strike a blow. "I'll…tell Ben…hello." Valek panted, trying to fill his lungs.

Owen's grip turned painful. "Did you murder my brother?" Anguish and anger creased his face.

So much for the theory that Owen ordered their deaths. "Not me…another…assassin."

"What about Loris and Cilly?" Rika asked.

"Them…too."

"He's lying. He killed them all. They were a threat to Yelena," Rika said. "Finish him."

"If I'd assassinated Ben…I'd be bragging about it…especially now."

Owen shook his head. "He's just delaying the inevitable. It'll be easy to learn if he's telling the truth. Goodbye, Valek. Oh, and here's something to think about during the few seconds you've left to live. Yelena's next."

MARIA V. SNYDER

12

JANCO

"What's your rush?" Maren asked.

Janco hustled her along the hallways of the castle. The need to hurry pulsed in his veins. "Something's not right," he said.

"What are you talking about?"

"Outside Valek's office. That darkness was...odd...weird. I felt strong magic. And his knife was on the floor. Didn't you see it?"

"No. I was—"

"Too busy sleeping. And that was strange, too."

"Yeah, I guess." Maren remained quiet for a while. "Do you think something happened to Valek?"

Did he? He considered the clues. "Yes."

"But he's immune to magic."

Janco forgot that Maren didn't know about null shields. No time to explain it to her. "Yeah, well, Owen could have shot him with a dart of Curare."

"Where are we going?"

"To get Ari. We need reinforcements."

"You need a couple magicians to fight them."

"Ari's got the best aim with the blowpipe. Curare works on magicians, too."

"But can't that one guy move objects with his magic? A dart wouldn't reach him."

Janco skidded to a stop. "Oh, hell."

"And I'm sure they're gone by now."

They wouldn't wait for Janco to figure it out and return. What to do? Janco closed his eyes. He ejected his chaotic thoughts, suppressed his worry and fear for Valek and concentrated on the logic. If Owen killed Valek, the Commander would be upset, but if Valek disappeared… But he couldn't hide a dead body, it would stink after a few days. They could smuggle the body outside the castle by hiding it with an illusion. Too risky. Maybe they planned to keep him locked up. But where? And would they risk the possibility of Valek escaping? Probably not.

This was going nowhere. He switched his line of thought. Where was the one place the Commander had said was off-limits? The guest suites! Janco opened his eyes.

Maren waited with her arms crossed. "Got something, genius?"

He ignored the insult. "Come on." Janco ran and didn't bother to check if Maren followed or not.

Ari jumped to his feet when Janco burst into their apartment. "What's wrong?"

Janco raced to his room, grabbed his bag of tricks and dashed back. "Reema, stay here. Ari, come on."

"Weapons?" Ari asked.

"Got 'em. Let's go!"

Maren remained in the hall. Janco shot past her, heading to the nearest stairwell. Her and Ari's pounding footsteps sounded behind him.

"Are you going to tell me what this is about?" Ari asked him.

MARIA V. SNYDER

"He thinks Valek's in trouble," Maren answered.

"Thinks?"

Maren explained about the oddness in the hallway outside Valek's office. It didn't take Ari long to reach the same conclusion.

"The three of us can't fight three magicians," Ari said.

Janco reached the stairs and bounded up them three at a time. At the fourth floor, he stopped, putting his hand up to signal all quiet. He peered down the hall. Empty.

Giving Maren and Ari the wait signal, he crept down the corridor until he reached the turn that would lead to the guest quarters. A quick peek confirmed no one lurked in the shadows. But a creepy-crawly sensation brushed his skin.

Magic nearby. Lovely. At least it wasn't the sharp pain of an active illusion. Janco returned to his friends. He explained his plan in a whisper, then dug into his bag of tricks.

Ari raised his eyebrows when Janco handed him a blowpipe and darts.

"Just in case," Janco said. Then he gave Maren the most important item. "Make sure it gets as close to the action as possible."

"What if there's no action?" she asked.

"Then we find it," Ari said. "No stopping until Valek's safe."

Janco flashed his partner a grin. While Maren might doubt him, Ari was all in.

In silence, they ghosted through the hallway. When they reached the door to the guest suites, Janco knelt on one knee. He twisted the knob. Locked. Janco whipped out his lock picks. Using the one with the mirror, he inserted it under the door and confirmed no one guarded the door. A cool breeze blew over his hand and voices murmured from inside.

"A window is open," Janco whispered. "We'll have to move fast."

Inserting his diamond pick and tension wrench into the lock, he aligned the pins in record time and slowly turned the cylinder. Even though every nerve tingled with the desire to hurry, he eased open the door. It about killed him to move that slow.

Owen, Tyen and Rika stood in front of the window with their backs to the door, talking. Strange, but good fortune for him. Where was Valek? He scanned the rest of the room.

"...Valek," Owen said.

Janco's gaze jumped back to the others and he spotted his boss through a gap between Tyen and Rika. Valek sat on the ledge with Owen gripping his shoulders, talking to him. Pushing the door wider, Janco entered the room and signaled Ari and Maren to follow.

Owen said, "...Yelena's next."

"Now!" he yelled at Maren.

The three magicians whipped around just as she threw a glass ball at their feet. It shattered on impact. A knockout gas hissed from the broken shards, fogging the area. But the breeze from the outside would soon clear the air. Then they'd have three pissed-off magicians.

Owen and the others stumbled to the ground. "Ari!" Janco pointed to the prone magicians. "Curare."

But Ari raced through the fog to the window instead. The empty window! Shit. Fear burned in his gut. Janco held his breath and dashed after Ari.

His partner leaned out. Oh no. Janco joined him, preparing to see the worst.

Ari held Valek's arm as the man dangled in midair. The big man's arm muscles strained with effort. Janco reached for Valek's other arm. Together they heaved their boss into the room.

MARIA V. SNYDER

"They're reviving," Maren yelled.

"Go," Valek ordered.

They sprinted for the door and didn't stop until they reached Valek's suite. Valek unlocked the door. Or tried. His hands shook and the key rattled in the lock. Ari nudged Valek aside and finished the task. The housekeeper had lit the lanterns, but the main living area was empty.

Valek called for Yelena. He raced up the stairs, then returned a few minutes later, wild-eyed and frantic. "She isn't here. Owen said she's next. We need to search the castle!"

Ari blocked Valek. "Owen didn't have time to set a trap for her."

"But what if he's looking for her right now?" Valek tried to push past, but Ari clamped a hand on his shoulder.

"He won't just grab her in front of witnesses. He'll have to plan. Let's just take a moment and think. Okay?" Ari guided him to the couch.

Valek just about collapsed onto the cushions. Concerned by his boss's stunned expression, Janco rummaged for the good stuff in Valek's corner cabinet. No one said a word as Janco poured healthy shots of whiskey into four glasses. He handed one to each. They clinked the glasses together and downed the alcohol in one gulp.

Fire burned his throat and warmed his stomach. Janco refilled the glasses.

Valek stared into his, swirling the amber liquid around. "That's the closest I've come to..." He pulled in a deep breath, then raised his glass to them. "Thank you."

"Thank Janco," Maren said. "He's the one who figured it out."

"Yeah, but I couldn't have done anything without you and Ari."

"We're a team. This is what we do," Ari said.

They drank. This time Janco sipped his.

"Now we can concentrate on finding Yelena," Ari said. "Has anyone seen her since she returned from her ride with Reema?"

No one had.

"We'll divide the castle into sections and each take one," Valek said.

"No can do," Janco said. "If one of us runs into Owen or his goons, we'll be in trouble." He scratched his goatee. "We should stay together. Let's list the places she's most likely to be." He glanced at the dark windows. "Supper's over. How about the washroom?"

"Or she could have gone to say goodbye to Reema and found her alone," Ari said.

Valek stood. The whiskey appeared to have steadied him. "Let's go."

They left the suite. As they headed down to the washrooms, Janco asked Valek, "Are you going to report the attack to the Commander?"

"No. Owen will spin a tale about how I tried to sneak into his rooms."

"But we saw—"

"What, exactly?" Valek asked.

Janco recalled the scene in the guest suite. "He had his hands on your shoulders."

"He'll claim he was trying to help me. You didn't witness my abduction. All you had to go on was a creepy feeling in a dark hallway. No. It would be pointless to report the incident to the Commander."

"How did he manage to capture you?" Maren asked.

Valek exchanged a look with Ari. The big guy nodded and Valek explained to Maren about the null shields.

It didn't take her long to understand the danger. "So that means he can trap you at any time?"

"Unfortunately. And he can also suffocate me with that blasted shield." Valek increased his pace.

Janco wished he'd brought the bottle of whiskey along as they checked the washroom, then their apartment, where they found Reema curled up in a chair fast asleep. They searched the stables, the kennels and visited Yelena's friend Dilana, the seamstress. With every stop, Janco's alarm grew twofold.

They visited Valek's office, just in case. Valek's knife remained in the hallway. He picked it up and a murderous expression settled on his face. If Owen had been standing there, no doubt Valek would have rammed the blade into his black heart.

While there were plenty of places left to look, there was no logical reason Yelena would visit them.

"Owen must have her," Valek said in a deadly tone. "I'll kill him."

13

YELENA

Blue. The liquid in Medic Mommy's vial was blue. Blue for baby. I navigated the hallways of the castle without any thoughts on my destination. Lanterns glowed, painting blue shadows on gray stone walls. I clutched a list of foods and drinks that would aid in the baby's healthy growth. The words had been written in blue ink.

Deep down, the news wasn't a shock, but rather a confirmation. Yet the part of me that wanted to automatically dismiss the idea had been a loudmouth, shouting over the quiet knowledge.

Bad time or not, I wasn't able to change the past. Based on my calculations and Medic Mommy's experience, I was about six weeks along, which meant I had a few months before my body revealed the truth to others. The baby was due in seven and a half months and right in the middle of the cooling season. Hopefully by that time, Owen would be turned into a memory. A "remember when" that had a happy ending.

What a crazy day. I wondered if Valek would still consider my news a cause for celebration. So much had happened since I first suspected.

A baby.

I imagined a little boy with bright blue eyes and black hair. The scamp would be causing trouble at every turn. Janco would soon be the favorite uncle, and Junior would probably learn how to throw a knife before he learned how to dress himself. Or perhaps a little girl with curly black hair. She'd be in the midst of trouble and have Valek wrapped around her finger. Ari would spoil her rotten. And she'd learn how to pick a lock before she could read.

I arrived at the kitchen. Laughter and the clatter of dishes vibrated through the double doors. A spicy roasted meat aroma enticed me onward. Steam puffed from buckets of water as the staff scrubbed pots. I'd missed supper while visiting the medic.

Sammy, the head chef, spotted me hovering near the door and waved me over to his workstation. It gleamed, but his all-white uniform sported a number of gravy splotches and other stains.

"Did you stop by to say hello or to scrounge for food?" he asked.

"Both. And to thank you for the delicious sweet cakes. The best you've ever made. You added something new, didn't you?" I sat on one of the stools.

"Yup. Guess what it is." A devilish grin spanned Sammy's youthful face.

At age twenty, he was the youngest person ever assigned as head chef for the Commander. A pang of grief pressed on my heart for the previous chef, Rand. A friend who had betrayed me, and then saved me.

"Lemon juice?"

"Aww, you're no fun." He pretended to pout.

"Then you should ask someone who wasn't trained as a food taster. Why did you add it?"

"The lemon juice reacts with the baking powder, causing

the batter to bubble, and it makes the sweet cakes lighter and fluffier."

"And yummier." I smiled. "Speaking of food, is there anything left over from supper?"

He opened one of the ovens built into the stones above the huge hearth that dominated the center of the kitchen. Grabbing a protective mitt, he pulled a pan out along with the mouthwatering scent of braised beef.

Sammy picked up an oversize metal spoon, ladled two heaping servings and slid one over to me along with a fork. "Nice to have company while I eat."

"Thanks. Do you always wait this late?"

"Yup. This way I know everyone's fed and no one's gonna interrupt me."

The meat just fell apart and melted in my mouth. Sammy chuckled at my unladylike moans.

"This is fantastic. What's the occasion?"

Sammy sobered. "The Commander's guests requested it."

Figured Owen wouldn't be happy with standard fare. And this was the perfect opportunity to learn what the gossip network had discovered. "Does the Commander usually let his guests decide?"

"No. Usually, he lets me plan the menu unless there's a special occasion. Then he orders the meal. But these three have been a giant pain in my ass since they've arrived."

"Really?"

"Yup. They complain about everything. The meat's too hot. It's too cold. Too much bread. Not enough cheese. They also have the poor housekeepers in a tizzy."

"Why?"

"They've taken over the entire guest wing and refuse to let the housekeepers into certain rooms. And they fuss if their beds aren't made early enough and if the chamber pots aren't immediately emptied."

"Has any of the staff complained to the Commander?" I asked.

"No. The Commander gave orders that we were to ensure that their every need was met, no matter what. And no, he's never said that before. Not even when the Generals are visiting."

Not too surprising, if Owen had somehow managed to influence the Commander despite the null shield woven into his uniforms. How long ago did Leif provide the protection? Could Owen have done it four and a half years ago, when he'd first been captured in Ixia? I'd have to ask Leif. But would his answer come in time? Before, I'd contact him through a super messenger and have instant communication. Now it would take a week at least. If my magic ever returned, I'd never take it for granted again.

"Anything else strange going on with them?" I asked.

Sammy chewed thoughtfully. "Yup. They took a bunch of the housekeepers' buckets and filled them with dirt. And they've been burning lots of wood. But not in their rooms, 'cause there's not enough ash."

"Buckets of dirt?"

He shrugged. "Probably in the rooms they blocked from the staff."

Sammy's gossip confirmed that Owen had brought along a few of those Harman saplings and were growing them inside. It made sense if the tree was used to the warmer Sitian climate. Plus, it would take a few weeks for Owen to build a glass hothouse.

As Sammy prattled on about the various hookups among the servants, I wondered if Valek could sneak into the guest suite and steal one of those saplings. Eventually Sammy finished his stories and started yawning. His day started hours before dawn. I bid him a good-night and headed to Valek's suite.

Only a few people traveled the corridors. It was later than I'd thought. By the time I reached the turn into the shortcut through the servant's wing, the halls were deserted.

"Yelena!" Valek called from behind me. He sounded relieved.

I turned.

He ran up to me. "Where have you been?"

"In the kitchen, talking to Sammy. Why? Is something wrong?"

"I've been searching all over for you."

Not quite an answer. "Aren't you supposed to be guarding the Commander?"

"He refused the extra protection."

"Then what—"

"Come on." He grabbed my wrist, tugging me the opposite way. "Janco and Ari found something interesting in the guest wing and want you to look at it."

"Is it a tree growing in a bucket of dirt?"

Valek's grip tightened. "How did you know?"

He sounded accusatory rather than impressed. Strange. "The gossip network. Why else do you think I was in the kitchen?"

"Oh. Well, now you'll get a chance to see it up close."

He hurried through the hallways, dragging me along and going the long way. I stumbled and his nails dug into my skin as he yanked me upright. "Ow. Valek, slow down."

"No time."

I glanced at my arm to see if he broke the skin and I almost tripped again. The long thin fingers clutching my wrist were not Valek's, but a woman's. Yet when I focused on the rest of the body, it appeared to be Valek, which meant...

MARIA V. SNYDER

An illusion! And only one person in Ixia had that ability. Rika.

After a brief moment of panic, I settled my nerves. Illusions couldn't harm me. As long as she didn't have any surprise talents, I wasn't about to let her haul me to her cohorts, where I'd be outnumbered. I dug in my heels, slowing our progress.

"Come on," she said.

Recalling my self-defense lessons, I broke her grip. Then I kicked her in the ribs with a side kick. Rika flew back, and I took off. She yelled, but I ignored her. However, at the end of the corridor, Owen and Tyen stepped into view, blocking my escape. Oh no. My pulse jumped in my throat as fear zinged through me.

I glanced over my shoulder. Rika clutched her side, but she stared in my direction. They wouldn't get me without a fight. Increasing my speed, I aimed for the space between the men, hoping my momentum would allow me to break through.

Except they were also an illusion. I sailed right by them and slammed into the far wall. Pain spiked my shoulder, but I didn't bother to slow or to look back as I ran all the way to the main entrance of Valek's and the Commander's suites. Valek's rooms were the safest place for me.

The guards reached for their weapons when they spotted me. I stopped and gasped for breath. It had been a while since I'd had to run for my life. Guess I'd need to add that to my training schedule.

When no one appeared behind me, I explained about the illusions. "Even if it looks and sounds just like Valek or the Commander, don't let them pass unless you inspect their key for the diamond insignia. Understood?"

"Yes, sir."

"And the same goes for me." I dug my key from my pocket and showed the row of diamond shapes etched into the round, flat section. The Commander's paranoia came in handy from time to time and I doubted Rika would know about the symbols.

"Yes, sir."

"Has the Commander retired for the evening?" I asked.

"Yes."

"Is Valek with him?"

"No."

"Have you seen Valek tonight?"

"Yes. He was here briefly with his second-in-commands. But he hasn't been back since."

"Thanks." I debated if I should search for him, but decided it'd be too dangerous. He'd return to his suite eventually.

When I entered, I spotted four empty glasses and a bottle of whiskey. I considered pouring myself a large portion, but Medic Mommy advised me to avoid alcohol. Too bad.

Instead, I stirred the fire to life and filled the teapot with water. Waiting for Valek proved difficult, so I rummaged through his piles of books for something to distract me. I found one titled *The Art of the Lie*, by Hedda Bhavsar, that instructed readers how to lie convincingly and how to spot liars. Useful information.

Once I had a steaming mug of tea in hand and the book in the other, I settled into a comfortable position on the couch and used my cloak as a blanket. Since it was longer and heavier than she was used to, Reema had been happy to return it to me. She liked the new one I'd purchased, and it fit her much better.

Despite the fascinating subject, I didn't read too long before my eyelids gained weight and the words blurred together on the page. Head nods came next. Giving up, I set the book down and stretched out. After all, Medic Mommy had lectured me on getting the proper rest. I'd finish reading later.

A shuffle woke me, sending fear zipping down my spine.

MARIA V. SNYDER

Valek wouldn't be so noisy. Under the cover of my cloak, I reached for the switchblade strapped to my leg and grasped the handle. I peered between slitted eyelids. Embers glowed from the dying fire. I'd been asleep a couple of hours. No other sounds disturbed the quiet. I waited for an attack, but nothing happened.

Unable to remain still any longer, I jumped to my feet, brandishing my weapon. The room was empty. Or so I thought.

Valek sighed my name. He stood by the door, blending in with the dark wood. He hurried over to me, but I backed up and assumed a defensive stance. His expression of relief transformed into confusion and he stopped a few feet away.

"What's wrong?" he asked.

"What shape did you make with the napkins for Leif's wedding?" I asked.

"Are you—"

"Just answer the question."

Understanding smoothed his features. "Swans, but I can make flowers, as well. Which would you prefer for our wedding?"

I sagged with relief. Closing my switchblade, I stepped into his arms. He hugged me tight. And for a long moment, he said nothing.

"Did they try to trick you with an illusion?" Valek finally asked, releasing me.

"Yes." I explained about the incident with Rika.

"Thank fate you escaped. Seems we were wrong to assume Owen'd wait to attack us."

Alarmed, I asked, "Us?"

"Yes, I had my own run-in with him." Valek detailed his ambush and near-death experience.

"Run-in? He almost killed you!"

Valek didn't deny it or dismiss it with his usual bravado,

which worried me even more. "Is that why you were standing by the door? Did you think I was another trap?"

"No." He paused. "I needed...a moment. The guards said you were in here, but I didn't quite believe them until I saw you. And then..." Valek pulled me close. "We searched half the castle. I thought Owen had you."

"I'm surprised you didn't go after him." And glad.

"I wanted to, but Ari stopped me."

"Did he sit on you?" I teased. That earned me a smile.

"No. He used logic."

"Yay for logic."

"I better go and tell them you're safe. They're waiting with the guards."

"The guards?"

"Yes, I insisted they remain there. It was difficult since Ari and Janco won't let me go anywhere on my own."

"That's good. Stronger together, remember?"

He hesitated for a second, then said, "I need to tell Ari he was right."

"It could be worse."

Valek waited.

"It could be Janco who was right."

"Ah, yes. That would be worse."

Ari and Janco were happy to see me and I gave them each an extra hug for saving Valek.

Maren refused to hug me. "Save that mushy stuff for your boyfriend."

Much to Janco's disgust, Ari limited his gloating. "It's wasted, just wasted on you!"

Ignoring his partner, Ari said, "We'll be back at dawn to escort you to your meeting with the Commander. Then we'll stay with you until you and Yelena leave."

MARIA V. SNYDER

"We're leaving?" I asked Valek in an icy tone.

"Didn't he tell you?" Janco asked.

"There wasn't time." Valek frowned at him.

"That's our cue to say good-night," Janco said, pulling Ari and Maren with him as they left.

I stared at Valek, waiting.

"We're leaving tomorrow."

"Why? What else happened?" The now-familiar throb of fear pulsed in my chest.

"The Commander has given you a choice," Valek explained.

"That isn't really a choice." I couldn't cut all ties with Sitia and my family to be the Commander's Sitian Adviser.

"And since Owen has made his intentions clear, you're safer with me. So you're coming with me to investigate those Storm Thieves."

I drew breath to speak, but Valek interrupted me with a kiss.

"Let's just go to sleep. It's been a hell of a long day," he said.

"That bad?"

He pressed his hand over my heart. "Except for this joy. Yes."

I put my hands over his and then pulled it down so his palm rested on my abdomen. "How about this?"

He stared at me. "Are you sure?"

"Medic Mommy confirmed it."

He beamed. "I've changed my mind. This is the best day of my life! When?"

"Middle of the cooling season."

Valek swept me up in his arms, spun me around, laughing. "We're going to be a family!"

Snuggled together in bed, we exchanged information about what we'd discovered that day and discussed the Commander's orders.

I mulled everything over and found a few troubling in-consistencies. "If Owen is controlling the Commander, then why would he send you to the coast and ensure I'd return to Sitia? Owen wants us both dead. It'd be easier if we remain in the castle."

"But Owen's attempts to kill us failed. Maybe he wants us out of the way so he can work on his plans without us inter-fering." Valek stifled a yawn.

"You received your orders from the Commander before Owen's ambush."

Valek pushed up on his elbow. "That's right. Are you think-ing Owen *isn't* influencing the Commander?"

"No. The Commander has been acting too erratic. Yet..." I struggled to grasp the significance. He'd been horrible to Valek, almost as if he wanted to drive him away. "Did you tell him about the Storm Thieves?"

"Yes."

And that gave the Commander a reason to send Valek away! "I think he's trying to protect us."

"Sorry, love, but I'm too tired to follow your logic. Pro-tect us from what?"

"From Owen. From himself."

"But wouldn't Owen know and stop him?"

He had a point. I speculated further—all I could do with-out my magic. "Maybe Owen doesn't have complete control yet. Maybe the Commander is hoping we'll get help before he succumbs to the magic."

Valek lay down. "That's a lot of maybes. Although I rather like the idea of the Commander trying to protect us. It's bet-ter than the alternative."

I agreed. It didn't take us long to fall into an exhausted sleep. Dawn came way too soon. Valek left for his meeting and I packed my meager belongings. I finished in no time.

MARIA V. SNYDER

Instead of fretting over a dozen different things, I sat on the couch and resumed reading *The Art of the Lie*. The book included instructions on how to read a person's body language by spotting small gestures and tics that revealed a liar.

A shutter creaked loudly. I stood and grabbed my switchblade. Onora climbed through the now-open window and stepped into the room. At least I hoped it was her and not another illusion.

She held her hands wide, showing she was unarmed. "I'm sorry if I startled you, but the guards wouldn't let me in."

"And you couldn't wait?"

"I wanted to talk to you in private before you left."

"Okay, but indulge me first. What is the one thing Janco hates?"

She laughed. "Janco hates many things, but he has a strong aversion to sand. He also despises magic and ants. Did I pass?"

I doubted Owen would know all that about Janco. "Yes." Gesturing to the couch, I asked, "Would you like some tea?"

"Yes, please." Onora sat on the opposite end. "I know you're worried about being fooled by an illusion, but there is no way Rika or anyone else would be able to climb in through Valek's windows."

"That difficult?" I added more water to the teapot.

"Yes, and he has a couple...interesting booby traps." She pulled her sleeve back to reveal a cut along her forearm. "Knives hidden under fake stones being one." Blood snaked to her wrist.

"Let me get you a bandage."

"No need. It's not deep." Onora tugged her shirt down, covering the wound and avoiding my touch.

She wore an all-black, tight-fitting sneak suit similar to Valek's, except it lacked a hood. Plus, her hands, feet and face remained uncovered. Morning sunlight streamed in through the open window.

"Someone may have spotted you on the castle's walls," I said.

"I doubt it. Most people don't look up."

"True." But knowing Valek, he had probably assigned an agent to watch the walls.

I poured two cups of tea and handed one to Onora. "You wanted to discuss something?"

She sipped her tea. "Valek informed me this morning that…" Onora gazed at her lap. "That Captain Timmer is in the Commander's dungeon, and that I would have the honor of executing him at the fire festival in front of the Commander's entire army."

I suspected this Timmer had been the one to assault her, and the Commander wished to make him an example. "Why you? Why him?"

Her foot juddered, swinging back and forth like an excited puppy's tail. "He's the bastard I should have assassinated a year ago."

"Why didn't you?"

"I… Shit." She set the teacup down with a clatter and surged to her feet. "I tried, but every time I got close to him… I just…couldn't. My failure's been haunting me. I was so convinced his death would make everything go away. But then you claimed it wouldn't. And…"

I waited.

Onora stabbed a stick into the fire. Sparks flew and ash swirled. "And I…panicked. What if I can't kill him? What happens if this…" She pounded a fist on her chest. "This hardness inside me doesn't dissipate with his death? What if it spreads instead, turning me as hard and cold as the castle's stones?"

MARIA V. SNYDER

Ah. I drank my tea, stalling for time as I mulled over her comments. "You knew before I said anything that death wasn't the right solution. That's why you couldn't assassinate him."

"But he should die!" She punctuated *die* with a powerful thrust of her branch. The logs shifted, rolling to the back. Her anger spent, she sat on the floor, crossing her legs.

"And the Commander agrees with you. His soldiers are warned of the consequences of abusing their power, and Timmer will be executed, either by your hand or another's. Yet that won't untie the knots inside you. You need to determine what you're afraid of and confront it." I lifted my cup. "I know. Easier said than done, and if I had my magic and your permission, we may have been able to untangle you this morning."

She stared at the flames. They flickered as if agitated.

Memories of my efforts to expel my fear rose to the surface of my thoughts. Terror and pain no longer tainted these memories. Instead I drew strength from them, and Onora needed to know I shared a similar experience. I told her about the torture and rape I'd endured. "Reyad blamed me for the abuse. If only I'd listened better or tried harder, then I wouldn't suffer. He led me to believe that I was no longer a person, but an empty shell to be used. I slit his throat, not to stop him from hurting me, but to keep him from abusing my sisters in the orphanage. I knew murder would land me in the Commander's dungeon, awaiting execution, and I welcomed it."

"How did you get past all that?" Onora asked in a low tone.

"With the realization that I was in control of my life and body. Me. Not him. That I was no longer a victim and should stop acting like one. I also had help from my friends. And I drew strength from Valek's love. I still do."

"I don't have—"

"Yes, you have friends. Janco may be annoying, but he'd drop everything in a heartbeat to help you. You have me and

Gerik—who I suspect cares for you more than he lets on. And the fact Valek hasn't killed you yet is an encouraging sign."

She laughed. "To quote Janco, 'I feel all warm and fuzzy inside.'" Then she sobered. "What am I to do about Timmer?"

"The fire festival is six months away, so you have time to decide. In the meantime, I suggest you visit the captain." Before she could reply, I said, "And I think going to talk to the young women who Timmer abused after you left is a good idea, as well. Valek has their names. Make sure you get them before we leave."

Onora gave me a mulish look, but she said, "Yes, sir."

"Good. I want a report about your progress when I see you again."

"I heard you're leaving for Sitia. Does that mean you decided not to become the Commander's Sitian Adviser?"

Interesting. Valek hadn't trusted Onora with my real destination. I wondered who else knew besides Ari and Janco. "Yes. That shouldn't be a surprise."

"It isn't."

We shared a smile. Then I asked, "Have you noticed a change in him since we've arrived?"

"Yes. He's harsher and no longer wishes to hear advice from me or his advisers. And before you ask, the Commander hasn't confided to me about what Owen is planning."

"Would you tell us if you knew?" I asked.

"Not if the Commander ordered me to keep quiet."

"Fair enough. How about if you knew Owen was using magic on him? Would you tell us then?"

"If you can prove that is the case, then I would, to save the Commander."

"Good to know. Too bad all I know is that Owen is growing those Harman saplings in the guest suite. But I have no idea why."

MARIA V. SNYDER

"How do you know this?"

I explained about the kitchen staff. "They're rarely wrong."

"Would getting a branch of one of those plants help you?"

"Yes, but Valek says it's too dangerous. They probably surrounded them with a magical barrier that would alert them if someone crosses it."

"Do you think they'd relax once you are gone?" Onora asked.

"No. Don't try it. It's too dangerous. I'll ask my father about it."

But Onora's contemplative expression failed to dissipate. She thanked me for the tea and my time. The guards at the main entrance weren't pleased that she'd bypassed their security, but she ignored them.

Valek entered the suite close to noon. He carried a stack of uniforms. When I asked about his meeting with the Commander, he said, "The more I interact with him, the greater my certainty that he's being influenced."

"Even though the Commander has a magic detector?"

"What would happen if Owen put a null shield around it?"

Interesting. "It would no longer flash when magic was used, but it would have sparked when he pulled power to create the null shield."

"In that case, he could just distract the Commander. Owen's rather quick with those bloody things." Valek frowned.

"What about the null shields woven into the Commander's uniforms?" I asked.

"Would that protect his head, as well?"

"Yes."

"Is the shield skintight?"

"I'm not sure. Leif has been experimenting with them. And that glass magician, Quinn, can attach one to a glass pendant."

Valek handed me the uniforms, but seemed distracted. "What would happen if Owen touched your skin while you wore protected clothes?"

I considered. "Are you thinking that once Owen's fingers are past the shield, he could use his magic on a person?"

"Yes. The shield blocks magic, but not physical objects."

And magic would work inside a null shield bubble as long as the magic wasn't directed at something outside the bubble's walls. "He'd have to channel the power through his body and to the ends of his fingertips. Difficult to do, but not impossible. That is *if* the shield doesn't go through his hand, but rather flows around it like invisible water."

"Would Leif know?"

"If he doesn't, it wouldn't be hard to find out."

Tugging his sleeve down, Valek fiddled with the cuff. "Speaking of hands, it was interesting about the illusion Rika tried to trick you with, and how you noticed her fingers didn't match the rest. Do you think it was the physical contact that negated the magical effects?"

With everything that had happened since then, I'd forgotten about that. "If it did, then I would have been able to see her whole body under the illusion and not just her hand."

"Unless it's just the part that is in direct contact with you. Perhaps what's blocking your magic will block others', as well."

Interesting indeed. Could there be a bright side after all? "I can experiment with that when I'm back in Sitia." I'd love to neutralize the bastard with a touch. Thinking about Owen... "What happens after we deal with the Storm Thieves? Are we going to Sitia?"

Valek's expression hardened. "If I leave Ixia, it will be an act of treason."

"You said the Commander is under Owen's influence."

"I know, but I'm still hoping to repair my relationship with

MARIA V. SNYDER

the Commander." He stepped close and cupped my cheek with his hand. "It'll never be the same as before, but I don't wish to destroy any chance I have to retire on a positive note."

"Retire?" That was new.

"Someone has to change diapers while you're saving the world, love."

My heart melted over his willingness to retire for me and the baby. "Me? Save the world? So you're a comedian *and* an expert diaper changer. Wow, did I hook a keeper or what?"

He bowed. "You have the total package."

"I'd swoon, except I'm guessing I don't have time."

"No. The boys will be here soon to escort us to the stables." Valek pointed to the clothes I held. "You'll need to change into an Ixian adviser's uniform in order to blend in once we're away from the castle." Valek retrieved his own pack and sorted through the contents.

As I added the solid black pants and shirt with two red diamonds stitched onto the collar to my pack, I mulled over our conversation. "What will I do then? I can't return to the castle and I'm not going to sulk about Ixia, hiding." And do nothing.

Valek didn't answer. And I realized why he remained quiet.

"You don't really need me at the coast. It makes more sense for me to travel to Sitia. Then I can experiment, consult with Leif and my father. It—"

"No. Too dangerous."

"It's dangerous to give Owen time to set his plans in motion."

"We have time."

"How do you know?"

Valek folded his black sneak suit. "We have until the fire festival." Gathering an impressive number of knives, Valek slid them into various pockets in his uniform and into hidden places in his knapsack. "It's not like the Commander to make an execution a public spectacle. Just hanging the man for abusing his power is enough of a deterrent. News would eventually spread to even the remotest post."

A tendril of unease snaked around my heart. "You think the Commander has another reason for requiring all his soldiers to be at the fire festival?"

He met my gaze. "Yes."

"And this reason includes Owen?"

"Yes."

When I considered how close Castletown was to the Sitian Citadel, the tendril thickened and squeezed. "They're going to invade Sitia!"

14

VALEK

"We need to warn Sitia," Yelena said.

"Of what? Our gut feeling? We've no proof, love."

"But the Commander's army might invade."

"And they might not. Besides, I'd hang for treason if I warned Sitia of an attack."

"I won't."

"You wouldn't hang for treason, but the Commander would consider you an enemy of Ixia and send an assassin after you. We'll just have to ruin Owen's plans well before the fire festival."

"How? We need to consult with Leif and my father about those Harman saplings. And the null shields."

Valek loved watching Yelena puzzle out a problem. Her brow crinkled and he suppressed the desire to smooth the ridge with a kiss. "I've a loyal and skilled agent who is going to deliver messages for us. Once Leif responds to your missive, she'll bring it to us in MD-1."

Yelena frowned.

"What's wrong?" he asked.

"Where in MD-1?"

"The northern coast."

"Too far. Once Leif learns Owen is in Ixia, he'll return to the Citadel. Even if your agent had the fastest horse in Ixia, it would still take her twelve days to travel that distance. And messages aren't effective. If Leif doesn't understand something, it will be a twenty-four-day wait until he does. Plus, you can't brainstorm ideas."

"No." The word sprang without thought from his primal core. The place deep down inside him that screamed, *You will stay with me!*

"You know it's logical."

To hell with logic. "We're stronger together. You said so yourself." Ha. She couldn't logic her way out of that one.

"Yes, for when we go against *Owen*. Not against a gang of Storm Thieves. I'll just be in the way."

"Fine. I'm coming with you to Sitia."

"You can't."

"I'll wear a disguise."

"And what happens when the reports keep coming in from MD-1 about those Storm Thieves?"

He crossed his arms, refusing to acknowledge her point.

She answered for him. "The Commander learns you committed treason."

"I'll stay in Sitia."

"And let Owen win?"

Determined to remain stubborn, he kept silent.

"All right. We let Owen win, and he eventually convinces the Commander to invade Sitia, where *we'll* be living. You, me and our child. How long do you think Sitia will last? I guess we could go into hiding, wear disguises and live in constant fear. That's a healthy environment to raise a child." Her tone indicated it would be anything but. "And we both know it's a matter of time before the Commander hunts us down."

Damn it all to hell! Valek growled every single curse he

MARIA V. SNYDER

knew as impotent fury surged through him. At this moment, he hated logic. He wanted to take his knife and stab it through its cold calculating heart. Why couldn't he be selfish and irrational for once? Damn it all to hell!

"I'm not happy about it, either. But I won't be gone long," Yelena said in a soft voice. "We can rendezvous and return to the castle together."

"Have you forgotten there's an assassin after you?" he asked.

"I'll head straight for the Magician's Keep. I'll be safe there."

"Then take Ari and Janco with you. Please."

"Will the Commander agree?"

"I'll make sure he does."

"All right."

He pulled her into a hug as he accepted the inevitable. "This is the last time we say goodbye."

"Don't say that. We have many more goodbyes and hellos left."

"I meant—"

"I know, and that's a sweet sentiment, but even you know it's impossible."

"You mean you won't let me lock you in a tower so you can never leave?"

She gazed up at him. "Tempting…but no."

"You'll promise to be extra careful?"

"Of course."

They finished packing just as the guard knocked on the door to inform them that Ari and Janco had arrived. The man retreated back to his post. Valek slung his pack over his shoulder and grabbed Yelena's.

He grunted. "What's in here? Rocks?"

"Books. And don't you start being all…" She tugged on the handle. "I can carry it."

"Being all what?" Keeping a firm grip on her pack, he strode to the door.

She hustled beside him. "Being all…my-wife-is-pregnant-and-she-can't-do-anything…overprotective."

"Me, overprotective? You must have mistaken me for another man," he teased.

She swatted him on the arm.

"You're the one who had to pack books." Valek waited while she opened the inner door. "What kind of books?"

"Ones about how to spy and stuff."

"Nothing's better than actual training."

"I know, but I can still learn a few new tricks."

"Tricks?" Janco asked as they exited the main entrance.

"Yes. You'll need your bag of tricks," Valek said. "You, too, Ari."

"Why?" they asked in unison.

Valek explained their new mission. "All you have to do is protect Yelena."

"Easier said than done," Janco muttered, then shot her a sweet smile. "What about the Commander?"

"After you pack, we'll swing by his office and I'll obtain permission. I'm sure he'll want to ensure she arrives in Sitia without incident. She may no longer be the Liaison, but he wouldn't risk a diplomatic incident. At least, not yet." He fervently hoped.

As they headed to Ari and Janco's apartment, Valek asked Ari about Reema.

"She left this morning," Ari said.

"Any problems?"

"None."

"She *loved* her gifts," Janco chimed in.

"What gifts?" Yelena asked.

MARIA V. SNYDER

Valek swallowed a groan as Janco listed the various weapons they'd given the girl.

"Opal's going to kill you," Yelena said.

"Not me," Janco protested. "Ari bought them. I just gave her a set of lock picks."

"Ari?" Yelena turned to him.

"Sitian knives are too flimsy. She's going to need a quality set."

"For what? To defend against the other eleven-year-olds in her class?" Anger turned her words sharp.

Ari hunched his shoulders. "To defend against those who would use her to get to you."

Which was the reason Reema was at the castle in the first place. Yelena snapped her mouth shut. Then she exhaled. "You're right. Sorry, Ari."

"And we all know Reema's going into the family business," Janco said.

"Family?" Yelena rested her hand on her stomach.

Before anyone noticed her unconscious gesture, Valek tugged her hand away and laced his fingers through hers. Excitement about the baby tapped a quick tempo in his heart, but a deep bass of worry also played along. He kept his expression neutral.

"Yeah. You know…" Janco swept his arm out, indicating all of them. "Us. She's the next generation of sneak." He grinned with glee. "I almost feel sorry for those future criminals. They won't know what hit them."

"So we're all sneaks?" Ari asked.

"Sneaks, spies, defenders, heroes, masterminds, tenacious bastards—it doesn't matter what you call us. We're the ones who will do whatever it takes to stop those who believe they're entitled to wealth and power at the expense of others."

"The family business," Yelena said, smiling. "I like that. Well said, Janco."

Valek squeezed her hand in agreement. For once Janco didn't preen.

The boys packed in record time. Valek wished his admittance into the Commander's office matched their speed. Eventually the Commander allowed him to enter and heard his request.

The chair creaked as the Commander leaned back, studying Valek. "Granted. Have them collect information on the Council before returning to Ixia."

"Most of the Councilors will recognize them," Valek said.

"They can still get a sense of the Council's mood and look for signs of an invasion. Tell them to look for a possible way to get our agent inside. Perhaps one of the Councilors needs a new adviser."

"Yes, sir."

Relieved expressions greeted him when he exited the Commander's office. "Did you expect him to say no?" Valek asked.

"Yes, actually," Ari said. "He's been giving you such a hard time since you returned from Sitia."

"Yeah, but without us underfoot, there will be two fewer obstacles in Owen's path," Janco said.

Good point, but Valek wouldn't say it aloud and risk Janco gloating. "You might be safer in Sitia."

"Doubtful," Janco muttered.

Yelena flicked his left earlobe with her finger.

"Ow!"

Now she shot him a sweet smile.

"Kids, behave," Valek admonished, but inside the knot of worry for his heart mate eased just a bit. Janco and Ari would do everything in their considerable power to keep her safe.

The four of them left the castle and headed toward the

stables, where Maren and Onora had been waiting for them. On the way, they picked a rendezvous location and estimated a date to meet.

"Don't go back to the castle without me," Valek ordered.

"Same goes for you," she shot back.

When Maren and Onora came into view, Yelena said, "Here are two more members of our family."

The women sat on bales of straw stacked near the entrance. Both Kiki and Onyx had been saddled, and their travel supplies were packed. Valek glanced at Maren.

She shrugged. "We were bored. Where have you been?"

He explained about the change in plans. "Onora is now in charge. The Commander wants reports twice daily."

A subtle flinch of surprise meant Onora hadn't expected that.

"Consult frequently with Maren," Valek added.

"Yes, sir."

When Ari and Janco sought the Stable Master for horses, Valek pulled Onora aside. "Keep a close eye on the Commander. As close as he'll allow. And send me a message if anything odd or strange or bad happens. Also, if you learn of anything that will affect his or Ixia's safety."

"Yes, sir."

"Did you have a nice chat with Yelena?"

Her gaze snapped to him. "Did she tell you?"

"No. The agent who had his crossbow trained on your back as you climbed the wall told me."

"Why didn't he shoot me?"

"He recognized you and once you reached the window, he knew you weren't an illusion."

She touched her arm. A small white bandage peeked from underneath her sleeve.

"Did you visit the medic?"

"It's just a scratch."

"Go see her right away. I treat my blades with scum. You'll get an infection if you don't clean the cut properly."

"Yes, sir."

"I'm quite impressed that when you climbed to the Commander's suite that first time you didn't encounter any of my hidden blades." Valek studied Onora, seeking a reaction. "And it was quite the coincidence that Sergeant Gerik was assigned to cover the wall that evening."

Onora didn't blink, or even breathe, for that matter.

Gotcha. Valek drove his point home. "Gerik must have recognized you, since you both grew up in Silver Falls and you joined the army at the same time. Too bad he was assigned to another unit."

"Why didn't you…"

"Arrest him?"

She nodded.

"And split up a highly effective team? No. You'll need loyal people working with you if you're going to take over my job."

The prospect of being promoted failed to crack her serious demeanor. Perhaps she'd learned enough about his position to realize the danger and constant headaches.

Valek and Onora rejoined the others. The Stable Master had brought The Madam and a thick-chested dark brown horse with a white diamond on its forehead.

"Is it okay to send The Madam along with Kiki?" he asked Onora.

"Yes. She'll help Janco get through his lonely nights without his beloved Beach Bunny."

Janco made a rude gesture at her. As Ari and Janco saddled their horses, Valek warned Maren and Onora to keep away from Owen. He also reminded them of the various operations in progress. "And select an agent for the undercover job. Ari and Janco will be sending you more information."

"Don't worry, Dad," Maren said. "We won't burn the house down or invite our friends over for a brew party while you're gone."

"We'll probably be at the rendezvous point before you, so message us if you need backup," Ari said to Valek.

"Yeah, feel free to share the fun," Janco added.

"I'll be on the coast," Valek replied.

"Ugh. Forget it. That's not fun."

"I'll bring you back a souvenir. A bag of sand, perhaps?" he teased.

"That would be fabulous. Then I can dump it into Ari's bed so he can experience the joy of coastal living—the unique sensation of sand in your sheets."

"Would it help me understand why you named your horse Beach Bunny?" Ari asked.

"Shut up."

While they finished packing their saddlebags, Valek drew Yelena away from the others. He put his hands on either side of her face and kissed her with the full depth of his love, wishing to communicate the vast extent of his passion and his desire. He'd have gladly given her his magical immunity if it were possible to keep her and their baby safe.

When they broke apart, Yelena gasped for breath. Her green eyes shone. "A few more kisses like that and I might agree to be locked in a tower."

"Then expect many more when you return." He traced her bottom lip with his thumb. "Hurry back, love."

"I will."

Mounting Onyx, Valek exchanged one last smile with Yelena, then spurred his horse forward. He'd already lost more than half the day, and he planned to be at the first travel shelter by sunset. As the distance from the castle grew, the warmth from his kiss with Yelena drained away. Dread, worry and an emptiness rushed in its place.

Instead of brooding, he concentrated on making up time. Traveling in Ixia was different than in Sitia. In the south, even small towns had inns, and the population sprawled from one city to the next. In Ixia, the farmers lived in town and walked to their fields every morning. The town borders were more defined to make it easier for security to patrol the perimeter and ensure everyone remained where they should.

Instead of inns, travel shelters had been built in Ixia when the distance between cities required travelers to stop for the night. Security patrols frequently checked them for unauthorized people. As an adviser to the Commander on horseback, he shouldn't be questioned as much.

Valek headed northwest. As soon as he'd passed the outer wall of the castle, he was officially in MD-6. The Commander governed all of Ixia, but he directly controlled the complex and Castletown. Both were located in the southern point of MD-6, which was ruled by General Hazal.

It would take Valek approximately nine days to reach the coast of MD-1. He'd have to cross the northeastern section of MD-8 to get there. The reports about where the Storm Thieves had hit listed many of the towns along the northern section—a place Valek knew well. He'd learned the assassin arts at the School of Night and Shadows. The complex had been built on top of a cliff facing the Sunset Ocean and near the most northwestern point in MD-1. The terrain to the south smoothed into gentle dunes, allowing fishermen to trap crabs and hook sea cod. A few miles inland, farmers raised herds of bison that thrived in the colder climate.

Valek urged Onyx into a gallop as the irrational part of

him tried to outrun his memories. But the vision of his father's leather tannery rose despite his efforts to quell it. His parents' house was near the area being targeted by the thieves. Valek had left twenty-eight years ago. The sound of his father's voice still remained clear despite the years. He'd never forget when his parents told him never to return. They hadn't approved of his desire to seek revenge on the men who murdered Valek's three brothers. And Valek had honored their request and stayed away.

Of course, he'd assigned agents to watch over them and protect them if needed. But he didn't want a detailed report. All he wished to know was that they were alive and safe. Nothing else was relevant. Details would be a painful reminder of a time he'd rather forget. And soon he'd have his own family— or rather, another addition to his eclectic family, if he agreed with Janco's assessment.

Valek reached the shelter before the sun fully set. The bloated half disk colored the sky with orange and red streaks. A couple horse stalls with a few bales of straw and buckets for water leaned against the structure. He removed Onyx's saddle. It weighed a ton. With only four hours of sleep in the past three days, Valek felt every pound. And when he considered everything that had happened with Yelena, the Commander and Owen, he was rattled, exhausted and overwhelmed.

While Onyx ate, Valek groomed him and filled a water bucket. When he finished, he patted his horse. "If you smell or hear anything, can you please alert me?"

Onyx bobbed his head.

"Thanks." He fed him a peppermint.

No one else was in the shelter. Valek doubted he'd have company, since he'd only seen a few security patrols on the road. The one-room building resembled all the other rest stops in Ixia. Valek tossed his pack onto a lower bunk far from the door. The distance would give him time to react if anyone entered with ill intentions.

After a meal of sliced cheese, nuts, meat jerky and bread—typical travel rations—Valek collapsed on the narrow bed. Already he wished the mission was over. He planned to stop the thieves as quickly as possible and return to the rendezvous location just as fast. If Yelena didn't arrive in a reasonable time, he'd go to Sitia and find her.

Not even committing treason could stop him.

After eight days of hard riding with only brief stops to rest and feed Onyx, Valek arrived at the garrison near the northern coast of MD-1 by late afternoon. He needed to check in with the local patrols in order for them to leave him alone as he conducted his investigation. Besides, a hot meal, a bathtub and a real bed sounded too good to pass up.

The guards at the gate snapped to attention and just about wet themselves when Valek told them his name. High-ranking officers were fetched and a private arrived to take charge of Onyx. Despite the private's assurance to take good care of his horse, Valek followed the young man to the stables to ensure Onyx received the proper attention.

Pausing at the entrance, Valek remembered the first time he'd arrived at this stable twenty-six years ago. He had reported to work minutes late, and the Stable Master had boxed his ear. It had been his first undercover operation, and he learned so much working as a stable boy. Back then, the King ruled Ixia, and all the officers had horses, so he'd not only been busy, but had a perfect spot to keep track of the comings and goings of the soldiers. Best of all, he'd assassinated the three men who had murdered his brothers, and their captain. No one had suspected the stable boy, and it was many years later before the garrison learned who had killed the men.

Satisfied Onyx would be taken care of, Valek allowed the garrison's commander, a Colonel Ransley, to escort him to his private dining room for supper. Four older officers and two younger lieutenants joined them for the meal. Most of the King's soldiers had switched their loyalties to the Commander during the takeover. It hadn't been hard to convince them once they learned they'd earn higher wages and receive better benefits and respect, as long as they followed the Commander's Code of Behavior.

From the occasional scowl directed his way, Valek figured a few of the older men had been stationed here when Valek had caused such panic over the mysterious deaths.

Once they were seated around an oval-shaped table, servers poured them glasses of wine and placed plates filled with steamed cod and salted seaweed. Colonel Ransley swallowed a large mouthful of wine before asking, "What brings you to this remote corner of Ixia, Adviser Valek?"

Conversation ceased as the others waited for Valek's answer.

"I've been getting reports about a gang of thieves that strike when it storms," he said.

Ransley scoffed, "It's just a bunch of kids, stealing for kicks."

"Yet you haven't stopped them." Valek studied their expressions.

"The local security forces can handle it," an older major said. "Besides, they've only stolen petty stuff. When the fleet goes out, the incidents will stop."

"Petty?" Valek asked. "I don't think the weapons taken from the security office in Gandrel are insignificant."

The major glanced at Ransley, who covered his surprise. Ransley cleared his throat. "Are you sure this information is accurate?"

Valek's tone turned icy. "Do you think I'd journey all this way for a mere rumor?"

"No, sir," Ransley was quick to reply. "It's just we hadn't heard about the hit on Gandrel."

"The thieves might be intercepting messages to the garrison," Valek said.

"Wouldn't they block information traveling to you, as well?" the old major asked.

Turning to the idiot, Valek bit down on his temper. "My corps are well trained, Major. They wouldn't make the rookie mistake of trusting the wrong messenger."

"But they couldn't find the Storm Thieves, either," one of the young lieutenants piped up.

The others froze in horror, but Valek pointed his fork at him. "You're right, Lieutenant. My corps couldn't catch them. Every time they set a trap, the thieves avoided it." His gaze met each man at the table. "Someone is providing them with insider information. It could be one of my agents, or one of the local guards. There is also the possibility that the thieves have discovered a way to spy on the authorities. Since my men were unable to determine the source of this leak, I decided to aid their efforts." Valek resumed eating.

"Why do you believe you will have more success?" the major asked, his tone skeptical.

Valek stared at the man with what Yelena called his killer look.

The major dabbed at his mouth with his napkin in an attempt to hide the red splotches spreading on his face. "Er… yes…no doubt you will… My apologies, sir."

Ransley changed the subject. "We have a promising young man that you might wish to recruit into your corps, Adviser Valek. He's a skilled swordsman and smart, too."

Letting the major off the hook for now, Valek made the appropriate inquiries about the swordsman. He wondered if any women had been promoted in this garrison and decided

MARIA V. SNYDER

to check into that, as well. The King had frowned on female soldiers, claiming they were too weak to fight. The Commander held the opposite opinion and recruited many loyal and fierce women into his army when he took control of Ixia.

After supper, Ransley escorted Valek to the guest quarters. The two-room suite contained a bedroom and a living room. The lanterns had been lit and a fire danced in the small fireplace. Comfortable and clean. Valek approved.

"Colonel, while I'm investigating I'll leave my horse here, and I'll also need to borrow a couple uniforms." His black-and-red adviser's uniform would stand out among the black-and-white colors of MD-1. Each Military District had its own color combined with black.

"Of course. I'll be happy to provide anything you need."

Valek thanked Ransley as he ushered the man out the door. Changing into his sneak suit, Valek slipped from the guest quarters and ghosted through the garrison's buildings. He found a comfortable and hidden location to watch the back gate. He'd divulged his mission to his fellow dinner guests for a reason. And, after a few hours, the reason approached the gate and talked to the guards, who laughed and waved him through.

Too easy. Valek slid from his hiding spot and followed the man, certain he'd lead him right to the Storm Thieves.

A half-moon peeked from behind a layer of thin clouds, casting enough light to navigate the narrow road. Aside from the occasional glance over his shoulder or the infrequent times he stopped to listen to the night's sounds, the man didn't appear concerned about the possibility of being tracked as he headed straight to the coast.

The familiar cool scent of salt air reached Valek before the distant crash of waves. The expected turn to the southern towns didn't happen. Interested, Valek closed the distance between them so he wouldn't lose his quarry. After a few more hours, Valek guessed the man's destination. Clever. Very clever.

Sure enough, near dawn, the man entered the outer boundary of the School of Night and Shadows. Or what had once been the school. When the Commander took over Ixia, work for assassins in Ixia had dwindled. Hedda eventually closed the school instead of taking the offer to work with Valek and the Commander. But they'd recently discovered from Onora that Hedda hadn't retired, and had actually been training a few students.

Fresh grief for his old teacher rose. Onora had killed Hedda. Probably because she wouldn't divulge the name of the client who had hired an assassin to target the Commander.

Memories stirred as Valek kept the man in sight. When he'd first arrived on Hedda's doorstep, the school had plenty of students. Now the place appeared deserted—although he doubted it was. In fact, this location would be a perfect spot to run another illegal operation, like stealing during storms.

The man disappeared into the main building. In this part of MD-1, cliffs lined the Sunset Ocean, and Hedda had built her school to resemble the rocky terrain, painting all the structures in the complex to blend in with the surrounding grayish-white landscape.

The sky brightened as dawn's first rays chased away the blackness. Valek looped around to a little-known entrance. From the undisturbed and thick coating of salt and rust on the combination lock, he guessed no one had come through here in years. Good thing the corrosive salt air eventually turned metal brittle. Valek broke the lock in two and slipped inside.

He paused, letting his eyes adjust to the darkness. Voices bounced off the stone walls. Concentrating, he detected two speakers, but the words were garbled. Valek tracked the conversation until he understood the speech. He listened next to an open door. Yellow lantern light spilled into the hallway.

"...no one followed me. Stop worrying so much," a man said in a placating tone.

"You're an idiot. You just killed me," a woman responded with a twang that Valek would never forget.

"Relax. Valek's not here for you, but I thought you'd like to know he's in the area," the man said.

Valek stepped into the room, surprising the man, but not Hedda.

"I'm closer than you think. And she's right," Valek said. "You are an idiot." Then he turned to his former teacher.

Hedda stood behind her desk with a knife already in her hand. All but a few fiery red strands of her hair had turned gray. Wrinkles etched her forehead and drew her mouth into a frown.

"Hello, Hedda." Unconcerned about the blade, Valek strode closer. "Nice to see you alive and well."

She inclined her head politely. "King Killer." Her grip tightened on her weapon. "Did the Commander send you?"

15

LEIF

"They're trying to grow Theobroma-resistant Curare?" Leif repeated. "Are you sure?"

"Yes," Esau said. "This..." He waved the thin branch. Its oval-shaped leaves bounced with the motion. "...is a cross-breed of the Theobroma tree and the Curare vine. If this grows pods, the Theobroma seeds might contain Curare. If you press those seeds, you might get a Curare that can't be neutralized by Theobroma."

Sitia's army would be unable to defend itself against the paralyzing drug. The Commander's soldiers could invade without any resistance. The thought of having to wear a uniform and obey his Code of Behavior soured Leif's stomach. "So you don't know if they've been successful?"

"I'd have to wait until it produces pods that are ready to be harvested, and then test it." Excitement raised Esau's voice at the prospect.

Leif studied the specimen. Owen had escaped this compound but was unable to take these plants with him. However, he'd cleaned out his other hothouses. This might be the only sample they had. "How long until the pods are ready?"

"Oh, I'd say about...three, maybe four years."

Somehow, Leif didn't think Owen or the Commander would give them those years. But then again, it would take Owen the same amount of time to supply his men with the resistant Curare.

"What about the other crossbreed plants?" he asked his father.

"One at a time, my boy. One at a time. Is that dinner?" Esau gestured to the tray Leif held.

"Supper, Father. You worked through dinner." Leif set the tray on the ground. "When it gets dark, come inside the farmhouse. I'll have a bath ready for you."

Already chewing on an apple, Esau nodded, but his gaze had returned to the greenery surrounding him. Leif left, knowing he'd have to return and fetch his father or the man would work through the night. When his father immersed himself in a project, Leif's role was simple—take care of Esau's needs.

Esau decided he needed to catalog all the plants in the hothouse, along with the investigation of the crossbreeds. Over the course of a few days he determined that Owen's gardener had crossed a few medicinal plants.

"Very clever," Esau said. "This way one plant will take care of two symptoms. Less to pack!"

"Do you recognize the person who did the crossbreeding?" Leif asked. "Is it someone from our clan?"

"No to both questions. However, I suspect it is someone from the Greenblade Clan. They have forest experts who have been crossbreeding trees to grow a harder wood for buildings."

"But how are they getting the jungle plants?"

"We can't patrol the entire jungle, Leif. Curare and Theobroma grow all over and are just as accessible at the border of the Cowan Clan's lands as well as deep in the interior."

At least it wasn't one of their clan members. Small comfort. He'd hoped his father would recognize the gardener helping Owen.

Esau spent a total of six days working in the hothouse. On the last day, he shouted for Leif, who'd been grooming Rusalka. Leif raced to join his father. Esau had leaves caught in his hair and dirt stained his forearms, forehead and knees.

"Come see what I found!" Esau grabbed his elbow and tugged him inside the hothouse. "Back here. I almost missed it."

Leif crouched down to avoid being smacked in the face by a branch. Near the back right corner, Esau pulled him to his hands and knees, and they crawled the rest of the way.

Esau stabbed a finger at a Theobroma tree. "See that?"

"Yes. So?"

His father pointed to what appeared to be a large knot on the lower trunk "Look! This is where another Theobroma tree has been grafted onto this tree."

"Okay. What's so special about that?"

Esau huffed. "It means that this second tree doesn't need as much time to mature as the first one because the roots and trunk are already established." When Leif failed to produce an appropriate reaction, he continued, "It means that instead of waiting three to five years for the Theobroma tree to mature and produce pods, it will grow pods in just a *year*."

Wow. That meant... "And will double the number of trees growing pods?" Leif asked.

"Exactly!"

"Increasing the production of Theobroma is what the Council has asked Bavol to accomplish."

"Then message Bavol and tell him to come here. He needs to see this!"

And it also implied Owen's stock of Theobroma may be twice the amount they'd estimated. Had he sent it to the

MARIA V. SNYDER

Commander along with the Curare? What if Owen used the grafting to grow Theobroma-resistant Curare? Would they be able to use the Theobroma after they extracted the Curare? Leif asked his father.

"It's possible, but I won't know for sure until the trees mature."

Leif hurried to the farmhouse to contact Irys and ask her to talk to Bavol. Before he reached the porch, a voice called his name. A young messenger stood outside the gate waving a sealed envelope. He thanked the girl and tipped her. The scent of lavender tickled his nose, and the part of him reserved for worrying about his sister relaxed a fraction. He waited until he was inside before ripping it open.

After reading the first sentence, his concern returned, along with fear. Owen was a guest of the Commander, staying at the castle in Ixia. With Yelena! She was supposed to be safe there with Valek. Instead she was in just as much danger as when Owen had captured her.

Leif raced up to his room. He pulled the super messenger from his pack and sat on the edge of his bed. Drawing on the magic inside, he reached for Irys. She allowed him through her defenses right away.

Good timing, Leif. I was just about to contact you. Do you have any news?

Plenty, he said. Leif filled her in on what he'd learned from Yelena. *I'm going to Ixia. Send Hale and two other magicians and have them meet me at Yelena's cabin in the Featherstone lands. Do you know where it is?*

Did she ask for help?

No, but neither she nor Valek can defend against Owen, Rika and Tyen.

I'm sorry, Leif, but I can't spare the magicians. In fact, the Coun-

cil has ordered you back to the Citadel again. *They want your report in person.*

But Yelena—

Must be safe, or else she wouldn't have sent you that message. You need to convince the Council of the danger.

If I return to the Citadel, it will be to gather magicians to travel with me to Ixia. Yelena's helped so many people, I'm sure I'll have plenty of volunteers.

Talk to the Council first, and then I'll help you recruit.

Irys's desperation shrilled in his mind like an out-of-tune violin.

That bad?

Yes. I need your help.

All right.

Thank you. Did your father discover anything useful?

Leif told her about the various plants Esau had identified. Her reaction to the Theobroma-resistant Curare matched his. *And Bavol must come and see this grafting technique.*

He can't leave the Council sessions. Would it be possible to bring your father and the plants to the Citadel?

It's too cold. The plants will probably die before we arrive. But I'll ask him.

Please tell him it's very important.

Now she was scaring him. Leif had known Irys for most of his life, and she'd always been rather unflappable and stoic. *Irys, what's really going on?*

I'll explain everything when you arrive.

A classic dodge. *Come on, Irys, it's me.*

How soon can you get here?

If we leave tomorrow, we'll be there in seven days. But you didn't answer my question.

Be extra careful on your journey. She paused. *We've…lost a number of magicians.*

MARIA V. SNYDER

Lost? Like they're missing, or they're dead?

Both.

Holy snow cats, Irys! Why didn't you tell me that right away?

The Council doesn't want to spread panic needlessly.

Well, if there's a time to be panicking, I think this merits it. Don't you?

She ignored his sarcasm. *Get home as soon as you can.*

Yes, sir.

16

YELENA

My lips still burned from Valek's kiss. The intensity of it seared into my soul like a red-hot iron branding his name right on my heart. The idea of being locked in a tower with him no longer sounded so terrible. If my magic never returned, what else would I do aside from raising our child? I might be content...for about a week.

Valek mounted Onyx. He met my gaze, and his smile promised a reunion worth waiting for. Then he was gone, leaving behind a cloud of dust. The rest of the world returned, appearing duller.

"Yelena," Onora said.

I focused on her. "Yes?"

She held out a roll of parchment. "I drew this for you."

Suppressing my surprise, I took it and unrolled the sheet, revealing a picture of a tree drawn with charcoal. Each oval leaf had been carefully detailed, along with the precise lines and shading of the bark. I half expected it to sway in the breeze.

Why would she— I gasped. "It's the Harman tree, isn't it?"

"Yes." Onora's tone was matter-of-fact.

She'd gone into Owen's suite and sketched one of the saplings, despite the danger. Impressive and brave. "When?"

"This morning. Right after I talked to you."

"Did anyone see you?"

"No. And I didn't touch the trees or go near them, just in case there was a magical alarm."

"Smart. I want to admonish you for taking such a risk, but..." I waved the picture. "This is perfect. You are a talented artist."

She shrugged away the compliment. "Will it help your father identify the tree?"

"Yes. He'll be ecstatic. And then he'll bug me to invite you to the jungle to go on an expedition with him and draw plants. To him, that's the ultimate experience, and he doesn't understand why others aren't jumping up and down at the prospect."

Onora laughed. It was a small burst of sound as it escaped her tight self-control. "I might actually like that."

"When all this mess with Owen is resolved, consider yourself invited."

"Thank you."

I tucked the picture into my saddlebags. Ari and Janco finished readying their horses.

The Stable Master gave Ari's horse a pat on the neck. "His name's Diamond Whiskey, 'cause of that diamond-shaped blaze on his forehead. But we all call him Whiskey for short. Take good care of him and make sure he returns with you. The Commander's partial to him."

Ari paused in midmount. "Why did you pick him, then? I can take another."

"He's the strongest of my lot."

"That's a polite way of saying you're fat, Ari," Janco said.

Ari and the Stable Master ignored him.

The Master pointed to Kiki and The Madam. "I also picked him 'cause he gets along well with the girls."

"Being able to get along is a good quality to have," I said, giving Janco a pointed look.

He batted his eyelashes at me—Mr. Innocent. "Hey, I'm the epitome of a team player."

I suppressed a sigh as I swung into my saddle. Janco in high spirits meant more high jinks. However, no matter how hard I tried, I really couldn't consider that a bad thing.

"Come on, Epitome," I said. "Mount up. I'd like to cross the border before dark."

We arrived at the northern gates of the Citadel late at night on the third day. Since I didn't know Leif's current location, I'd thought to check with Irys about his whereabouts to see if he'd already left the farmhouse.

Surrounding the Citadel was a high white marble wall broken only by four entrances. Janco had wanted to stop at an inn a couple hours ago, but the thought of sleeping in my own bed had given me a burst of energy, and we pushed on.

By the guards' slow response to our calls, I guessed we had woken them. Two men exited the guardhouse to talk to us, but two others headed into the Citadel at a fast pace—so it was a shift change, not a case of sleeping on the job. Much better, considering the Commander's plans.

The guards were members of the Citadel's security forces. Since I wasn't ready for the Council to know I'd returned from Ixia, I'd pulled my hood over my head and planned to give them fake names. I'd inform the Council of my return once I learned of their state of mind from Irys.

"Names?" the taller of the two asked.

"I'm Elliona Featherstone. This is Yannis and Pellow Moon." I hooked a thumb at Janco and Ari. Their pale skin matched most Moon Clan members.

The man asked a number of detailed questions about our

reason for visiting, how long we planned to stay and where we were lodging. He wrote all our answers down with slow strokes of his quill in a ledger. Then he consulted another book before he allowed us to enter the Citadel. The whole exchange took much longer than normal.

Once we were out of sight of the guardhouse, Janco rode alongside me. "That's new. When did they start with the cross-examination at the gate?"

The last time I'd arrived, I'd been waved through. I calculated. "Sometime in the last forty days."

"Do you think it's because the Commander now has Curare?" Ari asked me.

"No. In that case, they would have doubled the guards at the border, but we didn't see any unusual activity on the Sitian side."

"Do they know Owen's in Ixia?" Janco asked.

"Leif may have messaged Irys."

"Is Leif back from Broken Bridge?" Ari asked.

"It's possible. We'll ask Irys once we reach the Magician's Keep."

"I'm *so* looking forward to being in the Creepy Keepy again," Janco muttered sarcastically. "Can't we crash in Leif's apartment? Mara won't mind."

"She will if an assassin climbs through her window," I said. "He might get my blood on her pretty yellow curtains."

"I guess it's the cold, hard floor of your room in Irys's tower, then."

"The Keep has comfortable guest quarters. I'm sure—"

"Not a chance, sweetheart," Janco said. "Valek said 'protect.' We're not letting you out of our sight. Except...you know...when..." He blushed and spurred The Madam into a faster walk.

The Citadel was a large, rectangular-shaped city divided

into six quarters. The northwest and southwest quarters contained a maze of residences. The two middle quarters resembled a giant bull's-eye with an impressive market right at the center. A diverse selection of goods imported from all over Sitia and Ixia were sold in its many stands. Large-scale businesses and factories ringed the market in ever-widening circles. The Magician's Keep with its four towers occupied the entire northeast corner of the Citadel, and the Council Hall, government buildings and Councilor's residences were located in the southeast quarter.

At this late hour, only a couple people hurried through the streets of the Citadel, but I knew various members of the Helper's Guild hid in the shadows cast by the street lanterns. Fisk, the young man in charge of the guild, would be informed of my arrival well before anyone else. Good thing he was a friend and would keep the knowledge to himself.

Firelight blazed from a few taverns where voices buzzed and an occasional burst of laughter tumbled from open windows. We soon passed the outer ring that consisted of inns and taverns and entered the quieter and darker loop of factories.

After a few minutes, the cool breeze shifted and Kiki stopped. She reared up and snorted, signaling trouble. Without conscious thought, I yanked my bo staff from its holder on my saddle just as Ari and Janco drew their swords.

Dark figures rushed from the shadows and blocked our path. My pulse rate increased as I counted over a dozen. Too many for the three of us.

"Ambush," Ari said.

"Ya think?" Janco pulled on the reins, backing The Madam closer to Kiki and Whiskey.

We turned around. More figures stood on the street behind us. There was just enough light to reveal the swords and daggers gripped in their hands. At least two aimed crossbows at

MARIA V. SNYDER

us. I scanned the buildings on each side, seeking an alley to escape down. Instead, I spotted more ambushers.

We were trapped. Anger mixed with fear. Those two guards hadn't been rushing home after their shift. Idiot!

"We're on horseback. We can charge them," Janco said.

"And get bolted," Ari said. "I don't think so."

"Drop your weapons and dismount," a deep male voice ordered. He strode forward and into the faint light. Two silver captain bars glinted on his shoulders—Captain Romas.

"They're the Citadel guards," I said to my friends, relaxing. Then, louder, I asked Romas, "Why have you ambushed us? We've done nothing wrong."

"You mean other than giving false names at the gate?" he asked.

Uh-oh. We were recognized. "I don't—"

"Save it for your hearing. Yelena Zaltana, Ardenus Ixia and Janco Ixia, you are all under arrest."

"You can't still be mad at me over that little incident last season," I said, referring to when Romas and a unit of his men tried to stop Leif, Hale and me from leaving the Citadel about a hundred years ago. Or so it felt.

He grasped the hilt of his sword. "It isn't about *that*."

Oops, I shouldn't have reminded him. "Is it for lying to the gate guards? You can't—" I tried.

"No. For conspiring with the enemy, for espionage and for treason. Now drop your weapons and dismount, or my archers will knock you off your horses."

And that answered my question about the Council's state of mind regarding me. Kiki tensed. One word from me and she'd shoot forward and trample anyone unfortunate enough to be in her path. However, I'd been hit by a crossbow's bolt before. If it didn't kill me, it'd still mean an excruciating trip to the infirmary.

"Orders?" Ari asked me.

"It's clearly a misunderstanding," I said, lowering my bo. "No need for bloodshed." I threaded the staff back on my saddle and dismounted. "Do as he asks."

Although they grumbled, Ari and Janco returned their swords to the sheaths attached to their saddles before swinging down.

"Step away from the horses," the captain ordered. "Hands on your heads."

Before I complied, I whispered, "Kiki, once they have us, take The Madam and Whiskey to the Keep, please."

Staying together, we moved a few feet down the road. Romas instructed us to kneel and then his men closed in to secure our hands behind our backs. A shout rose as Kiki lurched forward, scattering guards. The Madam and Whiskey kept pace with her.

"Sir?" someone called.

"Let them go," Romas said. He grabbed my arm and jerked me to my feet. "We've only orders for these three."

"Who signed the arrest order?" I asked him.

"You'll be shown a copy of the arrest affidavit when you're processed. Let's go."

The captain kept his hand clamped around my biceps as they marched us through the streets. I imagined one of Fisk's helpers reporting to him about our arrest. Would Fisk even be surprised? Or had he heard about the arrest warrant through his network?

A list of recriminations spun through my mind. I should have stayed at an inn as Janco had wanted and then visited Fisk in the morning when the traffic through the gates would have hidden us. Too bad I hadn't thought of this sooner. I'd grown lazy, relying on my magic. Being extra cautious, paranoid even, was no longer a habit of mine. At least my stupid mistake didn't get us killed. Not this time.

Instead of leading us to the Citadel's jail, Romas escorted us to the holding cells in the basement of the Council Hall. No surprise that the members of the Council had signed the order to arrest me and my companions on sight. And I probably shouldn't be shocked that they didn't incarcerate me in the Keep's special cells—the ones that blocked a prisoner's magic. By now, news of my condition had probably spread throughout the Citadel and Sitia.

While they searched Ari and Janco and removed a substantial pile of weapons and lock picks, they only performed a quick pat-down on me—an interesting side effect of being considered harmless. They found my switchblade, but nothing else.

We were locked in three adjoining cells, the guards departed and the metal outer door clanged shut, leaving us in utter blackness. I groped for the bed and tried to get comfortable on the thin mattress. The silence didn't last long.

"Ah, just like old times," Janco said. "Oh, wait. What am I saying? It's just like almost every time I'm with you, Yelena. Don't you get tired of being arrested *all* the time?"

"You're exaggerating," I said.

"Oh, that's right. I forgot about our last mission. We weren't locked up, just tied down. My mistake."

"Give it a rest, Janco," Ari said.

"Yeah, well, it seems every time I'm in Sitia, I'm thrown into jail. Do you think they'll stamp my frequent-visitor card? I think I get a prize if I've been in them all."

"What's the plan?" Ari asked. "Do either of you have a set—"

"This place gives me the *creeps*," Janco interrupted, warning us of magic in use nearby.

A magician was probably listening or monitoring us in some way. Lovely.

"Everything gives you the creeps," Ari said, but he didn't sound as exasperated as usual.

"Not everything. There are a few things that don't bother me."

"What about you, Yelena?" Ari asked.

They had switched to talking in code. I replayed their comments in my mind, teasing out the true meaning. Ari was about to ask if we had a set of lock picks and from Janco's recent comment, I guessed he did.

"There are a couple things that give me the willies, but being locked in a cell isn't one," I said. In other words, yes, I had two sets of lock picks on me, but we should stay put. I'd hoped to convince the Council of our innocence, and escaping would be a guilty action.

"Do you think we'll have visitors?" Ari asked.

"I'm sure Master Magician Irys will stop by in the morning to explain what's going on."

"As long as that annoying little bloodsucker doesn't show up, I'll be happy," Janco said.

He referred to The Mosquito, an assassin who'd been hired to kill me. I'd also be happy to never encounter him again. "We've only just arrived. It's doubtful he knows we're here."

"News spreads fast." Concern laced Ari's voice.

"We won't be here long," I tried to assure him.

"Have you been in here before?" Janco asked.

"Yes, to visit Opal when the Council was worried about her glass-siphoning powers." Which meant I knew the layout of the cells and building. "She scared them and they kept her well guarded."

"Do we scare them?" Ari asked.

"Not as much." It'd be difficult to break out, but not impossible. However, I hoped to avoid the necessity of escaping. "Just let me do all the talking."

Ari's deep laugh echoed on the stone walls. "Good luck with that."

As I predicted, Irys arrived with our breakfast. My appetite disappeared when her harsh demeanor failed to soften after the guards left. She stood on the other side of the bars and studied me. Deep lines of worry scoured her forehead and dark circles ringed her emerald-colored eyes. Wearing her official purple silk magician's robe, she had pulled her long once-black-but-now-painted-with-gray hair into a neat bun.

"Yelena, why didn't you message me you were coming?" she finally asked.

"I didn't have time." I tapped my ear and gave her a questioning look.

"No one can hear us. I've made certain of that. Now will you tell me the real reason you tried to sneak into the Citadel last night?"

"I wasn't sneaking. I just wanted to avoid a confrontation with the Council before I had a chance to talk to you."

"I see. And how did that work out for you?"

"Wowzers," Janco said in awe. "That's some impressive sarcasm!"

"Zip it, Janco," Ari growled.

"Yes, I realize I made a big mistake," I said. "But Owen Moon is in Ixia, and we need help."

"You mean like the help I needed to convince the Sitian Council of a few impossible things, like Owen being alive despite the Commander's assurance to the contrary, and that the Commander funded an illegal Curare manufacturing facility in Sitia and now has barrels of the drug at his disposal? Like the help I could have used to explain why our Liaison headed to Ixia along with every person who could have enlightened the Council about what had happened in Lapeer? That type of help?"

Her words cut right through me. And the fact they were true gave them a sharper edge. Red-hot guilt welled from the wounds. "I'm sorry, Irys. After the encounter with Owen I..." I tucked my tail between my legs and bolted, yipping in fear. "I felt safer with Valek. I'm sorry I didn't return sooner."

Her anger lessened. "And I must also apologize. The last three weeks have been a nightmare."

No kidding. The formidable Master Magician appeared as if she stood on a crumbling foundation. "Aside from the obvious problems with the Council, what's wrong?" I asked.

"While the Council has been debating how to respond to the Commander's allegedly bold moves with Curare and Owen, the antimagician sentiment, which had been simmering in the background for the past couple of seasons, has now boiled over. Councilor Jewelrose has proposed a new system of keeping track of magicians and overseeing what they can and can't do and when. It's similar to a military structure, but more restrictive." Agitated, Irys paced. "The Councilor claims magicians are dangerous and that we need to be regulated and controlled by the Council."

I glanced at Janco through the bars. If anyone would be happy about keeping a leash on magicians, it would be him. He mouthed, *Too easy.*

Irys continued, "Bain and I and a few other Councilors had enough votes to veto the idea, but..." She stopped. "However, I'm pretty sure another group has decided to implement it. I've been hearing rumors about a cartel."

My relief over the veto disappeared in a heartbeat. "What do you mean?"

She yanked at the sleeves of her robe and smoothed the fab-

MARIA V. SNYDER

ric. I'd known her for eight years and recognized her delay tactic.

"It must be bad," I said.

Lifting her gaze, she met mine. "In the last six weeks, four magicians have been assassinated, and twelve are missing."

The horror of her words hit me with such force that I groped for the bed as my legs lost the strength to hold me up.

"Assassinated how?" Ari asked her.

"Puncture wound to the jugular. We suspect The Mosquito. But the assassin could be using his signature move in order to throw us off."

"Where are the attacks happening?"

"All over Sitia. There's no pattern that we can discern."

I shot to my feet in terror. "Leif?"

"He's fine. I communicated with him two days ago. He's on his way to the Citadel." She relayed Leif's information about my father's discoveries and Owen's whereabouts. "Leif planned to recruit a rescue party to save you from Owen, Yelena." Irys laughed. It was a dry, humorless sound. "I never thought I'd *ever* say this, but our magicians might be safer in Ixia."

"Only if they join Owen," Janco said. "Probably not a bad idea, since he's gonna be our Overlord."

"Your faith is heartwarming," Ari said drily. "Have there been any incidents inside the Citadel, Second Magician?"

"No. And we have sent messages to all our magicians, ordering them back to the Keep."

"That could be exactly what this group *wants* you to do," I said. What was that old cliché…something about fish in a barrel?

"But with the Keep's thick walls and towers, it is almost impenetrable. Not to mention the increase in magicians. Surely they wouldn't attack us there." Her tone failed to match her confident words.

"Who says they're gonna let them *get* there?" Janco asked. "If it was me, I'd set up ambushes on all the major roads to the Citadel and pick them off one by one."

Irys pressed a hand to her forehead and closed her eyes as if enduring a wave of pain.

"Real nice, Janco," Ari muttered.

"What'd I say?"

"You need to warn all of them of the possibility of an ambush," I said to Irys. The desire to add *Leif first, please* pushed up my throat.

Her eyes snapped open. "Of course. I'll do it right away."

"You mean you'll do it after letting us out of here, right?" Janco asked with a hopeful tone.

"I can't. The Council wishes to interrogate you regarding the incident in Lapeer."

"If they just wanted information, why charge us with treason and sign an arrest warrant?" I asked.

"Your actions right after looked suspicious, and when you add in your attempt to sneak into the Citadel with two known Ixian spies...let's just say they're not taking any chances. Not with magicians being assassinated."

Janco huffed. "If we were here on official Ixian business, you wouldn't have caught us."

"Not helping," Ari said.

"Will they drop the charges after I explain what happened?" I asked Irys.

"At this point, I've no idea."

Lovely. "Then what should we do?"

"Talk to the Council. Then escape as soon as you can. It's not safe here."

MARIA V. SNYDER

17

VALEK

Valek considered Hedda's question. Up until five minutes ago, both he and the Commander had been under the impression that Onora had killed Hedda when she refused to name the client who'd paid for a hit on the Commander.

He scanned her office. Spartan and neat—just like when he'd been a student here, she kept her personal effects in a hidden apartment. But nicks marked the furniture, a chair arm had broken off and bald spots littered the area rug. Despite the uniform requirement for all Ixian citizens, Hedda wore a faded gray-green mottled tunic and pants. Patches dotted the threadbare fabric.

Remaining behind her desk, Hedda clutched her knife. Her informant from the garrison sidled next to her. The young pup brandished a sharp dagger. Valek would have been impressed if the man's arm wasn't shaking.

"If the Commander sent me, Hedda, we wouldn't be having this conversation," he said, showing her his empty hands.

She didn't relax. "Then why are you here?"

"I followed your man, hoping he planned to warn the Storm Thieves about my presence."

"I didn't *see* him," the man said in his defense.

"Of course you wouldn't, you idiot. Valek was my best student. The only person to come close is Onora." Hedda's frown deepened as she gazed at Valek. "You killed her." It wasn't a question.

"Actually, no. Do you still keep a bottle of blackberry brandy in your desk?"

Hedda's knife disappeared. "I do."

Valek turned to the idiot. "Report back to the garrison before you're missed."

"Yes, sir." The man paused in the doorway. "Sir, are you...?"

"Going to discipline you?"

He nodded, and his Adam's apple bobbed as he swallowed.

"Let me guess. You've been exchanging information for instruction from Hedda, right?"

His grip on the knob tightened in surprise. "Yes, sir."

"Do you wish to become an assassin?"

"Oh, no, sir. I just wanted to improve my skills. The garrison's master of arms is...old, sir."

"I'm not about to punish ambition, but I suggest you work on spotting a tail."

"Yes, sir." He bolted.

Hedda settled behind her desk and produced a bottle of brandy. She poured the deep red liquid into two glasses as Valek sat in the chair facing her.

"You've changed," Hedda said, handing him a glass.

"Oh?"

"The old Valek would have made him suffer for a few days, waiting to find out if you'd inform his commanding officer or leave him one of your infamous black statues." She downed her drink in one gulp, then poured herself another. "The old Valek would have killed Onora for getting so close to the Commander."

MARIA V. SNYDER

"I'll admit, I was tempted to get rid of my competition, but she's proven to be quite the puzzle. And you know me and puzzles. That hasn't changed."

"Good to know." Hedda sipped from her drink.

"And while I'm truly glad you're alive, I'm wondering why Onora informed us of your unfortunate demise."

"I've no idea."

"No?" Valek swept his arm out, indicating the shabby room. "Perhaps it's because there wasn't a client. You probably haven't had a client since the takeover. And after years of resentment, you finally had a student you could send after the Commander. And what better time than when I was in Sitia."

"You always did have such an active imagination, King Killer."

"Then how about this? When the Commander ordered her to murder this…er…shall we say *mystery client*, she returned. But Onora couldn't kill you. You took her in after she'd been abused, taught her to fight, to stand up for herself, to no longer be afraid. Instead, she reports your death and you agree to go into hiding." He drank his brandy, savoring the burn of the spicy blackberry flavor.

She raised her glass. "That was an entertaining tale, but you of all people should know I don't ever divulge the names of my clients."

"But you are training new assassins, even though you've claimed to have closed the school and retired."

Pressing her lips together, she gave him a shrewd look. "I have to keep my skills sharp."

That was more information than he'd expected. "And if I sent you a promising student or two in the future, would you turn him or her away?"

Surprise flashed in her light green eyes. "No."

"Then I'll add you to my payroll."

"What about the Commander?"

"I'll handle the Commander."

"Are you going to report me?"

"No need."

"You *have* changed."

He quirked an eyebrow. "For the better?"

"I think that your blind loyalty to the Commander is no longer so…blind. And I think the change is due to your heart mate."

"I'll take that as a yes." He finished his drink.

Swirling the liquid around her glass, she stared at it. After a few moments, she met his gaze.

"Since we have an agreement, you should know your story has one error," Hedda said.

"Really?"

"Remember how I helped you find the men who murdered your brothers, but I never sent you after the King as you desired?"

At the time, he'd been making her too much money assassinating targets for *paying* clients, and she believed he'd be caught trying to get close to the King and executed. "Yes. What's this—"

"I also didn't send Onora after the Commander."

Valek kept his expression neutral as his thoughts whirled. He didn't like what they dragged to the surface. Straightening in his chair, he leaned forward. "You're saying *Onora* wanted the Commander dead?"

"Yes."

And you've left Onora with the Commander, you idiot. His heart thumped. But he ignored the panic. Onora had had multiple opportunities to kill the Commander. Plus, she wore his mark, given when she'd sworn to be loyal.

"I found it quite interesting that she changed her mind and

chose not to kill me, even though I was the only one who knew her true mission," Hedda said.

Valek noted her use of the past tense. "Instead she concocted a story of your demise. Risky."

"Compassionate. As you said, I aided her in her time of need."

He tapped a finger on the edge of his empty glass. "The Onora puzzle takes another unexpected turn."

"I'm sure you'll figure her out. You always do." She splashed a generous amount of brandy into his glass. Hedda raised hers and said, "To solving puzzles." They clinked.

The alcohol left a fiery trail down his throat. "Speaking of puzzles, have you heard anything about these Storm Thieves?"

"I may have. It's probably just gossip and rumors," she hedged.

Valek dug a gold coin from his pocket and set it on the desk. "How about now?"

She snatched it in one quick motion. "Damn foolish kids." Jabbing a finger at Valek, she scowled. "I knew they'd eventually attract too much attention."

"They've been rather successful for a bunch of foolish kids."

"That's because no one had linked their petty and seemingly random crimes until recently. Because, like most criminals, they grew bolder and hit bigger targets, and it was just a matter of time until…" Hedda swept a hand, indicating Valek.

"Do you know where they've been operating from?"

"No. No one does. That's why they still haven't been caught."

"Do you know who is involved?"

"Well… I've heard rumors."

Valek understood the hint. He dropped another gold coin on the desk. This one disappeared as quickly as the first.

"They're a group of teenagers—mostly the children of fishermen. The thefts started at the beginning of the cooling season, when the fleet arrived in port waiting for warmer weather and calmer seas."

So a bunch of bored kids taking advantage of the storms, but they'd been rather smart. Too smart. Valek suspected a more experienced person led them. "Anything else?"

"I've lived on the coast all my life. In sixty-two years, we've never had a cold season like the one we just had."

"What do you mean?"

"I mean, we've always had plenty of snow, rain, wind and fog. This past year, we've had more storms, but they don't last near as long and they always rage overnight."

Valek considered. "The Commander has allowed Storm-dancers up on the northern ice sheet."

"And they tamed the nasty blizzards sweeping down from the north, but these others are blowing in from the west."

Ah. "Magic?" He'd suspected it before, but not for the storms.

She shrugged. "Maybe. You've killed all my magicians, so I can't say for sure."

He didn't bother to correct her. The Commander had ordered their executions soon after the takeover, but they'd had more than enough time to escape to Sitia. Valek had made sure of that.

Thanking Hedda for the information, Valek reminisced with her for a while before he left. "Keep your low profile, and when your young idiot is ready, have him request a transfer to the Commander's company."

She smiled. "His name is Gannon."

No surprise he was the one Colonel Ransley mentioned as showing promise.

As Valek hiked back to the garrison, he mulled over all he'd learned from Hedda. He concentrated on the Storm Thieves,

MARIA V. SNYDER

putting himself in their place. Bored and physically able to climb ropes and rigging on heaving seas, the young fishermen would have no trouble scaling a wall. They'd also been on boats most of their lives, knew the currents and tides and could spot all the warning signs of approaching foul weather. Valek had no problem believing they were the thieves; however, the fact that his corps hadn't been able to catch them or discover their hideout didn't fit. Magic could explain it. Or an older leader. Or both.

When he returned to the garrison, he checked on Onyx. The black horse's coat gleamed and his tail and mane had been combed. Onyx snuffled Valek's empty hand, searching for a treat. Valek laughed when Onyx's ears dropped in obvious disappointment. He fed the horse a carrot before swinging by the canteen in time for supper.

The loud rumble of voices dwindled and then ceased by the time he'd grabbed a bowl of clam stew, a hunk of bread and a wedge of cheese. He scanned the tables of soldiers. Predominantly male, most of them averted their gazes. However, in the back right corner, a table full of female soldiers ate. Much to their terrified surprise, he joined them. The first thing he noticed was they were all low-ranking, and not a commissioned officer among them.

Once they recovered from their shock and overcame their fear of him, they answered his questions about the garrison's male-dominated leaders.

"Is it true that half of the Commander's personal guard are female?" asked a woman who introduced herself as Sergeant First Class Jaga.

"Yes. And half of his advisers. In fact, the Commander would be upset with the ratio at this garrison. What happened to all your colleagues?"

"Transferred. We stayed because we have family nearby," Jaga said.

"Any inappropriate behavior, Sergeant?"

"No, sir."

She didn't hesitate or exchange glances with her colleagues, which meant she told the truth. Good. He asked her about the higher-ranking officers.

"They've been here for ages, sir. All promoted from within."

"I see." The garrison was way overdue for an inspection. It was partly his fault for avoiding the area all these years. "I think it's soon time for an update and some fresh blood."

They smiled.

"It won't be until after the hot season." And only if the Commander didn't declare war on Sitia.

"It will be worth the wait, sir," Jaga said.

Valek finished eating and returned to his rooms. A pile of MD-1 uniforms waited for him on the small table. He checked for intruders before collapsing on the bed.

The next morning, Valek changed into a basic laborer's uniform. The black pants had a row of white diamonds down the outside of each leg. A row of white diamonds cut across the chest of the black tunic. Throughout Ixia, laborers were men and women who filled in where extra people were needed for a project or job. They had a variety of skills from construction to harvesting crops, and they frequently traveled from one city to another. In other words, the perfect cover for Valek.

He transferred a few things he'd need into a well-worn rucksack, tied his hair back with an old piece of string and altered his appearance just enough to throw a casual observer off. Most Ixians only knew his name and wouldn't recognize him. When he exited the garrison, he stopped and rubbed dirt over the white diamonds on his clothes. Satisfied that he looked the part, Valek headed southwest to Gandrel, where the most recent and boldest burglary had occurred.

Six hours later he arrived in town. He reported to the local checkpoint and showed them his papers.

"Reason for visit?" the man asked in a bored voice.

"Repairing fishing nets for the fleet," Valek answered. Once the cold season ended, the fishermen spent the warming season readying their boats.

The man grunted, stamped Valek's paper and handed it back all without once glancing at Valek. If the rest of the security personnel matched this man's attitude, then no wonder the Storm Thieves had no trouble stealing their weapons. Pathetic.

Valek visited the Sail Away Inn next. The innkeeper rented him a room, but the few other workers ignored him. Extra laborers usually arrived at the coast at this time of year. Since supper was a couple hours away, the common and dining room were empty. He waited in his room. It didn't take long for a servant to knock. She carried towels and a bath kit for him.

Opening the door wide, Valek stepped aside, letting in Agent Annika, who explained about the amenities of the inn until the door closed.

"Where?" Valek asked.

"Four-fifteen Cannery Road, second floor, sir. There's an entrance in the back, through the alley. Endre's there now. His shift doesn't start until later."

"Thank you."

She nodded and left. He followed soon after. Every town in Ixia had at least one inn and a security office—the two best places to gather information. Valek had an agent in both. Larger cities warranted more agents. And the agents shared a safe house or apartment as a base for their covert operations.

The yellow paint peeled from the wood of building number four-fifteen, which was wedged in the middle of a row of houses. The pungent odor of fish guts fogged the street. Valek looped around to the alley and climbed the metal ladder to the apartment.

Endre yanked open the door before Valek reached it. The burly man held a dagger, but his fierce expression smoothed with recognition.

"Welcome, sir," Endre said as Valek entered the small unit— half of it was living space, the other used for work.

Valek noted with approval the maps of the area covering the table with the thieves' targets already marked. Times, dates and stolen items had been listed next to each.

"Any news, Endre?"

"Since the hit on the security office, no other incidents have been reported, sir."

"Any progress on finding the thieves' hideout?"

"No, sir. Security officers from Gandrel, Krillow and Coral Caye have searched every cove, building, boat, port and wooded area."

Valek studied the map. "Looks like they hit every town along MD-1's coast. I thought the targets were random."

"At first they appeared random, but reports were slow coming in from some towns. They didn't make the connection to the storms right away. But even so, if you look at the times and dates, there's still no pattern."

"And no one knows where and when they'll strike next?"

"No, sir. But Annika is working on finding a few informers. She'll report back here after the supper crowd."

"Tell me about the theft of the weapons."

"They struck in the middle of the night during a nasty downpour. The guys on duty didn't hear a thing and frankly didn't think the thieves would have the gall to rob us. Up until that hit, the Stormers took mostly money, equipment,

MARIA V. SNYDER

tools and food. But they left nothing behind but puddles on the floor."

"Stormers?"

"It's what the officers call them."

Ah. "Any boot prints?"

"No. Just the water."

"Fresh or salt?" Valek asked.

Endre's thick eyebrows smashed together like two caterpillars butting heads. "We didn't check. I'm assuming fresh from the rain. Why would it matter?"

"You tell me."

He ran a hand over the short bristle of his black hair. "Salt would mean they came up from the beach."

"Or waded in from a boat."

"Not this time of year. It'd be suicide."

It would be dangerous for ordinary thieves. But what if one of them used magic to navigate the seas? He recalled Opal's description of how the Stormdancers harvested energy from the storms. They kept a bubble of calm around them as they worked to avoid being swept out to sea. Valek wondered what the Stormdancers did during their off-season. Kade and Heli helped with the blizzards in Ixia, but one of the others might be helping these thieves.

Valek tucked the thought away to investigate later and returned to the break-in. "Forced entry?"

"Yeah, crowbar on the back door and on the weapon lockers."

Not professionals, or they would've used lock picks. Valek considered. "Do you have a complete list of what's been stolen?"

"Yes, sir." Endre hunted through papers lying on a desk and pulled one from the pile. "I copied this from all the reports. After the weapons were stolen, the Gandrel office took the lead on the investigation. All the other offices have sent their incident reports to us."

Interesting. "Where are these reports being kept?"

"In a conference room. The captain formed a team of investigators and we've been working in there, poring over all the information."

"You don't sound too impressed."

Endre grinned. "They're not us, sir. I can only do so much with these guys. Now, if you were on the team with Annika, then..."

Nice to know Endre had such confidence in him. "Then when can I get in there to take a look at those reports?"

"*You* can get in there anytime, sir."

"I'd prefer to remain incognito if possible." And as long as the news of his arrival hadn't already spread to the Storm Thieves. While he'd been following Private Idiot slash Gannon to Hedda's school, another mole could have sent a message to them.

"Oh, then late at night would be best. I'm on the graveyard shift tonight. If you can get into the conference room without being seen, I can make sure no one bothers you. You'll have to leave before the morning shift arrives at dawn."

"All right, then expect me after midnight."

"Yes, sir."

"Do you have any more information?"

The big man gestured to the desk. "Annika and I have been writing down what we've heard and other bits of news." He brandished the list of stolen goods.

"May I?" Valek held out his hand.

"Of course, sir. Here." Endre handed the list to Valek.

Valek scanned the items. Missing money and jewelry were expected, but others like wood, saws, nails, paint and teacups were not. He sat at the desk and read through the other papers. Endre and Annika had collected a nice variety of facts, including ruling out the initial suspects—a gang of teen troublemakers. Five young men and three young women had had run-ins with the local security for fighting, drinking and vandalism. However, they all had alibis for the storm thefts.

After an hour, Valek rejected the idea of bored teens as the culprits. No. The Storm Thieves were organized and had a precise plan. The building supplies meant their hideout either needed major repairs or they'd built a place. But any new building would have been found during the search.

Repairs? The salt air was corrosive. Each structure in a coastal town needed a new coat of paint every couple of years, and replacing rotted wood was a typical renovation. But why this much wood? Unless both the exterior and interiors had been rebuilt. Would the guards notice this during the inspections? He asked Endre.

"It depends on the person. Some of the officers are more observant than others, sir. The reports on the searches might mention something like that."

Guess he'd have to wait until later. In the meantime, what else needed repairs? Fishing boats. Just like the buildings, each boat needed extensive upkeep, and they'd been searched. Unless the boat was out to sea at that time. Suicide, unless magic was involved. Assuming a magician was on board, Valek mulled it over and found a flaw in his logic. The fishermen would notice if a boat sailed away during the storm season. They'd think the captain was insane and talk about that "damn fool" at all the local taverns.

No. The Storm Thieves couldn't risk such odd behavior. Unless… Valek straightened. Unless they left *before* the storm season and never returned! They'd be considered lost at sea. No one would suspect them because they were all dead. A perfect alibi.

Valek asked Endre if any boats had disappeared during the fishing season.

"There are always a few that don't come back. The Port Master in each town would have those records. Also Annika might know. When a ship is lost at sea, everyone gathers at the inn." Endre paused. "Why is that important?"

He explained his theory.

"That would be a right smart trick. But why go to all the trouble? Living on a ship ain't fun."

"Are there places along the coast only accessible by boat?" Valek asked.

"Yeah. There's a few. Up north there's a couple coves hidden in those cliffs. Do you think they could be there?"

"It's possible. Or they could be stocking up for a journey to Sitia." Which would be a safer place for the magician to live.

"That's too dangerous. Out of dozens of ships, only one has crossed the Rattles intact."

But would a boat with a Stormdancer aboard be able to? Valek considered. The Rattles extended over a hundred miles into the Sunset Ocean from the knob of land jutting from the southern coast of MD-1, which was also the western edge of the Snake Forest. It twisted over underwater rocks, contained pockets of shallow water and created unpredictable riptides and strong currents. The sound of the turbulent water reminded sailors of rattlesnakes when they shook their tails in warning. And it fit perfectly with its location at the end of the Snake Forest.

A Stormdancer influenced the weather and not water, so Valek doubted having one on board would make a difference in an attempt to cross the Rattles. One thing Valek did know—the Storm Thieves must have a grander scheme than stealing in mind. Once he figured that out, they'd be easy to find.

Annika arrived with two steaming containers of seafood chowder for them. Valek's stomach lurched in sudden hunger as the tangy, fishy aroma reached him. She served Valek first, but she gave Endre a sweet dimpled smile with his bowl. Ah. They'd been working together too long. In the past, he'd break them up and assign one to the other side of Ixia. But as Hedda had said, he'd changed. Valek no longer believed love or romance negatively affected an agent's ability to do his or her duty. In fact, he thought it made them a stronger team.

Pah, you've gone soft, old man, Janco's voice sounded in his head. He ignored it. Instead he asked Annika about the boats that had disappeared this year.

"There's always a bunch that wreck or sink or catch fire," she said. "Mostly those have a few survivors, but there were two that sailed from Gandrel and never came back. The *Starfish* and the *Sea Serpent*."

"Do you know who captained the boats and worked on them?"

"No, sir, but the Port Master will have all that information."

"Can you get the names for me without anyone knowing?"

She hesitated, then glanced at Endre. "Do you have any sleeping juice left?"

"Yep."

"Then that would be a yes, sir," she said to Valek. "The Port Master is a frequent customer."

"What about the other towns?" Endre asked him. "There have to be other boats that disappeared."

"The Stormers are from Gandrel."

"How do you know?" Annika asked.

"You tell me," he said. "What's changed?"

She stared at the map in concentration. A section of her long brown hair fell in front of her face, and she tucked it behind her ear with an impatient tug. Her darker skin tone reminded him of Yelena.

Annika tapped on the map with her finger. "Stealing weapons from a security office is a dangerous hit." She met Valek's gaze. Long eyelashes framed lovely brown eyes. "There are a number of offices along the coast, but they picked Gandrel's because they're very familiar with the town. There's no need to worry about getting lost while a storm rages when you know every street, and the chances of encountering an officer are smaller when you know their patrol patterns."

Valek grinned. "Exactly."

After Endre finished his chowder, he left to report to work. Valek asked Annika about the local gossip. "Anyone mention my name?"

"A few noticed you arriving in town, but they all assumed you're here to help with the nets."

Good. "How about speculation over these Stormers?"

"Lots of that, from the ridiculous—ghosts living in the clouds—to the mundane—local kids taking advantage of the weather. A couple folks think the security officers are making a big deal for nothing. So far, I haven't heard anything of value."

Annika returned to her job at the inn. Valek waited thirty minutes before finding a spot at the bar of the inn's common room. He ordered an ale and listened to the various conversations around him.

"...best net caught on the blasted rocks and shredded like wet paper."

"I wanted to ring his bloody neck..."

"I'd bet Nichel's boy is behind all this trouble. Damn kid never did listen."

"...fat cats at the garrison. You'd think they'd help us with these bastards."

MARIA V. SNYDER

When Valek finished his ale, he inquired about work, and one of the boat captains said he needed an extra pair of hands. Then he climbed the stairs to his room, changed into his sneak suit and slipped out the window. He spent the next three hours reading reports. A couple of comments from the searches snagged his attention, and he wrote a list of buildings and shipyards to recheck. Overall, there wasn't any information that challenged his theory.

Good. The sooner he could solve this and reunite with Yelena, the better.

Over the next couple days, Valek helped repair nets. His nimble fingers and skill at tying knots earned him a favorable reputation. The fishermen soon relaxed and Valek listened to their gossip. Eventually he steered the conversation to the lost ships.

"Everyone knows the risks you take when you step on that boat." Pug looped new twine around a tear. His fingernails were black and he smelled like brine. "You expect a few losses, but it's a heartbreaker regardless."

"Yeah," Joey agreed. He was one of the oldest men on the crew. "And sometimes you can guess who's not coming back. I told Nell not to take on such a young, inexperienced crew, but she wouldn't listen. What you get in energy and stamina, you lose in experience and plain old good sense."

"Poor Nell." Pug tsked. "At least those tadpoles didn't leave behind younguns, but I'm sure their parents are beside themselves."

Valek remembered Nell's name from the *Starfish*'s manifest. Annika had copied it along with the *Sea Serpent*'s last night while the Port Master had been slumped over a table at the inn, snoring. The list of names hadn't meant anything to him, but learning the crews' ages helped. A person with children and a spouse wouldn't be as likely to pretend to disappear at sea so he or she could become a thief.

After a few more questions, Valek would have bet money that the *Starfish* was the Storm Thieves' ship. Now the next step would be to find it. There hadn't been a break-in in over three weeks, and most of the fishermen believed the weapon raid was the last one. Only thirteen days remained until the start of the warm season and the first safe day that the fleet could set sail.

Valek figured the Storm Thieves would make one more raid before lying low for the fishing seasons. He needed to review the stolen items again. Once he determined what was next on their list, he could anticipate their destination.

"We better finish this net today," Pug said. He gazed at the sea. "I don't like the look of those clouds."

"Could be a big blow." Joey massaged his stiff fingers.

"Any idea where it will hit?" Valek asked.

"If it's big enough, it don't matter. The whole coast gets punched," Joey said. "If it's smaller, then you follow the waves."

"The waves?"

"Yeah. If the storm's coming right at you, the waves are parallel to the shore, lined up like rolling pins on my granny's table. If the waves are angled to the right, the storm's moving north. Angled left means south."

Valek studied the waves lapping under the dock. Rolling pins.

"Too soon to tell," Joey said. "Look in the morning."

"When will the storm hit?"

Pug squinted. "Tomorrow...maybe tomorrow night."

Valek needed to hurry. He didn't have much time to prepare.

18

LEIF

As he traveled to the Citadel, Leif's thoughts kept returning to Irys's comment about the twelve missing and four dead magicians. And Irys's lack of intel about the attacks gnawed holes of worry in his guts, ruining his appetite. Irys could only speculate why—to regulate all the magicians. As for who, she suspected a group of influential and wealthy people was behind it, but she had no evidence.

The timing of the incidents matched with Yelena's loss of magic. Almost right after she'd been shot with that damn poisoned arrow, the Cartel—Irys's name for them—started their aggressive campaign against magicians. The only suspected member of the Cartel was Bruns Jewelrose, who'd hired The Mosquito to assassinate Yelena and supposedly the other four magicians. And perhaps he'd also targeted Ben Moon and Loris and Cilly Cloud Mist.

Unable to solve the puzzle while traveling, Leif forced his brooding thoughts to a different topic. Too bad yet another worry popped to the surface. Yelena. Through the super glass messenger, Irys told him the good news—that she'd returned to the Citadel with Ari and Janco—and the bad—she'd been arrested and interrogated by the Council.

Irys urged Leif to hurry so he could verify her story. Leif also carried detailed drawings that his father, Esau, provided to show the Sitian Council what Owen had been growing. Esau had refused to leave the glass hothouse until he had finished his investigation and found someone to properly care for the plants while they were gone.

Meanwhile, Yelena waited for Leif's arrival instead of escaping. She wished to regain her positive status with the Council. But every day she remained in the jail, the greater the danger.

Sensing his mood, Rusalka picked up her pace. They rode on the main east-west route in the Featherstone lands. In two more days, he'd be home, but if he pushed it, he might shave off half a day. Of course that meant arriving late at night, when all the Councilors would be asleep, so he'd have to wait until morning to talk to them.

He grinned. Leif knew exactly how he wanted to spend those hours. In bed with his wife, Mara, who made the plainest housedress appear to be the height of fashion. Just wrapping his arms around her would ease the ache pulsing deep in his chest. And he'd breathe in her scent—the light aroma of ylang-ylang flower, combined with the sweet fragrance of the living green—and be home.

Instead of overnighting in an inn, Leif decided to stop to rest for just a couple hours. He'd find a merchant camp to join. The caravans tended to avoid the expense of a real bed and bivouacked along the road. With the warm season a few weeks away, many had started their first deliveries of the year.

A couple hours after sunset, Leif caught a whiff of molasses followed by the bitter tang of fear. Rusalka broke into a gallop as the shrill sounds of a horse in distress pierced the air.

When they turned a corner, a cloud of emotions struck him. Panic and fear the strongest. In the faint moonlight, he identified the black shapes. Horse. Wagon. Person.

MARIA V. SNYDER

As they drew closer, the shapes sharpened. Overturned wagon. Man about to be trampled by a panicked horse.

High-pitched squeals and cries emanated from underneath the wagon. The man shouted at the kids to be quiet. "You're scaring the horse."

Too late. Leif stopped Rusalka fifty feet before the scene. Her presence might make it worse. At least the children quieted to whimpers.

The man lurched forward in an attempt to grab the reins, causing the horse to rear again. Idiot didn't know anything about horses. Leif dismounted, then approached slowly.

"Back away or you're going to get hurt," Leif ordered the man in an even, nonthreatening tone—more for the horse than the idiot.

The man whipped around. "Oh, thank fate! Can you help us?"

"Yes. Stand over there." Leif pointed to a safe spot.

"But my children—"

"Will be fine, if you do everything I say."

The man backed away to the place Leif had indicated. Leif drew in a breath and studied the horse's body language. A wildness shone in its eyes as its sides heaved. Foamy sweat dripped from its body and it blew air from its nostrils. One of the wooden supports of the wagon had snapped in half, but the horse remained tethered. Crates littered the ground behind the overturned wagon.

Leif inched closer, keeping in the horse's line of sight. He projected calming emotions, not sure if it'd work on a horse, but figured it couldn't hurt. Talking to the horse in a steady voice, he approached. The horse shook, but didn't rear. Leif kept his soothing tone and reached for the reins. He grasped them in his left hand. Then he stroked the horse's nose and kept talking.

When the horse's sides slowed and it no longer arched its neck, Leif said to the man, "Move slowly and come take the reins."

The man followed his directions. Keeping his hands on the horse, Leif slid them back to the hitch.

"Daddy, what's going on?" asked a little girl.

"Just wait, sweet pea. We need to free Doggie."

Doggie? Leif glanced at the man.

"We let the kids name him," he explained.

Better than Beach Bunny. Leif unhitched the wagon while keeping contact with the horse so it wouldn't spook again. Then he removed the harness. It was slow and tedious work, but eventually, he freed Doggie. Leif led the horse to a nearby tree, then covered Doggie with his cloak to keep him warm until they could walk him to cool off. He returned to help the man free his children.

They lifted the broken wooden bed and four figures scrambled out as they righted the wagon.

Leif turned. "Is everyone all right? I've bandages and..." The kids were much taller than he'd expected, and the father pointed a loaded crossbow at Leif's chest. Unease swirled into alarm.

Stupid.

"And?" the armed man prompted.

"And I just aided in my own ambush. Didn't I?" Idiotic.

"You're quick. It took that Hale fellow ages to understand."

They have Hale? Why didn't Irys tell me? He swallowed his fear and concentrated on the five assembled before him. No emotions emanated except from the "father." The others must be wearing null shields. "Why go to all this trouble? You outnumber me."

"Where's the fun in that? Besides, if you caught a whiff of an ambush, you'd have been long gone."

MARIA V. SNYDER

If it's fun you want...let's see how fun it is when your clothes are on fire. Leif concentrated.

"Oh, no, you don't. Frent."

A puff sounded right before a prick of pain burned on Leif's neck. He yanked the dart from his skin, but knew it was too late. "Rusalka, go home!"

She galloped by as the woods spun around him. Sinking to his knees, his last thought before the darkness rushed in was of Mara. Their reunion would have to wait. He hoped.

19

YELENA

Five steps. Turn. Five more steps. Turn. I paced along the twenty-seven iron bars of my cell. Even though I had used all my skills as the Liaison and convinced the Sitian Council I hadn't been involved in espionage, treason or conspiring with the enemy, they still required my brother's testimony in order to release us.

Five days. We'd been locked in here for one, two, three, four, five and turn, days. Leif had better hurry.

"You're going to wear a hole in the soles of your boots," Ari said.

I glared at him. He'd taken a philosophical view of the entire endeavor, using the time to rest. He'd claimed we'd need our energy for our eventual escape, which we'd already planned in detail so we could bolt at a moment's notice. Of course it helped his calm attitude that Irys had smuggled in a couple of swords for him and Janco, just in case The Mosquito tried to take advantage of my incarceration.

"Yeah, better to do something constructive with your time," Janco said.

Janco exercised by grasping the highest crossbar with both hands and pulling his body up off the floor. He'd taken his shirt off, exposing long, lean muscles rippling with the effort. Scars crisscrossing his back, arms and chest resembled a street map of a dense city. And he'd named each scar in remembrance of where and when he'd sustained the injury. The healed gash on his stomach and the matching mark on his back, he'd named "Yelena," for the time he'd been run through with a sword and almost died. Janco swore I'd healed him.

"Pacing is also a form of burning off excess energy," I said to Janco.

"I'm not burning. I'm keeping in shape. While Ari's muscles turn to fat, mine will remain strong and ready for action."

Ari shot to his feet. "I'll show you ready for action." He reached through the bars and clamped his huge hands around Janco's narrow waist. With one yank, Ari pulled Janco off the bars and held him suspended over the floor.

Janco sputtered and tried to break his partner's hold. *Tried* being the key word. Without warning, Ari released him. Janco landed with an *oomph*. He recovered, but before he could squawk in protest, a clang echoed.

We turned to the main entrance of the jail. Irys strode in with two guards on her heels. One glance at her pale face and her fingers fretting at her sleeves, and I braced for bad news.

"Unlock the doors, now," Irys ordered the guards.

They moved to obey, starting with Janco's.

Perhaps *bad* was an understatement. I gripped the bars. "What happened?"

"Rusalka showed up at the Citadel without Leif," she said.

I pressed my forehead against the cool metal. Concentrating on not panicking, I drew in a few steadying breaths. "My father? Is he missing, too?"

"No. He remained behind to finish his investigation."

One good thing. I focused on the positive. "What's being done to find Leif?"

"As soon as I heard, I gathered Kiki and your other horses, along with Rusalka. They're waiting for you. Rusalka'll guide you back to where she…lost Leif. Janco, you will be able to track him, right?" The desperate hope in her voice almost cracked my composure.

"How long ago did Rusalka arrive?" Janco asked her.

"This morning. About three hours ago."

"Then we need to hurry." Janco grabbed his hidden sword from under the metal cot.

We joined Irys in the corridor. If the guards were surprised by the sudden appearance of the weapons, they didn't show it.

"Do you think the Cartel has him?" I asked her.

"I suspect they're behind it, but I've no proof."

Sprinting after Irys, we exited the building. Bain Bloodgood argued with a handful of Councilors at the base of the steps. A few shouted at us to stop, but we ignored them and mounted our horses.

"Let's go," I said.

Rusalka turned. We followed. The loud clatter of hooves over cobblestones vibrated in my ears. I let the sound drown out the voice in my head. Being very familiar with that voice, I knew it would list all the horrors that might have befallen my brother, remark on the slim chance of successfully finding him alive and comment on every other terrible scenario. That voice was rather creative when stressed and worried.

After a day and a half of hard riding, we reached the location of Leif's disappearance. A few hours of daylight remained.

Janco dismounted and examined the ground. Ari and I allowed him to do his tracking mojo while we walked the horses. They had set the brutal pace. Patches of sweat stained their coats. Their nostrils flared as they caught their breaths. Once their breathing smoothed, we watered and fed them. By this time, Janco had finished his investigation. He stood

MARIA V. SNYDER

in the middle of a number of scuff marks on the right side of the road, scowling.

"What did you discover?" Ari asked him.

"It wasn't a typical ambush." Janco pointed to clumps of grass and dirt between two trees. "Somebody went to considerable trouble to stage an accident. They overturned a wagon and made it appear as if it was stuck." He strode closer and crouched down. "And here's evidence of a freaked-out horse." Janco straightened. "They knew their mark."

"Janco," Ari warned.

"I'm trying to be dispassionate. Leif's my friend, too."

I concentrated on the information and ignored my emotions, which threatened to let that voice of doom speak. "Why do you think it was set specifically for Leif?"

"'Cause of the elaborate setup. Being a Sandseed horse, Rusalka would have alerted him of people hiding in the woods."

"Unless they were waiting downwind," Ari added.

"Not this time of year. The prevailing wind direction is from the west."

Ari and I exchanged a glance. Impressive.

Janco huffed. "Ya know, it's not all…tracker mojo. There's a lot that goes into it. And there's some good news."

My heart jumped. "You know where he is?"

"I wish. They headed west, but the road's surface is too hard packed and well traveled to distinguish their tracks from all the others."

"The *good* news," Ari prompted.

"There's no blood."

"That makes sense if he was taken by the Cartel. They wouldn't want to harm him until he refused to join them." And my stubborn brother would probably never agree to work for them. Which meant we had a limited amount of time to find and rescue him before The Mosquito bit.

"Another thing about the setup is they knew Leif would be on this road at a particular time," Janco said. "Who else knew his location, other than Master Irys?"

"Bain and the Councilors, who might have informed their aides," I said. Plus all the people who bribed the aides for intel. In other words, too many.

"Janco said they continued west. We didn't pass them on the road, or else Rusalka would have smelled Leif. Is there another road that branches off this one?" Ari asked.

I considered. "There's a shortcut about a day west of here that leads to the main southern road. That route follows the western edge of the Avibian Plains, but they could have veered off into Stormdance or Greenblade lands. And they have a three-day head start." Frustration welled.

"That's also the way to the Jewelrose lands," Ari said.

"*If* Bruns Jewelrose is dumb enough to amass his magician army in his own backyard," Janco added. "I doubt he's that stupid."

"What's our next move?" Ari asked.

Guessing would get us nowhere; we needed reliable information. I stifled a groan. My earlier mistake—the one that had led to us sitting in a cell wasting time for five days—returned for another kick of recriminations. "Fisk."

"But if he knows where Leif and the others are, why doesn't he tell the Council?" Ari asked.

"For the same reason we don't trust the Council," Janco said.

"And the reason is?"

"They're ineffective idiots!"

"He probably doesn't have any proof," I said. "These are wealthy businesspeople who have a great deal of influence and power. Fisk has probably cobbled together bits of information from his sources and determined what's going on." At least I fervently hoped so. "We need to talk to him. Let's go." I stepped toward Kiki, who grazed nearby.

Ari grabbed my shoulder, halting me. "No."

"But time—"

"We haven't slept in over a day."

"We've been resting for five days."

"A few hours is all we need."

"Leif—"

"Leif's clever. He'll play along, knowing we'll come rescue him. But you won't be able to help your brother if you're exhausted."

I peered at him. He'd gone from using *we* to *you*, meaning *me*. "Let me guess. Valek—"

"Doesn't have to order us to protect you. You are family. That goes beyond orders."

When we reached the Citadel two days later, we split up, just in case the guards at the gate had been ordered to look for groups of three. Janco circled around to the southern gate with Rusalka, while Ari and I headed for the eastern entrance. We merged with the early-morning traffic and sidled behind a large caravan of wagons. The guards didn't even glance at us as we passed through.

While the benefit of having busy streets helped us enter unnoticed, the crowded roads slowed our pace. It'd been six days since Leif had been taken, and the desire to scream at all these obstructions clawed at my throat. Then the need to ensure no one followed us to Fisk's headquarters delayed us further as we snaked through the streets.

Fisk's building resided in one of the outer factory loops southwest of the market. By the time we rendezvoused with

Janco near the narrow alley that led to the door, all of my pent-up frustration and worry pressed on my skin from the inside. If Fisk couldn't help, I'd explode. His Helper's Guild members would be cleaning Yelena bits off their ceiling, walls and floor for days.

"Any trouble?" Ari asked his partner.

"None." Janco scrunched up his nose.

"Then what's wrong?" I asked.

"Yet another stinkin' alley. The smell is bad enough, but the place is also reeking with magic. I thought Fisk was a regular kid."

"He is." Although I wouldn't call a seventeen-year-old a kid. "He probably hired a magician to hide the guild's entrance with an illusion."

"Why?" Ari asked.

"Problems with the criminal element. Their cheap labor force, also known as the homeless children and the desperate, have been too busy working and earning money by being a part of Fisk's guild, so the crime bosses have been making it difficult for the helpers. Leif offered to help, but Fisk insisted he'd handle it on his own. The young man's a bit stubborn."

"Stub…born?" Janco sounded out each syllable as if saying the word for the first time. "Gee, I don't know anyone who is stub…born." He stared at me.

"Just for that, you get to go into the stinkin' alley first," I said.

"Yay for me." He rubbed his right ear. "What about the horses?"

"Ari, can you stay with them until we find the door?" I asked.

"What if it's a trap?"

"I'll scream really loud and you run and get backup," Janco said.

"It's not a trap. It's Fisk." I dismounted.

"Yeah, well, Fisk is a businessman, and I'm sure he has other clients who will pay—"

"No. Not Fisk." I kept my tone even despite my anger. "Before you remind me of my…inability to wield magic and how I have to be paranoid and trust no one, it's *Fisk*. Got it?"

"Yes, sir." The big man set his jaw.

"While I'll agree that Fisk wouldn't ever betray or harm you for money, Yelena—" Janco swung down from The Madam's saddle "—I also think Ari has a point, even though he didn't communicate it well. Everyone is vulnerable. If I was a ne'er-do-well, I'd find a person's weakness and exploit it in my favor. Like when Owen found your weakness by kidnapping Leif and forcing you to steal the Ice Moon. Fisk is no exception."

"You're right." Before Janco could gloat, I added, "Ari didn't express it well. My apologies, Ari."

"Just be extra careful," he said. "Janco, if you sense any magic inside Fisk's headquarters—"

"We'll make a super-quick exit." He handed The Madam's and Rusalka's reins to Ari.

Janco entered the alley and I stayed a step behind him. The rank smell of urine and rotted garbage stung the inside of my nostrils, causing nausea to roll in my stomach. Our boots crunched on broken glass. Fist-sized spiders skittered behind heaps of trash. All, I hoped, part of the magical illusion. I kept my hand close to my switchblade just in case.

"You always take me to the fanciest places, Yelena. You really spoil me."

"Anyone who can use *ne'er-do-well* in a sentence deserves every comfort."

Janco grunted, but I wasn't sure if it was over the joke or because of the magic. He stopped, turned to his right, held up his hands and walked through a brick wall, disappearing. I followed, bracing for impact even though I knew it was illusion.

We entered an alcove. Remembering the series of knocks Leif had used during our previous visit, I rapped on the door. If they'd changed the pattern, we might be in trouble.

A small peephole opened. "Kinda early for a visit," a young girl said.

"It's never too early to lend a helping hand," I replied.

The peephole shut with a bang.

"Talk about paranoid," Janco whispered.

Nothing happened. I resisted the urge to pound on the door with the sides of my fists. Then a metallic snap sounded and the door swung wide.

A girl no older than thirteen gestured us into a foyer. "Lovely Yelena, you honor us with your visit." She tucked her long brown hair behind her ears. "Master Fisk has been expecting you."

And probably wondering why we didn't come sooner. I scanned the three rooms that branched off the foyer. On the right, the rows of bunk beds for the helpers were empty, and so was the classroom on the left. The enticing aroma of sweet cakes floated from the kitchen located straight ahead.

"Is Fisk in his office?"

"No. This is our busiest time of day and everyone is at the market helping shoppers. However, I sent Cricket to fetch him. Come and have breakfast while you wait. Amberle's making sweet cakes."

Another delay. I clasped my hands together to keep from shouting at the girl that we didn't have time to eat. With my fingernails biting into my skin, I said, "We have another person outside with our horses."

"Then I will direct him to the stable."

Interesting that she already knew his gender.

MARIA V. SNYDER

"You have a stable in here?" Janco asked, glancing around with a sharp gaze. Probably marking all the exits.

"Not exactly. It's on the other side of our building and is part of the White Rose Inn. However, we have an…arrangement with the proprietor of the White Rose, and there's a convenient door into our headquarters from the stable."

"I'd better go instead. Ari's not gonna trust you." Janco asked for directions.

"Tell the stable boy Hilly sent you."

Janco nodded and left. I followed Hilly to the kitchen. It opened up into an expansive kitchen with rows of long wooden tables to the left of the hearth. Amberle waved hello with her spatula.

Hilly gestured to a table, grabbed a plate, filled it from the stack of sweet cakes next to Amberle and set it front of me. The nausea caused by the odors in the alley transformed into ravenous hunger. I thanked her and dug in as if I hadn't seen food in days. Somewhat true. Cold road rations didn't count as real food, and my appetite had been nonexistent between my worry for Leif and the morning sickness the medic had warned me about.

Once I stopped shoveling sweet cakes and took a breath, I realized that in spite of my concern for my brother, I must ensure the baby remained healthy by eating regularly and getting enough sleep.

By the time I'd finished my meal, Janco and Ari arrived in the kitchen from another direction.

"This place is huge." Janco straddled a bench opposite me.

Ari sat next to me. The wood bowed under his weight and I tipped toward him.

"The horses?" I asked Ari.

"Fine."

Hilly served them and sat down next to Janco. While they ate, I asked her why only a few remained in the building.

"Oh, there are others," she said. Her brown eyes sparkled. "Headquarters is never empty. I'm told it's like a hive with bees flying in and out all day."

Janco paused. "And if you upset the hive, will you get stung?"

She grinned, showing her teeth. "Oh, yes. Many times."

"Nice." He scratched his ear. "But not many people can find this place. There's magic all around the outside, but thank fate the inside is clean."

"These are...uncertain times, Master Janco."

He preened. "*Master* Janco. Did you hear that, Ari?"

Ari and I ignored him. Instead, I studied the girl. Hilly knew his name, and she was here instead of working the busy market.

"You're one of Fisk's information collectors. Aren't you?" I asked.

Hilly smoothed her skirt. "I just answer the door."

"Ha." Janco stabbed a forkful of sweet cakes at her. "Don't try the innocent act, kitty cat. I invented that act ages ago."

"Too bad you never could pull it off," Ari mumbled.

"Zip it, Ari." And then to Hilly, "I spotted you hiding in the shadows the night we were arrested and again when we left the Citadel a few nights ago."

She gazed at him. "You're lying."

"Navy blue tunic and pants, scuffed black boots and the handle of your dagger is patterned with stars."

Her mouth gaped for a second, before she pressed her lips together in annoyance—a typical reaction after dealing with Janco.

"Don't worry about it, kitty cat. You're good—not as good

as me, but no one's perfect." He flourished the fork before sticking it in his mouth.

"That ego is going to get you killed someday," Ari chided.

"Pish." Janco faced Hilly. "After we were hauled away by the Citadel's guards, did you return to Fisk or did you wait to see if anyone else watched the spectacle?"

"What would you have done?" she asked.

"Patience isn't my thing, but a smart spy would stick around and see who the other curious cats are."

Ah, clever. He phrased it in a way to prod her ego into giving us information.

"I may have seen another...cat slinking away," she said.

"Oh? Do you know who this cat belongs to?"

"It depends."

Janco leaned forward. "Depends on what?"

"On how many coins you're going to give me for the intel."

"Gotcha," Ari said.

I laughed at Janco's sour expression. "How about two silvers for the name?" I asked.

"Six, and I'll tell you who also watched you leave to find your brother."

"Three."

"Five."

"Four."

"Deal." She held out her hand.

I placed four silver coins in her palm.

"The cat returned to a well-dressed man wearing a necklace with a large red jewel. The man was staying in the Council's guest quarters. He stepped from the back entrance to talk to the cat."

"Can you describe him?"

"It would be better for you to see him. I can tell you where to find him."

"For a few more coins?" Janco asked.

"Of course. Feeding everyone in the guild isn't cheap," she snapped.

"Well, if it wasn't for Yelena, you wouldn't even have a guild," he shot back.

I held up my hands. "I'm happy to pay. That's the whole point—to provide services in exchange for payment." I gestured, indicating the room. "So those without homes and families have food and shelter." Smiling, I added, "I'd no idea it would expand into a guild, and, for that, you have Fisk to thank." I handed her two more silvers.

Hilly said, "The man sits in on most of the public Council sessions and he's staying in number three-oh-six."

"Do we want to have a look?" Janco asked.

Tempting, but rescuing Leif was my priority. "Let's talk to Fisk first."

"What about the person who took an interest in us when we left the Citadel?" Ari asked Hilly.

"It's the same cat."

I mulled over her comments. Could the cat be The Mosquito, reporting to Bruns Jewelrose? Then why didn't the assassin try to kill me when I was locked in a cell? Probably because his prior attempt in the Fulgor jail hadn't worked. And all he needed was patience. No doubt another opportunity to target me would arise.

Ari touched my sleeve. Concern creased his face. "That cat may have followed us here from the east gate." Ari had chased the same logic as me.

"Unfortunately, Master Ari is correct," Fisk said, entering the kitchen. "A man—or should I say your cat—is keeping an eye on the White Rose's stables right now."

I stood. "I'm so sorry, Fisk!"

"No need to apologize, Lovely Yelena. The man has been

sniffing around here for the last three weeks. Seems he assumed that when you returned to the Citadel, you'd pay me a visit *before* being arrested." A gleam of amusement touched Fisk's light brown eyes. "Kudos to you for doing the...unexpected. It may have saved your life."

"How?" Janco asked.

"Think about it," Ari said.

Janco tapped his fork on the edge of the plate for a minute. "Oh. If we came straight here, he would have surprised us, but now we know his exact location, but he *doesn't* know we know."

"Not bad, Master Janco. I'd hire you if you were available. You could train under Hilly."

The girl smirked at Janco and handed the six silver coins to Fisk. She curtsied to us. "Please let me know if I can be of any more assistance." Then she left.

Fisk pocketed the coins. "Always wonderful to see you, Lovely Yelena, but I fear you bring us bad news?"

"Let's talk in your office," I said.

We trailed him down a long hallway that ended with a door. Fisk unlocked it and ushered us inside. The large two-story room also housed a living area and a loft above his office.

Janco sat in one of the two nubby red armchairs and Ari took the other. I perched on the edge of the black-and-white couch. A glass sculpture of two hands spread out like wings sat on the table between the two chairs. It was one of Opal's magic detectors. Nothing flashed within its core, which meant no magic was in use. Plus Janco appeared to be relaxed.

Fisk remained standing, making him seem taller than his normal six feet. "What happened?"

No way to break this news gently. "Leif's been taken."

He gripped the back of the couch. "When? Where?"

I told him about the ambush.

"Oh, no." Fisk sank to the couch. "I'd thought he'd be safe."

"Why?" Ari asked.

"He has that…smell thing."

"Doesn't matter if they used null shields," I said. They had their uses, but were a big problem when abused. A strange thought popped into my head. What if the Cartel did gain power over all the magicians? They'd be able to regulate those shields, but would they use them for the good of Sitia or for their own plans?

I shook my head. It didn't matter, because we'd stop them. We had to. "Do you have any information about the disappearances?"

Fisk hesitated.

"I'll pay you, of course."

"No. It's not that at all. Leif has aided me so much over the years, and I will do everything I can to help you rescue him."

"Then what it is?"

He took a breath and met my gaze. "Not all the magicians are missing. A few of them are in hiding."

20

VALEK

A storm brewed over the Sunset Ocean, and Valek had a day and a half to prepare. His theory about the Storm Thieves being the crew of the *Starfish*, which was reported lost at sea, meant they'd use this incoming storm to cover their approach to land. But many questions still remained. Which town did they plan to target? Would they use a dock or send a skiff to a beach? And then there was a good chance they wouldn't arrive at all. It'd been three weeks since their last break-in.

Valek returned to the apartment on Cannery Road after supper. Endre snored in the bedroom and Annika worked at the inn. Valek reviewed the information gathered and the list of stolen items. Ignoring the jewelry and money, he concentrated on the others. He considered the basics—food, water, shelter.

Endre had said living on a boat would be difficult. If he assumed they'd found a place to live—a cove hidden in the cliffs, perhaps—then the Storm Thieves had enough supplies to build a couple structures. That covered shelter.

Fresh water was too essential to steal, so Valek figured their location had access to a stream or river that flowed toward the ocean. He checked the map of the coast and discovered that all of the rivers that emptied into the ocean had towns built around them. Which made sense for shipping supplies up the river to cities inland.

He considered the cliffs in MD-1. Would fresh water run under the cliffs and not be marked on the map? Possible. And no one would notice a settlement that was inaccessible by land. However, during the fishing season, they'd be visible to the fleet. Unless they used camouflage. And that would explain the fifty gallons of gray and green paint stolen from Krillow. The hidden cove moved to the top of Valek's suspected location list.

As for food, the Storm Thieves had stolen basics like grain, rice, corn, flour, sugar, but they also took seeds and gardening supplies, which meant they planned to plant crops. No way a cove could sustain plants, unless it was huge. A sandy-rocky soil covered most of the coast, and farmable land started about ten miles inland. So much for the cove idea.

Valek tapped the map with a finger. He chased a memory of a conversation with one of the Stormdancers. Something about islands out in the Jade Sea… They were too small for a settlement because of the unpredictable storms. What if the Storm Thieves built their base on an island in the Sunset Ocean? With their magician keeping the storms at bay, they'd be safe. And no one would suspect they lived there.

Excited, Valek scanned the coastal map. Dozens of small islands were marked on the chart. It'd take seasons to check them all, and news would undoubtedly spread about the search, alerting the Storm Thieves, who could use a storm to keep the searchers from reaching their island. Plus they could have discovered an uncharted island. Deflated, Valek leaned back in the chair. Finding the island would be impossible.

He returned to the list of stolen items. What was missing? What did they need to sustain a settlement? Medical supplies had been taken from an infirmary in Coral Caye, casks of ale missing from a tavern in Lattice Beach, pots and glassware from a inn in Draggan and—

Valek shot to his feet. He flipped through the information Endre and Annika had collected, looking for the report on damages sustained during the storm thefts. Once he found it, he scanned the pages. A henhouse had collapsed during one storm and all the chickens had escaped. During another, a gate blew open and a dozen sheep had run away and had presumably drowned. Four milking cows had disappeared when a storm had knocked down a wall of a barn. What if these animals had been stolen instead? That meant the Storm Thieves still needed beef.

Once again Valek consulted the map. Where was the closest steer farm to the coast? He located one about three miles south of Gandrel and approximately a half mile inland. Gotcha!

When Annika returned and Endre woke up for his night shift, Valek ran his theory by them, seeking flaws in his logic.

"Those cliff coves aren't big enough for livestock and crops," Endre said.

"Are you sure there aren't any missing steers listed in the reports?" Annika asked.

"I checked all the information twice," Valek said. "But I'll read through the ones in the security office again tonight, and tomorrow I'll see what the locals have to say about the islands."

"You think they'll strike tomorrow night?" Endre asked him.

"If not tomorrow, then during the next storm. The Stormers need to have all their supplies before the fishing season starts in twelve days. We need to be in position regardless."

Valek spent another late night in the security office's conference room. With his theory in mind, he scanned the incident reports looking for anything that would dispute his logic.

Finding nothing, he returned to the inn for a few hours' sleep before reporting to the dock to join the repair crew.

The waves no longer lined up like rolling pins. Instead, they titled to the right.

"The worst part of the storm's gonna miss us," Joey said.

"Heading north, right?" Valek asked, tying a knot. Disappointment slowed his movements. More time spent away from Yelena.

"Yup. But the one right behind it might blow over us."

Valek paused. "Two close together? Is that usual?"

Joey cracked his knuckles. "Yup. They're called twins. We get them from time to time. They either follow the same path, hitting the same place one right after the other—those we call identical—or they diverge and go separate ways."

"Let me guess, those are called fraternal."

"You catch on quick."

Pug snorted. "Nothing quick about that, old man. Let's see if he can guess what we call them when they hit the coast at the same time?"

"Conjoined?" Valek guessed.

"Nope. We call them double trouble, and you hope that your boat don't sink and your house don't blow away during one of those nasty buggers." Pug shuddered. "Good thing they're rare."

"I've seen two in my lifetime," Joey said. "That's more than enough."

"Can you tell where the second twin will strike?" Valek asked Joey.

"Not yet."

Valek contained his impatience. He listened to their banter, their mild teasing and fish tales.

"…kid sunk like a stone, I had to fish him out with a net."

"…caught them hiding under the sails, lazy buggers."

MARIA V. SNYDER

"I spotted the wreckage in the water and I thought Smelly drowned, but we found 'im on Hook Island, sunnin' hisself on the beach. He was pissed we got to 'im so fast. Old Smelly thought he'd get a vacation." Joey coughed a chuckle.

"Could he have lived on the island?" Valek asked.

"For a couple days, sure, but he'd run through the food right quick. Nothing grows on them except berries, and you have to be real quick to catch one of them seabirds."

"Do ships wreck on those islands often?"

"Sometimes in a storm, but the fleet avoids them in bad weather. We'll check 'em when a ship's been reported missing, but it's rare we find anyone. Smelly's an exception."

"Yeah, he's an exceptional stinker. The man eats nothing but raw fish," Pug said.

Valek kept a comment about Pug's briny odor to himself. "Do you check them all?"

"Nah. Just the ones in the fishing grounds," Joey said.

"Does anyone use those islands?"

"Are you planning on building a vacation home?" Pug laughed. "If so, I've a deed I can sell you for ten golds."

Valek shrugged, playing down his interest. "Just making conversation."

"Ignore Pug," Joey said. "Those islands are only good for a rest or when you have to make repairs. A few have fresh water, but no one stays for long. Even a mild hot-season storm can swamp 'em and you're swimming."

"Or clinging to the treetops. Remember we found Fawlon tied to a branch?" Pug asked.

"Oh, yeah. Smart fellow, Fawlon. Too bad he died of thirst."

As they traded stories of other poor fellows, Valek mulled over the information. It seemed the Storm Thieves could live on an island as long as they had a magician to keep their settlement from being swamped. A Stormdancer would have to be back in Sitia by the heating season or the dancer would be missed. Was it another magician from Sitia or someone new? Joey said the crew of the *Starfish* was young.

What if one of those teens developed magic? Magic wasn't tolerated in Ixia, so the person had one of two options: escape to Sitia, or hide his or her power from everyone. But then there was the chance the person would grab too much magic and flame out. According to Irys, only those with amazing self-control could prevent that without any training.

If nothing happened during the storms, Valek planned to investigate all the crew members. It was a tiresome, tedious chore, but it might uncover a clue to the Storm Thieves' whereabouts.

After the fishermen rolled up the repaired nets, Joey pointed a crooked brown-spotted finger out to sea. "The first storm's headin' for the cliffs. But it looks like his twin is turnin' toward us. It'll hit tomorrow night, but I'll know better in the mornin'." He patted Valek on the shoulder and lowered his voice. "You catch those Stormers, boy. They're a nuisance." Then he limped across the street to the tavern.

So much for being subtle. Janco's incredulous voice sounded in his head. *An old man saw right through your cover? You're slipping, boss.* Good thing Janco was in Sitia with Yelena.

Valek stopped at his room to grab his pack before returning to the apartment. When Endre woke and Annika arrived, he reviewed his plan with them.

"I'm going north to keep an eye on the storm just in case. I want you both to watch the steer farm tonight. Get familiar with the layout of the barn, fields and the route to the coast. It'd be easier without a storm raging."

"Yes, sir," they said.

Endre rubbed his stomach. "If we want to keep our covers, we need an excuse for leaving work early."

MARIA V. SNYDER

"Not..." Annika covered her mouth with her hand.

"I'm not happy about it, either," he said.

"If it's any consolation," Valek said, "you only need three drops on your tongue, and it'll wear off in half an hour."

Endre rummaged in one of the kitchen's cabinets and removed a small glass vial filled with a brownish-yellow liquid. He crinkled his nose. "It even looks like vomit. Where do you find this stuff, sir?"

Valek grinned. "I've a source in Sitia who makes it for me." Leif always brewed potent concoctions, but he never bothered to improve the taste or smell. "Take the vomit tonic right before you leave. It will kick in once you're at work."

"Kick in?" Annika gave him a pained look.

"Sorry, I couldn't resist."

After the moon disappeared behind the thick bank of storm clouds, Valek headed north along the coast, following the waves. Since it was too dark to see the path, he carried a bull's-eye lantern and kept a small beam of light trained on the ground in front of him. He peered into the inky blackness of the ocean, searching for a ship's light. Nothing.

The edge of the storm reached land. Rain tapped against his black cloak. The castle's seamstress, Dilana, had soaked the material in a liquid wax to help repel water, but Valek had learned from experience that, with enough time, it would become waterlogged.

Gusts of wind blew ashore, flapping his cloak and threatening to extinguish the lantern's flame. Even though he pulled the hood over his head, the salty spray stung his eyes and burned his nose.

The rolling sand dunes along the coast turned rocky and steep. A blast of air from the north meant the cliffs must be ahead, deflecting the storm's wind. Even though he was unable to spot the sheer bluffs in the darkness, their massive presence loomed over him.

Valek retreated, finding a spot that he'd pick if he was on a boat and searching for a place to land. Then he hunkered down, closed the lantern's slide and waited.

He wondered what Yelena, Ari and Janco had discovered about the glass-house plants. It had been thirteen days since they parted. Was she on her way to the rendezvous point? Worry for her and the baby swirled.

At least she hadn't reached him with one of her desperate mental calls. Thrice before, she had been in dire trouble in Sitia and reached for him in a blind panic. Her frantic fear had ripped through him like a giant monster's sharp claws. Each time, he'd opened himself to her, loaning his strength and immunity to her across the miles. It had saved her life, and those times had been the only ones where they magically connected. Except now... His blood ran cold. Without her magic, would Yelena be able to reach him? Probably not.

What the hell was he doing here? Crouching in the rain, hoping to spot a gang of young thieves. Was this important to him? No. Catch these thieves and more would just pop up someplace else. He needed to be with his wife, even if she wasn't in danger. He'd let his job keep them apart for far too long. All he had to do was retire, and once free of the Commander's orders, he'd assassinate Owen.

Valek stood and wiped rain from his eyes. He turned and halted. A sigh escaped his lips. As much as he wished to go, he'd never leave a job unfinished. He revised his to-do list. Catch the Storm Thieves, retire, assassinate Owen. He returned to his position and tried not to fret over Yelena. After all, she was resourceful and smart. Plus Ari and Janco would never let her out of their sight.

Hours later, a light bobbed on the water. Valek watched

MARIA V. SNYDER

it with keen interest. The light broke into two points. The second one appeared to head for shore. As it drew closer, it clarified into four lanterns. The yellow glow revealed a large rowboat with four figures rowing and four others holding the lights. When they reached the shallow water, the rolling waves around the boat smoothed flat. Valek squinted. No rain or wind buffeted the craft, either. Sticky magic pressed on Valek. One of those eight must be the magician. Despite his earlier claims of not caring about these thieves, excitement warmed his chest.

Two men jumped out and pulled the boat's prow onto the beach. There was enough light for Valek to distinguish male and female, but not enough to observe facial features. Three men and two women hopped onto the sand. They carried two of the lanterns. Exchanging a few words with the woman in the boat, the five then strode across the sand, heading inland.

The men pushed the craft into deeper water and leaped in. Picking up the oars, they rowed toward the light still bobbing in the ocean. The water under the boat remained smooth despite the storm surge, which meant the magician had stayed with the rowboat. Valek'd bet a gold coin it was the woman sitting in the stern. Valek moved closer, risking being spotted to get a clear view of the magician. She was young. Sixteen, maybe seventeen years old. Pretty with long dark hair. At least she wasn't one of the Stormdancers.

Unable to follow the rowboat in storm-tossed seas, Valek trailed the group that had been dropped off. If they were a raiding party, then why did the boat leave? Perhaps they planned to rendezvous later at another location. That would be rather smart.

As the Storm Thieves traveled east, Valek recalled the map of the area. No towns or farms had been built here. There was nothing of value to steal. Maybe they'd hidden a stash of goods and were retrieving their stolen supplies. After hiking two miles, the Storm Thieves turned south, paralleling the coastline. The wind eased and soon it stopped raining.

When they bypassed Gandrel, the half-moon shone through a film of wispy clouds. Valek suspected that the Storm Thieves were headed to the steer farm. Instead of relying on the storm, they might be attempting to steal the cattle later tonight when everyone was asleep. An unexpected move. Again, he suspected their leader wasn't an average thief.

But how would they transport the animals? Someone would hear the hooves on the wooden planks of the dock. And he doubted they would bring them back to the beach where they'd landed. That boat was too small unless they carried one steer at a time. In that case, they'd have to make multiple trips, but no one would be searching for them up there. Now the question remained, were the Storm Thieves clever enough to make it work?

A quarter of a mile before the steer farm, they turned east, not west as expected. Curious, Valek closed the distance between them. After half a mile, the five hurried down an overgrown lane and into a barn with a sagging roof and weathered wood. Valek looped to the back of the dilapidated structure. A rusted chain wrapped around the handles of a set of warped doors. An oversize padlock cinched the chain tight.

The barn had only one exit. Good. Scrawny pine trees surrounded the area. There were no other buildings or lights visible. Lantern light glowed through the two dirty windows. Valek peeked inside. The Storm Thieves set up bedrolls. The glass garbled their words, but their tone suggested a relaxed, easy banter. Interesting.

Valek found a hidden vantage point and waited. Nothing happened. They remained inside. Right before dawn, he checked on them again. They slept in a circle around one of

MARIA V. SNYDER

the lanterns. It still glowed. The faint light illuminated their young faces, ranging in age from fifteen to nineteen.

A heaviness pressed on his shoulders. These kids had ruined their futures by being a part of the Storm Thieves. No spouse or children for them. The Code of Behavior didn't give second chances.

He mulled over the reason they hid in the barn. That second storm would hit the steer farm tonight, and these five would already be there to lead the cattle to the ship, saving time. And with the noise of the wind and waves, no one would hear the animals' passage over the dock. Shrewd. Very shrewd. And perfect for him. He knew just what to do.

Valek returned to the apartment. His cloak, uniform and hair were stiff with dried salt and sand. The cold air had soaked into his bones. He stirred the coals in the hearth to life and added logs. Then he washed up and changed into his adviser's uniform.

An hour after dawn, Endre and Annika arrived. They reported a quiet night.

"The owner's not too concerned about a theft," Endre said. "Except the house, none of his barns, sheds or gates are locked up. I guess he's relying on the brands on his livestock."

"Brands don't help when the cattle disappear," Annika said.

"Speaking of disappearing," Valek said. "I've a job for your security force, Endre. How many soldiers are there?"

"Five others beside me."

"We need more. Can you recruit from neighboring forces?"

He shook his head. "My captain can, but she's not going to do it because I ask her to."

"Then I'll ask her. Let's go."

"Now?"

"Yes, I'll explain on the way."

"What about me?" Annika asked.

"Find a seamstress, a bolt of a solid dark fabric and five gallons of sculpting clay. Bring them to the station as soon as you can." Valek didn't wait to see her reaction. He strode from the apartment with Endre close behind.

Detailing his discoveries and his plan to Endre, Valek hurried through the empty streets. Everything had to be in place by the time the storm arrived.

Captain Tahnee scowled at Endre—the newly revealed spy in her domain—but she sent messengers to Krillow and Coral Caye with Valek's orders.

"I'll need Endre and one other to go with me to arrest those kids," Valek said to Tahnee.

"You'll need more than that. There's five of them," she said.

Valek waited.

"Fine. Mikus," she barked.

A slender soldier no more than twenty years old snapped to attention. "Yes, sir!"

"You're with them."

His face paled. "Yes, sir!"

She pressed her lips together for a moment as if swallowing a sigh. "What can we do while you're gone?"

Valek listed a number of tasks. A dubious expression creased her face, but she agreed and organized the rest of her staff. Valek asked Endre to fetch five pairs of manacles, then they headed to the abandoned barn.

"They're young, so you shouldn't have any problems," Valek explained. "You are going to go in first, rouse them, manacle their hands behind their backs and make them kneel."

"Is that really necessary?" Endre asked. "They're just a bunch of kids."

Mikus sucked in a breath, as if he couldn't believe Endre dared to question Valek.

"I want them scared and off balance," Valek said. "I'm going

MARIA V. SNYDER

to make an entrance and terrify them. This way they will divulge all they know. For this age group, it's more effective than goo-goo juice."

"Ah, nice." Endre's tone held approval.

Grabbing the end of his shirt, Mikus twisted the fabric.

"Mikus, I encourage my agents to ask questions so they can understand what's going on. I also value their input. If Endre thought my plan sucked, he'd say so and explain why he believed that without any consequences."

"Oh." Mikus's voice squeaked. "And…would you change your plan then?"

"Depends. If Endre's reason had merit, then yes. If I didn't agree with him, then no." And that had been the same relationship the Commander and Valek had shared until recently. Perhaps Yelena had been on the right track regarding the Commander's unusual behavior. Had Valek missed vital clues from Ambrose? It was something to consider after he dealt with the Storm Thieves.

They reached the overgrown path. Valek signaled for silence, then he motioned for them to wait while he checked the barn. Keeping close to the trees, Valek approached the structure and looked through the window. The teens hadn't moved. He fetched Endre and Mikus.

When they drew close to the door, Valek mouthed, *Go!* The two men yanked their swords and barged into the barn, yelling at the teens to get against the wall. Valek remained outside as shouts and cries sounded. A clang of metal followed a curse.

One young man darted out. Valek tripped him. He sprawled in the dirt, but not for long. He scrambled to his feet and by the time Valek neared, he'd spun with a dagger in his hand. Quick little scamp.

The scamp brandished the weapon. "Don't come any—"

Valek kicked the boy's wrist, sending the knife flying

through the air. He pounced, grabbed the scamp's arm and twisted it behind his back. Valek grasped his shoulder to steady the boy.

"Keep still," he ordered his prisoner, "or I'll break your arm." Valek tugged it higher to emphasis his threat.

The scamp gasped in pain.

When the noise from inside the barn subsided, Valek pushed the boy ahead of him. "Move."

They entered. The other four knelt with Endre and Mikus standing behind them. The Storm Thieves' faces whitened another shade when they spotted their friend.

"You missed one," Valek said.

"Sorry, boss." Endre strode over, snapped the manacles on the scamp and dragged him to join his associates.

Valek gazed at the five with what Yelena called his cold killer expression. "Congratulations, your antics during the last couple seasons have caught *my* attention." He waited a beat. "Do you know who I am?"

They kept quiet.

"Endre, tell them."

"You are Adviser Valek. The Commander's *assassin* and right-hand man."

His name had the desired effect on all but one. Panic flared in four sets of eyes, but the scamp glared—a challenge.

Valek said, "Tell me the plan for tonight."

They glanced at the scamp.

"Don't say a word," he ordered them.

Ah. The scamp was in charge. Valek drew one of his knives from his sleeve with his right hand while palming a dart with his left. He grabbed the closest thief by her arm and yanked her upright, pricking her with the dart. She squealed in fear.

Placing his blade on her neck, he said, "Tell me the plan for tonight."

MARIA V. SNYDER

"You're bluffing," the scamp said. "It isn't a crime to sleep in an abandoned building. You got nothing on us."

Valek stared at him a moment before returning his attention to the girl. "What's your name?"

"Sa...Sadzi." Her eyes glazed.

"You should have picked better friends, Sadzi." He turned and stepped in front of her so he blocked her from the others. Drawing his knife arm back, he stabbed at her, sending the blade into the gap between her arm and side. The other girl screamed. Sadzi buckled as the sleeping potion kicked in. Valek grasped her shoulders, trapping the knife and keeping her upright as he muscled her out the door. He dumped her to the side, but her motionless boots remained visible to those inside.

Valek pulled a bloodstained handkerchief from his pocket. He pretended to wipe blood from his hands when he returned to the others. Mikus's mouth gaped, as shocked as the Storm Thieves.

He waved the cloth at the door dismissively. "She soiled herself. Quite the stink." Valek studied them one by one. The other girl burst into tears under his scrutiny. Yelena's voice sounded in his mind, admonishing him for being mean.

Sliding another knife from his pocket, Valek said, "Tell me the plan for tonight."

Terrified, they started talking at once, rushing to explain the plans.

Back at the station, they processed the thieves. The security officers searched them and gave them coveralls to wear before locking them in the cells.

The scamp scowled at Valek when Endre laid the still-sleeping Sadzi on a bunk. "I knew you were bluffing."

Valek didn't bother to reply. Instead, he checked on the preparations. Annika had arrived with the supplies and a seamstress. The older woman tsked and rubbed the knuckles on her right hand as he explained what he needed.

"I don't know if it'll work," she said.

"That's for me to worry about. Can you do it by supper?"

"Yes." She unrolled the bolt of black fabric on the conference room's table.

Captain Tahnee showed Valek what her staff had found. "They don't look authentic."

"Leave that to me. Annika, did you get the clay?"

"No one had clay, but I brought you quick wood. It's a putty the fishermen use on their boats to plug small leaks. It hardens fast, so it should be good by tonight."

"Wonderful." Valek pried the lid off the bucket. He gave everyone a job and then set to work on his own task.

Around noon, Annika brought chowder for everyone. The spicy scent caused Valek's stomach to cramp with sudden hunger. He hadn't eaten since yesterday. After downing the chowder, he returned to work. The hours sped past.

Endre interrupted Valek at supper time. The soldiers from the other towns had arrived. He gathered everyone in the conference room. Each town had sent five officers, which brought the total number of people available to ambush the Storm Thieves to eighteen—not counting the seamstress, who had finished her part and left. He hoped it would be enough.

Valek explained the plan, picked people to fill certain roles, then set a schedule for small groups to leave for the rendezvous location. Satisfied with the progress, he resumed his assignment, completing the last item around sunset and four hours before the Storm Thieves landed.

His group included Annika and Endre. They were the last to leave the station, leaving only Captain Tahnee to deal with any problems in Gandrel. Valek checked to make sure they

MARIA V. SNYDER

had everything. No one said a word during the trip to the steer farm.

Once they arrived, everyone knew what to do. They prepped and moved into position just as it started to rain.

A thrill of excitement shot through him. The trap was set.

The storm raged, soaking Valek's hair and clothes. The fishing boats banged and screeched against the wooden pilings as they pitched in their docks. Flags flapped in the strong wind, adding to the noise. Waves raced under the planks, sending up salty sprays when they collided with the support beams.

Annika waited at the end of the pier. She watched for the Storm Thieves' ship's light. According to the teens in custody, the ship would appear during the height of the storm. It would tie up to the dock, lower the gangplank and the scamp and his crew would lead five stolen steers onto the ship. Then they'd raise the gangplank and cast off, with no one the wiser until morning.

Valek acknowledged the beauty and simplicity of the Storm Thieves' plan. He looked forward to interrogating their leader. Perhaps Valek would learn a couple new tricks.

Two quick flashes of light pierced the darkness—Annika's signal.

"Get ready," Valek said, and his order was relayed to the others.

The four other teams of two pulled on their disguises. Valek and Endre draped the black cloth the seamstress had sewn around them.

Annika appeared. "They're close." She wore Sadzi's clothes and had styled her hair the same way as the girl. "Where's the rope?"

"Here." Valek handed her the end. The lead was tied around the steer's head. Or rather, the mask of a steer's head that he wore. Not quite an exact replica. He'd done his best to make all five look lifelike, using bones from the butcher shop and the quick wood. Between the darkness and the storm, he hoped no one would spot the deception until it was too late.

"Let's go," Annika said.

Valek and Endre crouched over. Endre grasped Valek's waist and they moved forward. Behind them, the other four teams should be doing the same. The "steers" were each led by a handler who wore one of the captured Storm Thieves' clothes.

Halfway down the pier, Valek spotted the ship. Lanterns blazed from its upper deck. Unlike the other boats rocking on the heavy seas, the Storm Thieves' ship remained steady as if traveling over calm waters. A large commercial vessel, it was under full sail. An impressive sight.

The white fabric of the sails caught a wind that wasn't as strong as the storm's. The magician not only controlled the sea, but the storm, as well. Talented.

Annika slowed, keeping the small "herd" away from the lanterns' bubble of light until the gangplank was lowered. The storm stopped, reducing the noise. The ship approached and four figures jumped onto the pier. Ropes flew over the gap and were secured to the pylons. Voices shouted an all clear and the gangplank eased toward the dock.

"Sadzi, come on! Hurry!" a man called from the top of the gangplank.

Annika kept her pace. When the thud of the plank hitting the pier sounded, she sped up. Two others joined the man. Valek drew his blowpipe. Behind him, Endre pulled his sword.

Stepping into the light, Valek tensed as he encountered thick magic. He scanned the rigging and decks, counting opponents. The magician stood on the bow with her arms stretched to each side.

Laughter reached them. "That has to be the ugliest-looking

MARIA V. SNYDER

steer I've ever seen," a man said. "Did you feel sorry for him, Sadzi?"

Annika kept quiet.

"Looks like he's limping, as well," another voice said. "Jibben isn't gonna be pleased."

"They're all walking weird. Did you hobble them, Sadzi?"

"Hey, they're not—"

The jig was up. "Now," Valek yelled, throwing off the fabric and yanking off his mask.

The three men standing at the top of the gangplank stared at him in shock for a few seconds. Long enough for Valek to reach the gangplank. Behind him, he knew the others tossed off their disguises and pulled their swords. He couldn't see it, but by the way the men in front of him blanched, gasped and finally cried an alarm, it must have been quite the sight. Valek grinned. He loved a good surprise.

"Ambush!" one of the Storm Thieves yelled, drawing his sword.

The magician dropped her arms and turned. Valek loaded his blowpipe and aimed at the closest man. Then he shot the other two in rapid succession. He yanked his sword, then rushed them, exchanging a few parries before they wobbled as the sleeping potion took effect.

Yells sounded from the dock. Valek turned. Huge waves of water crashed over the pier, swamping his backup. Annika, Endre and two others had reached the gangplank, but the rest clung to the rope rails as whitecaps slammed into them. Valek had to neutralize the magician and stop the water attack.

Boots pounded on the deck. Four armed Storm Thieves rushed toward him and more poured from the wheelhouse. Valek gestured for Endre, Annika and the two with them to engage the four. He sheathed his sword and raced to the bow.

Two young men dropped from the rigging. Brandishing

daggers, they blocked his path to the magician. Valek tucked the blowpipe into his pocket and drew a knife with a flourish to distract them while he palmed a couple darts. They hesitated for a second, glancing at each other.

"Come on, boys, let's see what you can do," Valek said, sliding his feet into a fighting stance.

The bigger of the two advanced. He held his weapon in his lead hand. Rookie. Valek used a roundhouse kick to knock the weapon from his opponent's grasp, then he shuffled in closer, punched the teen in the solar plexus and pricked him with a dart. The boy fell back on his butt with an *oomph*.

Not waiting for his friend to gain his feet, the second teen charged Valek. The boy's speed made up for his lack of finesse. They exchanged a few jabs and parries and Valek would have liked to test the extent of his opponent's skills, but the sounds of fighting grew louder and, after a quick peek at the ruckus, he saw that Endre and the others were outnumbered.

Valek blocked the next jab with his left hand, grabbed the teen's wrist, stepped back and as he yanked the Storm Thief toward him, Valek kneed him in the groin. The poor boy collapsed to the deck. Not very sporting, but time was critical.

When he neared the bow, another Storm Thief landed in front of him. Valek didn't bother engaging him. He simply bowled the teen over, jabbed a dart into his neck and continued.

The magician faced him. A heavy stickiness engulfed him. The waves pelting the dock disappeared. Good. He guessed she couldn't multitask. Valek waded through the magic, approaching her. Balls of water flew at him, but instead of slamming into him, they veered wide, missing him. She sucked in a breath of surprise. Fear soon followed. The young lady backed up and grabbed the railing.

Valek had a second to wonder what she planned before

MARIA V. SNYDER

the ship lurched violently under his feet. The bubble of calm popped and the storm surged in. Yells and cries of alarm emanated from the fight on deck. He swayed for a moment, teetering off balance, but years of training kicked in and he adjusted to the motion. Smart move, sweetheart.

The magician clung to the wood rail as if her life depended on it. She stared at him with intense blue eyes. When he closed in, her magic disappeared,

She sank to her knees and said, "Please, don't kill me."

In that moment, with her wet hair pressed to her head, she looked twelve years old—someone's beautiful daughter. A vision of Yelena holding a baby girl flashed in his mind. He dismissed the distraction. Valek had no intention of killing her, but what to do with her?

"Stop the storm, and I'll think about it," he said.

"I can't. I only control the water."

"Then restore the calm."

The waves around the boat smoothed and the rain ceased. The ship settled.

"Is someone controlling the storm?" he asked.

She bit her lip and gazed past him. Valek glanced at the battle. All his people had reached the deck, and they had the upper hand. No surprise, considering the ages of their opponents. Experience trumped youth in most cases.

"It's over," he said. "Cooperation is the best way for you to stay alive."

Sitting back on her heels in defeat, she said, "My brother can call the storms, but he's not on board."

"Where is he?"

"On the island."

Valek kept his stern expression, despite the thrill of having guessed right. "You will take us to the island."

Now panic filled her expression. "I...can't."

He waited.

"I… They will kill him."

Not what he expected. "They?"

She swept her arms wide, indicating the boat. "The people who hijacked our ship and forced us to help them."

21

LEIF

A searing pain in his head roused Leif to consciousness. Harsh sunlight waited on the other side of his eyelids, so he kept his eyes closed. He cataloged his woes. The dried-out piece of leather that had been his tongue meant he hadn't drunk any water for a while. The headache meant no food, either. Plus, he suspected a hangover from the sleeping juice. Leif guessed he'd been knocked out for a few days or more. Vague memories rose of being awake for short, blurry snatches to eat stale bread and gulp tepid water.

When the sharp pulses in his temples dulled to a loud throb, Leif opened his eyes. Bright side—not a cell. He lay on a bed in a small, neat room. One window, one night table, no decorations on the white walls and one door currently shut. Dark side—his arms had been pulled up over his head and his wrists were secured. Probably to the headboard, which would match his feet, since his ankles were tied to the footboard. Also a null shield surrounded him, blocking his magic.

A steady hum of unease vibrated through him. Not outright fear. At least, not yet. He still wore his own clothes. The lock picks hidden inside might come in handy. His captors would have to let him up at some point. Right?

As the hours dragged by—each one slower than the previous—Leif worried they'd forgotten him. Or they planned to let him die of thirst. No. If they'd wished him dead, they could have ensured he'd never wake up. This was all part of their scheme to drive the point home that they were in control. Leif kept his thoughts positive. His main objective—stay alive until an opportunity to escape arose or rescued arrived. No doubt Yelena would search for him.

The scrape of metal jolted Leif from a light doze. The knob turned and the door swung inward, admitting a tall man in his late forties. Two bruisers entered behind him. One carried a chair, the other a tray of food. Swords and daggers hung from their belts. The wonderful aroma of beef caused Leif's head to spin. An effective way to torture him would be to withhold food.

The man studied him while Leif assessed his captor. Short black hair combed back with streaks of gray at the temples, and sharp features that would be considered appealing by the ladies. His posture oozed confidence, and, if the jewels in his rings and the monster ruby hanging from his neck didn't tip a person off, then the expensive silk clothes tailored to enhance his muscular build indicated the man had money—lots and lots of money.

Leif waited for the man to speak.

"Aren't you curious about what's going on?" the man asked.

"I am." The words croaked from his dry lips. "But I figured I really wasn't in a position to demand answers."

The man laughed. "Refreshing. You're the first to realize that so soon. The others hollered and blustered, thinking their *status* as magicians had any influence over their situation." He gestured.

Bruiser One placed the chair next to the foot of Leif's bed. Then he pulled a key from his pocket and unlocked the re-

MARIA V. SNYDER

straints around Leif's wrists before stepping quickly back. His meaty paws hovered near his weapons. Everyone in the room tensed, waiting for Leif's reaction.

He sat up and rubbed his arms, working the feeling back into his hands. Weak from days without food or water, and with his ankles still secured, he had no option but to play nice—for now.

The man approached and held out his hand. "Bruns Jewel-rose."

The name sliced through Leif, igniting anger. This was the son of a bitch who had hired an assassin to kill Yelena. He drew in a breath to calm down, reminding himself to play nice and stay alive. He grasped Bruns's hand. "Leif Liana Zaltana."

They pumped once and released—just like a couple of businessmen meeting for the first time. Weird.

"It's a pleasure to finally meet you," Bruns said, sitting in the chair. "Your résumé is quite impressive." He snapped his fingers.

Bruiser Two brought the tray over and placed it on Leif's lap. It contained a bowl of stew, a hunk of bread, cheese, a spoon, napkin and a large glass of water. No knife.

Bruns said, "Go ahead and eat. I'm sure you're starved."

Leif hesitated. "And in exchange?"

"All I ask is that you hear me out. That you don't form an opinion until I'm finished."

Glancing at his bound ankles, Leif said, "What if I've already formed an opinion?"

Bruns inclined his head. "That is an unfortunate necessity. I've learned that a demonstration of my abilities and resources is far more convincing than a discussion. You cannot deny that my network was able to neutralize a powerful magician such as yourself rather easily."

A protest over the word *easily* pushed up his throat, but he swallowed it down. The ambush had been expertly set to appeal to his instincts and bypass Rusalka's abilities. "Did you neutralize my sister?"

"No. My sources say Onora, the Commander's new assassin, did."

He scoffed, "Your sources are wrong."

"Unlikely."

"Why would the Commander do that?"

"That's all part of my explanation." Bruns waited.

Playing nice meant listening to his captor's crazy theories and perhaps pretending to agree with him.

"All right, Bruns. I'll listen to your…pitch." Leif picked up the glass and gulped half the water. Ahhh. Welcome back, tongue.

"The Commander is preparing to invade Sitia. We know this because he has gone to great lengths to secure Curare, stockpile null shields, nullify the Liaison and is harboring Owen Moon, a known rogue magician."

Stockpiling null shields? That was news to Leif. Filling the spoon with chunks of beef and potatoes, Leif shoveled it into his mouth. Not bad. Not the best he'd ever tasted, but up there in the top five.

"The Commander ordered the hit to block the Liaison's magic so she would no longer be an asset to the Sitian Council. Without her magic, the Commander could invite her to be one of his advisers and, with the added appeal of being with her heart mate, it would be a tempting offer. Valek would also be happy. And it's important to the Commander to keep him happy. He's vital to their security. That's also why Onora didn't kill Yelena. That would have sent him on a quest for revenge."

Bruns crossed his legs. "With me so far?"

"One question. Why did you hire The Mosquito to assassinate Yelena?"

"To cause strife in Ixia by sending Valek on that quest for revenge. We hoped he'd assume the second attempt was connected to the first and discover the Commander sent Onora. Plus Yelena has classified information about Sitia. The last thing we wanted was for her to give it to the Commander. We're trying to *protect* Sitia."

Protect Sitia by murdering Yelena? That was very twisted logic. "Who's we?"

"I'm getting to that. Considering the Commander's hatred of magicians, Owen Moon's presence is harder to explain. He must have something rather significant that the Commander can use when he attacks Sitia.

"The Sitian Council has almost all this information, yet they still argue and discuss and get nothing done. Yes, I know they tasked your Councilman to increase production of Theobroma, but that will take years. We don't have years. We have a year at most."

Leif stopped chewing. A year? Even with the grafting technique, they'd never be ready in time.

"Frustrated with the Sitian Council's refusal to accept the facts and act, I contacted a number of friends and colleagues. We formed our Cartel and brainstormed ideas on how to protect Sitia from being invaded. First we listed our assets. Our army doesn't stand a chance—we lack discipline and numbers. But we have magicians and super messengers.

"Except the magicians don't know how to fight or work with an army. Some of them can't be counted on to help because they're selfishly pursuing their own agendas, which is why the Commander can stockpile null shields. It's incomprehensible to me why a magician would create something that can be used against him. It's like giving your sword to your previously unarmed enemy, and then being surprised when he stabs you with it!"

Bruns stopped his tirade. He drew in a deep breath then continued in an even tone, "We decided to stop the randomness and the stupidity. The idea is to gather *all* the magicians into one unit, train them how to fight and use their magic to gain information. Organize them to maximize their efforts during a war and stop them from selling null shields to the enemy. It's the only way we will prevent the Commander from conquering Sitia."

"The Council does use magicians—"

"Only a handful compared to how many there are. And how many like Owen Moon have caused us trouble over the years? Dozens?"

Names sprang to mind, but Leif resisted the temptation to list them. Instead he considered Bruns's idea. He gestured to the bruisers. "And this is your way of gathering all the magicians? Ambush and imprison them until they hear your speech? Then what? Join or die?"

Bruns smiled, revealing a row of straight white teeth, but no humor shone in his gray eyes. "Those who have been recruited by the members of the Cartel had no need for a demonstration of our resources. They recognized the danger and agreed to train."

"And the ones that don't agree?"

"They're persuaded. I can be very convincing."

Leif imagined Bruns's persuasion techniques involved threats, torture and isolation. Good thing he'd finished the food, or he would have lost his appetite. "How about the four who were assassinated? Are they the ones you couldn't sway?"

"No. They were the troublemakers. No amount of logic or appealing to their patriotic sense of duty would ever entice them away from being selfish, greedy problems. We didn't bother to waste our time with them."

Harsh. "And you sent The Mosquito to Lapeer to assassinate Ben Moon and Loris and Cilly Cloud Mist."

"Yes. They were easy–to–solve problems." Bruns's tone remained reasonable, as if they discussed business.

That brought the total number of murdered magicians to seven—playing nice might be harder than Leif had thought. He switched to a safer topic. "Why didn't you try logic and reason on me?"

"I'm doing that right now."

"No. I meant why the ambush, the...demonstration?" At least Bruns hadn't called it a kidnapping. He detested that word.

"Ah. I see. In your case and in a few others, we determined that your loyalty to the Council would make it much harder to convince you. That it would take us some time to demonstrate our sincerity in protecting Sitia."

"A few others? Like Hale?"

"Yes. And those who work closely with the Council and Master Magicians on various operations."

"Is Hale...?" Leif couldn't say the word. He'd grown fond of the stiff—quite the surprise.

"He's fine. Another reason for the extra measures is so you don't warn the Council until we're ready."

"But they already know about the Cartel and the missing and dead magicians."

"Yes, but they don't know *who* is involved or where our base of operations is located."

So The Mosquito hadn't informed his boss about revealing Bruns's name to Yelena when he failed to assassinate her in Fulgor's jail. That little detail might just save Leif's life. "If they do find out who's involved, they'll know to search Jewelrose lands."

"I believe you're fishing for information. And I'm insulted that you'd think I'd be fooled that easily."

"Can't blame a guy for trying."

"If you wanted a tour of the compound, all you had to do was ask." Bruns stood and smoothed his tunic. "First, some safety information. These two gentlemen are armed with blowpipes and darts filled with Curare. Their aim is remarkable, even at a distance. They will be accompanying us. Understand?"

"That they'll shoot me with Curare if I try to escape? Yes, that's quite clear."

Mister Business frowned at him as if he'd used crass language. But he gestured to Bruiser One. The broad-shouldered man unlocked Leif's ankles. Leif noted which pocket the key disappeared into. Valek's lessons on how to pick a pocket just might come in handy. Leif rubbed feeling back into his feet. His boots had been placed beside the bed. He wondered what had happened to his cloak and machete as he tied the laces.

When Leif stood, a brief spell of weakness flushed through him. He'd need more than one meal to return to full strength. Bruiser Two opened the door and, with Bruns in the lead, followed by Leif, the four of them entered a hallway. The null shield remained around him. Too bad. He'd hoped it was attached to the room.

The hallway's white walls held no decorations, just a series of closed doors on both sides. Leif counted a total of forty.

"This is the barracks for the magicians," Bruns said.

Did he expect to fill the entire building? That would be quite an accomplishment. At the end of the corridor, they descended two flights of stairs and walked into the sunlight. Leif squinted until his eyes adjusted. The warm air smelled of wood smoke and leather. A green fuzz lined the tree branches, but he'd have to examine the buds closer to see where in Sitia he might be. Bigger buds would mean he was farther south. Of course, that only narrowed down his north/south location. East/west would be harder to discern without more geographical information.

Bruns strode around the compound, pointing to the various buildings—stables, armory, infirmary, dining hall—with pride. Leif memorized the layout. It resembled a military base and even had a three-story-high marble wall surrounding it. Leif wouldn't be surprised if Bruns had commandeered the Jewelrose garrison.

Soldiers marched in unison, wearing olive-colored fatigues. Others practiced a variety of fighting techniques in a large training area.

Bruns showed him the armory. "We've been developing new weapons." He picked up an oversize bow. "We've discovered the bigger the bow, the farther an arrow will fly, giving us an advantage." Placing it back on the table, he drew Leif over to a pile of leather. "This is going to be made into protective clothing. It resists punctures and will stop a dart of Curare from reaching a soldier's skin!"

When they left the armory, a young soldier ran up to Bruns and handed him a red flag. "They're ready for you, sir."

"Wonderful."

Bruns led him outside the compound. The bruiser brothers closed in on Leif, staying a mere foot away. Unfortunately, the null shield remained. Leif wondered if it had been woven into his clothing. Only one way to find out, but he'd wait until he was alone to strip.

Now the air held the faint scent of the sea. The Jewelrose clan did have a thumb-shaped bit of land that extended into the Jade Sea. And, if he remembered correctly, the area was rather isolated. In fact, just north of it was the Lion's Claw Peninsula, where the Bloodrose cult had lived for years in relative obscurity, until Opal discovered their illegal activities and stopped them.

Reaching a pasture with a wooden fence, Bruns halted. A forest lined the north and west sides. Dozens of soldiers crouched on the southern side.

"Watch this," Bruns said. He leaned against the fence and waved the flag. Gesturing to the soldiers now climbing through the wooden rails, he said, "That's one of our platoons. And in the woods is a mock Ixian army about the same size."

When the platoon reached the halfway mark, arrows sailed from the forest. Instead of slamming into the soldiers, they stopped in midair, as if hitting an invisible barrier, and dropped to the ground. The platoon increased their pace. Two people called enemy positions. Branches shook, dislodging archers.

Within minutes the platoon had penetrated the forest and captured the Ixian soldiers.

Bruns beamed. "See how effective we can be when we have magicians fighting alongside soldiers?"

Leif tried hard not to get swept up in Bruns's enthusiasm. But damn. That was one hell of an impressive demonstration.

22

YELENA

"How many are in hiding?" I asked Fisk. With all the bad news, it was nice to hear something good.

Fisk shot to his feet as if he needed to move. He paced behind his couch. "Five of them. Once the word spread that magicians were disappearing and dying, they came to me to help hide them."

"With that cat slinking around your headquarters, are you sure they're still safe?" Janco leaned forward in his chair.

"Yes. But the requests have stopped, and I fear he's responsible."

I mulled over the information. "So we still have seven missing and four dead magicians."

"Eight, if we count Leif," Ari said.

My heart squeezed. Leif wouldn't become a statistic. I'd make sure of that.

"And they're just the ones we know about," Fisk said. "It's not like they all work for the Council or the Master Magicians. They're spread over the eleven clans of Sitia."

"Who would know if there are more missing?" Ari asked.

"Does it matter how many?" Janco asked. "I'd think the more important question is *where* are they?"

"Not if they've joined forces with the Cartel." Ari gestured. "We wouldn't get a warm welcome if we showed up to rescue them and they have no intention of leaving, and oh, by the way, they outnumber us, so now *we're* captured."

I held up my hands, stopping Janco's retort. "I think we're getting ahead of ourselves. Fisk, do you know how long the Cartel's been recruiting?"

"I heard rumors starting soon after you left for Fulgor eight weeks ago."

Almost a full season.

"But they could have been at it for much longer," Ari said. "We should assume that once the rumors started, they no longer cared if word spread."

Good point. Unfortunately. "Any ideas where they're... gathering?"

Fisk strode over to his desk. He leafed through a stack of papers, pulled one out and returned. "Hilly's been keeping an eye on the people who have been associating with the man who was so interested in your whereabouts, Yelena." He sat on the couch and handed me the paper. "I've been identifying them. This one..." He tapped the blank space next to a description of the man with the large ruby pendant. "I just received confirmation on his name. He's—"

"Bruns Jewelrose?" I guessed.

"Yes. Friend of yours?"

"Hardly. He hired The Mosquito to assassinate me."

"Odd." Fisk's brow crinkled.

Janco laughed. "That's not odd. That's just another typical day for our girl here."

Fisk ignored him, but I scowled at him.

Unaffected, Janco said, "You know I'm right."

Fisk continued, "I mean, why kill you and risk getting

Valek involved? That would be dangerous. Plus, he already neutralized your magic."

Ari and Janco glanced at me. Not many people knew that the first attack hadn't been The Mosquito, but Onora following the Commander's orders to test Valek. Perhaps Bruns had learned this and hoped my death would send Valek after Onora or the Commander.

"Bruns knows that I will rescue Leif, despite not having magic," I said. "And that I have powerful friends to help me." I stood. Time to answer at least one question. "Fisk, do you have a window that faces in the same direction as the stable?"

He grinned. "You want to take a look at that cat hanging around?"

"Yes. Except I suspect he's not a cat."

Fisk led me to the loft above his office. Navy blue curtains covered two long, narrow windows. He pointed. "The glass is tinted, so no one can see you."

"Handy."

"Opal's father made them for me. They're getting popular with people who want extra privacy."

I eased the curtain aside carefully, just in case the movement drew attention. Late-morning sunlight warmed the cobblestones below. The street appeared to be empty. Half a block south, there was an entrance to an alley. Perhaps the cat hid inside the alley's shadows.

"He's good," Fisk said, standing behind me. "Look at the second-floor windows on the third building to the left across the street."

I followed his directions. Sure enough, a figure in dark clothes stood behind the panes of glass.

"Is that your Mosquito?"

"I can't see his face." I considered. Even if he wasn't the assassin, the man still worked for the Cartel and could provide information about Leif's location. "We need to set a trap."

We returned to the living area and I explained my plan to lure the cat from his lair.

"Too dangerous," Ari said. "There's only three of us."

"I can provide as many people as you need. No charge," Fisk offered.

"We can't put a bunch of kids in danger," Janco said.

Fisk huffed in annoyance, but before he could educate Janco about the skills of his people, I said, "That would be wonderful." I calculated how many helpers I'd need. "Six should be plenty. How soon can they be in position?"

"Give me an hour. In the meantime, make yourselves at home." Fisk left.

"I still don't like it," Ari said as he swung up into Whiskey's saddle.

Janco mounted The Madam. "This is going to be fun."

"You said that about the Bejin ambush, and look how that turned out." Ari gathered the reins.

"There's just no way to stifle a sneeze once it reaches a critical level. Besides, no one was hurt."

"No one was arrested, either."

Janco waved a hand. "Details, details."

I helped Hilly into Kiki's saddle. She wore my cloak with the hood pulled down low over her forehead. "Listen to Ari and ignore Janco."

"Hey."

She smiled. "Will do."

The three of them left the stable, heading toward the Magician's Keep. I remained in a dark shadow with a view of the street. Would the cat follow them? It depended on his powers of observation.

"He didn't take the bait," Fisk said, standing next to me.

"Give it a few more minutes. He might have slipped out the back entrance."

We waited. After five minutes, there was still no movement and no signal from Tweet that he'd left the building. It seemed the cat realized Hilly hid under my cloak, even though we were of a similar size and build.

"Time for Plan B," I said. "Shall we?"

Fisk grinned. "We shall."

We peeked from the stable, glancing left and right as if searching for witnesses. Then we strode into the street, going in the opposite direction as Ari, Janco and Hilly. I wore a Helper's Guild uniform and had arranged my hair into a bun similar to Hilly's. We followed a predetermined route that appeared to be random, as if we were checking for a tail, but it allowed Fisk's helpers to relay information to us. The guild members knew every shortcut and alley in the Citadel and could reach certain intersections faster than us.

"Ah," Fisk said, catching sight of one of his helpers. "Smart kitty is following us."

"How soon will everyone be in position?"

"Let's take the scenic route and give them time to prepare."

As we continued walking through the streets, Fisk played tour guide, filling me in on the various buildings and businesses. "A few businessmen have copied me and converted the abandoned factories into living spaces. It has improved the living conditions in the Citadel's two resident quarters, and having four families live in one house is a thing of the past."

"That's wonderful news."

"It is, but there's still criminals and those who prey on the weak. If I can only expel them, then everyone can live in peace."

"It's a lovely goal, Fisk, but I've learned there will always be criminals. You can arrest them and prevent certain crimes, but they'll never be completely gone. They're even in Ixia, despite the Commander's soldiers patrolling the streets and watching the citizens. It's human nature."

"I guess you're right, but I'm still going to try."

I touched his arm. "Just please don't get yourself killed."

He placed his hand over mine and squeezed. "That's not in the plan."

"So that means you'll ask for help when things get too hot?"

His shoulders stiffened with a familiar stubbornness, and he dropped his hand. "Well…"

"Fisk, it's not a sign of weakness to ask for help. We're friends, and that is what friends do. Help each other."

"But then I should pay you like you pay me."

I shook my head. "Not how it works."

"Why not?"

"You need the money to run your business and give your helpers food, clothing and shelter, which is very important. Me, Ari, Janco, Valek and Leif don't need the money. We are paid and have all the necessities in life."

"I still feel like I'm taking advantage of you."

I lightly smacked the back of his thick skull. "Then donate some money to Child Services."

Fisk made a rude noise.

"They're inefficient because they don't have enough staff or resources."

"I'll think about it."

Progress! I let the subject drop. We walked in silence for a while. A few other people strode along the streets Fisk had chosen. Some nodded to him in greeting; others smiled. I spotted one of his helpers lurking in an alley, but she faded from sight once Fisk met her gaze.

"They're ready," he said.

My heart fluttered as my hand rested on my abdomen for a moment. I'd been the bait before. However, this time, I had a baby to keep safe. If Valek ever found out… No. Not going there. I concentrated on the plan.

Fisk took a few turns, then led me to an alley's entrance. He made a show of checking for a tail before we dashed inside. When the alley's rank fragrance turned my stomach, I thought of Janco whining about the stench. The alley deadended, but a few doors surrounded us. Fisk produced a key and stepped toward the one on the right.

"Hold it right there," a familiar voice ordered.

I spun. The Mosquito stood about twenty feet away. He aimed a crossbow at us. I wasn't expecting that particular weapon, but we could adapt.

"Hello, Kynan, or do you prefer to be called The Mosquito?" I asked.

"You don't really think Kynan is my name, do you?" He didn't wait for an answer. "Perhaps you did, since you believe I'm not very bright and would follow your Ixian friends."

"It was a good decoy," I said in my defense.

He huffed with amusement. "Maybe at night or if I was half-blind. Her posture on Kiki didn't match yours."

I'd say his powers of observation ranked pretty high. "You need to get a life if you've been watching me that long."

"I told you before. I don't give up, and I always finish a job before moving on."

I glanced at Fisk. He held his hands to the side.

"The boy can go," The Mosquito said, gesturing with his weapon.

Fisk hesitated.

A twang snapped, sending the bolt right between us. I jerked in surprise as the tip struck the building behind us. By the time we returned our attention to The Mosquito, he had loaded another bolt.

"You're not fast enough, boy. Now go on. Fetch help for Yelena."

"Go ahead, Fisk," I said.

Fisk frowned, but he strode past The Mosquito, who kept his weapon aimed at Fisk until he disappeared from view. Then he swung it back to me.

"That's new." I gestured to the crossbow. "What happened to your ice pick?" I asked.

"I learn from my mistakes. I'm not getting close to you until I'm sure you don't have any of those darts hidden in your clothes."

"Then it's in my best interest to keep you at a distance."

He laughed. "Yes, that would be right. But you're in luck. The game has changed."

"Funny, I'm not feeling very lucky." Actually, I was quite confident—one gesture from me and The Mosquito would be squashed.

"Cute. My client has changed his mind about you. Instead of killing you, he wants to talk to you."

"So he can kill me later?"

"All I know is you get a free pass this time. I don't have orders for next time."

I considered his offer. "Does your client have my brother?"

"Yes."

"Will he exchange him for me?"

"No. And if you're thinking you can use your...truth serum on me to get the location of your brother, I've no idea where my client is keeping him. My knowledge is limited just for that very reason." He shot me a sour look.

"I'm guessing Bruns...or rather your *client* isn't happy you blabbed." I couldn't resist needling him.

The Mosquito tightened his grip on the crossbow. "Is that your answer?"

"Where does Bruns wish to meet?"

"I don't know. I'm to inform him of your response, and then he'll tell me the location."

Smart. This way I couldn't detain him until after I'd learned the meeting place. Unless he lied about the extent of his knowledge.

"And I know all about your trap." The Mosquito glanced up at the windows on the second story. "Should I wave to the Ixians?"

Busted.

"You really do think I'm an idiot."

"Not anymore," I said.

He smiled. "Your answer?"

"Tell Bruns I'll meet with him."

"Excellent." The Mosquito backed away. He paused at the entrance, checked for an ambush and disappeared.

I replayed the encounter in my mind, but really couldn't determine a way that it could have gone any differently.

Fisk arrived with a handful of his helpers. "You let him go?"

"I didn't have much of a choice." I explained what had happened.

"I've assigned a team to keep an eye on him," Fisk said. "Maybe he'll lead us to his boss and where they're holding Leif."

"He's intelligent, so I doubt he'd be that careless. But it doesn't hurt to try."

The door into the alley swung open and Ari and Janco arrived. The red splotches on Ari's normally pale cheeks warned me. I braced for his lecture on the dangers of meeting with Bruns. He didn't disappoint, listing a number of horrific and creative outcomes. Janco had rubbed off on him.

"...not listening, are you?" Ari asked.

"I got the point. You're not happy and neither am I, but I see no other way."

"What do we do while we wait?" Janco asked.

What indeed? "We need to update Irys and..." My stomach soured. "And Mara. She needs to know what's going on."

"Can we trust the guards at the Keep not to turn us in to the Citadel's security forces?" Janco asked.

For the first time since I'd come to Sitia, I truly didn't know. "Fisk, can one of your helpers deliver a message to the Second Magician?"

"Yes. In the meantime, you're welcome to stay with me. I've guest rooms."

"Fancy," Janco said.

Pride momentarily eclipsed my anxiety for Leif. Fisk had turned into such a fine young man.

Irys and Mara arrived after supper. Both wore worried expressions. Mara fisted the fabric of her skirt. We settled in Fisk's living area. He had left earlier and hadn't returned. I sat next to Mara on the couch and held her cold hand in mine. Janco leaned against the door and Ari occupied the other chair across from Irys.

"No," Mara said when I'd finished detailing my conversation with The Mosquito. "You can't sacrifice yourself for Leif." She smoothed the wrinkles over her lap.

"It's not an exchange.," I assured her. "He just wants to talk. Plus we can follow him after—see if he'll lead us to Leif."

"And if he doesn't? What if something goes wrong?" Ari asked.

"Then I'll have a *talk* with him," Irys said. Her steely gaze promised results, and the magic detector flashed in response. "Let me know when the meeting is scheduled."

★ ★ ★

While we waited for a message from The Mosquito, my thoughts turned to Valek. It'd been sixteen days since we'd parted. I wondered if he waited at our rendezvous location or if he still hunted the Storm Thieves. Should I send a messenger? I asked Ari and Janco.

"If you do, he won't worry why we're not there, but if he hears about Leif, he'll come here," Ari said.

Not good. He needed to stay in Ixia. "What if I say we've just been delayed?"

"He'll come regardless." Janco crinkled his forehead in confusion. "You act like that's a bad thing. He can flatten that Mosquito."

"The Commander has forbidden him to leave Ixia," I said.

"That didn't stop Valek last month," Janco said. "He disobeyed a direct order from the Commander when he traveled to Lapeer to help you. Valek's never done that before. His loyalties have changed, so unless you're at the rendezvous location soon, expect to see him."

I played with the butterfly pendant Valek had carved for me. If Janco had noticed that Valek's priorities had switched, then it must be obvious to the Commander. No wonder he'd come down so hard on Valek.

"Then we'll have to conclude our business with Bruns as soon as possible," I said.

"No problem. We'll rescue Leif, bring down the Cartel and be home in time for our afternoon naps," Janco snarked.

I stood and slapped him on the back. "That's the spirit!" However, my insides churned with dread. This Cartel might be beyond our ability to stop, and convincing the Sitian Council would require more proof than we currently had. Drawing in a deep breath, I cleared all the things I couldn't control from my mind and focused on the most important issue: rescuing Leif.

Fisk drew on his network of information gatherers to collect any bit of news regarding the Cartel's location. They kept an eye on the businessmen who were suspected of having ties to the Cartel. Irys gave permission to Lindee, Fisk's accountant, to access the Citadel's records room. According to Fisk, she had a sharp mind and was a genius with numbers. Perhaps she'd find a bill of sale for a building that could be traced back to the Cartel.

I organized the intel, searching for clues and weak links, and tried to piece together their plans. Ari and Janco frequented the taverns in the government quarter, listening to the gossip.

The Mosquito's messenger arrived four long days after the encounter in the alley. The young boy waited outside for a reply. The letter said:

The meeting is now. Follow the boy. If you don't arrive in thirty minutes, my boss will be gone.

"No way," Ari said, reading over my shoulder. "We won't be able to have backup on site."

"I think that's the point," Janco said. "It's a trap."

"You can follow me to the meeting place, then send one of Fisk's helpers to fetch Irys. I'll delay as long as possible."

"No." Ari shook his head. "It's—"

"Our only chance to find Leif." I gestured to the papers spread on one of the kitchen tables. "There's nothing here." I stood and wrapped my cloak around my shoulders.

Ari and Janco scrambled to grab theirs, but Fisk stopped them.

"You're too noticeable. Let my people do the honors, and

MARIA V. SNYDER

they'll relay Yelena's position to you. You'll only be a minute behind her. I promise."

Ari straightened to his full height and peered down at me and Fisk. "First sign of trouble and we're coming in. Understand?"

"Yes, sir." I hurried outside and found the messenger. "Where are we going?"

The boy shrugged. "All I know is to go east." He turned right and headed east.

After a few blocks, another boy waited. His instructions had been to lead me south until we reached a third boy. Then a fourth, fifth, sixth and seventh. I had kept track of my whereabouts despite the serpentine route. But once we'd traveled into the southwestern resident quarter of the Citadel, I lost my exact location in the unfamiliar labyrinth of streets. We reached a dilapidated section. Wooden boards covered the windows and doors of the buildings. Broken glass and trash coated the walkways. The air smelled rancid.

The eighth boy led me to a broken-down shack. "Inside," he said.

I hesitated. "Are you sure?"

"Yes." He pulled open the warped door, revealing darkness. "After you."

Bruns hadn't said to come unarmed. I yanked my switchblade from its holder and triggered the blade.

The boy smirked. "Good luck with that."

Bracing for...well, anything, I entered. The floor creaked under my boots. After two steps the door clicked shut, and I stopped, unable to see in the utter blackness. He brushed past me and then swept aside a curtain. We stepped into a room filled with sunlight that streamed in from two skylights high above. I blinked at the expensive furnishings, rugs and solid walls. If I didn't know any better, I'd think I was in the living room of one of the Sitian Councilors and not in the poorest section of the Citadel. The shack must be an illusion to keep the neighbors away.

The boy indicated the couch. "Please have a seat. Can I get you something to drink?"

"Uh, no thanks."

"Mister Jewelrose will be here shortly." The boy disappeared through an alcove on the left.

I peered through the single small window facing a narrow street. A row of houses slumped against one another. A few people sat on porches or pulled wagons over the cobblestones. No familiar faces. I hoped Fisk's people hadn't lost me.

"My estate outside Kohinoor has a much better view," a male voice said behind me.

I turned. A tall, well-dressed man with graying black hair and gray eyes strode toward me. He held out his hand. "Bruns Jewelrose."

Without thinking, I shook it. "Yelena Liana Zaltana."

"Pleasure to meet you."

"Not from what I've heard."

He smiled. "That was just business, Yelena. Nothing personal."

I gaped at him. How could he believe that? I recovered from my shock. "I disagree. You hired an assassin to kill me. That's *very* personal."

"You were an obstacle to be eliminated, but now the situation has changed."

"Yay for me." Sarcasm sharpened my tone.

"Now, now. No need for that. Have a seat and we can discuss my proposal."

I remained standing. "Not until you tell me what happened to Leif. Is he okay? Where is he?"

"You're jumping ahead. Sit down and—"

"Not until I know Leif is alive and well."

Bruns tsked over my stubborn refusal to play nice. "All right." He settled on a leather couch and crossed his legs. "Come on in," he called.

A door opened, and Leif strode into the room. An intense relief washed through me, and I swayed. He rushed to hug me, keeping me upright. I clung to him. Was he real?

"Took you long enough," he said. "Good thing the food is delicious."

Yup. It was him. "Are you okay?"

"I'm fine."

"Good. I'm going to get you out of here." Somehow. I hoped.

"Thanks, but I don't need to be rescued."

I pulled away. "What?"

"I've joined the Cartel."

23

VALEK

"Are you talking about pirates?" Valek asked the young magician.

She knelt on the bow of the ship, soaking wet. "I guess. They pretended to be in distress, and we pulled alongside their ship to help. Except they boarded our ship. They had swords and they killed Nell and our first mate." She closed her eyes for a moment as if enduring a wave of pain. "And then tossed their bodies overboard."

"Did they know about your and your brother's magic?"

"I...don't think so. No one knew except Nell. She taught us how to control it, and then we helped her avoid the storms. Until...they came."

Someone must have known about the siblings. The pirates had targeted their ship for a reason.

The young magician drew in a deep breath. "We tried to use the storms and water to escape, but the...pirates caught and separated us. If one of us doesn't obey, then they will kill the other."

Valek doubted they would have carried out the threat. The siblings were too valuable to the pirates. But the girl was sixteen at most and didn't have the experience to recognize a bluff. Or the confidence to use her magic effectively.

"That's why you can't go to the island. As soon as Jibben sees you, he'll kill Zethan."

"Then we'll make sure he doesn't see me."

Endre arrived. Blood splattered his face and stained his tunic. "All are secured, boss."

"Any causalities?"

"Nah. Minor cuts and bruises. Most are kids, but there are a few adults in the mix." Endre glanced at the girl. "What about this one?"

"She's been spinning quite a tale." Valek told him about the pirates. "What do you think?"

"It explains quite a bit. And we can check the island."

"All right. Find crew who can sail this ship and who are willing to help us for a reduced sentence. Secure the others below. Have Annika find those steer disguises. We're going to need them."

"Yes, sir." Endre dashed away.

Valek studied the girl. Something about her blue eyes and sharp features seemed familiar. "What's your name?"

"Zohav."

"Are you willing to help us?"

"Do I have a choice?"

"It's in your best interests. If your story is true, and you were forced to steal, then you won't be arrested for theft."

Annika arrived with a mass of sopping-wet cloth. "They were all swept into the ocean when the waves attacked us." She frowned at Zohav. "Mikus is fishing the masks out now."

"Wring as much water out as you can and hang them to dry."

"Is there going to be another performance of Valek the steer?" Annika asked with a smile.

Zohav sucked in a sharp breath and scrambled away from

him. She released her control of the waves and the ship bucked on the suddenly rough seas. When her back hit the bow, she huddled in a tight ball.

"What did I say?" Annika grabbed the railing to keep from falling.

He considered. "My name."

"You are the most feared man in Ixia," Annika agreed.

"It can be tiresome."

"Then you should stop eating babies for breakfast."

He laughed. "But they're so delicious."

Annika swatted him on the arm. "Behave."

Valek returned to the problem at hand. The seas remained choppy, but the rain and wind had stopped when the storm moved inland. "Tell the others to prepare to reprise their roles as steers once we reach the island."

Annika nodded and strode away.

Valek approached Zohav and she cried out in terror. He crouched down to her level. "Your magic failed to work on me. Who did you think I was?"

"I thought…you were protected with…with one of those… shields," she stuttered. "You…you're going to kill us." It wasn't a question. "That's what Jibben threatened to do if we ever escaped—report us to *you*." Zohav hugged her knees to her chest. "I'm not going to help you murder my brother."

"Zohav, I'm not going to kill you or your brother."

"You're lying."

"Look at me," he ordered.

With obvious effort, she met his gaze.

"I promise that if your story is true, then I will ensure that you and Zethan are escorted to Sitia." Valek knew that would make Yelena happy, plus it was the right thing to do.

She shook her head. "I don't believe you. You've murdered thousands and are pure evil."

MARIA V. SNYDER

Thousands, eh? His reputation had expanded another order of magnitude.

"You're not reaching my brother." Huge waves crashed over the rails, as if to prove Zohav's point.

She planned to sink the ship. No doubt she loved her brother. Valek pulled a dart from his belt and pricked her arm.

Fury replaced her fear. "Poison! I knew you were going to kill us."

"Sleeping potion. Good night, Zohav." Valek waited until she slumped over, then gathered her in his arms.

He carried her to the main deck. Endre had assembled a crew willing to help sail the ship. In fact, they appeared eager to free their friends.

Valek handed Zohav to Endre. "Find a safe place for her to sleep off the potion while I brief the others."

"Yes, sir."

Valek explained his plan to the ship's crew. It followed the same idea as when they'd ambushed the ship. He and the soldiers would be disguised as the steers. Annika and the other handlers would resume their roles.

"We'll extinguish all but one lantern so it's too dark to see. Once we reach land, my soldiers will attack and neutralize the pirates. The crew will climb into the rigging and keep out of the way," Valek said.

"There are more of them than you," one boy called.

"How many more?" he asked.

"At least thirty."

A little less than double. "I don't expect that to be a problem. Make good use of your darts," he instructed his soldiers.

"What about Jibben?" another boy asked. "He's huge and deadly with his sword. I saw him cut one of his own men in half."

Nice guy. "Leave Jibben to me."

NIGHT STUDY

"Please kill him," a teen girl said.

"You think he deserves to die?" Valek asked.

"Yes. He locked my older sister in his room. She escaped twice. The first time they caught her hiding in the woods, and the second time she ran into the ocean and drowned herself."

A heaviness pulled on his heart. He could well imagine what the poor girl had endured. "I'm sorry."

"Why? It's not your fault."

"Ah, but it is. I'm in charge of keeping Ixia safe for all its citizens."

"That's impossible. My ma says there will always be sharks in the water. Nothing you can do about it except be careful where you swim."

"Your ma sounds like a smart lady."

"Yeah, she is. I miss her."

"Then we should cast off and take care of these sharks so you can go home."

The girl saluted him with a bony hand. "Aye, aye, Captain."

The ship rocked back and forth as it crested one wave after another. Some of the soldiers turned green, and a few rushed to vomit over the rail. They raced the sunrise to the island. If the sun rose before they landed, they'd lose the element of surprise. When the boys in the mast signaled that they neared the dock, Valek and the others donned their disguises.

Thuds vibrated through the ship as it bumped against the wooden pylons. The young teens hopped off and tied the ropes.

A gruff voice smashed through the clatter. "Why's the ship moving? Where's that bitch Zohav?"

"She got sick, sir," one of the boys said. "She's down below."

Good thinking. Valek approved.

"What took you so long?"

MARIA V. SNYDER

The same boy said, "One of them steers freaked, sir. Devil to get him on board."

Another smooth reply. The boy had recruitment potential.

"Hurry up with that gangplank," Gruff ordered.

The crew scrambled to comply. The boy paused near Valek. "That's Jibben." Then he hurried away.

Happy that he wouldn't have to chase Jibben down, Valek wrapped his hand around the hilt of his sword and thought of that girl's sister. The gangplank eased toward the dock, revealing a number of men and women. Valek had seconds to assess the enemy before they realized they faced armed soldiers and not a herd of beef. He counted six pirates on the dock and another four on land. The others must be nearby. Perhaps in the woods. They'd want to hide the buildings from the ships that passed by, but wouldn't want to be too far from the dock.

A big brute stood with his thick arms crossed over his chest. Two long braids flowed over his shoulders and a sharp curved blade hung from his leather belt—a cross between a scimitar and a cutlass. The brute had to be the infamous Jibben.

"What in hell? Who picked these scrawny steer?" Jibben asked.

Next to Jibben, a tall man with colorful tattoos along his arms peered at them. "They look...odd, Jib." He pointed. "That one's wearing boots."

And that was his cue. Valek yelled and tossed off the still-damp material. He ripped the mask from his face before drawing his sword. The soldiers followed his lead. They rushed onto the dock in a wedge formation.

The pirates cried a warning, called for backup and drew their weapons in time to meet the rush. While surprised, they didn't panic like the crew of the ship. His men bypassed Jibben, who squinted at the melee, confused, until Valek approached him. He smiled, revealing sharp teeth. Jibben appeared quite calm. So much for Valek being the most feared man in Ixia.

"Ah, the Commander's attack dog. I heard you were in town."

Valek wondered where he'd gotten the intel. "Then why did you send your crew to steal the steers?"

The man kept his smile, but tightened his grip on his strange sword in response.

"Was it greed or stupidity?" Valek asked. "Probably both. You really don't need those steers, but you just *had* to finish your shopping list." He tsked. "Greed and stupidity, the downfall of so many."

"Shut up." Jibben swung his sword, aiming for Valek's neck.

Valek ducked and spun, hooking his heel behind Jibben's left boot. But the man's stance was as solid as a tree trunk. Jibben swiped down at Valek's head. Valek rolled to the right and regained his feet. Okay, time for Plan B.

Jibben pressed his advantage, keeping his longer blade in motion like a pendulum on a clock. Valek backed away until he neared the edge of the dock. Timing it just right, Valek stepped forward and parried Jibben's swinging weapon with his broadsword. The man's curved blade slid right along Valek's, and its tip stabbed right into his abdomen.

Valek gasped as pain ringed his waist.

"Your fancy moves won't save you here." Jibben twisted his wrist.

Before Jibben could disembowel him, Valek jabbed his sword into Jibben's thigh. The man growled, shuffling back.

"At least I know enough to disarm my opponent first, then claim victory." Valek rubbed the fingers of his free hand along the cut on his stomach. Despite the searing burn, the injury wasn't deep. Relief energized him.

Now that Valek had an idea of what that curved blade

could do, he changed the line of his attack from head-on to an angled approach. Jibben was strong like Ari, but also surprisingly quick. Not as quick as Janco, but only a few could make that claim.

This time, when Valek parried Jibben's sword, he deflected the blade down. The tip of the curved sword missed him and Valek was able to cut into Jibben's arm. When he blocked Jibben's blade, knocking it high, Valek nicked the man's thick leg. Each near miss increased Jibben's frustration, causing him to make small but critical mistakes. Blood soon soaked the brute's sleeves and pants. The man swayed.

Valek tried his takedown again, spinning and hooking his heel. Jibben landed with an *oomph* and Valek pricked him with a dart filled with sleeping potion. When the brute relaxed, Valek stood and surveyed the scene.

Most of the soldiers held their own, but a few struggled with their opponents. Valek helped those in need as they advanced inland. The sun rose and the trees cast long shadows. He engaged in a couple fights that ended in a few moves. Jibben should have trained his crew better. Weaving in and out of the other matches, Valek pricked the pirates with darts.

The last pirate fell not long after the sun's arrival. Endre searched the buildings, while Mikus compiled a list of the stolen goods they found. Two other soldiers interviewed the young teens, who had been smart enough to keep away from the fighting.

Annika pointed to Valek's shirt. "You're bleeding."

"It's nothing."

She pulled a first-aid kit from her pack. "Sit."

He recognized that tone. It meant business. He sat on the steps leading up to the door of one of the island's cottages. All the structures but one had been built atop tall pylons, probably in case the island was swamped with water. It would take a fierce storm for the tide to reach the living areas of the buildings.

Annika inspected his wound and decided it needed to be sealed. She pulled his shirt off before he could stop her. If she noticed his still-healing heart-shaped scar, she didn't say a word. Instead, she concentrated on her task by cleaning the cut and applying Rand's glue.

To distract himself from the pain, he studied the structures the pirates had built. Arranged in a circle around a giant fire pit, the one-story cottages appeared to be for housing and storage. One oversize building had a ramp leading up to the first floor—probably for the livestock. All the surfaces had been painted with gray, green and brown paint in a camouflage pattern that blended in with the surroundings. The color combination would probably work during all seasons. Further proof that Jibben was no fool.

The island's trees had been cleared farther out to make room for the crops. Small green shoots poked through the newly plowed dirt.

Valek spotted Endre and waved him over for a report.

"We defeated all the pirates, sir," he said. "The kids have corroborated Zohav's story. There's another ship docked on the back side of the island. It's the *Sea Serpent*."

Ah, the other one that had been lost at sea. "Secure the criminals in the *Starfish*'s hold. And get the names of all the survivors. We'll match them to the manifest and ensure none of the pirates are pretending to be a victim. And find Zethan—he's Zohav's brother and should be among the teens."

"Yes, sir. We also found a few older teens locked in a jail, but we couldn't find a key and the lock is…complex."

"Once Annika is done, I'll open it. Have the soldiers load the stolen goods onto the other ship. Also find a crew for both ships. We'll set sail as soon as possible."

MARIA V. SNYDER

"Yes, sir."

By the time Annika finished, the cut throbbed. "Thanks," he said, donning his ripped shirt.

"What should I do now?" she asked.

"Check the others. Make sure no one else is wounded."

"Yes, sir."

Valek found the jail. It was on the ground floor of the only building not set atop tall pylons. The pirates hadn't cared if the occupants drowned during a storm. Inside, four grubby boys stood on the other side of a row of bars. The rest of the cell had been constructed with thick wooden planks.

Purple bruises marked the prisoners' faces. Their shirts had been torn, and dried blood stained the fabric, as well.

"I take it you're the troublemakers?"

"Who wants to know?" a tall boy with black hair and blue eyes demanded.

The boy resembled Zohav and must be her brother, Zethan.

"The person who is rescuing you," Valek said. He pulled his various lock picks from hidden pockets and worked on the complicated mechanism. After a few minutes, it popped open and he swung the door wide, letting them free. "Give your names to the sergeant. We could also use crew for the ships, if you'd like to help all of us get home."

Three of the boys grinned and took off, but Zethan remained.

"Where is my sister?" he demanded.

Magic swelled around him, pushing against Valek. He held his ground. "She's safe."

"I want to see her. Now."

"You're not in the position to be demanding anything, Zethan."

Zethan jerked back. "How did—"

"Zohav told me. She was worried that I'd kill you."

"Why?"

"Because of that magic you're gathering around you right now."

Recognition was followed by fear. The power disappeared. His control was impressive.

"Are you…?" Zethan asked. His voice barely a whisper.

"Going to kill you?"

He nodded.

"No, and don't call me a liar. I've already been accused of that by your sister. Trust me or not, just keep it to yourself, along with your abilities. Understand?"

"Yes."

Valek waited.

"Uh…yes, sir."

He led Zethan to the *Starfish*. Jibben remained on the dock, but his throat gaped open and blood pooled around him. The pirate's curved sword lay next to him, covered with the bright red liquid. Someone had slit Jibben's throat with his own weapon while Valek was busy. He had wanted to interrogate the pirate, but other than that, he wouldn't mourn the man's death. Perhaps the girl with the bony arms had taken matters into her own hands, meting out justice for her sister.

They boarded, and Valek escorted Zethan below. When they reached the Captain's quarters, the teen gasped and rushed to Zohav's side.

"What did you do to her?" he asked Valek.

"Relax, she's sleeping. Stay with her until I come for you. And if I feel any magic, no matter how small, you'll be joining her. Understand?"

"Yes, sir."

Valek paused at the threshold. With the siblings side by side, he realized they must be very close in age. "Are you twins?" he asked.

"Yes, sir."

MARIA V. SNYDER

"Do you have any other siblings?"

"An older brother."

"Does he have magic?"

"No, nor do our parents. We're the only ones."

Unlikely, but he'd go along with it for now.

They arrived at the port in Gandrel by midafternoon. Anxious to get on the road, Valek put Endre in charge. "Interrogate everyone and have the pirates processed by the security office in Gandrel. Once all the goods are distributed to the rightful owners, you and Annika are to report to the Castle to be reassigned, since your covers here have been blown."

"Yes, sir." Endre gave Valek what Janco would describe as the sad-puppy-dog look.

He suppressed a sigh. "Because you and Annika work so well together, I'll find a post that needs two agents." He'd either gotten soft, or it was just the idea of seeing Yelena soon that made him...nice. Bah.

Endre grinned. "Are you leaving now?"

"Yes. I'm taking the magicians to the Castle."

"Are you going to visit their parents first?"

Annoyed, Valek snapped, "Why would I do that?"

"They believe their children were lost at sea. I'd think it would be a kindness to stop by and let them see their kids for a couple hours."

A refusal pushed up Valek's throat, but he swallowed it down. Endre was right. Valek went to collect the twins, who had remained in the *Starfish* as ordered. Zohav had woken. She leaned against her brother, who had his arm around her shoulders. Good. They could leave right away. He questioned them on the location of their home.

"Our family knows nothing!" Zohav cried. "They have no magic. Leave them alone."

Her fear of him was growing tedious. "Fine. We won't visit them, then. Guess you don't wish to say goodbye."

"We live up near the northern ice sheet in MD-1," Zethan said.

Zohav yanked away and glared at her brother.

At least their home was close to the garrison. "Say goodbye to your friends. We're leaving in ten minutes. I'll meet you on the dock." Valek left.

Instead of going to the dock, he stayed on deck, drew his blowpipe and a couple darts from his pocket, and leaned over the rail opposite the pier. Sure enough, the large porthole in the Captain's quarter's below swung open, and Zohav glanced out. Magic thickened the air around him. Then the water next to the ship flattened and hardened. Interesting.

Valek watched as Zohav then Zethan climbed from the window and stood on the flat water. Impressive. At their age, that level of control was unheard-of. The Master Magicians were going to be thrilled.

"Where are you going?" Valek asked.

Zohav gasped and clutched Zethan's arm as he looked up at Valek. The boy's face creased in chagrin. Valek brandished the blowpipe. "Unless you wish to drown, come up here. Now."

Zethan said something to Zohav. She shook her head. Valek loaded a dart into the pipe and pressed the weapon to his lips. He aimed for the boy. If he shot her, they'd drown for sure. Zohav noticed the motion. She scowled at Valek. At least it was better than terror.

Then the flat water rose, lifting the siblings to the deck. Valek extended his hand and helped Zohav onto the ship as Zethan hopped down lightly next to her.

"Any more escape attempts, and I will knock both of you unconscious and transport you to the Citadel like two sacks of flour. Understand?"

MARIA V. SNYDER

"Citadel?" Zethan asked.

"Yes. I told Zohav I would escort you both there."

"He's lying. He's going to take us to his Commander so he can publicly execute us."

This was going to be a long trip. "Let's go. I want to reach the garrison before dark."

Valek stayed a step behind the siblings. They glanced at him from time to time, but kept quiet. They didn't arrive at MD-1's garrison until well after supper.

Colonel Ransley welcomed him back with a hot meal and an offer to give the siblings their own rooms.

"No, thank you, they stay with me," Valek said. Then he filled him in on how the Storm Thieves were apprehended, but didn't mention Zethan's and Zohav's magic.

"We haven't had a problem with pirates in decades," Ransley said. "No wonder the coastal security forces had a difficult time locating them."

Exhausted from staying up two nights with little sleep, Valek declined drinks with the Colonel. "We're leaving early in the morning. Let the stable boys know I'll need Onyx and another horse saddled and ready to go."

"Yes, sir."

In the large guest quarters, Valek dragged one of the four beds over to the door, blocking it. "I'm a very light sleeper," he warned the twins. "Sounds, movement or magic will wake me." Valek drew two daggers, one for each hand, and stretched out on the bed. "I'd suggest you get some sleep. Tomorrow is going to be a long day."

As he closed his eyes, he wondered if Yelena waited for him at the rendezvous location. Valek calculated how long it would take them to reach it, including the fact that the twins would slow him down. Ten days if he was being optimistic, twelve if he wasn't.

A whispered argument woke him in the middle of the night.

"...not being nice. You're putting our family at risk, Zee."

"Don't you want to see Mother, Father and Zeb? When we were captured by Jibben, I thought I'd never see any of them again."

"Of course I do. But they think we were lost at sea. Isn't that better than knowing we're going to be executed?"

"He said—"

"Don't be a fool. The law is clear. Plus he has executed hundreds of magicians. Why would we be the exception?"

Normally Valek encouraged such exaggerations—fear was a powerful motivator—but this time, it irked him. He pushed up on one elbow. "I've killed twenty-three magicians, and if you two don't shut up and go to sleep, I'll add two more to my total."

He lay back down. The number had been an estimate. When he'd been dispatched to investigate reports of a teen with powers, he'd arrived and soon after, the person with magic disappeared. However, no one knew he'd arranged for him or her to escape across the border. Everyone believed he'd killed the teen. Even the Commander.

Hedda and Arbon had both accused him of blind loyalty. And while he'd been loyal to the Commander all these years, he hadn't been as blind nor as completely obedient as everyone assumed.

When Valek arrived in the stable the next morning, Onyx and a gray horse named Smoke were saddled and ready for travel. Zohav and Zethan kept their distance while the stable boy tied on their bags. They'd acquired fresh uniforms and a few personal items from the garrison's commissary.

Valek petted Onyx's neck, then checked his legs for hot spots. His coat gleamed and the black horse appeared healthy.

MARIA V. SNYDER

"Tell Smoke to follow you," he said to Onyx before mounting. "Zethan, you'll ride Smoke, and Zohav, you're with me."

The girl frowned, but she listened to the stable boy's instructions and soon settled behind Valek. Zethan also received a quick lesson on how to mount and steer the horse. The boy grinned in anticipation. Just like Valek's older twin brothers—Victor had been cautious and protective, while Viliam had rushed headlong into any adventure.

Valek turned to Zohav. "Which way?"

She pressed her lips together, but then told him to follow the road that headed northeast.

Eager for the exercise, Onyx set a fast pace. Valek glanced at Zethan, who bounced in the saddle, but appeared to be enjoying the speed.

When Onyx finally slowed, Valek rode beside Smoke. "How did you end up on the coast?" he asked Zethan.

Zethan glanced at his sister, as if seeking permission to speak. After a brief hesitation, he said, "After we turned fourteen, it became obvious that we both had magic. Our father searched for a teacher to help us learn how to control it before anyone found out. Nell…" He paused and swallowed, staring at his hands, gripping the reins much harder than necessary. "Nell taught us these last two years. She has…had the ability to call the wind, and she used it when sailing or to beat all the other fishing boats to the prime spots."

"What are your abilities?" Valek asked.

"Zee," Zohav warned.

"It doesn't matter now, Zo. Besides, he rescued us from the pirates."

"We're still prisoners."

"She has a point," Valek said. "You should never tell your enemy the extent of your powers, or he'll find ways to counter them." Like trapping you in a null shield, Valek thought sourly.

"I guess," Zethan agreed. "Although I don't know how someone could counter a storm. I can call them and then direct their paths."

"Zee!"

Valek suppressed a smile. "Actually, Stormdancers could turn your storm into a gentle rain."

"Really? What are Stormdancers?"

Valek explained the magicians to Zethan. "The Commander has even allowed Kade Stormdance to harvest the energy from the blizzards sweeping down from the northern ice sheet."

Zethan groaned. "Great. The one year I don't have to shovel snow, and I'm trapped on some island in the middle of the Sunset Ocean."

"I don't believe the Commander would let a magician into Ixia," Zohav said.

Valek twisted in his seat. "That's three. Call me a liar one more time, and you'll be turned into cargo. I also expect an apology when you finally understand."

Zohav stared at him, not backing down an inch. Almost all of her fear of him had been transformed into anger. In the sunlight, the blue in her eyes sparkled like sapphires. He suspected if he flattened his gaze into his killer's demeanor, she'd become frightened once more. But he'd rather have her angry than scared. He faced forward, and their conversation became limited to directions to their town.

They stopped briefly at noon for a quick dinner. The Colonel had provided full travel rations for the three of them.

Zethan couldn't contain his curiosity and asked, "What other types of magicians are there?"

Valek explained about the Master Magicians and the various magical abilities of the others. "Some people have what's called a One-Trick, which is one ability that is more instinc-

MARIA V. SNYDER

tive than learned. They don't have to worry about flaming out or being influenced by other, more powerful magicians."

"Flaming out? Should we be worried?" Zethan asked.

"No. You're in control of your powers, and you have Nell to thank for that. Otherwise, you would have grabbed more and more power until it overwhelmed you. By that point, the Master Magicians in Sitia would have sensed your presence and dispatched an...assassin to end your life before you flamed out. When a flameout happens, you not only kill yourself, but you ruin the power blanket for the other magicians."

Zethan rocked back on his heels. "Wow."

"You know an awful lot about magic and magicians. Is that so you can *counter* them?" Zohav asked.

"Knowing your enemy is always important, but I learned most of this from my heart mate, who has magic."

Zohav gaped at him. "*You* have a heart mate?"

"Who has magic, Zo. Magic! He's not going to kill us or she'll get mad at him. Right?"

"She would indeed."

"What about those twenty-three others you assassinated? Does she know about them?" Zohav asked.

"Yes. In fact, she has neutralized a number of magicians, as well. Just because a person has magic doesn't mean they're good people. Think about what Jibben did using your magic. Can you imagine what he'd do with his own?"

Their queasy expressions said it all. Lecture over, Valek wrapped the remaining cheese, packed it away and mounted Onyx.

Before Zohav stepped up, she said in a low voice, "I'm glad you killed Jibben."

"Me, too. Bastard got what he deserved." Zethan slashed a finger along his neck.

Valek didn't bother to correct them, and it was a quiet ride to—"Icefaren? You live in Icefaren?" he asked.

"I told you it was near the northern ice sheet," Zethan said. "Not many towns up here."

True. However, Valek never considered that they lived in his hometown. In his mind, only two people lived there—his parents, and no one else. According to the reports from his agents, his parents still resided in Icefaren.

Zethan spurred Smoke next to Valek. "I'll take point. If that's okay?" The teen had become comfortable riding a horse pretty quick.

"If you're about to fall off the horse, grab his mane and not the saddle," Valek instructed. "You won't hurt him, and a saddle can move with your weight."

"Mane, not saddle. Got it." Zethan pulled ahead.

Onyx stayed right behind Smoke, and Valek kept his attention on the boy. Falling off a horse at speed could be deadly, but he was glad to see Zethan had a natural grace and good balance.

When the horses stopped at a gate, Zethan jumped off Smoke and cleared the fence in one long stride. Zohav made an *ah* sound, slid from the saddle and took off after her brother. They raced to the house.

It was only then that Valek realized where they were. He stared at the familiar house as ice replaced the blood in his veins. His stomach cramped as visions of his murdered brothers flashed in his memory. With an extreme effort, he reigned in his emotions. Of course his parents had moved. His father was sixty-three by now and must be retired, and his mother was sixty. The five-bedroom house and adjacent tannery was too big for the two of them.

A door banged. Valek grabbed the hilt of his sword and turned. Two men stepped from the tannery. The older man stopped and stared at Valek as if he'd seen a ghost. Valek's heart pushed against his ribs and lungs as if it was a bubble about to burst. The pressure made it impossible for Valek to draw a breath.

The young man glanced between them. "Dad, what's wrong? Who is he?"

24

JANCO

"What do you mean, you *lost* her?" Ari demanded of one of Fisk's Helper's Guild members.

Janco put a hand on his partner's meaty arm. "Easy, big guy. You're scaring her." The poor thing looked to be about eight years old and fifty pounds. He'd seen sand spiders bigger than her.

"I don't care. We shouldn't have let a bunch of kids keep track of Yelena."

"I doubt we could have done any better. That relay system was genius!"

Ari glowered. "Valek charged us to keep her safe. If she—"

"Keeping her safe is almost impossible, and Valek knows it, Ari. Now, let me handle this." Janco crouched down to the girl's eye level. "Can you show me where you last saw her?"

She nodded and turned. They followed her through the busy streets of the Citadel and into the quieter residence quarters. She headed southwest and zigzagged through a maze of alleys and streets. No wonder she'd lost the trail. This place was a tracker's worst nightmare. Well, an average tracker. Janco was far from average.

The girl stopped at an intersection. "I turned this corner and...poof, they were gone."

He glanced around. From this point, there were four narrow alleys that branched off in different directions. He checked each one for any signs of Yelena—a peppermint or dart or bit of milk oat she might have dropped. No luck. Yelena probably assumed they were close behind her. Janco considered the timing and thought they should be nearing the final destination. He checked each narrow path. At the end of the third one, he found a chewed toothpick, as if someone had waited there.

"How many relays did they have?" he asked the girl.

"I counted seven before I lost her."

This one might be the last relay. From this point there were two alleys. Unable to find anything to distinguish one from the other, Janco picked one and closed his eyes. He inhaled, drawing the air slowly through his nose. Nothing but garbage and the typical city stink. He repeated the action in the other road. Same odors, but this time he also detected a faint whiff of lavender.

"This way," he said, hurrying down the tight throughway. It ended in a round courtyard with five different exits.

An uneasy, crawly sensation tickled his skin. Magic. Faint magic. Janco concentrated, seeking that unsettling...substance. Once again he closed his eyes and moved toward the nebulousness that repelled him. The creepy crawlies increased when he faced south.

He led Ari and the girl down an uneven sidewalk. Weeds grew between the cracks and glass crunched under his boots. The broken windows had been boarded over and the houses appeared to have been abandoned and left to squatters.

"I don't think you'll find this area listed in the guide book," Ari said.

"It's a little-known spot that should remain little-known,"

Janco agreed. Plus it hurt his scar. The pain increased, then lessened after he walked past a run-down shack. "You've got to be kidding me."

"What's wrong?" Ari asked.

"The complete and utter lack of creativity. That shack is an illusion."

"Okay, let's go." Ari yanked his scimitar and charged toward it.

Janco stepped in front of him. "Hold on. We don't know what's on the other side. And it might trigger an alarm." He paused as he realized *he* was being the sensible one. How about that? There was a first time for everything. Janco herded them back to the courtyard and out of sight. "Spider Girl, go fetch Fisk and as many of his minions as you can. Pronto!"

She flipped him the finger, but scurried away.

"Now what?" Ari asked.

"The illusion is hiding another building, so we case the joint. See if there are any other entrances. These houses are all jumbled together. They have to be connected."

"All right. I'll loop around back and you take the roof."

Janco eyed the sagging rooftops—some peaked, others flat. "If you hear a tremendous crash, that would be me falling through the shingles."

Ari didn't bother to reply. He slipped around the row of houses without making a sound. Janco sighed and studied the closest dwelling. The drainpipe looked sketchy, and the wooden siding bowed outward as if the house had been stuffed full. The corner of the building might be okay to climb up, as long as the nails hadn't rusted through.

A skittery feeling brushed his back. Janco spun around, searching for the cause. The courtyard was empty. He scanned the windows, but no one watched him. However, he couldn't shake the certainty that someone or something had a keen

MARIA V. SNYDER

interest in him. Ignoring the strangeness, he scaled the two-story structure and reached the roof.

Keeping low and testing each step before he put his full weight on it, he headed toward the shack. A number of squeals, squeaks and groans followed his progress. He wondered if any of the residents would investigate the noises or if they'd think it'd be safer to remain indoors. In this neighborhood, he guessed they'd stay inside.

As he drew closer, the quality of the roofs changed. The timber beneath his boots no longer dipped with his weight. The outer layer still resembled a patchwork, but the foundation was strong. His scar tweaked with pain just as he reached a smooth, flat roof with two skylights—quite a surprise.

Janco tiptoed closer, then laid flat on his stomach to peek inside. It took a few seconds for his eyes to adjust to the darker interior. He clamped down on a shout. Yelena lay on a couch below. She appeared to be sleeping, or maybe paralyzed by Curare. Janco fervently hoped it was one of those two, and that she wasn't dead. Before he could move, four men arrived. They carried a wooden crate with them, and then they lifted Yelena and packed her inside it, as if she were a piece of furniture!

He stared in shock as they wheeled the box from the room. *Must. Follow. Box.*

Janco had no memory of his trip back to the courtyard.

"Slow down, you're not making any sense," Ari said. "What's this about a box?"

Fisk and his minions arrived.

Janco explained what had happened. "We need to find that box. Spread out and search."

"Won't work," Fisk said. "This place is a labyrinth, and if you know the layout, you can get from one end to the other without being seen. If she's in a box, then they're not planning on keeping her here."

"Which means they're probably putting her on a wagon along with other goods to smuggle her from the Citadel," Ari said.

"The west gate," Janco said. "It's the closest."

"And the most obvious," Fisk said.

"But they don't know I know." Janco thumped his chest.

"Good point. Fisk, can you show us the shortest way to the gate?"

"Of course." He gave orders to a couple of his minions and then took off at a jog.

"What if we're too late?" Janco asked, keeping pace with Ari. "Or we don't spot it? There was nothing remarkable about that particular box."

"Think positive."

They reached the gate after two lifetimes. Fisk told them to wait while he bribed the guards to let him look at the logbook. Janco fidgeted, unable to endure even a few seconds of delay.

When Fisk returned, he said, "No wagons have left this afternoon. I sent my people to watch the north and south gates while we keep an eye on this one."

The three of them split up so they covered all possible angles. Fisk took the high ground to look down into the wagons. Ari was stationed outside the gate. And Janco waited in the shadow of the guardhouse. If a covered wagon arrived, Janco would peek under the tarp before it left.

In the end, it wasn't a box that tipped Janco off. It was the driver of the wagon. He just about fainted when he spotted Leif chatting with the gate guards. Stunned for a moment, Janco only had time to slip under the tarp before the wagon pulled away.

MARIA V. SNYDER

25

YELENA

I woke with a horrible headache and my mouth as dry as sawdust. Confused, I peered at my surroundings. The simple room had a night table, a single bed, one door and unadorned white walls. Not Fisk's colorful guest room. Something wasn't quite right. I couldn't move. Curare!

Panicked, I thrashed and stopped when I realized my movements were only limited, not paralyzed. Just my hands and feet had been secured. What did it say about my life when I took comfort in that?

Taking a few deep breaths, I calmed my racing heart. I concentrated on the facts. My symptoms matched being drugged with sleeping potion. Concern for the baby burned, and it triggered other worries. And then I remembered. Leif! He'd been captured. Yet that wasn't completely true. He was okay, but not okay. My thoughts spun and I closed my eyes. Perhaps I'd wake a second time and everything would be clear.

The doorknob rattled, and I opened my eyes in time to see Leif enter. He carried a tray of food. My relief at seeing him fizzled when Bruns Jewelrose and a couple goons followed him into my room. My memory jerked to life, and my arm burned where my rat bastard of a brother had pricked me with sleeping potion. I glared at Leif.

"I had to do it," Leif said. "You wouldn't listen to reason, and Bruns was worried Ari and Janco would find us."

"That's because nothing Bruns said was reasonable," I said.

"I thought the same thing at first. But you really need to see what he's done here. It's wonderful." Leif used the same tone he used to describe a delicious stew.

"Do I have a choice?"

"Of course," Bruns said. "Just finish hearing me out, and then decide."

"And if I still think you're a raving lunatic?"

Bruns pressed his lips together and smoothed an invisible wrinkle on his sleeve. "Then we'll discuss your options."

"Options, eh?" My imagination produced a number of horrific scenarios. I quelled my emotions. In this situation, I suspected logic and cold calculation would be required. "All right. I'll listen."

Leif smiled. One of the goons placed a chair near the bottom of my bed while the other freed my wrists. I sat up and resisted the urge to check my clothing for my lock picks and switchblade. Bruns sat in the chair.

Leif placed the tray on my lap. "You'll feel better once you've eaten. The chef is an artist. Everything he makes is divine."

I started with the water, draining half in one gulp. Bruns explained his theory about the Commander's imminent invasion. I half listened as I tried the stew. Leif hadn't been exaggerating. The broth had a nice balance of sweet and spicy. After I swallowed, I picked up on a subtle aftertaste. It tasted familiar. It took me another three bites to identify the substance. Theobroma.

Putting the spoon down, I reached for the water.

"Something wrong with the food?" Bruns asked.

MARIA V. SNYDER

"No. My stomach is still unsettled," I lied. "You were talking about Sitia's assets…" I prompted.

Bruns continued with his logical yet warped reasoning for protecting Sitia. I glanced at my brother. His expression was one of rapt devotion. No surprise, considering he'd probably consumed mass quantities of the Theobroma-laced food. The substance lowered a magician's resistance to magical influence and rendered a person without magic very susceptible to suggestion.

I listened to Bruns's well-rehearsed speech and agreed to take a tour of his facilities. They freed my ankles.

"Before we go, I'd like to talk with my brother. In private," I said.

"Of course." Bruns stood and flicked invisible dust from his pants. "We'll be right outside waiting for you." He left with his goons.

Leif stepped back. "You're not going to get upset again, are you?"

"No. I understand what's going on here."

Relief smoothed his features. "Finally! Isn't Bruns a genius?"

Not the word I'd use, but I had to choose my words with care. "Leif, there's a good reason why you love the food. It's been cooked with Theobroma."

His brow crinkled. "You must be mistaken."

"You know I have a sensitive palate." My survival had depended on it when I'd been the Commander's food taster. "Take a bite."

He did. Concern flashed, then he smiled. "Of course! It makes total sense. The Commander has Curare, and Bruns wants to protect our soldiers. If they're hit with a dart, the Theobroma will keep them from becoming paralyzed. I told you he's a genius."

So close. "But the substance also has other effects. That's why you're helping Bruns."

"No, it isn't. He wants to protect Sitia and so do I." Leif crossed his arms and stiffened into his stubborn stance.

But his gaze held a tiny seed of doubt.

"Come on, Bruns is waiting for us." Leif opened the door. Wrapping his hand around my upper arm, he escorted me out.

Bruns glanced at each of us. "Is everything all right?"

"Yelena is still not convinced," Leif said. "But I'm sure she'll come around in a few days, just like I did." He frowned at me.

I kept my expression neutral, but inside I allowed hope to grow. Perhaps my comments would snap my brother out of it.

Bruns showed me his garrison and demonstrated an impressive mock battle. His ideas and concerns for Sitia's battle readiness were sound; it was his execution that lacked basic morals. Leif remained Bruns's biggest cheerleader.

As we watched a training session, I asked Bruns, "Why did you change your mind about me?"

"My reasons were twofold. Assassinating you always came with the risk your heart mate would trace the hit back to me. When the Commander sent his other assassin after you, I'd hoped he'd think the second hit was also ordered by the Commander, and therefore it'd be a major upset in the Ixian leadership."

I kept quiet about just how much of an upset there was between Valek and the Commander right now. "And the second?"

"Your brother convinced me that your knowledge and intelligence would be an asset, despite the fact you no longer have magic. Also, the Commander has blocked your magic somehow, and we need to learn how he achieved this. If he can do it to you, he'll do it to the others. And while I'm all for no more magicians..." He frowned. "We need them for the upcoming invasion."

MARIA V. SNYDER

What a swell guy. He had a few things wrong, but I wasn't going to correct him.

"And there's also your knowledge of Ixian tactics and their military that will aid us."

Ah. I wondered what Bruns would do if I told him Valek suspected the Commander planned to invade after the Fire Festival a mere six months away. Probably freak out and kidnap every magician in Sitia. We looped back to the magicians' barracks.

"I realize it's quite a bit to take in," Bruns said. "I'll give you a few days to think about it before asking for your answer." He indicated the two goons who had stayed close by for the entire tour. "They will remain with you to answer any questions you might have. Feel free to explore the garrison. The dining hall is open all day."

"What happens if I decide not to join and wish to leave?" I asked.

Bruns's smile failed to reach his eyes. "I don't think that will be an issue."

"And if it is?"

"You're a smart girl, Yelena. You know there are always casualties during a war."

Before I could respond to the threat, Leif linked his arm in mine.

"Come on, sis, you're exhausted. You'll think better tomorrow. I'll fetch you supper."

Leif escorted me to the white room. The goons trailed us, but remained in the hall. Probably taking up flanking positions by the door, which Leif closed.

"Don't bother bringing me any food," I said. "I'll find my own."

"You're being paranoid. Bruns is—"

"Killing magicians, hiring assassins, kidnapping people and committing treason."

He glowered at me.

"You tasted the Theobroma. Come on, Leif, think about it."

"You're wrong."

I almost groaned in exasperation. "Okay, then prove it. Stop eating the food for a couple days and see if you still feel the same way about Bruns."

Leif gasped. "Stop eating?"

"At least find food that isn't tainted by Theobroma. Can you do that for me?"

He met my gaze. "And if I prove you wrong, will you join Bruns?"

"Yes."

Over the next three days, I tested the limits of my imprisonment. The goons bookended me whenever I left my room and kept within two paces of me at all times. Leif brought our meals to my room. It was mostly fruit and raw vegetables— the only edibles not tainted with Theobroma. He ate with me and griped about the food, but he was determined to prove me wrong.

Even with all the various war preparations going on, I spent most of my time in the armory. A number of the new weapons fascinated me, and I practiced with a few at the range. It was amusing to see the goon brothers so tense and ready to tackle me should I aim a weapon at them. Amusing and infuriating, since they completely blocked any opportunity for me to escape.

I also had to fight against the constant barrage of positive thoughts about Bruns and his efforts. Suspecting a magician able to mentally communicate these good feelings to everyone, I asked Leif about it when he brought supper that night.

"I didn't notice it before, but..."

"But what?"

"Oh, for sand's sake! You were right. Since I've been Theobroma-free, it stinks big-time." He speared a piece of broccoli with his fork. "Happy now?"

"Yes!" Relief flowed through me. "What's been going on?"

"There are magicians arriving daily who are already on Bruns's team. I'm guessing his recruiters are using Theobroma to convince them."

That was disturbing. "How is he getting to them?"

"Probably the same way he's doing it here, by spiking their food."

"Do you know where we are?" I asked.

"Krystal Clan's garrison, near the coast."

"Do you know where the other training areas are?"

"No. But I've been Bruns's best buddy, and I'm hoping to be part of his inner circle soon. He's assigned me to convince you to be on our side, so you're going to have to spout the bullshit to keep my cover."

"Can't wait," I said drily.

"I hope you're a better actress than that, little sis, or we're all in trouble."

As we finished our meals, I had an idea. "Is there any way to swap the Theobroma for a substance that tastes like it, but doesn't have the same magical properties?"

"I wish. Theobroma is one of a kind."

"Do you have a plan?"

"I suggest you play nice, show up for meals and pretend to be influenced by Bruns."

"Then what?"

"We gain his trust and find the chink in his armor. Then we send a message to Ari and Janco and Irys."

It sounded easy, except... "We can't eat the food in the dining room."

"But I can't keep coming here. Bruns is getting suspicious." Leif rubbed his chin. "And frankly, I'm sick of eating nothing but fruit and vegetables. I'm friends with Alvar, the chef—let me see what I can do." He stood, squeezed my hand and turned to go.

I made a quick decision. "Leif."

"Yes?"

"Make sure you get plenty of food. I'm eating for two."

He jerked as if I'd slapped him. Then a range of emotions crossed his face—surprise, excitement, worry and then concern. "You shouldn't have risked the baby for me!"

"I couldn't *not* try to rescue you."

Leif wrapped me in a hug. "I'm sorry. I shouldn't have yelled at you. Congrats, sis. Does Valek know?"

"Yes."

"Then we'd better escape before he sends the entire Ixian army to rescue you."

The next morning I met with Leif in the dining room. He had two plates of scrambled eggs and bacon waiting for me. I thanked him before shoveling the food into my mouth. Leif filled me in on how he'd offered to help Alvar with the morning rush and managed to snag a few servings of eggs before they were glazed with a *special* sauce.

"Holy snow cats! There's Dax Greenblade." Leif gazed over my shoulder.

I crushed my napkin in my hands to keep from turning around. Was he captured? "Does he have goons with him?"

"No. Just a goofy smile, and he's heading this way." Leif leaned forward. "Remember, we love Bruns."

"Leif! Yelena! So this is where you two have been hiding," Dax said. "I should have known you'd be where all the action is."

I glanced way up at the tall man with light green eyes. For him, I didn't need to fake a smile. He'd been my first friend when I'd been a student at the Magician's Keep. "Hi, Dax! Did you just arrive?"

"Yup. Isn't this place great? Much better than that stuffy old Keep, where we don't do anything but study. What a waste of time. Now we can contribute to the welfare of Sitia."

"Yes, isn't it wonderful?" The words tasted like ash on my tongue.

"That looks yummy," Dax said. "I'm famished."

I grabbed his wrist before he could leave. "You can have the rest of mine. It's still warm."

"Great." He dug into my plate with abandon.

"So how did you hear about this place?" I asked.

"One of the students, I think," Dax said between mouthfuls. "This is good, but not as good as the Keep's."

"Really?" Leif asked.

"Yeah. We got a new chef and her dishes are…divine!"

Nausea bubbled in my stomach. I met Leif's equally horrified gaze. If Bruns had managed to put Theobroma into the food at the Keep…

"I don't remember a new chef," Leif said. "When did she start?"

"Oh, a couple weeks ago, I think." He shrugged, oblivious to our alarm.

I sagged back in my chair. Everyone at the Keep ate their meals at the dining room, including Irys and Bain, the two most powerful magicians in Sitia.

Leif used a series of subtle hand signals, telling me to stick to the plan.

I replied, *What plan?*

Get Bruns to trust us.

And then?

We stop him.

That's not a plan.

Do you have anything better?

No.

Discouraged, I said goodbye to Leif and Dax. I scanned the faces in the dining room as I left, searching for more magicians from the Keep. I recognized four others. At this point, I thought only the Commander's army could stop Bruns. But what if he couldn't?

I was so preoccupied, I tripped and sprawled on the floor.

Before my goons could help me, another soldier swooped in and lifted me to my feet. "Are you all right?" he asked.

I met Janco's gaze without visibly reacting. Inside, my heart was doing a jig. "Yes. Just a bit clumsy."

"Not your fault—there are *lots* of people in here. It's hard to move."

My depression lifted. Help had arrived! "All the better for when we go to war."

"True. Bruns will lead us to victory."

I took a step, but wobbled and fell into Janco, who caught me with ease. He'd dyed his hair red and wore a fake ear that covered his scars.

"Don't eat the food," I whispered in his good ear before straightening. "Guess I must have tweaked my ankle." I gestured to my goons and let them support me as I limped from the dining room. Ha! *How's that for acting!*

My elation over seeing Janco faded as I realized that even with more people on our side we still didn't have a clue how to stop Bruns.

Bruns joined me in the armory the next day. I'd been practicing using one of the new blowpipes that had scoring in the barrel to improve accuracy and distance. Too bad the dart wasn't filled with poison. That would have been a quick way to solve the problem of Bruns.

MARIA V. SNYDER

"I heard you twisted your ankle. How are you doing?" Bruns asked.

I smiled at him. "That's so sweet of you to ask. It was a minor sprain. Nothing a good night's sleep couldn't take care of."

"Wonderful. Leif tells me you've changed your mind about me," Bruns said.

It about killed me, but I stretched my lips wider and beamed at him. "Yes, I was being so silly. I mean, once I thought about it, I wondered why I would protect the Commander when he fired me as the Liaison."

"Oh? I hadn't heard that. Let's go to my office and have a little chat."

"All right."

With his arm linked in mine as if we were old friends, he led me to the main administration building in the center of the garrison. Before entering, Bruns ordered my goons to remain outside. As we climbed to the top floor, I searched my memory for any bits of information that I could give to Bruns about the Commander.

We arrived at a waiting room, complete with a pretty secretary. She handed him a stack of papers and mentioned a number of people who had been looking for him.

"I'll deal with them later. Can you bring us a pot of tea, please?"

She jumped to her feet. "Yes, sir."

Opening a door behind her desk, Bruns escorted me into his vast office. It occupied the rest of the fifth floor. The sleek furniture was made of ebony wood. My boots sank into lush carpets, and the opulent paintings had gold frames. Floor-to-ceiling windows covered the entire back wall. Unable to resist, I gazed at the view. Sunlight glinted off the Jade Sea in the distance. Right below were the training yards and armory.

"Did you buy the garrison?" I asked, pressing my hand on the glass.

"No. Councilor Krystal agreed that we needed to prepare for war and offered it to me."

"How many other Councilors are helping you?"

"I believe I'm supposed to be asking the questions." Bruns's voice held a dangerous tone.

Uh-oh. I turned. "Sorry! I shouldn't ask such obvious questions. Of course *all* the Councilors support you. You're going to save Sitia."

Bruns relaxed. "Sit down, Yelena."

I sat in one of the leather armchairs. The dark maroon color reminded me of dried blood. Bruns tossed the papers on his desk before sitting across from me.

"Do you know where Valek is?" he asked.

An easy question. "Not exactly. When we parted, he was headed to the coast of MD-1 to deal with Storm Thieves."

"How long ago was that?"

I calculated. "Twenty-three days."

"Do you think that's enough time for him to finish?"

"I don't know. It depends on how smart the thieves are."

"Is it possible that he followed you to Sitia instead of going to the coast?"

"Uh..." That would mean he'd lied to me. Valek might not tell me everything, but he wouldn't lie to me. "It's possible, but not probable."

"Why do you say that?"

"Because you're still alive." Even though it was the truth, I regretted the comment as soon as it left my mouth.

Bruns stilled. "I see."

Thank fate his secretary entered with the tea. She set the tray on the table between us and poured two cups.

"Thank you, Tia."

She gave him a bright smile and left the room.

"Shall we toast?" Bruns picked up his cup.

I grabbed the other and held it up.

"To honesty, no matter how brutal," he said.

An odd toast, but I tapped my cup against his and sipped the hot liquid, which tasted strongly of Theobroma. I set it down.

Bruns questioned me about losing my magic and what I'd learned. Again, I didn't see a reason to lie. "I've no idea what happened."

We discussed potential causes. I'd explored all of them before, but I figured my openness would reinforce my I'm-on-your-side act.

"Is there something wrong with the tea?" Bruns asked.

"It's a little too hot."

"It should have cooled by now."

I picked it up and sipped a tiny bit. "You're right." Holding the cup, I rested my right arm in my lap.

Bruns surged to his feet. "Do you really think I'm an idiot?"

"Excuse me?"

"Your guides are very observant. It didn't take us long to guess why Leif always brought food to your room. I suspected when you first woke. As the Commander's food taster, you must have a sensitive palate. You can stop the act." Without warning, he grabbed my left wrist and pain pierced my forearm.

A dart was stuck in my skin. "What...?"

"I believe you call it goo-goo juice. Leif unarmed you while you were sleeping and gave me all your nasty darts filled with Curare, sleeping potion and goo-goo juice."

My head spun as fear clawed my stomach. I set the tea on the table to avoid spilling it in my lap.

Bruns knelt in front of me. "Now, let's talk."

26

VALEK

Valek stared at his father and then at the young man next to him. The one who resembled his dead brother Vincent. Or rather, how he would have looked if Vincent had lived four or five more years. And it clicked why Zohav and Zethan seemed so familiar. His parents had more children after he'd left.

Strong emotions strangled Valek, rendering him mute. He hadn't seen his father since he was thirteen and left to seek revenge for the murder of his brothers. Since his parents told him never to return.

"Dad, what's going on? Who is he?" the young man asked again.

Valek's father ignored the questions. He walked toward Valek with his brown-eyed gaze locked on him and as paralyzing as Curare. Gray had replaced his once-black hair, and wrinkles lined his leathery face. A part of Valek noted that he wore a tanner's uniform as required, but various colored dyes had stained the white diamonds.

Relaxing his grip on the hilt of his sword, Valek dismounted and stood at the gate. He clamped down on the maelstrom of shock, pain, fear and grief that raged inside him. Instead, he channeled the calm detachment he'd learned to rely on during times of great danger.

When his father reached the other side of the gate, he opened it and said, "Welcome home, son."

Those three words slammed into him. He rocked back on his heels, and only Onyx's solid body behind him kept Valek upright.

"Son? What are you talking about?" the young man asked. His voice squeaked with alarm.

"This is Valek, the Commander's chief of security and your older brother," his father said. "Valek, this is Zebulon."

Zebulon's shocked expression meant his...their father hadn't mentioned Valek before. And he wondered if Father had told him about Vincent, Viliam and Victor.

Just then his mother yelled from the house, "Kalen, Zeb, get in here! The twins are back! They're alive!"

Without a word, both men bolted to the house. Valek sagged against Onyx, glad for the few minutes to collect his wits, which had scattered when his father called him *son*. Completely unexpected, the word woke the small boy who had hidden deep down inside him. The child who craved his parents' love and approval and wished to be held and comforted. And although he tried to shove that young boy back into his slumbering coma, the damage was done. Valek suddenly needed Yelena's touch and her strength. With her support, he could endure this encounter. Without it—he might lose control of everything.

Valek pulled in a few deep breaths, knowing he didn't have much time before the entire family came spilling from the house. No matter what happened, the twins still needed to go to Sitia. However, he suspected leaving after only a few hours would be impossible for all concerned.

As predicted, five people streamed from the house. His

mother led the way straight toward him. She held a large kitchen knife and her expression was not welcoming. Not at all. Anger and determination emanated from her blue eyes— the mother bear protecting her cubs. She'd saved his life. And the nail-shaped scars still marked his shoulder from when she had held him back from attacking the soldiers who'd murdered his brothers.

Valek fought the instinct to grab his knives in the face of her charge. The others shouted after her to stop and think and calm down, but her stride never wavered. She halted on the other side of the open gate and brandished her weapon. The others fell silent, or rather held their collective breaths.

"You will *not* harm my children. You will *not* take them away," she said.

"I have no intention of harming them." Glad his voice didn't shake, he added, "Now that I know who they are, I will ensure they are protected once they're in Sitia."

"What do you mean, *now* that you know?" Mother demanded. "You've known all along." She gestured with the knife. "You've sent your spies to watch us since the takeover."

"I sent them to *protect* you, not *spy* on you. They are only to report if someone comes after you because of me. Not about your personal life." Valek glanced at his three…siblings. "And I take it you didn't tell your new children about your old children?"

"They know about the others, but not you. You're an assassin. The Commander's killer. Everyone hates and fears you— they didn't need to know they are related to an abomination."

The word sliced into him. He encouraged others to feel that way about him, but hearing it from his mother had an unexpected impact. Recovering, he asked, "And how did you explain my agents?"

"We made them part of our family. The kids and the neighbors think we hired them," his father said.

Not a bad idea, except for the fact that his agents' covers had been blown for years and Valek hadn't known.

"I don't care if you've been protecting us," Mother said. "They are *not* going with you."

"Calm down, Olya. Let's go inside and talk about this." Father placed his hand on her shoulder, but she shrugged him off.

"They *are* coming with me," Valek said. "Either we do this the hard way, and you'll have no time to spend with them. Or the easy way, and you'll get...the rest of the day together." A day of pure hell for him. Another day away from Yelena.

"I'll go with him," Zethan said.

"No! He'll kill you. That's what he does. It's all he knows," Mother accused.

That was the breaking point. Valek moved. In a heartbeat, he unarmed his mother. "If I'd planned to kill them, they'd be dead by now." He handed the knife to his father. "Now spend time with your children. We're leaving in the morning." Valek met Zohav's gaze. "You know what I'm capable of. Try anything—"

"And we'll go to the Citadel as cargo," Zethan finished. "Got it."

"Citadel?" his father asked Valek.

"Actually, the Magician's Keep. They need to learn the extent of their magic."

"Why are you doing this?" His father yanked on his shirt with his big callused hand—a nervous habit that had endured the years.

"Because his heart mate would be angry if he didn't," Zethan supplied.

His father didn't react to Zethan's comment. Instead, he squinted at Valek with his shrewd I-see-right-through-you expression that came from years of raising rambunctious boys. "That's not the entire reason."

"Let's just say it will be beneficial for Ixia. Despite the rumors, I'm not just a killing machine." This he said to his mother. "I do guard the interests of Ixia." *And my family.* But Valek wouldn't voice that aloud. "Go on." He shooed them away. "No sense wasting time."

They shuffled back to the house, appearing a bit dazed. Needing to move, lest his thoughts and emotions ambush him, Valek led Onyx and Smoke inside the gate. He fed them and gave them water. Then he groomed them. Every inch, until they practically glowed.

A door banged behind him. Valek spun and yanked a knife. Standing in the tannery's entrance was Patxi, one of his corp. The man held out his stained hands. Valek relaxed and gestured Patxi over.

The tall man fidgeted under Valek's scrutiny. "Sorry, boss, but this was the best way to protect your family. I'm with your father all day and sleep in the room above the shop. If something happens, I'm right here."

"And Milya?"

"She helps in the house and stays in the guest room."

"How did—"

"Your father discovered the agents long ago. When you assign new agents, we just take over the jobs. You can't be too surprised, sir. You had to get your canny intuition from someone."

Appealing to his ego—nice tactic. "Do you wish to be reassigned?"

"No. I've a feeling your visit today is going to cause a bit of a problem from the locals. I want to make sure Zeb doesn't get into any trouble."

"Is he a troublemaker?"

"He's a fighter. And stubborn. Won't back down ever. I've taught him a few moves to keep him from getting completely clobbered at the tavern."

Interesting. "Recruitment potential?"

"Yes. And now he knows you're his brother, it's probably safer for him to get the full training."

"Okay. Thanks."

Patxi nodded and returned to the tannery. By the time Valek finished cleaning the horses' hooves, the sun hung low in the sky. Now what? Having no desire to see what had changed inside the tannery, Valek looped around it.

The three graves remained in the place that was scarred into his memory. Their names had been chiseled into the black granite headstones lined up in a row—Victor, Viliam and Vincent. At the end sat another, smaller stone without a name. Had his parents put that there to represent him? Perhaps it was better to believe that he was dead instead of an abomination.

But his father's words—*welcome home, son*—didn't match that sentiment. However, the knife in his mother's hand clearly did.

He knelt next to Vincent's grave. Running his fingers over the cold stone, Valek envisioned Vincent's face. Grief surged through him. Valek wondered for the millionth time how his life would have been different if his brothers had lived. An idyllic scene with all of them older, married with children, gathered around the huge dining room table, laughing, teasing, complaining, arguing. His mother spoiling the grandchildren, his father teaching the next generation how to tan and dye leather.

Then the questions would start. Would the King's family still be ruling Ixia? Would the monarch's corruption make that homey scene impossible? Would he have been content to work in his father's tannery? Would he be a different person?

And the most important question: Would he have met

Yelena? The answer to that one was no. When he focused on her and their baby, then all this didn't hurt so much. It still smoldered deep inside him, and he still wished his brothers hadn't been killed. But the promise of having a family again pushed him past all the heartache and grief. Motivated him to find a way to get Ixia and Sitia back on good terms, so his future of laughter, teasing, debates and love would be…not quite assured, but would have much better odds.

"Thought I'd find you here," his father said.

Valek straightened and wiped the dirt from his knees.

"I think of those boys every day." His father tucked his hands into his pockets. Staring at the gravestones, he rocked on his heels. "Those soldiers that were killed about two years later…were they the ones?"

"Yes."

Father lifted his head. "And that Captain who died in the woods?"

"He ordered his men to pick a family to use as an example of what happens when you don't pay your taxes to the King."

"And you lodged a complaint with the King?"

"Everyone knows I assassinated him. Why are you asking?"

"Rumors can't be trusted."

Valek waited.

"I want to hear it from you."

"That I'm a killer, like Mother said? Yes. I am. I personally delivered my complaint to the King, Queen and the entire royal family."

"How did it feel? Once you finished…complaining."

"Satisfying and freeing. But by then, it wasn't all about revenge. I'd seen the rot and the deaths the King and his family were responsible for. I agreed with the Commander's vision for Ixia. He'd never murder a child because his parents couldn't afford to pay taxes."

MARIA V. SNYDER

"True. And my taxes were reduced after the takeover."

"Is that why you had more children?" Valek couldn't resist asking.

"No. We were devastated and lonely. Our house had been full of four energetic and boisterous boys and then…all gone. So quiet. Your mother didn't think she'd conceive, but Zeb was born four years after the takeover, then the twins three years later." He rubbed a hand over his face. "When their magic started causing problems, I'd thought you'd show up and…"

"Here I am."

"Later than expected, and not before we thought we lost them, too."

Dark shadows of grief haunted his expression. More than any one person should be asked to bear. But that was the problem with grief. No one ever asked for it. It arrived with its bags already packed for an extended stay. It settled into your best guest room and demanded to be waited on all day long, and when it finally shuffled out the door, it left behind permanent scratches on your furniture.

Valek wished to ease his father's pain. "They'll be…safer in Sitia. I'll make sure they learn how to protect themselves."

"Thank you. Come inside and get something to eat."

"No thanks. I belong here with the dead." Valek pointed to the unmarked gravestone. "Mother would agree."

"That's not yours. It's for that damn dog Mooch. The twins were so upset when he died. Made me dig a grave and buy a stone. Never did get around to carving his name in it. And do you know what's really galling?"

Amused, Valek shook his head.

"Out of the dozen dogs we've had, that damn dog hated me. Bit me three times, and I couldn't do nothing about it or they'd get upset."

"Which explains why it remains unmarked."

He laughed a deep chuckle. "You always were a quick study of people. I'm sure it helps with your job."

"It does."

His father scuffed his boots in the dirt. "I've thought about you every day, too, wondering if you'd ever come home." A pause. "If you hadn't run into the twins, would you have returned?"

"You made it quite clear—"

"And you've never said something in anger that you regretted later? Never uttered the wrong thing when you were out of your mind with grief?"

Cracks appeared in Valek's calm demeanor. Funny how being threatened by a butcher knife hadn't affected him at all, yet his father's words had the same effect as a blow to his head, followed by a punch to his solar plexus, leaving him dazed and unable to suck in a proper breath.

"Assassins learn to shut off their emotions," Valek finally said.

"That's bullshit. If that was the case, then you wouldn't let the twins stay overnight, you wouldn't be here by your brothers' graves, you wouldn't have a heart mate. Should I go on?"

"No. You've made your point."

"Then what's the answer to my question? Would you have returned?"

He hadn't planned to, but with marrying Yelena, and the baby… "I don't know."

"Fair enough. Now come on inside."

"I… Mother would get upset. I'd ruin her time with the twins."

"Put that intuitive sense to work, boy. How would you

feel in her place? It's a lot to take in, and she's not going to see them again—"

"Why not? You can visit them during the hot season when the Keep's on break."

His father jerked straight. "But they'll be in Sitia. We can't…"

"You can if I help you. In fact, Sitia has tanneries, too. If you want to live there, I can arrange that, as well."

"You can?"

"I can." Even if he no longer worked for the Commander.

He gazed at Valek for a few heartbeats. "I'll think about it."

"When you decide, just tell Patxi. He'll get word to me."

Valek's father returned to the house. Movement seemed the best cure for his…confusion. Valek retrieved his pack from Onyx's saddle and built a small fire near his brothers' graves. It might be morbid, but to him it was comforting. The horses moved closer to the heat.

He boiled water and sorted through the travel rations, ensuring there would be enough to last. The crunch of footsteps sounded to his left. Valek jumped to his feet, knife in hand.

"Easy," Zethan said. "Just bringing you supper."

Valek slid the weapon back into its sheath as the young man stepped into the ring of firelight. Zethan handed him a fork and a plate with two slices of roast beef and a pile of mashed potatoes, all covered with a dark brown gravy. The smell alone was intoxicating.

"Did you draw the short straw?"

Zethan laughed. "No, I volunteered."

"Thanks." Valek sat next to the fire.

"I didn't bring you a knife to cut the meat, 'cause I figured you already have about ten of your own."

"At least." Valek smiled.

Zethan took that as an invitation to sit down. "Mother's

coming around to the idea of us leaving. Although Zohav doesn't believe you have the authority to let them come visit us."

Zohav's comment wasn't a surprise. "Consider it one of the perks of my job."

The teen pulled a half-burned twig from the fire. He sketched designs into the dirt with it. "What's it like at the Magician's Keep?"

Between bites of the smoky beef, Valek explained the five-year student curriculum. "You probably won't have to start at the beginning, but I'd guess you'd be there two or three years."

Valek answered a bunch of Zethan's questions before Zebulon arrived with a piece of apple pie.

"Zee, Father wants to talk to you and Zo alone," Zebulon said. "I expect you'll get the same lecture that you got when you left for the coast. Plus, a bonus warning not to get captured by pirates," he teased.

"You mean we weren't *supposed* to get captured? Why didn't he tell us that before?" Zethan brushed dirt from his pants before heading to the house.

Zebulon handed Valek the pie. "Mother said you can sleep in the house."

"Thanks, but I have my bedroll and I'm used to sleeping on the ground."

He shrugged. "Suit yourself." Then he sat on the other side of the fire. He poked at the wood with a twig. Sparks shot into the sky.

Valek waited while Zebulon worked up the nerve to ask the questions he held inside. He studied his...brother—still a difficult concept to accept. Around nineteen years old, Zebulon's personality appeared to be a mix of the twins, cautious like Zohav, but with a bit of a sense of humor like Zethan. Valek wondered if he had Vincent's mischievous streak. Perhaps when the man relaxed, his true personality would show.

Would any of them ever relax around Valek, the King Killer? He doubted it.

"What you mentioned to Father about moving south, does that apply to me, as well?"

"Of course."

"What if we decide to stay here? Can we still visit the twins?"

"Yes."

"Why do you care? You didn't even know we existed until today. You didn't care enough to ask your...agents how my... our parents were doing. How can we believe that you care now?"

Valek imagined Zohav had asked the same questions in the house. "I've many enemies. People who wouldn't hesitate to use my family in order to get to me. But only a handful of trusted people know where my parents live, and I've assigned agents to protect them just in case the information is leaked. If I didn't care, the agents wouldn't be here. As for not knowing about you and the twins..." Valek swallowed. "I...ordered my agents not to tell me anything because..." He gazed at the gravestones.

His father's comments about regret over harsh words repeated in his mind. Had his avoidance really been due to his parents telling him never to return or Valek's own fear that if they became a family again, he'd be vulnerable to the intense heartache of losing them, like the grief he'd experienced when his brothers died? Or was it just pure stubbornness? Or the fear of being rejected if he'd returned? Perhaps all three.

"Because I couldn't handle hearing about their lives continuing on without me and my brothers." Because it would mean they'd moved past the tragedy and grief, while he hadn't. When he'd told his father that killing the King had been freeing, he'd lied. Everything he'd done up to this point had been a result of that day. It was as if he'd been frozen in time.

Yelena had been the only one to reach him through the ice, drilling a small opening.

"What about now? Can you handle it?"

Could he? From the hole, cracks zipped along the frozen surface, creating a pattern. If he let his family through the barrier, would he shatter? Sweat raced down his back as a burning pain bloomed around his heart.

Unable to sit still, he stood and strode to the graves. He'd told his father that he belonged among the dead. That unmarked gravestone could easily be for him. He'd let Yelena in, but it had taken eight years for him to realize just how precious she was to him. The scar on his chest seared his skin. He knelt on Vincent's grave and traced his name with a finger. Valek leaned his hot forehead on the cold, hard granite.

This was what he had been for so long. Cold. Hard. Why was this so difficult? He'd faced assassins, rogue magicians, the Commander, criminals of all sorts, and would gladly face them all a second time rather than watch his family be destroyed again. Yet he saw the murders so clearly in his mind. He relived that day over and over and over and over. Even with all his efforts to keep Ixia safe, they remained dead. The family of his childhood was gone and would never be the same.

Could he handle it? A new family that wasn't just him, Yelena and the baby? A fire suffused him, and then it disappeared. Cold air fanned his face. Just as Janco had said, Valek had found a family despite being surrounded by ice. Yelena and the baby of course, but also a rather unconventional one that included Ari, Janco, Leif, Opal, Devlen and a number of horses.

Could he handle it?

Yes.

The admission zipped through him, and the invisible yet ever-present weight lifted from his shoulders. Breathing eas-

MARIA V. SNYDER

ier, he straightened. Zebulon remained by the fire, watching him with a worried frown, hoping Valek didn't go crazy and kill them all. Odd that Zebulon's thoughts should be so clear to Valek.

As he returned to the fire, the air smelled different. He picked up a number of scents—the ashy smoke from the burning coal, the earthy aroma of leather and the sweet odor of grass from the horses. Tendrils of wind caressed his face. The strangeness continued. He recognized distant sounds and his night vision sharpened, extending his range of sight. It was as if he'd been bundled head to toe in thick furs and had flung them off.

"You okay?" Zebulon asked.

"Yes." He focused on the flames, blocking the extra sensations. Then he addressed his brother. "The answer to your first question is also yes. I can handle it."

"Good." Zebulon laid another branch onto the fire. Then he met Valek's gaze. "I'm not sure I can. I'm pissed at Father for not telling us, but if everyone knew, we'd be targets."

"Which is why you're not going to tell anyone. This little visit—" Valek's hand traced a circle in the air "—is me checking that you don't have magical powers before I drag the twins to the Castle, where they will be executed. Understand?"

"Yes. And you need to understand that just because we have the same parents doesn't make us *brothers*."

"I know. We're strangers." He glanced at the graves. "We haven't ruined the laundry together or planned a prank or snuck out late at night or hidden from Father when he was furious. Those experiences are what forges a relationship."

"Yeah, and I'm too old to hide from Father."

Valek quirked an eyebrow at him. "Really? You don't suddenly find somewhere else to be when he wants to clean out the acid vat?"

Zebulon laughed. "True." He played with the shoelaces on his scuffed and worn boots. "You're not what I expected. Mother had us so worried when Zee's and Zo's magic started doing crazy things. We'd thought you'd arrive with an army and kill us all."

"Reputations are interesting creatures. I've nurtured mine so that most people fear me. They're easier to manipulate that way. However, I don't kill because I enjoy it or get a thrill from it. There was a logical reason for each one, and it was usually after all other options were tried or considered. I've no regrets over anyone I've assassinated. Some criminals just can't be redeemed—locking them in jail just gives them time to plan their next crime and hurt more people. But some can. In fact, a friend of mine was addicted to blood magic and did a number of horrible things in order to feed his addiction, but he pulled it together, turned his life around and is making amends."

"You have friends?"

He gave him a wry smile. "A few brave souls. Being with me tends to put them in danger."

"I bet."

Voices sounded to the left, along with the light bang of a wooden door. Valek sensed the twins and his parents approaching well before he should. Odd. Father fetched more wood and built the small blaze into a larger one while the other three settled around the fire without saying a word. Heat pulsed. Orange light illuminated the ring of faces, the family resemblance clear.

Valek braced for another emotional conversation, but his mother asked about the Citadel, the Magician's Keep, what the twins should pack and how much money they'd need.

He filled her in on what the twins would be doing. "Don't

MARIA V. SNYDER

worry about money. The Keep provides a stipend to the students."

Zohav hugged her knees to her chest during the explanation. She'd rather stay home with her family, but Zethan relished the idea of learning more about his power. If he'd known what he could do, those pirates wouldn't have stood a chance. This insight into both of them hit Valek with such certainty, it was as if he'd read their actual thoughts. His head ached with the ceaseless chatter and emotions.

Mother fiddled with the sliver clasp on her cloak. "Will you tell the Sitians they are your siblings?"

"No. Sitians fear and hate me as much as the Ixians do. They will be safer if everyone believes they are refugees from Ixia."

Mother frowned. "They had to get their magic from my father. No one else in our family has it."

"Yelena speculated that my immunity to magic might be a form of power," Valek said.

"Who is this Yelena?" she asked.

"My heart mate." Best to keep her status under wraps for now.

Zethan asked, "Does she think your immunity is a One-Trick power? Like Nell's?"

"It's possible."

His mother studied him. Her thoughts clear. Valek couldn't be that terrible if another person loved him. Unless she was a monster, too. "Tell us about her."

The pain in Valek's temples increased. Was it due to this strange…sensation…ability? With effort, he concentrated on describing Yelena's wonderful kindness and intelligence, and he ignored the extra thoughts, sounds and smells that threatened to overwhelm him.

"Why isn't she with you?" Mother asked.

"She's in Sitia. I need to catch up with her, which is why we have to leave in the morning."

"Does her family know she's your heart mate?"

Again Valek understood why his mother asked that question. Her desire to find others who didn't hate him might help her see him in a better light.

"Yes. In fact, her brother and father are currently helping me with a problem."

"What problem?" Father asked.

"Identifying a plant. It's important, but we don't know why. It could either be a poison or be used as a potential weapon." Like Curare.

"Would that be something we'd do as magicians? Help you with problems?" Zethan asked.

Both Zohav and Mother scowled at Zethan's enthusiasm, thinking the boy was going to get himself killed if he helped Valek.

Valek rubbed his forehead. What the hell was going on? Why were their thoughts so clear to him? Was it because they were family? Unable to answer any of those questions, he concentrated on Zethan's question instead. "I expect the Stormdancers will be very interested in you, and you'll spend your time with them. Those who help me have a great deal of training and skill. They frequently give up months of their lives to work undercover, and it's a dangerous life."

"Then why do it?" Zohav asked.

His gaze was drawn to his brothers' headstones. "Because evil is out there. We've witnessed its devastation. We know it must be stopped."

"And you're the only ones who can stop it?" Father asked.

"Yes."

"That's rather egotistical," Zohav said.

MARIA V. SNYDER

"It could be taken that way," Valek agreed. "It's still true, though."

"What happens when you're too old to fight?"

Valek noted the use of *when*. Nice to know his father didn't think of him as too old. "By then I hope the next generation will be trained and ready."

"And if they aren't?"

"Evil wins."

Considering the reception of his arrival, Valek's family stayed by the fire longer than he expected. After they left, he lay on his bedroll and stared at the stars. Exhausted, his head throbbed and he couldn't sleep. It was as if his skin had been rubbed off, exposing all his nerves.

So much had happened.

So many emotions.

Thoughts swirled in his mind, bits of conversation repeated, and he replayed his own reaction at Vincent's grave when he'd realized why he had avoided any mention of his family. What had happened to him? His senses had sharpened into a super awareness, and he flinched at every tiny noise.

Giving up on sleep, Valek stirred the fire to life. Perhaps a cup of one of Leif's teas would help soothe him.

It didn't.

By the time dawn arrived, Valek had gotten only a few hours of rest. He packed his bedroll and supplies. Concentrating on the task at hand and not the conversation going on in the kitchen, Valek saddled the horses.

The twins both carried a pack. His parents and Zebulon followed them from the house. While Valek secured their bags on the horses, the others said goodbye.

"We want to visit them at the beginning of the hot season," Mother said to Valek. "Can you arrange it?"

"Yes." If there wasn't a war between Ixia and Sitia by then.

"Good. We'll see how it is before deciding on moving."

"Smart," Valek agreed.

She snorted. "You make sure they're safe." It wasn't a request.

"Yes, sir."

"If anything happens to them, I'm holding *you* responsible."

Mortified, Zethan said, "Mother, he's not going to babysit us. We can take care of ourselves."

"As long as there's no pirates in Sitia," Zebulon said.

"Shut up, Zeb." Zethan punched him on the arm.

She ignored her sons. "And you bring this Yelena to meet us."

Another order, but one that meant so much more. "Yes, sir."

Mother gave him a curt nod, then she hugged each of the twins. Zethan mounted Smoke, and Zohav sat behind Valek. He clicked his tongue and Onyx trotted through the gate. Unlike the last time he'd left twenty-eight years ago, this time he planned to return.

Valek and the twins approached the rendezvous location four days into the warm season and eleven days after they'd left Icefaren. Eleven days of dealing with his super-active senses, the twins' questions, their thoughts and emotions, and worrying about Yelena. Was she there or not?

When they were half a mile away, Kiki's whinny shot right through him. Relief and joy to see Yelena infused him. Onyx broke into a run with Smoke right behind him.

Arriving with a cloud of dust, Valek stopped Onyx. Kiki butted her head against the black horse. Valek peered over her, searching for Yelena. Signs of a campfire and other evidence of camp littered the clearing. But no Yelena, no other horses, no Ari or Janco.

He turned stone-cold. "Stay on the horses and keep quiet," Valek ordered the twins. Dismounting, he freed his sword with his right hand while grabbing a dagger with his left.

One thing kept him from panicking. Kiki. She wasn't agitated or upset. A rustling sounded from the woods. He spun, then relaxed as his new senses spotted Fisk carrying a water skin. Fisk's presence meant bad news, but not immediate danger. By the time Fisk reached him, Valek had sheathed his weapons.

Before the young man could say a word, Valek demanded, "Where's Yelena?"

"She's been captured by Bruns Jewelrose."

A wave of icy fear washed through him, followed by a molten fury that promised Bruns would regret the decision to apprehend her. At least she wasn't dead. Valek focused on that, or else he'd lose the tight control he had on his emotions. "Ari and Janco?"

"Trying to rescue her and Leif. He was captured first and..." Fisk spread his arms.

"Do you know where they are?"

"Yes."

One bit of good news. He hooked a thumb in the twins' direction. "I need to take them to the Magician's Keep, then we can talk to the Master Magicians and devise—"

"You can't go the the Keep."

"Why not?"

"There's no one there."

27

JANCO

Janco touched his smooth chin for the billionth time. Gah. He'd had his goatee for years. He loved it, but shaving it had been part of his disguise. Janco's exposed skin tingled as if the entire garrison saw right through him. Plus his head itched from the red dye, and the fake ear made him sweat. One of these days, he'd impersonate a wealthy businessman for a change. He'd wear tailored silk clothing, expensive jewelry, be surrounded by a cloud of sycophants and... Who was he kidding? Grunts blended in; businessmen with minions did not.

Suppressing a sigh, he picked up a practice sword and sparred with a soldier wannabe. Keeping half his attention on the out-of-shape farmer, Janco watched the armory. Yelena and her thugs had disappeared inside not long ago.

One good thing about the training yard—no magic. Most of the outdoor areas were clean, but magic infected the barracks and canteen. He spent his nights sneaking into the various buildings or reporting information to Ari. The big guy remained on the outside to liaise with Fisk and his people.

Bruns strode toward the armory. By his stiff gait and the short swings of his arms, Janco figured he was either agitated or angry. Bruns entered the building and after a few minutes,

Bruns and Yelena left, walking arm in arm. They both smiled, but Janco didn't like it. Not at all. Something wasn't right.

He let the wannabe disarm him. "Sweet move, puppy dog. You're just too good for me. I'd better go find someone more my speed." His ego shuddered with the blow, but showing off his superior skills would be the opposite of blending in.

Janco slipped away from the training yard and followed Yelena and Bruns to the administration building. The two thugs remained outside. A good or bad thing? He wasn't sure. Finding an inconspicuous spot to wait, Janco kept an eye on the door.

To pass the time, he sized up the thugs and decided he could take them both by himself, if the ruckus didn't cause every wannabe to come running. The problem with this place was not being able to tell the grunts from the magicians. They all wore the same uniform, which was a sound military tactic. No sense letting your enemy know who to target. But his magic mojo failed to work as well here. The power flooded the buildings and he couldn't home in on the magicians.

They needed Valek. His ability to feel magic was more sensitive. Janco hoped Fisk would return soon. Kiki had only allowed Fisk to ride her. She had to be the one to go, since Kiki knew the rendezvous location and was smart enough to avoid the border guards.

Bruns poked his head from the door and barked at the thugs. They nodded and took off. Not good. Janco debated between following the thugs or remaining in his position. Footsteps sounded behind him. He spun, grasping the hilt of his knife and stopped.

"You should give a guy a little more warning," he said to Leif.

"I'm trying to keep a low profile."

"Aren't we all."

"Yeah, well, those two bruisers that just bolted are looking for me."

Concerned, Janco scanned the area for them. So far, so good. "How do you know?"

"We weren't as clever as we thought. Bruns caught on that we weren't eating the Theobroma-laced food. He just tried to use goo-goo juice on Yelena to get her to divulge everything she knows, but when I gave Bruns her darts and told him which ones had Curare, sleeping potion and goo-goo juice, I mixed them up."

"So Yelena is…?"

"Sleeping."

"And you know this for sure?"

"Yes. Hale used his magic to listen in on Bruns and Yelena."

"Then you need to escape. Ari's—"

"I'm not going anywhere without Yelena."

"But—"

"Listen. She'll eventually wake up and then he'll use the goo-goo juice on her.

"She'll blow your cover and tell Bruns about Dax and Hale's involvement. Tonight, the three of you need to leave. This is bigger than we can handle right now. I'll rescue Yelena and join you outside."

"Did you see the size of those thugs? No way you're getting to her without help," Janco said. "Where is he holding her?"

"In the cells under the administration building."

"Damn. There's only one entrance. We'll have to use the windows. It's going to be difficult."

"How about if I let them catch me during a rescue attempt? Bruns might think no one else will try to reach her. Is there a way I can hide lock picks or a weapon where they won't find them?"

"Brunsie is a smart cookie." Without thinking, Janco

MARIA V. SNYDER

scratched his fake ear and almost peeled it off. Aha! "Actually, there is a way that might work, if he doesn't kill you once you're caught."

"He won't. Yelena and I are showpieces. Bruns wants us loyal to his cause. If we're unsuccessful, he'll probably force-feed us Theobroma and blast us until we're mindless Bruns groupies."

"Isn't there an antidote? Can you use Curare to reverse the effects?"

"No. It doesn't work that way." Leif frowned.

"What about something else? Even poisons have antidotes." Leif stared at him in shock.

"What did I say?"

"Those plants…in Owen's glass hothouses. They… We…"

"What? Spit it out, man."

"We thought the one hybrid plant was Vossen, but it might be an antidote to Theobroma!"

"Too bad you didn't figure this out sooner."

"Once we're free, it'll be a place to start."

"Start what?" Janco asked.

"The revolt."

Janco returned to the barracks and grabbed a few things from the bag stashed under his bunk. Then he met up with Leif in an abandoned storeroom. He mixed the putty, matching Leif's skin tone, and set to work. When he finished, Leif had a couple lock picks and a number of darts hidden under patches of fake skin.

"Don't scratch them. And don't touch the areas when you're being searched," Janco instructed.

"Got it."

They reviewed the plan to rescue Yelena.

"Dax will leave the compound during supper and update

Ari," Leif said. "Hale will meet you on the south side of the administration building unless there are guards. In that case, he'll rendezvous with you outside the magicians' barracks."

"Good. You might as well stay here until midnight. Bruns has increased the muscle searching the garrison for you."

"What are you going to do?"

"I'm going to finish my reconnaissance. There are a few places I haven't checked, and if you think there'll be a revolt, then we're gonna need as much intel as possible."

"Be very careful."

Janco huffed. "I'm Mr. Careful."

"Uh-huh. How many times have you been—"

"I don't count. What's past is past." With a wave, Janco left.

Blending in with various groups of soldiers, Janco explored the infirmary and the stables. Without Leif to secure untainted food, Janco ate a few pieces of ancient jerky from his travel pack. He chewed on it forever.

The canteen buzzed with conversation and magic. Janco's scar tweaked with pain. Despite the power, Janco thought it was a good time to discover where the unmarked door in the back left corner led. It didn't have a keyhole or other evidence of a lock. The knob turned with ease as Janco, acting as if he used the door all the time, strode through and closed it behind him.

He stood on a small landing. Stairs led down into a tight stairwell, ending in grayness. There must be windows below, letting in the last of the daylight. Janco descended, zigzagging from landing to landing until he reached bottom. As he expected, small windows set near the ceiling ringed the basement.

Glancing around, he spotted a collection of chairs, stacks of wooden crates, barrels, a pile of tablecloths and a mound of potatoes—an obvious storage area for the canteen. Foot-

MARIA V. SNYDER

steps, the scrape of chairs and voices filtered down to him from above. There was another door at the far end of the room. Janco wove through the mess and considered it a win when he only banged his shin once on a broken leg jutting from a table.

This door also opened without trouble. Too bad trouble waited for him on the other side. Big trouble. Pain drilled through his skull.

28

YELENA

Disoriented, dry-mouthed and dizzy—the all-too-familiar aftereffects of sleeping potion. My blurry vision sharpened, along with the ache in my temples. I wished I hadn't opened my eyes, but I couldn't unsee the bars surrounding me or unsmell the wet, mucky dungeon stench mixed with the acrid odor of burned lantern oil—another aspect that I was well acquainted with.

Perhaps it was time to reexamine my life.

Bruns no longer knelt by me, and I no longer sat in a chair, but was sprawled on a pallet of straw. Better or worse? I pushed to a sitting position and groaned as intense pain danced behind my eyeballs. Nausea rolled, splashing up my throat.

Resting my head in my hands, I willed my stomach to settle and hoped the repeated dosing of sleeping potion hadn't harmed the baby.

"It's about time you woke up," Janco grumped.

Oh, no. "I'm not awake. Because you're not in here with me. You're outside the garrison, rounding up the cavalry."

"I hate to break this to you, sweetheart, but the cavalry is hanging with Bruns in the canteen, quaffing down Theobroma and kissing his rich ass." The strain in his voice failed to match his flippant tone.

I swiveled. Janco stood in the next cell. Even in the dim lantern light, a bright red bruise shone on his swollen right cheek. His fake ear was gone, replaced by bloody scratches. His uniform was torn and blood stained the fabric.

"Is it as bad as you look?" I asked.

"Worse."

"Don't tell me." I scanned the small cell, searching for a way to escape.

"I'm all for denial, but it won't last."

"Ignorance is bliss." I ran my fingers through my tangled hair. The lock picks were gone, along with the set I'd hidden in the uniform Bruns made all of us wear.

"He's smart, Yelena. And pissed off."

I spotted a cup of water near the door. At least he wasn't cruel.

"I wouldn't do that," Janco said when I raised it to my lips. "Unless you want Bruns to be your master."

Stopping, I sniffed the liquid. Theobroma muddied the water.

"Can you say *hunger strike*?" Janco joked.

His words slammed into me as I realized that the joke was on me. I had to drink and eat for the baby's sake. If we didn't escape soon, eventually I'd consume enough Theobroma to be turned into one of Bruns's supporters.

"Where are we?" I asked, setting the cup aside...for now.

"I thought you didn't want to know."

"Changed my mind."

"We are in the special holding cells under the administration building." He gestured to the four others—one next to him and three more across the aisle, which were all empty.

"Special how?"

"This place is saturated with magic. I can barely stand it."

"Do you have any of your...toys?"

"No. They took everything, and the building has only one entrance. It's probably surrounded by dozens of guards."

Alarmed, I asked, "What happened? How did you get caught?"

In a rough voice, Janco told me about Leif's plan to stage a fake rescue and his own reconnaissance. "...checking the basement of the dining room and..."

"And?"

He leaned on the bars as if they alone held him upright. Alarmed, I stood, reached through the bars and put my hand on his shoulder.

"And," I prompted again, but more gently this time.

"And I walked right into a nest of nasties. We gotta start confirming dead bodies, 'cause I'd like to avoid being surprised and mind-raped again." He scrubbed a hand over his face.

At first, he didn't make any sense. I repeated his words in my mind, picking up on the significant bits. "Who isn't dead?"

"The brother-sister team of horror who was with Owen and Ben."

A cold knot gripped my insides tight. "Loris and Cilly Cloud Mist?"

"Yeah, them."

That meant Bruns and the authorities in Lapeer had lied. No surprise about Bruns's deceit; I was more concerned about Captain Fleming in Lapeer. Had he been bribed or coerced, and why the ruse? "Are you sure?"

"No doubt," he said drily. "Loris is living below the dining room. He claimed his sister is alive, as well. She's at one of the Cartel's other garrisons."

"Was Ben with him?"

"No. I didn't see him."

I gestured to his bruise. "Did they—"

"Nope. I turned tail and hopped right on out of there like a good little scared rabbit. Made it about halfway through the dining room before he aimed his magical mind mojo onto the soldiers eating supper. At least I managed another couple steps."

I squeezed his shoulder. "You couldn't have predicted they'd be here. They were reported dead by Devlen—a reliable source."

"And Dev trusted the captain. Which ya think would be an okay thing to do, considering all Fleming did to help rescue us from Owen."

"I guess that's a puzzle to be sorted out later." If there was a later.

"Yeah. Too bad I knew *exactly* what was gonna happen when they dragged me to Bruns." He shuddered.

And now his mind-raped comment made sense. "Bad?"

"Oh, yes. They know everything, Yelena. Leif's hiding place, Dax and Hale's involvement, where Ari's located... *everything.*" His covered his pained expression with his hand.

While I wished to panic over the dire news, I suppressed the emotion so I didn't upset Janco any further. Pressing closer to the bars, I pried his hand away from his face and held it in both of mine. "Ari and the others are smart, Janco. Plus three of them have magic. They'll be okay."

He stared at our hands. After a long moment, he met my gaze. "What are you doing?"

"Uh...comforting you?"

"The pain's gone."

"See? It's working."

"No, not that." He pulled his hand free, scowled at the air, then grasped my fingers for another moment. Letting go, he signaled, *The magic disappears when you touch me.*

Like a null shield?

"Not quite," he said.

"Then what?"

Switching back to the silent communication, he signaled, *It's like…my ability to sense magic has been turned off. But when you let go, it returns.*

I concentrated, deciphering Janco-speak. *Like something is blocking your ability?*

"Yes, that's it!"

"Lovely." *I'm contagious.* I yanked my hand back and tucked it into my pants pocket.

No, that's a good thing. Janco bounced on his heels. *Think about it. If Brother Horror tries to read your mind, you can touch him and stop it!*

"I don't know." I considered. *Owen had no trouble using his magic on me.*

Did you touch him? Skin to skin? It didn't work on me until you grabbed my hand.

The horrific events that I'd been suppressing for the past two months sprang to life. Owen had tried to erase all my memories. Except he'd been interrupted, and the events that followed jumbled together into a blur of being dragged along behind him, then tossed onto the ground. Valek had arrived, and Owen pressed his fingertips to my forehead. His magic had sliced right through me like a bolt of lightning.

Yes, he touched me and almost killed me, I signaled.

Janco rubbed his chin. *Well…your blocking power was new then. Maybe it's growing stronger.*

Jolted by the word *growing*, I placed my hand on my abdomen.

Janco noticed the gesture and he grasped the bars, stiffening in horror. "You're—"

I pinched his lips shut. "Remember where we are."

He used the hand signals to admonish me for risking the baby's life and asked if Valek knew.

"Yes," I said aloud.

He relaxed, grinned and signaled, *Valek will bring an army to rescue you.*

If he can find us.

Not a problem. Fisk went to the rendezvous point to meet up with him.

Which Bruns knows about. Right?

His smile disappeared. "Right. I really screwed up." He flopped onto his straw pallet.

"You can't blame—"

He waved away my efforts to console him. I let him brood. Eventually he'd purge the guilt from his system and return to normal. Well, normal for Janco. Sitting down on my pallet, I mulled over our conversation and what had happened when I touched Janco.

Could the baby be responsible for my inability to connect with the blanket of power? Other female magicians didn't lose their abilities while pregnant, so it couldn't be. But I wasn't exactly like other magicians. Perhaps the combination of my Soulfinder magic and Valek's strong immunity created a void—an area of no magic!

I surged to my feet, unable to remain still. Perhaps as the baby grew, the area affected by the void also expanded. And by touching Janco, I included him in the void. Of course it was all speculation, and I had no way to test my theory right now, but it gave me hope that my powers might return once the baby was born. Considering my current predicament, I held on to that small comfort.

A clang of metal woke me from a light doze. Harsh voices emanated from the far right as a group of figures emerged from the darkness. Janco stood close to his door, his tense posture poised for action. But the group stopped before reaching Janco and unlocked the cell next to his.

The door squealed as it swung wide. The pack pushed Leif into the cell. I winced in sympathy as he hit the floor with a thud. By the time he regained his feet, they had slammed the door shut. And our chances of being rescued narrowed, along with my throat. I swallowed, but it didn't help.

When the group retreated, Janco said, "Welcome to the party."

Leif glared at him. His pant legs were sliced open, his shirt was untucked and torn, and bloody bruises marked his face.

"Are you okay?" I asked.

"I'd be better if it wasn't for Mr. Careful here," Leif growled. "Just couldn't keep out of trouble, could you?"

"I didn't expect to run into—"

"I know. They gloated about it as they tried to puree my brains." Leif ran a hand over his short hair, smoothing the strands down.

I bit down on a joke about his brains already being pureed. In this foul mood, Leif wouldn't appreciate it. Instead, I asked, "Did they get through?"

"No. Unlike Mr. Careful, I have strong magical defenses. Besides, it doesn't really matter. It sounds like he told them everything." Leif waved the ribbons of fabric that had been his pants. "They took my hidden surprises."

"Lock picks?" I asked.

"And my darts."

Janco slouched. "Sorry."

Leif jerked his thumb at the empty cells across the aisle. "Make sure you tell that to Dax, Hale and Ari."

"They're caught!" I sagged against the bars.

"Not yet. Bruns sent trained teams to round them up. It won't take long, since Dax and Hale have no military training."

"Ari won't be easy to catch," Janco said with pride.

"They have highly accurate blowpipes, remember? Ari can be the best swordsman around, but one well-placed dart filled with sleeping potion…" Leif spread his hands.

There's still Valek, Janco signaled.

"They're setting a trap for him," Leif said.

My head throbbed from all the bad news and from dehydration. I picked up the cup of tepid Theobroma-laced water and took a couple sips for a bit of relief. Both Janco and Leif watched me in silence. Their matching resigned expressions said it all.

Over the course of the next few hours, Bruns's hunting parties dragged in first Dax, then Hale and finally an unconscious Ari—one for each empty cell. Janco curled into a tight ball of misery, and I worried about Valek and Fisk, wondering if they'd avoid capture or walk right into Bruns's ambush.

I slept in snatches. Every little noise jerked me awake, convinced Valek had been seized. Ari groaned to life, groggy and surly. Explanations on how everyone had been apprehended were exchanged again. We also discussed escape, but Bruns's men had been thorough and no one had any lock picks or weapons. Rescue might be our only chance.

"No way they'd get Valek," Ari said. "No way."

"They have a dozen magicians that can weave a null shield in seconds," Leif said, shredding that last bit of hope.

When a loud bang signaled the entrance of another group of soldiers, ice coated my insides with dread. But only Bruns and a handful of guards walked in. Relief warmed me.

Bruns surveyed us while his men slid trays of food into each cell and added oil to the lanterns. No one said a word.

"You have a choice," Bruns said, breaking the silence. "Eat and drink the meals we bring, or not." He shrugged. "At this point, I don't care if you die of thirst. You've all been a pain in my side since the beginning. But know that after you've had a few meals here, you'll be welcomed to my team. And you won't be able to fake it, and there's no chance of recovery. I believe you're all familiar with the talents of Loris Cloud Mist." Bruns turned to leave.

"Is that why you didn't assassinate them? So they can work for you?" I asked.

"Yes. Not only does it make them grateful, but no one wastes time searching for the dead."

"You stole that idea from Owen."

"Yes, I did. And why not? The tactic has a little bit of life left in it. Of course, it won't work anymore." He swept a hand, indicating the cells. "But I don't need it to."

"Did you save Ben, as well?"

Bruns met my gaze. His expression remained neutral. "Eat your breakfast, Yelena. I told your heart mate I'd keep you alive if he cooperated. Don't go making me a liar, now."

It took every fiber of my willpower not to react to his comment. Instead, I said in a neutral—I hoped—tone, "Too late, Bruns. We all know not to trust what you say."

A half smile twisted his lips. "Fine. Believe what you will." He left, taking the guards with him.

Leif sniffed the food. "Don't eat it. We can last a couple days without food."

The enticing scent of warm cinnamon tea drifted to me. My stomach cramped with hunger. It'd been over a day since I'd last eaten. I lifted the mug and cupped it in my cold hands.

"Yelena," Ari said. He was in the cell across from mine. "Valek's not caught. I don't care how many magicians and null shields they have. Bruns does *not* have him." Pure conviction vibrated in his tone.

"Have you heard from him?" I asked. If he was close, I could wait.

Ari shook his head, his expression bleak. I calculated the distance to the rendezvous point. If Valek left right now, then it'd take him three days to arrive. Plus he'd need another day or two to figure out a way inside the base. Too long—I'd need to eat by then. I glanced at Leif, looking for guidance. Of all of us, he had the most medical knowledge.

My brother pressed his lips together, clearly unhappy. Then he signaled, *It's your choice. You can probably go another day, but no longer. Think about it. You can save yourself now and have another baby later.*

"No," I said as Ari gasped. He'd been watching Leif. I held up a hand, stopping Ari from voicing his questions about the baby. "I need another option."

"I don't have one," Leif said.

"I do!" Janco jumped to his feet.

The poor man hadn't said a word or moved since they had dragged Dax in.

Janco's hands almost blurred as he motioned. *Wouldn't Brother Horror's power not work on you because of that blocking thing?*

That's just speculation. I can't risk the baby.

You might not have a choice if we're here for a few days.

True.

"Can someone tell us what's going on?" Dax asked.

"It's better if you don't know," Ari said. He sank onto the pallet of straw in his cell. "Did you know about...that before you rushed off to rescue Leif?" he asked me.

"Yes, and don't yell at me. Leif and Janco already have."

Ari grunted, but kept quiet. I sipped the cooling tea. It tasted divine, warming me. However, I planned to wait another day before I ate the food. At this point, I didn't have any other options.

The following day passed in a slow trickle of nothing. Without a window, we marked time by the guards' entrance. Trays of hot food arrived, cooled, congealed and were replaced—three per day. I started eating after the fourth delivery. By that time, dizziness made it difficult for me to stand.

Leif made a few obvious gestures to explain to Dax and Hale why I risked being turned into Bruns's minion.

After two days, the others started drinking the Theobroma-laced water. They didn't wish to die. No one voiced what we all thought: *Where's Valek? Will he be here soon? Or has he been captured?*

Four days into our incarceration, Loris and Bruns accompanied the food. They stood in front of my cell.

"You're the only one who seems to have an appetite." Bruns peered at me in suspicion. "Why is that?"

I shrugged. "I don't have as much willpower as the others."

"Uh-huh. Loris?"

Instinctively I glanced at Loris, but wished I hadn't when he captured my gaze. Unable to look away, I fought against a heaviness pressing into my thoughts. I tried to jumble them, keep the answers from his reach like a mental game of keep-away. It worked until he increased his efforts. Then I counted numbers backward as Valek had taught me and recited lists of poisons. It only delayed the inevitable. Eventually, Loris's magic shone on all the corners of my mind, exposing everything. The blocking thing failed to work. Instead, a power-less humiliation spread throughout my body.

"And?" Bruns asked.

"She's pregnant."

While Loris held me, I was unable to see Bruns's reaction. However, through Loris, I sensed Bruns's surprise turn into cold calculation.

"Is Valek the father?"

"Yes, and he knows all about the baby. In fact, the two of them have exchanged marriage vows."

That statement triggered a wave of astonishment throughout the prison.

"Let me be the first to congratulate you, Yelena," Bruns said. "I'm looking forward to learning more about what you've been up to this last year. Is she ready?" he asked Loris.

"Yes. She's mine."

"Good." Bruns gestured to one of the guards. "Unlock her door. We'll take her to my office, milk all the information from her, then scrub her mind clean."

Right now I'd like to scrub the floor with Bruns's face. Loris laughed. "You won't feel that way for long. In a couple days, you'll be his new best friend."

"Gentlemen, say goodbye to Yelena," Bruns said. "The next time you see her, she won't remember you."

The door to my cell swung open.

Loris said, "Come."

The compulsion to obey pushed on my muscles, and I moved to his side. He broke eye contact and I almost swayed with relief. However, my body now followed his commands. Odd.

As we walked by Leif's cell, my brother said, "Remember Mogkan."

A strange way to say goodbye.

"Who's Mogkan?" Bruns asked, stopping.

"Tell him," Loris ordered me.

The strong impulse to divulge the information pressed on me. "Mogkan was a magician who wiped the minds of other magicians in order to steal their magic to increase his own power. He'd attempted to add me to his ring of power, but he failed."

"Ah, a little pep talk from your big brother," Bruns said. "Sweet, but this is very different. I'm sure Mogkan didn't use Theobroma on her, and she had magic then."

We continued to the exit, but Leif's gaze never wavered from mine. I hadn't told them everything about Mogkan, and with good reason. When Mogkan had attempted to turn me into a mindless slave, he could only control one part of me. Either my mind or my body. Never both. And I'd been eating Theobroma, except we called it criollo at that time. As for my magic, it had been a survival instinct that kicked in when I was trapped without options. Mogkan hadn't ever triggered that when we were together.

Could that natural resistance to Mogkan's magic apply to Loris's magic, as well? Leif's pep talk might just save my life.

The questioning spanned hours. It'd been late morning when we started, but now most of the afternoon was gone. I huddled in the leather armchair in Bruns's office as he grilled me on Valek, the Sitian Council, the Master Magicians and the Commander.

There was no need for me to talk as Loris plucked the information from my mind. Each of his forays for details sapped my strength. And the effort to prevent him from my thoughts only weakened my resistance to his probes. I transferred my energy to keeping that bit of free will alive and hiding a few important secrets. However, if this session continued much longer, I'd pass out from exhaustion.

"Yelena and Valek believe the Commander is planning to attack Sitia after the Fire Festival in Ixia. Which is about five months away," Loris said.

"Ah. Good to know," Bruns said. "Did they tell anyone else their suspicions?"

"No. They're waiting for more proof."

MARIA V. SNYDER

"Does she know where Valek is?"

Ha. I knew he'd lied about capturing Valek. Bruns lied with ease. I wondered who else he'd lied to.

Loris shot me a look.

You don't really think you and your sister are safe, Loris. Do you? You're magicians, and Bruns has made his opinion about people with powers quite clear, I thought.

Don't think you can manipulate me. I'm in control here, and I see right through your attempt to distract me. Loris turned to Bruns. "She doesn't know where Valek is. If he's not at the rendezvous location, she can only speculate at this point."

"And?" Bruns asked.

Black-and-white spots swarmed my vision, but I imagined Valek clinging to the ceiling right over Bruns's bed, waiting to drop down and kill him. A guess or wishful thinking? I'd let Loris decide.

Loris studied me. "She thinks he'll come after you."

Bruns considered. "It would be a sound strategy, provided I was the sole person in charge. However, it's a Cartel for a reason. Our plans involve a great deal of people, and my death won't affect it at all." He drummed his fingers on the armrest. "He's going to attempt to rescue her. We'll use her as bait."

I dug my fingernails into the leather as the room spun. Loris's grip on my mind loosened a bit.

"Right now she needs to rest and eat," Loris said.

"All right." Bruns stood and scooped me up in his arms.

I yipped in surprise. He carried me to a small room adjoining his office. No windows or other doors, but there was a single bed, night table and lantern. Bruns laid me on the bed and pulled a blanket over me. No doubt his gentleness was all part of a bigger plan. A bit of energy surged through me as I braced for his threat or warning.

"Get some sleep. I'll have a tray of food sent up along with your favorite tea. You must stay healthy for the baby," Bruns said.

"And a fat, juicy worm works much better as bait."

He smiled, but no humor shone from his gray eyes. "You think I enjoy this? I don't. I value life, Yelena. That's why we're doing what needs to be done in order to save Sitia."

"Your methods—"

"Harsh, I know. But we don't have the time to convince everyone the old-fashioned way. And it's a good thing the Cartel didn't hesitate, because we'll be ready to protect our homeland if the Commander's army invades us in five months."

"You're not the first person to think that, Bruns. Remember Master Magician Roze Featherstone? She believed she was protecting Sitia when she unleashed the Fire Warper and joined sides with the Daviian Vermin. Look what happened to her." Roze had been killed, and I'd confined her soul in a glass prison.

"I'm touched you're so concerned with my welfare. However, the reason Roze Featherstone failed was due to her reliance on magic and magicians. They're an unpredictable, egotistical and selfish lot and can't be trusted unless they're properly...indoctrinated."

"Indoctrinated? That's a fancy word for brainwashed."

"I certainly won't miss these little chats of ours when you've had your change of heart." Bruns glanced at Loris hovering in the doorway. "Command her to stay in bed until you or I give her permission to leave."

A heavy pressure pinned me to the mattress. The compulsion to remain under the covers drained the last bit of vigor I'd summoned. My eyelids drooped as Bruns and Loris left. The door remained ajar mere feet from me. But in my current condition, it might as well have been miles away.

Unreachable.

Voices woke me…later. I had no idea how long I'd slept, but my stomach growled, demanding food. I sat up. A tray of sliced fruit, cheese and ham slices sat on the night table, along with a glass teapot. Heat radiated from the pot—one of Quinn's hot glass pieces.

I wondered how Bruns managed to get one. Had he indoctrinated Quinn, as well? Many of the Keep's magicians had joined Bruns's ranks, but I hadn't seen the young glass mage among them. Perhaps he was at another garrison. It made sense for the Cartel to commandeer as many as possible.

About to pour a cup of steaming tea, I paused as a knock silenced Bruns and his visitor. The other man left and—

"Come in, General," Bruns said.

"I apologize for the road dust and mud, but Tia said you wanted to see me right away," a man said.

There was no mistaking that confident, sly voice. Cahil, or rather, *General* Cahil of the Sitian army. The man who had gone from my friend to my enemy when he discovered he hadn't been the King of Ixia's nephew, and the years he spent planning to retake his kingdom from the Commander had been wasted. Cahil had joined with Roze and the Daviians until the horrors of their kirakawa ritual switched his loyalty back to me, but we'd never regained our friendship. It was obvious why Cahil now reported to Bruns. Cahil hated the Commander and Valek and had been itching for a fight since he was six years old.

I set the pot down quietly, slid from the bed and crept closer to the open door in order to hear them better.

"…new information about the Commander," Bruns said. He repeated all the intel he'd stolen from me. "Seems the Commander might make his move after the Ixian Fire Festival."

"How did you learn all this?" Cahil asked.

"From a reliable source."

Ah. Interesting.

"That means nothing. Valek has spies all over Sitia. I wouldn't trust—"

"Yelena Zaltana provided it," Bruns said with an annoyance that bordered on anger.

"Now I know it's fake. She'd never—"

"She's in my custody." Again the clipped tone.

Silence. "Is it true? About her magic?"

"Yes, and that makes her just as susceptible to Theobroma as everyone else."

Cahil huffed. "She won't *ever* be like everyone else. Don't *ever* underestimate her."

"She is in our control," Bruns almost growled.

And then I realized, I'd left the bed despite Loris's order. His command pulled at me, but it'd been reduced to an uneasy feeling, as if it was starting to wear off.

"Then I suggest you don't wipe her mind."

"Why not? She's dangerous. You said so yourself."

"If she's cooperating with you, then use her. There isn't another person in Sitia with her unique knowledge of Ixia's security and the Commander. I'd bet she'd have good ideas about how the Commander plans to attack. Think about it. She's been working as the Liaison for years. Plus dating Valek." Cahil spat Valek's name as if it tasted rancid in his mouth.

"Not anymore," Bruns said.

A pause. A long pause. "What do you mean?"

"They're married and are going to have a baby."

I bit my thumb, waiting for Cahil's reaction. At one point in our relationship, he'd hoped for more than friendship.

"I see." Cahil's flat tone said more than his words.

"Now there's more at stake than her own life," Bruns said. "Which ensures her continued cooperation."

"Is there anything else?" Cahil asked.

"Yes. Where are we with the other garrisons?"

"We have taken over control of the ones in Moon, Featherstone and Greenblade. Master Magician Bain Bloodgood and the Councilors have been relocated to safety in the base in Greenblade's lands. Master Magician Irys Jewelrose is at the Featherstone Clan's, along with the stronger magicians. We believe the Commander's army will head straight for the Citadel."

"Have the magicians along the border with Ixia reported any activity?"

"Not yet. They each check in at dawn via the super messengers."

"Send them orders to keep an eye out for Valek."

Another longish pause. "You don't know where he is?"

"He'll be coming here regardless. I'd just like some notice on the timing."

"From my experience, he's probably already here, hidden among your soldiers with a dozen of his corps. And if he isn't, he can cross the border without alerting anyone. If I was you—"

"You're not. We have the situation well in hand."

"All right. Then I'll go check in with the garrison commander."

Boots shuffled on the floor.

"Cahil," Bruns called.

I imagined Cahil looking over his shoulder with his hand on the door.

"Yes?"

"What would you do in my place?" Bruns asked.

"I'd put a big bow on Yelena and deliver her to the Commander. It would keep both her and Valek in Ixia. Plus she'd hinder the Commander's efforts. Yelena wouldn't want war, and she'd do everything she could to stop him from invading."

Actually, that was rather smart. Cahil had matured since I'd seen him last.

"I'll think about it," Bruns said.

The door clicked shut. I returned to the bed, sliding under the covers. After that charged conversation, I suspected Bruns would want to peek in and make sure I'd remained asleep and under his control. I lay on my side, facing the wall with my eyes closed, just in case.

A heel scuffed the stone nearby. I kept my breathing deep and even, only relaxing once Bruns's office chair squeaked under his weight.

I mulled over all I'd learned as I nibbled on the ham. It had a glaze that tasted Theobroma-sweet. It didn't sound as if Cahil was being influenced by Theobroma and magic. He might have volunteered, or he could even be a member of the Cartel. I wondered if Bruns kept a list of the Cartel members in his desk. Probably not—he didn't strike me as someone who made stupid mistakes. No, he was smart enough to ask Cahil what he'd do about me.

And I would be happy to go to Ixia. But Cahil also said to use me first. Not that I really knew the Commander. Other than his secret, I hardly knew him at all. The man was intelligent, cunning and had the brilliant strategy and forethought to plan and then execute the takeover of Ixia.

The takeover of Ixia. I clutched the sheets as I repeated those words.

The.

Takeover.

Of.

Ixia.

MARIA V. SNYDER

Holy snow cats! The Commander wouldn't invade with an army and wage war. No. He'd plan a way to take over Sitia with little bloodshed. Just as he did twenty-three years ago!

29

VALEK

"There's no one at the Keep?" Valek repeated Fisk's comment because it didn't make any sense. "Are you sure?"

"Yes. They've all left, and my network followed them to three different garrisons in Sitia," Fisk said.

"Why?"

Fisk explained about Bruns's Cartel using Theobroma to influence even the Master Magicians to join his cause. The magicians had gone to support the soldiers and prepare for when the Commander attacked.

Valek glanced at Zohav and Zethan, still on the horses but close enough to hear their conversation. Both wore worried frowns, and both their thoughts sounded inside Valek's head. Zethan disappointed they probably wouldn't go to the Keep, and Zohav plotting a way to turn this news to her advantage.

Combined with Fisk's thoughts, Valek couldn't think straight.

"Stop it," he yelled at the twins.

"Stop what?" Zethan asked.

"Stop projecting your thoughts into my head!"

Alarmed, they exchanged a look.

"We're not," Zohav said.

"You've been doing it since we left home."

"No. We've had our barriers in place, blocking magic from our thoughts."

"Then how do I know you wished you brought more books, and Zethan wishes he'd sent a letter to Rosalie before leaving home?"

Again their gazes met. Both bewildered.

Fisk touched his shoulder. "Valek, you're immune to magic. Even if they were sending their thoughts, you should only feel the *magic*."

Fisk was right. Valek drew in a deep breath.

"But I *was* lamenting the fact I didn't have time to write Rosalie," Zethan said.

"Have you ever heard another person's thoughts?" Fisk asked Valek.

"No. Sometimes I can tell what a person is thinking by his body language, facial expression, direction of his gaze…things like that, but not actual thoughts."

Fisk turned to the twins. "You have magic?"

"Yes," Zethan said.

"Can you try it on Valek? Something benign."

Zethan turned to his sister. "Zo can."

She pressed her lips together, dismounted, grabbed the water skin and unscrewed the cap. Zohav stared at it. Water rose from the skin, forming a ball that floated in midair.

Valek would have been impressed, but the fact that he didn't sense her magic, that the stickiness didn't press on him, had him quite distracted. The ball of water approached him and then struck his chest, soaking his tunic.

"Touch the wet spot with your hand," she instructed him.

He pressed his palm to the cold fabric. Zohav's eyebrows pinched together and the water streamed from his tunic and re-formed into a ball.

"Wow," Fisk whispered. "That's amazing."

"What is?" Zethan asked. "That she can manipulate water, or that Valek's immunity is gone?"

"Both."

"Gone?" Valek fingered his now-dry tunic. "That's...that's a big leap in logic."

"Zo."

She glared at her brother.

"We need to figure this out. Besides, he's—"

"Confused," Valek said before Zethan said *brother*.

Stepping toward Valek, Zohav extended her hand as if for a handshake. "It's another test. It won't hurt."

That wasn't why he hesitated. He feared the results more than the pain. But he feared not knowing just as much. Valek grasped her cold hand. A strange tingle zipped through him.

"I sense the water inside your body," Zohav said. "Zee's right. You're no longer protected."

Valek let go of her and stepped back. Unprotected? The desire to draw his daggers pulsed. He craved their tangible weight in his hands. No immunity? The words repeated in his mind, but they failed to find a place to settle.

"What happened to his immunity?" Fisk asked. "Did you two do something to him?"

"No. Even if it was possible, we don't have that ability," Zethan said.

Fisk turned to him. "Did something happen to you? Do you know when it started?"

"I..." Valek pulled his thoughts together with effort. He searched his memories. During the raid on the pirates, he'd been fine. The trip to Icefaren had been quiet. And then... the shock of seeing his parents, the surprise of learning he had three siblings... No. He'd had his share of astonishments over the years without any consequences.

MARIA V. SNYDER

It had happened sometime that night he stayed by his brothers' graves. When he'd talked to Zebulon, and Zeb had asked if he could handle it. Handle the fact his parents had moved past the death of their sons and resumed living. When he realized he'd been frozen in time.

The scene of Valek kneeling next to Vincent's grave flashed in his head. That strange, light feeling that had cracked the cold, hard ice around him. Had it destroyed his immunity? Yelena speculated that his protection was a null shield that he had grafted to his soul when he witnessed his brothers' murder. Did finally making peace with that part of his life release his immunity? And if so, what did that make him now?

"Yes, something happened," Valek said to Fisk in a strained voice. "I can't…" He held a hand up, stopping any more questions. Then he bolted down the road until they disappeared from sight.

Time alone might help.

He needed Yelena. Desperately.

Valek stopped and leaned against a tree. Emotions surged. His world spun as if he'd been set adrift. Was this how Yelena had felt when she realized she couldn't access her magic? Perhaps someone had blocked his immunity? Not likely.

Muted steps sounded, and then a warm, soft nose pressed against his cheek.

Ghost No More upset.

Valek jerked as Kiki's thoughts filled his mind. He stared at her.

She pushed on his shoulder. *Go find Lavender Lady.*

Yes. They needed to rescue Yelena and Leif. *Can you hear me?* he asked Kiki.

Yes. Ghost No More.

The horses called him Ghost because of his immunity. Another confirmation that it was gone, and in its place…

Magic, Kiki said.

Mine? Is that why I can hear you? Or is it your magic?

Both.

When he returned to the clearing, Fisk had packed his bag. All three of them turned to him, waiting.

"Where's Bruns holding Yelena?" he asked Fisk.

"No."

"No?"

"You can't go in there like that."

"Like what?"

"Open to magic. You need to learn how to block other magicians, or Bruns's people will seize you as soon as you get close."

"It's important to block others," Zethan said. "It's the first thing Nell taught us, along with controlling our magic."

"But I can still hear your thoughts," Valek said.

"Yeah...about that." Zethan grimaced. "We think you might be either very powerful or you're pulling too much magic from the blanket of power and could..."

"Flame out and kill us all," Zohav said.

Valek stilled. He hadn't even considered the danger. What else was he missing? "Can you teach me?"

"It's not safe here," Fisk said. "By now Bruns probably learned of this location from Yelena. We need to return to my headquarters in the Citadel and plan our next move."

Fisk was right. No doubt Bruns expected Valek to rescue Yelena and Leif. And he was in no condition to fight Bruns's magicians.

"Can you keep it together until we arrive?" Fisk asked, misunderstanding Valek's hesitation.

"I can explain how to build a mental barrier as we ride," Zethan offered.

MARIA V. SNYDER

He'd have to keep a tight hold on the…magic. Too many people were depending on him. Valek strode to Onyx and mounted. "Let's go."

As the others prepared to go, Valek tried an experiment and sent his thoughts to Onyx, *Go fast to Citadel?*

No response.

Kiki? he asked.

He not Sandseed.

But he understands you.

Kiki speak horse, too.

Valek stifled a laugh. If he lost it now, he wouldn't be able to recover his composure. He was already sure the repercussions from this…turn of events would echo for a long, long time. Mulling it over as they headed south to the border, Valek found a bright side. He'd no longer be trapped by a blasted null shield. Wouldn't Bruns be surprised?

This time, he laughed aloud.

During the two-day trip to the Citadel, Zethan taught Valek how to construct a mental wall that would block other magicians from reading his thoughts and influencing him.

"You tapped into the power source instinctively, which is why you're hearing our thoughts," Zethan explained. "First you need to locate that link, that thread to the blanket of power." He gestured to the sky. "For me, it feels like a current of air, connecting me, which makes sense since I can influence storms. Zo says it's like a tiny stream of water. Block out all distractions and focus. Tell me when you've found it."

Valek concentrated. He smothered his worries, strangled his anxiety and silenced his doubts. In the resulting calm, a river of energy flooded him. "Got it."

"What does it resemble?" Zee asked.

"A…flow of…power, as if spraying from a pipe." Valek

struggled to describe the magic. "Almost like a bolt of lightning that doesn't disappear."

Zethan exchanged a wide-eyed look with his sister. "All right. Imagine a shield made of marble, or something that can block the lightning and protect you. Use the lightning to construct this shield."

"How?"

"Imagine you can grab the lightning and mold it into the shield."

Following Zethan's instructions, Valek closed his eyes, but he couldn't manipulate the bolts of power, no matter how hard he tried. Frustrated, he asked, "What else can I try?"

"I don't know," Zethan said. "It worked for me. What about you, Zo?"

She frowned at her brother, but it seemed more from habit than a real emotion. "I couldn't manipulate the water. Instead, I imagined my shield as a piece of leather and the magic as a dye that I applied to the leather, strengthening it." Another scowl—this one directed at Valek. "I assume you worked in Father's tannery when you were younger. Maybe that might work for you."

A good idea, except his power seared the leather and set it on fire—or rather, it did in his imagination. Leather wouldn't work. Marble didn't resonate with him, either. What could withstand the lightning and was part of him? What had helped him in his time of need? His daggers and sword—both made of steel. Yet that failed to work. The metal melted. What else?

Kiki jigged to the side of the road and a stone flew out from under her hooves, whizzing past his head. He almost groaned aloud, remembering the gray rocks he used for his statues. Envisioning a large hunk of the rock about the size of his head, Valek used the lightning to carve the piece into a black helmet with specks of silver that would protect him from magic. When he finished, he strapped the helmet on and peace descended.

"Better?" Zethan asked.

"Much. Thank you both, and you, too, Kiki."

Kiki flicked her tail, but didn't slow. They were within sight of the Citadel's walls.

They looped around to enter the east side in case Bruns had set an ambush on the west side.

"But remember, if a magician is more powerful than you and he has the ability to read minds, you're screwed. He'll grind that wall into dust." Zethan twisted his fist into his palm, demonstrating.

"You and Zohav don't have the ability to read minds. Right?" Valek asked.

"Yes. I can't reach out to others. But if you send your thoughts to me, I can hear them if I let you past my barrier."

"Unless I'm more powerful and can break through?"

"Right. The same is true for Zo."

"Zee!"

"Relax, Zo. If we're going to help rescue his heart mate, he needs to know our abilities and limits."

Surprised, Valek said, "You're not—"

At the same time Zohav said, "We're not—"

"Nonsense," Zethan interrupted. "Fisk just said all the magicians are gone. Who else is going to help?"

The boy made an excellent point.

"My network of helpers," Fisk said.

"Do they have magic?" Zethan asked.

"No."

"Then how are they going to resist Bruns?"

Fisk looked impressed.

"It's not our fight," Zohav said.

"Nonsense, Valek's our br...er...friend."

Valek would have to teach Zethan how to keep a secret. That was the second time the boy almost slipped up.

"I already know," Fisk said, as if he read Valek's mind.

"How to rescue Yelena and Leif?" Valek asked, hoping to distract Fisk.

"No. That Zohav and Zethan are your siblings. Don't give me that look, Valek. Anyone with a modicum of observation skills could see the family resemblance within seconds. Give me some credit. Besides, I have much more than a modicum of skills. You have to give me that."

"I'll give you credit for knowing the definition of *modicum*." Fisk laughed.

Valek's attention turned back to the problem of who would help him. The magicians at the Keep had left, but not all Sitian magicians stayed at the Keep. In fact, many lived in other cities. But according to Fisk, Bruns had been either recruiting them into joining his Cartel or drugging/strong-arming them.

"Fisk, do you know if there are any magicians not under Bruns's control?"

"There are a few in hiding, but they're too scared to get involved."

Valek didn't want to risk the twins—he'd promised his mother he'd keep them safe, but they might be his only option. Zethan's storm powers— Ah, of course! "What about the Stormdancers?"

"I'm not sure," Fisk said. "They're on hiatus until the heating season. Maybe Bruns missed them."

Valek hoped so.

They waited until well after dark to enter the Citadel. After they passed the gate, a young boy appeared from the shadows and approached Fisk. Fisk leaned over Kiki's saddle as the boy gestured and made quiet tweeting noises.

MARIA V. SNYDER

Fisk's expression turned grim. "What about the escape hatch, Tweet?"

The boy shook his head.

"What's going on?" Valek asked Fisk.

"Bruns has an ambush waiting for us inside *my* headquarters." A hard edge sharpened his tone.

"What about your people?" Valek nodded in Tweet's direction.

"Being forced to feed and take care of the *guests* until we arrive for the big surprise." Fisk's disgust was clear. He held Kiki's reins as if he'd like to wrap the leather around one of the intruders' neck.

"What's the escape hatch?" Zethan asked.

"An alternate way into and out of our headquarters. They haven't discovered its existence yet."

"How many of them?" Valek asked.

Tweet held up ten fingers, then flashed them again.

"Twenty?"

A nod.

He considered. They'd have the element of surprise if they used the escape hatch to get inside. But he still didn't like the odds. "Do you know if any of them have magic?"

Three fingers.

They'd need backup. Or would they? What if he allowed them to capture him? They'd think they were safe if he was contained in a null shield. Then they'd take him to Yelena. He wouldn't have to worry about sneaking in, just getting away.

"Where are they holding Yelena?" he asked Fisk.

"Krystal Clan garrison. About two days west of the Citadel."

"Near Mica?"

"Yes."

And north of the Stormdance Clan's lands. "Can you get null shields for your helpers?"

"No. Bruns stopped the magicians from selling them."

Damn. "What about the magicians in hiding? Do any of them know how to craft them?"

"One or two, but it'll take at least seven days to reach them." Too long.

"There might be a few of those glass ones that Quinn makes left inside the Keep," Fisk said.

Tweet piped twice.

"The Keep's being watched by Bruns's people," Fisk translated.

"Has the staff left, as well?"

Tweet nodded, but then gestured.

"Most of the staff didn't go to the other garrisons," Fisk said. "Just the magicians."

"Do you know if Leif's wife, Mara, was taken?"

The boy shook his head. He didn't.

Valek considered the information Tweet had provided as he spurred Onyx toward the center of the Citadel. He found an inn with a stable a couple blocks away. After the horses were groomed and settled, he rented two rooms.

Fisk and Tweet followed them upstairs. As soon as they closed the door, Fisk asked, "What's the plan?"

"You tell me," Valek said.

"I'm not one of your corps."

"You could be."

Fisk smirked. "You couldn't afford me." But then he sobered. "I can send a team to check the situation with the Stormdancers and bring them on board if they're able."

"Good. And?"

"And you will visit the Keep and see if you can find anything that will help us."

"What about us?" Zethan asked.

"Stay here for now." He held up a hand, stopping the protest. "I'm going to need you both when we implement the rescue."

"You have a plan?" Zethan asked.

"I'm working on it. First I need to see what resources are available. Tweet, can you find out if Mara is still in the Citadel?"

He nodded in agreement and left with Fisk, who planned to check on his helpers. Fisk promised to return in the morning for another planning session.

Valek instructed Zethan and Zohav to remain inside while he visited the Keep.

"What if you don't come back or are captured?" Zethan asked.

"Fisk or one of his people will take care of you."

"And if Fisk is caught, as well?" Zohav asked, ever the pessimist.

He handed her a pouch of coins. "Then stay here. I will send one of my Citadel spies to keep you safe until I return."

"But—"

"Don't worry, Zo," Zethan said.

She jabbed him in the chest with her finger. "You said the same thing when those pirates boarded our ship."

He spread his hands wide. "And look how it turned out! We're in Sitia!"

"And in the middle of a...whatever this is."

She had a point. As Valek left, he tried to put a name to what Bruns's Cartel had been doing. Recruiting only worked for those who hadn't been coerced, or for those who were too scared to say no. As for those being drugged to obey, they didn't have a choice—more like a hostile takeover.

He paused. A takeover. Under the guise that it was in order

to protect Sitia from the Commander's army. But a takeover all the same.

Valek didn't like where his thoughts led him next. The Commander's hints of massing an army had never made sense to him, and he suspected Owen had influenced that decision. What if that was all a show? What if Owen had made a deal with the Cartel? The Commander's distrust and hatred of magicians ran deep, but what if Owen and Bruns conspired to demonstrate to the Commander that they could control the magicians, make them obey and show that they no longer had any free will?

But they wouldn't be content to rule Sitia. Once they'd earned the Commander's trust, or used magic to hijack him, it'd be just a matter of time before they removed him from power. Then Owen would rule Ixia, and Bruns's Cartel would be in charge of Sitia.

His stomach churned, pushing bile up his throat. Valek tried to dismiss his speculation as nothing but that—an exercise in logic. However, the inner intuitive sense that hadn't ever let him down agreed with his conclusions.

A wave of despair washed through him. He paused in a shadow, leaning against a wall. He didn't have the people or the resources to stop it. Plus, his life had been turned completely upside down. His protection from magic was gone, and he had no idea how to use the power. But Valek knew if Owen and the Cartel won, there'd be no family for him. Yelena, the baby, all the people he cared for would be eliminated, including him. Basic strategy.

He'd find a way to stop it. Or die trying. Giving up was not an option. He pushed the despondency away. Pure determination fueled his steps. He stopped by the safe house and reassigned his agents. They would also aid in the rescue attempt, but for now, he sent them to protect the twins.

MARIA V. SNYDER

Two watchers crouched in the shadows near the Keep. Valek sensed there had to be more. He scanned the buildings opposite the Keep's entrance, searching for places he'd use for stakeouts. Ah. Three—no, four more observed from windows and roofs.

Unfortunately, the Magician's Keep was surrounded by a high marble wall. The four towers at each corner that rose above the walls had also been constructed with the slick stone, which made climbing impossible. And with only one entrance, the place was well protected. However, when the Daviian Warpers had invaded and taken control, that protection worked against the magicians. Which was why the Master Magicians decided to build another entrance known only to them, Yelena and Valek. He'd aided them on so many occasions that they'd grown to trust him. And he'd kept the secret from the Commander.

He ghosted along a row of factories and businesses that faced the west side of the Keep, ensuring no one followed him or was watching. Satisfied, he slipped through a narrow alley, unlocked the third door on the left, entered and secured the door. Torches and flint waited on a table nearby. He lit one and revealed a small landing with steps leading down into blackness.

Valek descended. At the bottom was a tunnel that crossed under the Keep's wall and ended in the basement of Irys's tower. Valek reached it without incident. He climbed to ground level and extinguished the torch.

Letting his eyes adjust to the darkness, Valek waited a few minutes before leaving the tower. A half-moon lit the sky. He passed the empty stables and cut through the overgrown pasture on his way to the glass workshop, hoping a few of Quinn's null-shield glass pendants had been left behind.

The quiet campus felt abandoned and...dead. As if the life

had been sucked away. Perhaps it was his imagination. When he was immune to magic, he would encounter sticky pockets of random magic whenever he visited the Keep. Janco called it the Creepy Keepy because he, too, sensed the power. This time, the name certainly fit.

The door to the glass workshop hung open—not a good sign. He stepped inside and broken glass crunched under his boots. Even the dim light couldn't hide the fact that the place had been ransacked. Scattered tools lay next to overturned gaffer benches. Bent pontil irons and crushed coal littered the floor. Valek hoped the damage had been done after everyone had left the Keep, because worry for Mara grew as he inspected her office—it looked as bad as the rest.

If there had been any of Quinn's pendants left behind, they had been smashed or taken. Valek checked the armory next. All the weapons were gone. No surprise. Inside the administration building, files had been strewn into a chaotic mess. Bain's and Irys's offices had also been searched, along with Bain's tower in the southeast corner.

Disappointed and sick to his stomach over the destruction, Valek headed back to Irys's tower, cutting through the center of the campus. He stopped at the Fire Memorial. It had been carved from stone to resemble a campfire's flames. Valek almost lost Yelena during the battle with the Fire Warper. Many people had died in the fight, and their names had been etched onto a plaque on the front side of the memorial. On another side was a list of the names of those who prevented the Warpers from taking control of Sitia. Valek's name was among them. The one on the back only had two names— Yelena's and Opal's. Without them, the Fire Warper would still be a threat.

Valek touched Yelena's name with a fingertip. *Stay strong, love. I'm coming.*

MARIA V. SNYDER

When he returned to Irys's tower, an impulse to visit Yelena's rooms flared in his chest. Instead of heading down to the tunnel, he climbed up to the third story. And stopped.

A ribbon of yellow light glowed from underneath the door. He pulled a dagger and a small mirror from his pockets. The long, thin handle of the mirror allowed him to peek under the door without tipping off the person or persons inside.

The scent of wood smoke wafted out as he bent to insert the mirror. From this angle, he caught sight of a small fire burning in the hearth and a single pair of boots in front of the couch.

Too curious to leave, Valek straightened, returned the mirror and tested the doorknob. Unlocked. Bracing for an attack, he entered the room. A dark figure stood next to the couch, looking in Valek's direction, but a wavy translucent shimmer hung between them and made it impossible for Valek to identify the person.

"Uncle Valek?" a young male voice asked. "How did you… Oh!"

The veil dropped.

Teegan rushed to him, throwing his arms around Valek for a quick hug. "I'm so glad to see you!"

"What are you doing here?" Valek asked his not-quite-nephew.

"Waiting for you or Aunt Yelena to show up."

"Why? And how?"

"Long story." Teegan raced around and packed up his meager belongings. "Tell you on the way."

"The way?"

"Yeah. On the way to wherever you're hiding."

Valek glanced around, spotting evidence that Teegan had been living here for at least a week. A pile of books teetered near the couch. He couldn't leave Teegan here, even though it was probably safer than the inn. "Tell me when we get there. We need to keep quiet."

"Okay." Teegan poured a bucket of water onto the fire, dousing the flames. Thick smoke boiled up the chimney. Teegan followed Valek's gaze. "It's too dark to see it."

"But not to smell it," Valek said.

"Oh. I hadn't thought of that."

"Remember it for next time. Let's go."

Many questions rose in his mind as Valek escorted Teegan through the tunnel and during the circuitous route around the Citadel. Only when Valek was satisfied no one followed them did he head to the inn.

Teegan stayed with the horses while Valek checked the rooms. His agent waited inside Valek's.

"Report," Valek ordered.

"All quiet. No trouble," the man said.

"Good. Get some sleep. We're meeting in the dining room in the morning. Tell the others."

"Yes, sir."

Valek fetched Teegan. Once the boy was comfortable, he said, "Tell me why you were alone in Irys's tower and spare no details."

"Do you know about the Theobroma in the Keep's food?"

"Yes."

"Then you know why everyone went basically crazy, believing the Commander is going to attack Sitia and they had to help fight. Convinced of the danger, groups of magician and students took off for the garrisons until only a few support staff remained. I didn't feel this compulsion, and I thought it was because I'm a student of Master Irys and she must be protecting me. But when I surprised her by showing up for a morning lesson, she determined that I must be strong enough to resist the magic, even with Theobroma in my body. Just like her and Master Bain."

Valek jumped on that bit of news. "Masters Irys and Bain aren't affected?"

"No."

"Then why did they follow Bruns's orders?"

"Because they didn't have anyone else but me to help them. Because they thought it better to pretend to be influenced and gather information until you and Aunt Yelena planned a way to stop Bruns's Cartel."

Such trust. Valek hoped not to disappoint them, but his main goal—rescuing Yelena—would come first. And then it hit him. "You have master-level powers!"

Teegan grinned. "I have to take the test first, but this kind of confirmed it."

Great news, except Teegan was only fourteen years old. Which reminded him... "Why didn't you go home and stay with your mother and father?"

"Master Bain thought the Cartel would be watching them, and it would be suspicious if I showed up there. Master Irys destroyed all record of my enrollment here, and she hoped the Cartel would assume they got everyone. Not many people knew I was working with her, and she told me to keep a low profile among the students. She sensed magicians would soon be under attack."

"So when Irys and Bain left..."

"I stayed and waited for you."

"What if someone saw your fire? Or decided to search the Keep?"

"I hid behind an illusion. Didn't you... Oh, that's right, you're immune, so you only felt the magic. If anyone else arrived, he'd see nothing but an empty room."

Valek had seen through the illusion. Did that mean he was

stronger than Teegan or that he was closer to flaming out? This wasn't the time to worry about it. "What if no one came?"

Teegan rummaged in his pack. "The Masters believed you'd come looking for these." He held up a handful of glass pendants.

"Are they—"

"Yup. Null shields. And if you didn't show, I planned to relive my days as a street rat and find Fisk."

Smart. Valek smiled. With Teegan and the pendants, they had a better chance of success. A crazy scheme to rescue Yelena and the others swirled to life. "Besides illusions, what else can you do?"

Teegan gave him a cocky little grin. "It'd be quicker to tell you what I *can't* do."

Oh, yes, this just might work.

Fisk and Tweet returned to the inn in the morning, and they gathered in a private dining room. Valek scanned the people sitting around the table. Two of his corps, Fisk, Tweet, Zethan, Zohav and Teegan. The majority were under eighteen and had no prior experience with subterfuge or fighting.

"I dispatched a team to the Stormdance Clan," Fisk said. "If there are Stormdancers who are willing to help, they'll meet us at the rendezvous location near the Krystal garrison."

Valek filled them in on Teegan's information. Relief touched all their faces when they learned of the Masters' resistance to Bruns's brainwashing.

"How many glass shields do you have?" Fisk asked.

"A dozen," Teegan said.

"Are there any more?"

"Not in the Keep," Teegan said.

Tweet gestured and piped a few notes.

"Good idea," Fisk said to the boy. "He confirmed that

Mara's still in the Citadel. She hired one of my people to carry her purchases from the market to her apartment yesterday. We can ask her if she has some of the glass shields."

"Was there anyone with her or in her apartment?" Valek asked.

"Are you thinking it could be another ambush?" Fisk asked.

"Anything is possible."

Shaking his head no, Tweet wagged his hands and tapped his forearm.

"She was alone."

"Good. I'll visit her tonight," Valek said.

They discussed possible scenarios and ways to infiltrate the garrison. Much depended on whether or not the Stormdancers would assist them, and if Mara had more glass pendants. The twins and Teegan consulted each other on what they could do with their combined magic. It gave Valek a few more ideas, which helped, considering everyone vetoed the plan where Valek walked into the ambush waiting in Fisk's headquarters and allowed them to capture him.

They formulated a basic plan, but more information needed to be collected before they could implement it. Satisfied, Valek ended the meeting, then he returned to his room to catch a few hours of sleep to prepare for another long night.

Under cover of darkness, Valek scouted the area near Mara's apartment building. No watchers lurked in the shadows. Just to be safe, Valek looped around to the back, climbed up to Mara's floor and entered through the hallway's window. Leif had learned how easy it was to open a window and ensured the ones in his apartment had extra security measures installed.

He debated using his lock picks on the lock. But it was late, and he didn't wish to scare Mara. Just to be sure, Valek slid his mirror under the door to check for intruders or ambushers. A small fire burned in the hearth and cast a warm amber glow on the furniture in the main living room. Seeing nothing amiss, he straightened and knocked lightly. After a few seconds, a shadow appeared under the door and an eye squinted through the peephole. He rested his hands near his daggers just in case.

The door swung open. Mara flew into his arms, squeezing him. "Valek! Thank fate!" She stepped back and blushed. "Sorry. Everyone's gone and I've been in a panic ever since. I figured all my friends and family had been caught."

He gave her a wry grin. "I'm not that easy to catch. Are you all right?"

"Fine. Do you have any news?"

Hating to disappoint her, he swallowed the sour taste in his mouth. "We're doing—"

A bang sounded behind him. Valek whirled with both his daggers in hand. The door across the hall gaped open, and armed men spilled from the opposite apartment. Almost twenty soldiers fanned out—ten on each side.

His comment about not being easy to catch had returned to haunt him. With twenty against one, they would have it easy. Valek, on the other hand—not so much.

30

LEIF

Hungry.

So hungry.

His stomach no longer rumbled, it *roared*. It growled and dug its sharp teeth into his gut, insisting, *Feed me!* He lay listless on the straw pallet, trying to ignore the scent of warm sweet cakes a few feet away. It masked the acrid stench of slop pots and body odor. For now.

Torture.

This was torture.

Worse than pain.

With nothing to distract him, he worried about Yelena, wondered how long he'd last before giving in, and wished for his favorite beef stew, and cherry pie, and Mara's pumpkin cake, and...

It'd been four days since Yelena was taken. Four days of sipping water and nibbling on a few bites of food to stay alive. Four days of silent discussions with the others about escaping. Nothing. They failed to find a weakness. A way out. Their one effort to grab the guards when they delivered the food had been a complete and utter flop.

By the fifth day, bouts of dizziness spun his cell, and his

legs shook when he stood. He'd have to decide if refusing to become Bruns's lackey was worth dying for. The scrape of the door roused him. Too soon for supper. He lifted his head.

Mara entered the jail with two guards on her heels.

His own woes disappeared in an instant as a cold knife of horror sliced right through him.

Leif surged to his feet and then grabbed the bars to keep from falling. "Mara…" His voice cracked in anguish.

Alarm and fear flashed in her golden eyes before she gathered her composure. She turned to the guard on her left. "You call this well? He looks half-dead."

"It's his own fault. He refuses to eat," the man said.

An odd exchange. Perhaps Leif was hallucinating. He certainly hoped the bruises on her beautiful heart-shaped face were an illusion.

Mara stepped closer to his cell. "Leif, you need to eat. No more hunger strike. Okay?"

Her sweet scent washed over him. "Mara, what's going on? Did they capture you?" he asked.

"Yes, but I worked out a deal with Bruns. He's really not that bad."

Another jab of pain pierced him. They'd brainwashed her, too.

"If I convince you to start eating, he'll free you. Bruns promised that we'd work together at the Moon garrison. Quinn Bloodrose is there, and I can assist him with his glass creations." She moved and reached her hand through the bars. "It's the best I could do."

He grasped it, twining his fingers in hers. Soaking in her warmth, he savored her touch as if it were the last time. "Sounds like you've given up."

"Bruns's men used the apartment across from us to ambush Valek." She bunched the fabric of her skirt in her free hand. "Valek managed to…kill a couple of them, but they

MARIA V. SNYDER

overwhelmed him. And I was…useless. Bruns is interrogating him now."

The news of Valek's capture slammed into him. Good thing she clutched his hand, or he would've collapsed from the blow. Valek had been their last hope.

"Start eating, please. For me," Mara implored him.

"All right," he said. "For you."

She relaxed, then pressed her face to the bars to kiss him. Her lips opened and he deepened the kiss.

"That's enough," the guard holding her arm said.

She rounded on him. "I haven't seen my husband in months."

"I've my orders."

"Fine." She jerked her arm free and smoothed her skirt. Mara turned to Leif. "At least we'll soon be together." Mara said goodbye and was escorted out.

When the door clanged shut, he sagged against the bars. A thousand emotions ripped through him. Fear dominated. Not for him, but for Mara.

"That was…unfortunate," Janco said.

For once the man didn't exaggerate. Leif glanced up. The rest of the inmates stared at him. No one said a word, but their thoughts were clear in their morose expressions. End of the road.

"Does that mean we're out of options?" Hale asked.

"Can we eat now?" Dax asked.

"Yes to both." Janco wasted no time in stuffing a sweet cake into his mouth.

Soon after, a group of soldiers carried an unconscious and naked Valek into the jail, dumped him into Yelena's empty cell next to Janco's, tossed a uniform onto his prone form and left.

Bloody, battered, bruised and with multiple cuts along his arms, legs and torso, Valek looked near death.

Janco reached through the bars and felt Valek's pulse. "It's strong."

They breathed a collective sigh of relief.

We're dead, Janco signaled.

Relax, Janco. Valek will have it all worked out, Ari said.

Valek didn't regain consciousness until after three meals had come and gone—a full day. He groaned and sat up, pressing one hand to his head and the other to his ribs.

"Welcome to the land of the living, boss," Janco said.

Valek glanced at them, then scanned the jail. "I think I prefer oblivion. It didn't hurt and it smelled better."

"Mara said you took a few out," Ari said.

"Is she okay?" Valek asked.

"Bruised and scared, but she said she made a deal with Bruns," Leif said.

"Good for her." Valek grimaced as he reached for the cup of water.

"Why do you say that?" Leif demanded. He crinkled his nose. There was something…off about Valek, and it wasn't the physical damage. Strange.

"It's a smart move on her part. I'd suggest you all do the same and make a deal with Bruns."

They glanced at each other in alarm.

Ari caught Valek's attention and signaled, *You're just saying that. Right? That's all part of the plan. Right?*

This—Valek gestured to his cell—*was not part of the plan. We were working on one, but it was in the preliminary stages.*

We who?

Fisk, his people and a couple of young magicians.

So we're screwed? Janco asked.

"Yep." Valek eased back into a prone position.

"Can I stop relaxing now?" Janco asked Ari.

31

YELENA

The past three days had been…strange or interesting, depending on the way I looked at it. Bruns had taken Cahil's advice and hadn't wiped my mind. Yet. Once he determined that my knowledge about the Commander was limited, Bruns no longer asked specific questions. In fact, my theory that he was just going through the motions of preparing for war strengthened the longer I spent with him. Which meant Cahil didn't know about it. No surprise, since it appeared Bruns had recruited Cahil and hadn't brainwashed him. So to keep Cahil cooperating, it would have to appear as if they prepared for battle.

I hadn't found any proof of my theory, but I kept an eye out for anything while I worked with Bruns on strategy. He planned to expand to the other garrisons in Sitia, indoctrinating them, as well. I hated helping him, but at the same time, the challenge kept my mind from imagining my brother and friends starving to death in the jail.

I'd been sleeping in the side room of Bruns's office and using the washroom in his suite downstairs. Every morning, Loris arrived and reinforced the magic holding me captive. Funny thing about that—for the next few hours, I couldn't refuse a command and I enjoyed the work, almost existing on an I-love-Bruns high, but as the day wore on, the magic wore off. From what I'd seen of Bruns's other minions, that didn't happen, and from the conversations Bruns had with Loris, it sounded as if once a person had been fully converted, they no longer needed to be influenced unless they had magic.

Perhaps I hadn't been fully rehabilitated yet. Or perhaps what had happened with Janco in the jail—that blocking power—had something to do with it. But I didn't touch Loris. Unless the baby really was a void and was slowly siphoning off the magic. My head ached with the possibilities.

The desire to bolt once the magic released its hold on me was strong, but I wouldn't leave without my brother, Ari, Janco, Dax and Hale. And I hadn't figured out a way to rescue them. Not yet.

On the fourth day, everything changed. Bruns called me into his office. I'd been helping in the armory that morning.

Mara stood on the other side of his desk. I froze in shock for a moment. No guards bookended her, and she appeared healthy, despite a few cuts and bruises on her face. Pure determination radiated from her—a side of Mara I hadn't seen before.

"You see? She's perfectly fine and has joined me. Tell her, Yelena."

"Yes, I'm assisting Bruns now. We have a lot of work to do in order to prepare for war."

"And it will be the same with Leif, if you convinced him to eat," Bruns said.

"He'll eat. As long as we can work together," Mara said.

He gave her a condescending smile. "Of course. I'm a businessman, and that was our deal."

Bruns called for his secretary, Tia, and asked her to escort Mara to the magicians' quarters to wait for Leif.

"It'll take a couple days. In the meantime, please make

yourself at home," Bruns said to Mara. "All meals are served in the canteen, and if you get bored, the cooks are always looking for help."

She nodded her thanks, met my gaze and held it a moment before leaving. Odd. The entire exchange was odd. Did I dare hope this was part of a larger scheme?

"You should be happy, Yelena. Now your brother won't die of starvation."

"I am."

"But?"

"You didn't seem to care if he lived or died before."

"Ah, true. However, working with you these last few days has made me realize why you, Leif and the others locked below have been so successful all these years. The level of intelligence is impressive. Now all I need is for Valek to break, and the Commander won't stand a chance."

"Excuse me if I don't believe you have him."

"Figured you'd say that. When we're done with him, I'll let you visit."

"Mighty nice of you." I gave him a tepid smile, but inside, worry bubbled. Bruns appeared way too smug to be lying.

He laughed. "Return to the armory. The Weapons Master is excited about your ideas. When you're finished, come back here."

Being in the armory had its advantages—access to weapons was at the top of the list. I stole darts filled with Curare and hid them in my clothes and room. Bruns never specifically said I couldn't. He was confident that his order not to escape included scheming, but it didn't.

At night, when the magic wore off, I could sneak down to the jail, disable the guards and free my brother and the others—I refused to believe Bruns had Valek. Denial kept me functioning.

Rescuing them from the jail would be easy. The hard part

would be leaving the garrison. Every entrance was well protected, soldiers patrolled around the buildings and magical alarms had been set on the walls. I could take Bruns hostage, put a knife to his throat and use him to get my friends released. Except it would only take one dart filled with Curare to neutralize me.

I sparked on another plan the morning of my sixth day. Simple, yet it just might work, if I had enough time to prepare. It would depend on when Loris intended to brainwash Leif and the others. I suspected soon. But it was the best plan I had so far.

That afternoon, Bruns ordered me to accompany him to the jail. By the way his chest puffed out and his eyes gleamed with glee, I assumed my days of denial were coming to an abrupt end.

When we entered, the first thing to hit me was the smell. After more than a week without bathing, the men reeked. I met Leif's gaze. He stood next to the door to his cell. He'd lost weight.

"You okay?" he asked.

I nodded. "You?"

"Fine. The food could be better, though."

Ah. They were eating. *Has Loris been here?* I signaled.

Not yet.

One positive. I moved on, and Janco gave me a halfhearted smile. And he might have said something, but my attention focused on Valek. His complexion made the color white look dingy. He clutched the bars, and from the purple bruises on his face and the gash on his forehead, I wouldn't be surprised if they supported his weight, as well. The desire to wrap him in my arms and heal him pulsed deep within me.

Unable to do either, I stood frozen while my heart dissolved. Valek kept his expression flat, but a blast of emotion pierced me when he met my gaze. I thought his voice sounded in my head, saying, *Sorry, love.* But I dismissed it as just my imagination. He wore a Sitian uniform like the others. Blood stained the fabric in more than a few places.

"Believe me now?" Bruns asked.

"Yes." Time to put on a show. I turned to him. "Why didn't you just prick him with goo-goo juice to make him talk? He has vital information about the Commander we can use."

"I did. It failed to work and so did torture."

It took all my self-control to stay put and not kick Bruns in the nuts.

"Next up. Threats." Bruns turned to Valek, who faced him. "Yelena, tell your *husband* what you've been doing these last few days."

"Helping you."

"Why?"

"Because we need to prepare for the Commander's attack," I said, while I signaled with the hand Bruns couldn't see—but Janco and Leif could. *Because I've no choice, you prick.*

"You follow my orders. Is that correct?" Bruns asked.

"Yes."

Bruns pulled a glass vial from his pocket. "Hold this." He handed it to me. "Don't drop it."

A pretty, deep purple liquid filled the container.

"It's an extract from the amethyst flower," Bruns explained. "It will kill the baby."

My grip tightened. All I could do. It was still early, and Loris's magic controlled my movements. But it didn't stop the panicked screaming inside my head.

"Drink it," he ordered me.

Terrified and unable to resist, I pulled the cork from the bottle and raised the rim to my lips.

"Stop," Valek growled.

"Stop," Bruns echoed to me.

The vial paused a few inches from my mouth. My blood slammed through my body as if I'd run for miles.

"You'll cooperate fully?" he asked Valek.

"Yes."

"Good. Yelena, put the stopper back in and keep that vial with you at all times. Understand?"

"Yes." Happy to comply, I shoved the cursed liquid into my pocket and out of sight. Purple was now an evil color.

"Eat," Bruns told Valek. "We'll have a chat when you've had some more time to recover. Any hint of trouble, and I'll order your wife to drink the extract. If I'm not happy with your answers or if I discover you lied, I'll—"

"I said I'd cooperate." There was a hard edge to Valek's voice.

"You better. The life of your child depends on it." Bruns strode away.

I stepped close to the bars, reached through and lightly pressed my hand to Valek's bruised cheek. He covered my hand with his own. His gaze showed his love as he turned his head and kissed my palm.

"Yelena, come," Bruns barked.

Leaving Valek caused me physical pain, as if my heart had been ripped from my chest. I followed Bruns, but glanced back when we reached the door. Valek watched me, and so did my brother and the rest. Their defeated postures and pained expressions matched. Unable to resist, I flipped them a thumbs-up sign.

No time left. I waited until Loris's magic ebbed, then I rushed to prepare. I could no longer be subtle. Tonight was my only chance to collect the rest of the supplies I needed for tomorrow night's rescue attempt.

Using Bruns's name netted me a number of items I nor-

MARIA V. SNYDER

mally would have stolen piece by piece to avoid detection. I hoped no one talked to Bruns.

All the next day, I tried to focus on the tasks Bruns assigned me. If I looked too distracted he'd inquire about my thoughts. That had led to embarrassing revelations, but today a disclosure would be far more than just humiliating.

As I worked in the armory that afternoon, testing the Weapons Master's new ultralight sword for female soldiers, Bruns arrived.

"Put the weapon away. We need to talk," he said.

My pulse skittered through my body. I wondered who or what had tipped him off. Or if he'd spotted the blowpipe hidden in my uniform.

On the way to his office, he said, "Captain Geffers tells me you've been asking questions about the training sessions outside the garrison."

Oh no.

"Why the interest?" he asked.

I chose each word with the utmost care. "They're our first line of defense, and I'm curious how well trained they are."

"Why are you curious?"

"A company of soldiers is trained to fight an enemy army of similar size, and I know from experience that a small group or just one person can cause havoc with a larger group that's not prepared."

"You mean guerrilla tactics? Or someone like Valek?"

"Both."

"And you think our soldiers need this more specialized training?"

"I don't know. That's why I was asking Captain Geffers, to see if we should consider it."

Bruns tapped his fingers on his thigh—a gesture I'd learned

meant he was deep in thought. "Do you think Valek would train our units?"

"Yes."

"But can I trust him?"

"Yes. He'd do anything to keep us safe."

"That's what worries me. With his immunity, he won't be influenced by the Theobroma."

"He gave his word to cooperate. That is more binding than magical coercion."

Bruns studied my expression. "Good to know."

He appeared satisfied with my answers, and I relaxed. When we reached his office, my fear returned in a rush. Ben Moon lounged on the visitor chair, waiting for us.

"I thought Owen ordered you to kill her," Ben said.

Ah, confirmation that Bruns was working with Owen. Being right didn't make me feel any better. In fact, my hopes of stopping the Sitian takeover plunged. Even if we escaped, we didn't have enough people or resources.

Bruns scowled at Ben. "I don't take orders from Owen." Then he glanced at me. "Are you surprised about Owen?"

"No."

"What tipped you off?"

"When I overheard your conversation with General Cahil."

"But Cahil believes we're preparing for a war."

"Exactly, and I know the Commander well enough to know he'd rather come in and take over Sitia the same way he conquered Ixia. There had to be a reason he didn't execute Owen."

"And *that's* why I didn't kill her." Bruns jabbed a finger at me. "She's been an invaluable resource."

"I wouldn't trust her," Ben said.

"She's under my control."

"Yeah, well, Owen thought the same thing, and look what happened."

"Owen didn't take away all her supporters. Besides, he's doing pretty good for a dead man, and soon he'll be in charge of Ixia."

"For sand's sake, Bruns, why don't you just tell her everything? That's another reason she needs to die. We've been successful with this plan because only three of us know what's *really* going on."

"No. I need her and Valek."

"Valek's alive, too? How stupid can—"

"That's enough, Ben. They are my guarantee that you and your brother won't double-cross me."

"Why would we do that?"

"To have Ixia and Sitia to yourselves."

Ben waved it off. "I don't want either. Too much work."

"That's fine, but in case you change your mind, I have two very capable people to send after you."

Ben huffed in amusement. "And they'll obey you? Yeah, right. As soon as they're out of your sight, they'd be gone."

"Yelena, tell him."

I met Ben's dubious gaze with the flat killer stare I'd learned from Valek. In a cold, emotionless voice, I said, "Bruns, it would be our *pleasure* to assassinate Ben and Owen Moon for you." This time, the truth tasted as sweet as my favorite breakfast.

Fear flashed in his eyes for an instant, then Ben grunted and faced Bruns. "Just remember who told you to kill them both. Is this why you wanted to meet? To gloat that you've captured them?"

"No. Valek agreed to cooperate, and I thought you should hear his information firsthand. It should be very helpful."

"If we can trust him."

"We can."

Explaining about the amethyst, Bruns ordered me to show Ben the bottle. I held it up. Then the three of us trekked down to the jail to interrogate Valek. Ben fussed about the stench until Bruns glared at him.

Valek answered every question. The information he provided, while true, omitted quite a bit. Impressive, considering the battered state of his body and mind. The session ended two hours later when Valek passed out. I worried that Valek wouldn't be physically able to escape later tonight, but I couldn't wait for him to recover. Even with Ben's presence at the garrison complicating things, I had to risk it.

Bruns kept me by his side as he played host to Ben that evening. I endured a long supper, an even longer discussion on how they would use Valek's information and then was sent to bed like a child while the "adults" conversed about important matters.

Glad to be released, I lay in bed and reviewed my plan, seeking gaps in the logic and other possible problems. My imagination had compiled quite the list of things-that-could-go-wrong by the time Bruns and Ben finished their conversation and retired for the evening.

I waited a couple more hours. Near midnight, I slipped from my room and crossed Bruns's dark office. I grabbed the doorknob.

"Bruns really is an idiot." Ben's voice pierced the darkness.

My breath locked as fear coiled around my body. I turned. "I was just—"

"Save it. I don't care what you were about to do. The fact that you can do it, despite Loris's magic, should be a surprise, but I've learned my lesson. Do you want to know what that lesson is?" Ben stepped from the shadows.

"No."

"Too bad, 'cause I'm going to tell you anyway. I've learned to never, ever underestimate you. And to never assume anything." He moved closer.

A strange weakness flushed through me.

"You've been consuming the Theobroma," Ben said. "So why isn't the magic working? Let's see…"

The compulsion to sit in Bruns's visitor's chair pressed on me. My body obeyed before my mind gave the command. Panic pulsed and urged me to run, scream or fight back. All was ignored.

"Goody. My magic works on you." He pulled a dagger from a sheath on his belt and stood in front of me. "I've imagined stabbing this knife into you a million times." Ben crouched down to my eye level. He poked my stomach with the blade's tip.

The pain failed to register over the sheer terror that gripped me.

"However, I think it'll be so much more fun watching you slice yourself to ribbons before you cut your own throat." Ben offered me the weapon. "Take it."

Unable to resist, I reached for the hilt. My fingers brushed Ben's as I wrapped my right hand around the hilt. In that instant, the compulsions disappeared. Without thinking, I grabbed his wrist with my left hand and hundreds of hours of knife-defense training kicked in.

I thrust forward, unbalancing Ben. He fell back on his butt as I sprang from the seat and followed him. Turning the knife around, I didn't hesitate to plunge the blade into his stomach, aiming the tip up to his heart, killing him.

It was brutal and ruthless. It was necessary to save myself and the baby. It was just what Ben wished to do to me—erase a problem permanently.

Should I be upset by the warm blood gushing over my

hands? By the final painful exhalation from my victim? By the stench of body fluids pooling under his dead body?

Yes—taking a life was never easy, no matter the circumstances.

But did I regret it?

No.

After I cleaned up, I filled a bucket with water and grabbed the basket full of soap, washcloths and clean uniforms I'd assembled and hidden in a supply closet. I carried them down to the jail. Now wasn't the time to worry about what could go wrong. There were two sets of doors and four guards between me and my family. Now was the time for action.

"What's this?" the soldier on the left asked when he spotted me lumbering toward him with my heavy load.

"Bruns wants the prisoners to wash up before the morning," I said.

"Now? It's the middle of the night."

"I don't question orders," I said. My tone indicated that he shouldn't, either.

"All right, give them here."

I handed the bucket and basket to him as his partner unlocked the door.

"Make sure they all clean up," I said.

"Yeah, yeah. We'll take care of it."

I left, but didn't go far. The second set of guards also grumbled about the time. While they transferred the items to the inner guards, I drew a blowpipe from my tunic and a handful of darts with extra-long needles. Loading the first one, I aimed.

With a sharp puff of air, I shot the closest man. It hit his arm, piercing the fabric. By the time he jerked with surprise, I launched another. Then in quick succession I hit the other two.

The Curare worked fast and, with only a minimal amount of yelling, they toppled to the ground, paralyzed. Sweet.

I tucked the blowpipe back in my tunic. It was a keeper. The rifling in its barrel had improved even my terrible aim. Take that, Janco!

Grabbing the keys, I unlocked the inner doors. I stepped into the lantern light and everyone turned guarded and worried expressions on me.

"You ready to get out of here?" I asked.

Smiles all around and a whoop from Janco. I moved from cell to cell, freeing them. Valek pulled me into a tight embrace. I closed my eyes and allowed myself a moment of comfort in his arms.

"How?" he whispered.

"Later," I promised. "Are you strong enough?"

"Yes." He released me.

"Good."

"What's the plan?" Janco asked.

I pointed to the bucket of water, which remained upright, and to the basket, which had spilled, scattering clothes onto the floor. "Clean up and change quick. Leif, can you and Hale weave null shields into the uniforms?"

"What about Mara?" Leif asked.

"Janco will fetch her. Do his uniform first."

Janco stripped off his shirt. "Where is she?"

I told him. "Tell her you're taking her to Leif. That we're all working for Bruns now and are leaving for an important and secret mission."

Leif found a uniform sized for Janco and concentrated on building a null shield on the shirt. Hale picked up another while Janco washed up. I turned my back when Janco yanked off his pants, giving them some privacy.

They didn't waste any time or energy asking me questions.

Their unconditional trust that I had it all worked out warmed me and terrified me at the same time.

Once Janco was dressed and ready, I said, "Meet us near the entrance of the main barracks. A platoon of soldiers are scheduled for nighttime maneuvers outside the garrison, and we need to join them before they leave."

"Got it." Janco touched his hip. "Weapons?"

"Take one of the guards'."

Janco stripped the men of their swords.

"Give Ari, Leif and Dax the others."

"What about me, love?" Valek stepped into my view. He sponged grime off his neck and bare torso. Large bruises stained his skin. Bright red cuts oozed blood.

Concentrating on the task at hand and not Valek's battered body, I pulled Ben's knife from my boot and gave it to him. His eyes gleamed as he appraised the quality of the blade.

"And me?" Hale asked.

"I hid a few more weapons near the barracks," I said.

Janco left to collect Mara.

"We only need to put null shields on three uniforms," Leif said. "Hale and I can erect ones around ourselves. Plus we can drop them just in case we need to use magic."

"Good, that will save time," I said.

"I need one," Valek said in a tight voice.

I spun around. Everyone stared at Valek.

"Just do it," he said to Leif. "I'll explain later."

"Uh… Yelena," Ari said.

Oh. Half-naked men. Right. I turned, but my mind kept whirling. Why would Valek need a null shield? No logical answer formed, and soon the men were ready to go.

I led them from the jail and along a route I'd scouted that kept us in the shadows. Except for the patrols, the garrison remained quiet. We stopped to grab the weapons before reaching our destination.

Unlike the rest of the garrison, activity and light spilled from the main barracks as soldiers prepped for their training mission and gathered outside. We waited nearby. My heart tapped a fast rhythm in my chest, sending pulses of fear along my extremities. Where were Janco and Mara? If we were caught, there'd be no second chance to escape.

Valek laced his fingers in mine. Comforted by the gesture, I squeezed his hand. But then I remembered what had happened with Ben. My touch had blocked Ben's magic. Would it do the same to Valek and remove his null-shield protection? I let go and shook my head at his questioning glance. If we escaped, we had much to discuss.

A commanding officer called the milling soldiers to order. They formed ranks. Come on, Janco. We needed to join the company soon. Very soon. What if they didn't show? Would I be able to leave without them?

Yes. For the baby, and for the others. This was the last opportunity for all of us.

My stomach twisted with pain as I gestured for us to leave our hiding spot. Leif and Ari refused to move. Stubborn, sweet idiots.

Then Leif faced the wrong direction. About to grab his arm, I stopped. Janco and Mara materialized from the shadows. Leif wrapped his wife in a bear hug.

"Did you take the scenic route?" Ari growled at Janco in a low voice.

While relief pumped through me, there was no time for explanations or hellos. I punched Leif's shoulder and pointed at the company now marching away. We scrambled to join, lining up at the end of the ranks. None of the soldiers in front of us appeared to notice or care about the additional people.

After all, we wore the standard Sitian military uniform. Mara appeared content to march next to Leif.

My heart rate increased as we neared the gate. The guards had swung the barriers wide to allow the company to pass. Just a few more minutes and we'd be outside the garrison.

When the head of the column approached the gate, the commanding officer shouted, "Round up."

The ranks split into two and broke into a run. One side peeled off to the left and the other the right, but neither crossed through the gate. Valek reacted first, drawing his knife as the others brandished their weapons. The soldiers looped back, forming a circle around us.

Trapped.

Surrounded.

Ambushed.

It didn't matter what word I used to describe our current situation, or how Bruns had figured it out. No, what mattered was Bruns's next move. And he was smart enough to conclude that only one option remained.

Death.

32

VALEK

Valek kept tight control of his emotions. He scanned the fifty soldiers surrounding them, assessing skills and searching for a spot where they might be able to break through to make a run for the garrison's gate and freedom. Motioning to Ari, Janco and Leif to form a wedge, Valek pointed to the weak link—a trio of teenagers standing shoulder to shoulder. Must be friends.

Just as he raised a hand to signal *go*, torches blazed to life, illuminating the area beyond their circle. More men flooded into the courtyard, cutting off their escape route. Ah, hell.

He met Yelena's gaze, and his heart lurched to see her so frightened. Something must have tipped Bruns off, and he'd been ready for them. If Valek hadn't been thrown off balance by losing his immunity and gaining magic, he never would have been ambushed at Mara's. Plus, it didn't help that pain still clung to his ribs, chest and back, and the blows to his head clouded his thoughts.

The ring of soldiers parted, and Bruns strode into view. He held a crossbow with a bolt already loaded. Pure fury radiated from every muscle of his body. This wouldn't be pretty.

"I don't know how you managed to disobey my orders, but it stops now," Bruns said to Yelena, aiming his weapon at her.

Valek shifted his weight, preparing to push Yelena out of the bolt's path. He'd gladly be skewered in her place.

"Loopholes," Yelena said with a calm voice.

"What?" Bruns asked.

"That's how. Loopholes in your orders gave me plenty of freedom."

"And you think by telling me this, I won't kill you?"

"You need me. You know Owen will double-cross you."

"No. No more. You'd just find another way to sabotage my efforts." Bruns wrapped his finger around the trigger and squeezed.

Valek tackled Yelena as a sudden gust of wind blew through the garrison. Bruns's shot flew wide and slammed into Dax's chest. The tall man crumpled to the ground with a cry of pain. Yelena struggled to go to her friend, but Valek pinned her down, covering as much of her body as he could with his own.

"Stay put," Valek said to her. "Bruns is reloading."

Another whirlwind hit, kicking up a large cloud of dust and extinguishing a number of torches. Lightning flashed, followed by a roar of thunder that shook the ground. A second blinding flash ripped through the air, sizzling. The main barracks caught fire.

"Hold your positions," Bruns ordered above the noise of the storm and the panicked yells of his men.

They obeyed until the third bolt struck the administration building. The stone wall exploded and sharp pieces bombarded those standing below. Thunder announced the arrival of a deluge. Sheets of cold water rained down, soaking everything and everyone in seconds.

Mass chaos ensued. It was a thing of beauty. One of the best distractions he'd ever seen. With no time to admire the results,

Valek helped Yelena to her feet. She ran to Dax, kneeling by his side. Dax stared at the sky with dead eyes.

Another flashing sizzle. A wooden shed burst into flames.

Valek pulled Yelena away from her friend, despite her protests. If they didn't move, there'd be six more dead. Seven, if he counted the baby.

Leif had his left arm around Mara, holding her close while his right hand clutched a sword. Her confusion was clear, but it appeared her love for Leif overrode Bruns's brainwashing. Ari and Janco crouched nearby, ready to fight off anyone who came too close. Hale had disappeared, but there was no time to search for him.

"Arrow formation," Valek ordered. "Head for the gate."

With Ari, Janco and Leif forming the V shape of an arrowhead, Mara, Valek and Yelena followed in a line. The three teenagers raced up to their group. Janco and Ari raised their swords, but the boys waved their hands, showing they were unarmed.

"This way," the middle one said. "Follow us."

Janco glanced at Valek.

"Fisk sent us."

In that case... "Go, go, go!"

The trio led them to a ribbon of calm. It was a narrow trail where the rain did not pound and the lightning bolts did not penetrate. It snaked through the chaos and Valek wondered if they followed the ribbon or if it matched their movements. Either way, they drew closer to the exit.

Unlike the others in the garrison, the line of guards at the gate held their positions despite the storm. They braced against the now-closed wooden barrier and each one was armed with a crossbow.

Still unnoticed, their group slowed. Yelena pulled out a

blowpipe. That would help, but it wouldn't be enough to incapacitate them all.

One of the teen guides yelled, "These guys don't have the balls to stop us!"

Janco rounded on the boy, ready to berate him for giving away their position, but a loud wet splat sounded nearby. It took Valek a moment to decipher the scene in front of him. Huge balls of water flew through the air and slammed into the guards at the gate, flattening each one.

It clicked. Zohav! His siblings and Fisk were rescuing them! Zethan controlled the storm, and a Stormdancer must be responsible for the calm.

Soon the gate was cleared of defenders and they sprinted from the garrison. They had to get as far away as possible and find a safe spot to hide. As they ran through the dark woods, Valek searched his memory for possible locations, but the effort needed to stay on his feet drained all his energy.

So used to being in charge, it didn't dawn on Valek that the teens continued to lead them.

The night turned into one long slog. Cold seeped into his bones as his wet clothes clung to his skin. At one point, Valek realized Ari's arm was around his shoulders, supporting him. Near dawn, they entered a cave and they all dropped to the ground in exhaustion. Soon after, Fisk arrived with Zohav, Zethan, Heli the Stormdancer and Teegan.

Smiles, hugs and slaps on the back were exchanged. Then introductions were made. Yelena shot him a shocked and questioning look when his relationship to Zohav and Zethan was revealed. He mouthed, *Later.*

"You saved our lives," Valek said to Fisk. "Thank you."

"Except for the jailbreak, it was a combination of a couple of the options we discussed with you back at the Citadel. Plus,

MARIA V. SNYDER

I had lots of help," Fisk said, gesturing to the twins, Teegan and Heli.

"How did you know we needed you tonight?"

"My helpers infiltrated the garrison. They wore null-shield pendants to protect them from the magic. They noticed that Bruns had a man following Yelena, so they followed the man. By his behavior, we suspected something was going down tonight, so we prepared to launch the plan."

Yelena made a disgusted noise. "And here I thought I was being clever."

"You freed us from the cells," Leif said.

"And led you right into an ambush."

"It worked out," Janco said.

"Not for Dax." Yelena's voice quavered. "Or Hale."

Valek pulled her close.

Janco ducked his head. "Ah, I'm sorry, Yelena. I liked Dax. He was a good guy. And we'll find a way to rescue Hale."

The silence stretched as they remembered Dax.

"It's been a hard night for everyone," Fisk said. "There are bedrolls, blankets and supplies in another cavern."

They set up a camp. Valek tried to help, but Janco pushed him down on a bedroll. "Relax, boss. You look half-dead."

"But—"

"It's an improvement from almost dead, but ya still have a long way to go."

Yelena arrived, and all his protests died as she lay next to him, spreading a blanket over them. She rested her head on his shoulder and he hooked his arm around her.

"We have lots to catch up on," she said. "Are there any more surprises you're hiding?"

"Yes, but I'm not hiding them. I just don't have the energy to explain right now."

"All right." She snuggled in closer. "We'll discuss it after we're rested."

But Valek wouldn't be able to truly relax unless… "Janco," he called as Janco hustled past. "We need to set up a watch schedule."

"Already on it, boss."

"Good." But Valek's mind still whirled with all that had happened. And this problem with Bruns and the Sitian takeover was far from over. Oh, no. It was just the beginning, and he had no idea how to stop it.

Despite his dark thoughts, Valek eventually drifted to sleep.

Cries of alarm jolted him awake. Valek jumped to his feet with a knife in his hand before he even deciphered the trouble. Armed soldiers streamed into the cave. Their hiding spot had been discovered.

Yelena stood next to him. She muttered a curse and pulled a blowpipe from her tunic. Ari and Janco met the charge head-on. Their swords cut down the first couple of soldiers. Zohav and Zethan retreated to the back of the cave, along with Heli and Teegan. It would be difficult for them to use their magical powers in the confined space of the cavern.

Fisk engaged the enemy, fighting beside Ari and Janco. Mara huddled by the fire while Fisk's three helpers threw rocks at the soldiers. The melee appeared to be evenly matched, until more of the enemy arrived.

Swiping a sword from a fallen man, Valek moved to intercept the new arrivals. He wondered who'd been on watch and realized Leif wasn't in the cave. A part of him worried about his brother-in-law, but once he reached striking distance, all his energy focused on the matter at hand.

With his first opponent, he sidestepped the man's sword thrust, shuffled in close and stabbed him in the stomach. No

MARIA V. SNYDER

time for finesse in this fight. Valek moved to the next soldier without waiting for the first to fall. A successful attack combined surprise, speed and intensity. Valek kept up the pace, but a part of him knew his injuries would eventually slow him down.

The clang of metal, cries of pain and smell of blood soon dominated all his senses, and the fights blurred into one unending skirmish.

Minutes…hours later, it appeared they had the upper hand. And that was when he spotted Yelena and Loris. When had that bastard arrived? And how did he get to her? Fury and fear mixed into a lethal combination and he stalked toward them, stepping over fallen bodies.

Loris held a knife to her throat and was retreating from the cave. He must have also figured out that the surprise attack would eventually fail.

"Don't come any closer, or I'll slit her throat," Loris ordered Valek. He stood behind Yelena, using her to shield his body.

Valek wondered why Yelena hadn't disarmed him. That move had been a part of her training. She even clutched something in her hands. The answer dawned on him when he met Yelena's gaze. Anger and helplessness blazed in her eyes. He stopped.

"Smart," Loris said. "Too bad you weren't smart enough to protect her with a null shield."

Ah, hell.

"Don't let him leave," Yelena said. "He's going to kill me regardless."

"Shut up," Loris said. He backed up a couple more steps.

Valek scanned the cave. Ari and Janco waited nearby. He lifted his eyebrows just a fraction. Then he returned his attention to Loris.

Tapping a finger on the hilt of the sword, Valek gauged the distance to the man.

"You're not getting out of here alive, puppy dog," Janco shouted.

Loris glanced at Janco. In that split second, Valek flipped his knife over and threw it at Loris. The tip of the blade pierced the man's left eye. He screamed and flailed. Valek shuffled close and disarmed Loris, freeing Yelena.

But before he could finish the man off, Loris tackled Valek to the ground and yelled, "Drink it."

As Valek struggled to push Loris off, Janco cried out. Yelena tipped the glass vial filled with amethyst to her lips.

"Don't!" Desperate, Valek finally broke away, lunged and knocked the bottle from her hands, but purple stained her lips. He'd been too slow. His world shattered.

Yelena's face creased in disgust. "Yuck."

How could she be so—

"I never liked grape jam." She wiped her mouth with the back of her hand.

Valek almost fainted with relief. "Was that one of the things we need to discuss?"

"Yes."

Loris moaned. Valek found his knife and slashed the man's throat, ending his ability to bark orders and his life. Then he pulled Yelena to him and held her tight, needing to breathe in her scent and just take a moment before he released her.

Valek scanned the cave, assessing damage. Everyone appeared to be okay, despite their collection of cuts, bruises and bloodstains.

"Pack up," he said. "We need to move to another location. This one's been compromised."

A shout from outside the cave drew his attention. More enemy soldiers already?

MARIA V. SNYDER

He, Ari and Janco raced to the entrance with their weapons in hand, preparing for a fight. The bright sunshine seemed incongruous to the carnage inside. A small group of people huddled over a prone figure. And then Valek remembered.

Leif.

His brother-in-law had been shot with a crossbow bolt. The wooden shaft jutted from Leif's chest an inch from center. Blood pooled underneath him. Unable to stand, Valek knelt beside him, feeling for a pulse. Weak. He sank back on his heels. Ah, hell.

Yelena's and Mara's cries of alarm roused Leif. His eyes fluttered open, focused on Mara. She crouched next to him and grabbed his hand in both of hers. Tears streamed down her face.

"I...tried to...warn..." Leif gasped. "...sorry."

"No," Yelena said with anguish, falling to her knees next to her brother. "You're not leaving."

"Don't think...I...have...a choice. Mara...I...love you." Leif passed out.

Yelena growled in frustration. "I'd give anything to have my magic back."

Magic! "Get Zethan, Zohav, Teegan and Heli," Valek ordered Janco, who hovered nearby.

Janco raced to the cave and returned with the twins, Heli and Teegan right behind him. Valek asked them if they could heal.

"No, sorry," Zethan said.

Heli shook her head sadly. "It's not part of a Stormdancer's power."

Teegan creased his brow, looking queasy. "I tried to heal a squirrel, but I killed the poor thing instead."

Silence followed the bad news.

"We can't," Zethan said. "But maybe *you* can."

"I…"

"Valek? What are you talking about?" Yelena demanded of Zethan.

Wordless, the poor boy stared at her.

The idea seemed ridiculous. He might flame out or end up injuring someone. Plus he'd never used magic before and had no clue how to wield it. But he was intimate with someone who did. He had to try, or he'd never forgive himself.

"Everyone except Yelena go inside the cave," Valek ordered. When they hesitated, he said, "Go now!"

They hurried to obey. Valek stripped off his shirt to remove the null shield Leif had attached, tossing it far away.

"Valek…?" Yelena began, but then she pressed her lips together. "Tell me what you need."

"I need you to imagine you have magic and you're going to heal Leif. Think of each step and how you'd use the magic to repair the damage. I'll follow your instructions. Be very specific."

She drew in a deep breath. "Imagine in my mind, right?"

"Yes. Visualize as much as possible." He reached for her hand, but she pulled away.

"Touching me will block your magic. Tell me when you're ready."

Valek grabbed the bolt in both his hands. "When I yank this free, start."

"Okay. Make sure you press your hand to the wound."

"Got it. One, two, three." Valek tugged the shaft from Leif's chest. Blood welled, pouring out. He covered the hole with his hand and dropped his mental barrier.

Yelena's instructions flooded his mind. He reached for the blanket of power. A bolt of energy pulsed, and power flowed inside him. The temptation to grab it all consumed him. Bruns and the Commander's plans to take over Sitia would be easy

MARIA V. SNYDER

to stop. Nothing could match his power. Nothing could harm him or Yelena or the baby.

"Focus on Leif."

Yelena's voice sliced through the greed. With effort, he extracted a small thread and sent it into Leif's wound. He matched the images in Yelena's mind of stitching skin and bone together with that glowing fiber of magic. One thing Valek did know how to do—sew. The other assassins hadn't called him the King Knitter for nothing. As he worked, pulling thread after thread to repair the damage, the images in Yelena's mind faded. Valek needed to reinforce the connection over and over. It was as if another magician sucked at the magic he used. Odd—but then again, it might be normal. He had nothing to compare it to.

"You got it. Keep going," she encouraged him.

Healing a wound involved more than he'd ever imagined. Broken bones needed to be fused together. Muscles woven back in place. Tissue smoothed. Veins repaired and reconnected.

Exhaustion flirted with him, but he shoved it aside.

"Blood," Yelena said. "He's lost too much. You need to generate more."

"How?"

"Inside the bones." She showed him a mental image.

He seized additional magic from the blanket to keep their link, then drew extra strands to induce Leif's bones to produce blood. And when his own body fatigued, he tugged a few more to energize him.

"The color is returning to Leif's face," Yelena said. "His pulse is stronger."

Valek removed his hand. A livid red scar surrounded with black, purple and green bruises marked Leif's chest.

Relief, joy and pride pulsed through Valek. He'd saved

Leif's life. With magic! The power still rushed through his veins, as if he'd drunk too much whiskey. Valek worked on his own injuries. The cracked ribs gone. The bump on his head erased. The bruised muscles and all the cuts, sewn together. He hadn't felt this good in a long, long time.

"Valek, stop!"

Valek focused on Yelena. Worry and love and gratitude and jealousy swirled in her mind. And that...tug. It sucked his magic, as if he'd sprung a leak. Good thing an unlimited power supply was so easy to reach.

The magic filled him, and he wrapped it around his body, layer after layer after layer, protecting him. Valek ignored Yelena's sharp tone. Her fear grated on him, so he broke their connection. Now he wouldn't lose any power to that leak. He'd keep it safe. And keep it from everyone. Owen and Ben Moon and all those who used it to harm others wouldn't be able to hurt another. No. Valek controlled the magic now, and he wasn't going to share. With anyone.

MARIA V. SNYDER

33

YELENA

Valek gathered too much power. He was going to flame out and kill himself and anyone nearby. I had to stop him, but wasn't sure how. Panic threatened to jumble my thoughts, but I wasn't going to lose him now. I yelled for Ari and Janco. They rushed from the cave.

Pointing at Leif, who stirred, I said, "Take him inside. Tell the twins, Teegan and Heli to come out here now!"

They didn't hesitate. An eternity later, the magicians arrived.

"Oh, no," Zethan said. "He's out of control."

Zohav backed away. "We need to take cover. It's not safe."

"Can you bleed off the magic?" I asked them.

Heli raised her arms and a gust cooled my sweaty forehead. "Some, but he's just drawing more."

I glanced at the twins. "How about you?"

"Are you crazy? You're going to get us all killed," Zohav said.

"Yeah, we can. Zo, that's our brother."

"But you heard Heli, it won't stop him, just delay the inevitable."

"Since I'm still learning control, I've been augmenting Zo's and Zee's powers," Teegan said. "We can bleed off more magic that way."

"Good. Use as much as you can. I'll do the rest." Grabbing Valek's shirt from where he'd tossed it, I put it on and held the material close.

Valek scowled at me as I approached him. The null shield in the fabric must seem like a hole in his cocoon of power. The air grew thick and viscous, and I struggled to get closer. Valek's gaze darted to the magicians, then back to me. He crouched as if preparing to fight, and no glint of recognition appeared in his gaze.

Nothing left to do, I yanked off the null shield. Magic slammed into me. I braced against it as if it were a gale. I concentrated on our love. On the matching heart-shaped scars on our chests. On all our times together. On our baby growing inside me.

He staggered. "I can't...stop."

"Send it back to the sky." I took another step.

"I...can't."

I searched my mind for an image Valek could use. "The magic is an ugly gray stone. Carve it. Shape it into a butterfly and let it fly to the sky."

His black hair clung to his sweaty face. He swiped it from his eyes. His muscles shook with the effort.

"Do it, or we will all die."

That seemed to rouse him. His gaze focused on a distant point. I twisted the fabric of his shirt in my hands. If this failed, I might have to use the null shield to sever his connection to the power blanket. But the magic he'd gathered would be released like a flameout, killing us. Unless he managed to return enough of it.

"It's working," Zethan said. "Keep going, bro!"

Valek sank to the ground. He fisted his hands and his brows creased with pain. I moved to within touching distance.

He met my gaze. Exhaustion and misery etched on his face. "Can't...do...more."

I glanced at Zethan.

The teen shook his head. "Still too much. But he disconnected."

"Go inside the cave," I ordered. And when they hesitated, I added, "Now."

Zohav grabbed her brother's hand and pulled him along. Heli frowned, but she left with Teegan.

When they were safe, I tossed the shirt aside and knelt next to my husband. Perhaps what drained Loris's magic from me would work for Valek. Reading my intentions, he shook his head and tried to scoot away.

"Risky," he rasped.

"I'm not leaving you."

"Go."

"No."

"Yelena, wait!" Zethan ran toward us. "Leif says I can share my strength with Valek. You and Leif have done it in the past."

True. "But we could both control our magic. Valek—"

"Lasted longer than he should."

"No," Valek said.

We both ignored him.

"Come on. Let me try," Zethan said.

"All right, but if he starts gathering more—"

"I'll disconnect."

"What if you can't?"

Zethan gestured to the shirt. "Use the null shield."

A temporary measure, and one that wouldn't save his life, but I agreed. We had to do something. Despite Valek's protest, Zethan grabbed his brother's hands.

"Send the power back," I instructed, imaging how I would release souls into the sky, including the pure joy of it—a feeling I'd missed.

I waited a lifetime. Deep lines of strain scored Valek's face.

"No," Zethan said. "Take the energy from me."

After another couple of centuries, Zethan wilted, but held tight.

"That's it," Zethan encouraged. "Almost there."

Picking up the null shield just in case, I fisted the fabric. It wouldn't be big enough to cover both of them.

"Just a…little bit more." Zethan's head dropped as if it was too heavy to hold up. "Stop." He opened his hands and pulled back, but Valek clung to him. "Stop." Zethan glanced at me with wide eyes. "He's drawing power again."

Dropping the shield, I grabbed both their hands, hoping the blocking effect worked with direct touch. Magic sizzled along my arms and ripped through me. The force pushed me back. Pain exploded in my head and a loud crack sounded. Then it all disappeared in a snap of black.

When I woke, I felt as if I'd been struck by lightning. I groaned, and Heli helped me sit up.

"Not lightning," she said. "I promise. But probably a mini flameout."

"Valek?" I asked.

"Still out," Heli said, pointing.

He lay a few feet away. I scooted over to him. His skin looked almost translucent, and dark smudges ringed his eyes. I smoothed his hair and trailed my fingers down his cold cheek. Someone had put the null shield back on him. Good.

"How long?"

"Four hours."

Not long, but I pressed my hand to my abdomen as a new

worry flared. Did the magical explosion harm the baby? I hoped not.

I glanced around. We were in a small wooden structure. Perhaps a barn or shed. "Where are we?"

"Empty cabin somewhere in the Krystal Clan. We had to find a new hiding place, and the big guy took charge."

"Ari?"

"Yeah."

"Where is everyone?"

"Ari and Janco went to fetch the horses. Fisk and his people left to return to the Citadel. Leif and Mara are in the other room with the twins and Teegan." She quirked a smile. "Leif mentioned something about cooking supper."

Which meant he'd recovered from his brush with death. Thanks to Valek. I checked his pulse. Steady.

"How's Zethan feeling?"

"Probably about the same as you, but he wasn't out as long."

Ah, youth. Ten years made a difference.

"Tea?" Heli asked.

"Please. And could you ask Leif to come?"

"Sure."

Leif brought the tea. Even though he was pale and haggard, he still smiled when I crinkled my nose over the smell of the tea.

"How are you feeling?" I asked him.

He rubbed his chest. "Sore, but I don't care. I'm happy just to be alive! That's the closest I've come to death." Leif glanced at Valek. "He certainly took his role as my best man seriously. Did you know Valek could do that?"

"No." I gazed at my husband. "We haven't had time to talk about anything."

"He'll wake. The man doesn't know how to quit." Leif studied my expression. "How are you doing?"

"I'm not sure." I asked him about the baby.

"I don't know. Let's ask Teegan."

"Teegan?"

"Yeah. Kid's impressive."

Leif fetched Teegan, who was happy to help. The boy gazed at me and said, "Two strong heartbeats."

That was impressive and a huge relief. "Thanks, Tee."

He grinned. "Anytime, but why are you siphoning my magic?"

Surprised and alarmed, I asked, "I am?"

"Don't worry. It's not like you're stealing it from me. It's just when I used my magic to...scan you, something pulled it. When I stopped, it stopped."

"Do you think it's the baby?"

He shrugged. "No idea."

"Hold my hand and see what happens."

Teegan grasped my hand and frowned. "It's like a null shield, blocking my magic." He released me as if I'd burned him. "Sorry, but that's...awful!"

"I know. But it gives me some protection." And perhaps a bright side to losing my ability to use magic.

I remained by Valek's side as one day turned into two. Leif brewed his healing teas, and I dripped spoonful after spoonful into Valek's mouth. My worry grew. What if he didn't wake up? Was this how he felt all those times our positions had been reversed? I think I preferred being oblivious rather than nauseous and on the edge of panic.

At the end of the third day, Ari called everyone into the main room for a meeting. We gathered around the hearth.

"We can't stay here much longer," Ari said. "Bruns has sent patrols to search for us, and we're too close to the garrison. Any ideas?"

"We report back to Ixia," Janco said. "They can come with us as...political refugees."

"You can't," I said.

"Why not? The Commander needs to know what's been going on."

"He already knows." I filled them in on Bruns's and the Commander's plans. "I'm pretty sure once they take over Sitia, Owen is going to kill the Commander."

"Holy snow cats," Janco said. "We're screwed."

Trust Janco to sum it up succinctly.

"We need to stop them," Ari said.

"How?" Leif asked. "There are nine of us, and a million of them."

"Ten." Mara elbowed Leif.

"Oh no, you're staying far away from danger," Leif said. "When I saw you in Bruns's custody, I almost died. I'm not going through *that* again."

"You were shot in the chest and almost died. So by that logic, you're staying away from danger, too." Mara's stubborn expression matched Leif's.

"We can hide on the coast near The Cliffs," Heli suggested. "No one lives there or would dare come there during the storm season."

"Are we really going to hide?" Janco asked. "That doesn't sound like us."

"What sounds like us?" Ari asked.

"Being in the thick of things, causing trouble and—"

"Being captured and thrown in jail," Zohav said. "Have you forgotten that they have magicians, Curare, Theobroma, weapons and garrisons full of soldiers?"

"Fisk and his people would help," Zethan said.

"And Loris is dead," Janco added. "I'm feeling pretty happy about that."

"Ben, too," I said, but unlike Janco, I didn't relish the fact that I'd been forced to kill him.

"Are you sure? 'Cause these guys have a tendency to fake their deaths, and I don't want any more nasty surprises."

"Yes."

"We could try to warn the Commander about Owen," Ari suggested.

"*If* you can get near him, and *if* you can block Owen's magic," Leif said. "And then what? The Commander still wants Sitia."

"The Commander doesn't want Sitia," Valek said from the doorway.

Relief poured through me, cleansing the worry away. I jumped up and rushed to him, wrapping him in my arms. "How do you feel?"

"Like I wrestled a snow cat and lost."

Leif took charge. He made Valek sit down and eat. When Leif was satisfied, he allowed Valek to explain.

"I don't think the Commander has any desire to rule Sitia," Valek said. "But he's probably afraid a rogue magician or magicians will take control of Sitia and invade Ixia. And with all the Sitian resources—magicians, Curare, Theobroma and the glass messengers—he knows he can't win a war with Sitia. Which is probably why he agreed to the Cartel's plan."

"Why does it matter if he wants to or is forced to invade Sitia?" Leif asked. "He's still going to invade."

"It matters because if we give him a good reason not to invade, he won't," Valek said.

"And how can we possibly do that? There's only ten of us," Zohav said.

"For now," Valek said.

Janco straightened. "You thinking of recruiting, boss?"

MARIA V. SNYDER

"Thinking about it, along with a few other…nasty surprises for the Cartel."

"Sweet."

Valek scanned their faces and then met my gaze. "It'll be dangerous."

"Suicidal," Zohav muttered.

Valek addressed the group. "It's your choice. Fisk can find you a safe place to stay until it's over."

"I'm in," Janco said.

Ari nodded. "Me, too."

"And me," Zethan said.

Zohav glared at her brother. "I'll help," she said in a resigned tone.

Leif met Mara's gaze. "We need to discuss it."

She huffed in amusement. "Where you go, I go. It's that simple."

I suppressed a smile.

"No way I'm hiding," Heli said.

"I'm already signed up," Teegan said.

Everyone looked at me.

"You need to think of the baby," Leif said.

"I am. And I don't want to raise our child in a world controlled by two power-hungry megalomaniacs. So I will do whatever it takes to prevent *that* from happening."

"And that would be a yes." Janco grinned.

"What's our first move, boss?" Ari asked.

"You and Janco go scout for a more permanent hideout. I'm going to need time to plan."

Janco jumped to his feet. "We're on it."

Valek recovered his strength a few days later, but we still didn't get a chance to talk about all that had happened while we were separated. Ari and Janco found an abandoned farmhouse inside the Stormdance Clan's lands. We traveled to the site in small groups, each going a different way. Reuniting with Kiki soothed my soul.

We planned to renovate the inside to suit our needs, but keep the outside in its dilapidated state. The horses would stay in a camouflaged structure in the forest nearby.

On the first night, Valek and I arranged our bedrolls and blankets in the largest bedroom on the second floor. We added coal to the small brazier, coaxing a little more heat. Most of the others stretched out by the fire around the central hearth downstairs, but we hadn't had any privacy in forever. Or so it seemed.

Even with so much to discuss, we spent the first couple hours getting reacquainted.

Finally, with our hearts beating in sync and our bodies pressed together skin on skin, we shared the events that had changed both our lives so drastically.

Valek explained about the Storm Thieves and discovering his new siblings. The epiphany by Vincent's grave.

"I had no idea letting go would have such…consequences," he said. "A huge weight lifted off my shoulders, but it took my immunity with it."

"I was right. You attached a null shield to your soul when you witnessed your older brothers' murders. Once you didn't need that protection, it returned to the sky."

"Rotten timing," he murmured.

"I wouldn't say that. Nor would Leif or Mara."

"I lost control and almost killed us."

"But you didn't. Next time—"

"There's not going to be a *next* time." He sounded like a sullen child.

"Yes, there will be. We need every advantage we can get. Leif and Zethan can teach you how to control it."

MARIA V. SNYDER

"I don't have to like it."

Amused by his tone, I said, "Look at the bright side. You reconnected with your parents and gained three new siblings."

"And you gained a mother-in-law."

Oh. Right.

"Not so amusing now, is it? I even promised her to bring you for a visit."

"Fighting Bruns's Cartel doesn't seem that bad now," I joked.

"Ha."

The silence stretched as I considered how much Valek's world had been turned upside down in the past two months. The Commander's mistrust, our marriage, the baby, his family, his lost immunity and the discovery of his magic. No wonder Bruns's men had been able to capture him at Mara's. Anyone else would have been unhinged by just one of those incidents.

"Your turn, love," Valek said. "Why does your touch block my magic? Not that I'm complaining. In fact, I love your touch even more now."

I told him my theory about the baby being a void. "But after my experience with Loris's magic and Teegan's comment, I'm not so sure anymore."

"Something drained the magic when we were connected," Valek said. "Is that what Teegan meant?"

"I think so. But if that was the case, then what did the baby *do* with the magic? I didn't regain my powers. Nothing happened. I don't think so, anyway."

"But this blocking power has grown stronger, right?"

"Yes."

"Perhaps the baby is channeling the power back into the blanket?"

"Perhaps."

"I guess time will tell if the baby's responsible for your lost magic, love. In the meantime, you can neutralize a magician with a touch. That may come in handy over the next couple months."

"As long as it doesn't hurt our baby."

"Of course." Valek rested his hand on my stomach. "That's what the upcoming battle is all about. Protecting our baby, giving him or her a chance for a peaceful life."

"No, it isn't."

"No?"

"It's about giving *all* the babies and *all* the people a chance for a peaceful life."

"You know that's impossible."

"I know, but wouldn't it be nice?" I asked.

"It'd be worth dying for."

★ ★ ★ ★ ★

MARIA V. SNYDER

ACKNOWLEDGMENTS

Even though I spend plenty of hours working alone in my writing cave, none of my books could have been written without the help and support from many people, including my readers. They're a constant source of joy and motivation.

Thanks to my trio of beta readers—Natalie Bejin, Judi Fleming and my husband, Rodney—my stories are as logical and error-free as humanly possible.

My agent, Bob Mecoy, and editor, Lauren Smulski, have been essential in guiding my stories and career. Thanks for all your hard work!

Speaking of hard work, no acknowledgment of mine is complete without a shout-out to all the talented people around the world who are part of Harlequin. Your efforts on behalf of my books are appreciated, and, if you're ever in my neck of the woods, stop on by, I'll buy you a drink.

I don't have a street team, but I do have loads of supporters who help spread the word about my books. They're invaluable and I thank them all, especially Alethea Allarey, Jaime Arnold of Rockstar Book Tours, Michelle Haring of Cupboard Maker Books and Sarah Weir.

Thanks to my family and friends for your continuing support. And thanks to my children, Jenna and Luke, for their patience and for not being too embarrassed by Mom's career and wardrobe choices.

I saved the best for last—my husband, Rodney. Without him, there would be no books. Thanks so much!